ALSO BY OWEN WEST

Sharkman Six

FOUR DAYS TO
VERACRUZ

A NOVEL

OWEN WEST

SIMON & SCHUSTER
New York London Toronto Sydney Singapore

SIMON & SCHUSTER
Rockefeller Center
1230 Avenue of the Americas
New York, NY 10020

This book is a work of fiction. Names, characters, places,
and incidents either are products of the author's imagination
or are used fictitiously. Any resemblance to actual events or
locales or persons, living or dead, is entirely coincidental.

Copyright © 2003 by Owen West
All rights reserved, including the right of reproduction
in whole or in part in any form.

SIMON & SCHUSTER
and colophon are registered trademarks
of Simon & Schuster, Inc.

For information regarding special discounts for bulk purchases,
please contact Simon & Schuster Special Sales at
1-800-456-6798 or business@simonandschuster.com

Manufactured in the United States of America

1   3   5   7   9   10   8   6   4   2

Library of Congress Cataloging-in-Publication Data

West, Owen, 1969–
Four days to Veracruz / Owen West.
p.   cm.
1. Americans—South America—Fiction.   2. Special operations
(Military science)—Fiction.   3. South America—Fiction.
4. Drug traffic—Fiction.   I. Title.
PS3623.E845F68   2003
813'.6—dc21   2003043216

ISBN 0-7432-2982-7

Acknowledgments

This novel was hatched in a Google Internet search and nourished by a number of people. So thanks . . .

To the incredible gang of adventure racers who dragged me along on Eco-Challenges around the world: Danielle, Kalin, Jennifer, Terry, Steve, Sarah, Darin, Kristin, Heather, Keith, Mitch, Alex, Shannon, Rand, Dan, and especially Monty and Robyn.

To my Everest teammates, especially Andy, Asmuss, Keiron, Russ, Jaime, Evelyne, Robert, Lopsang, Ram, Ellen "Little E," Chris, Purba for the most incredible physical feat I have seen, and Marco, the fastest man on the mountain in 2001—Requiescat in pace.

To my father and mother for ideas and assistance.

To my wonderful marathoning editor, Marysue, and of course the man who made it all possible, my agent Dan.

*To Susanne, the love of my life and partner
in all things adventurous.*

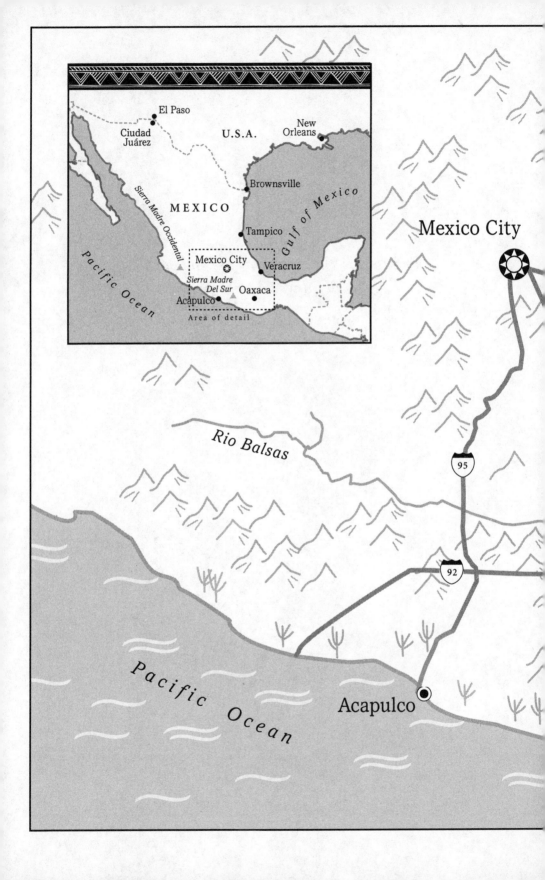

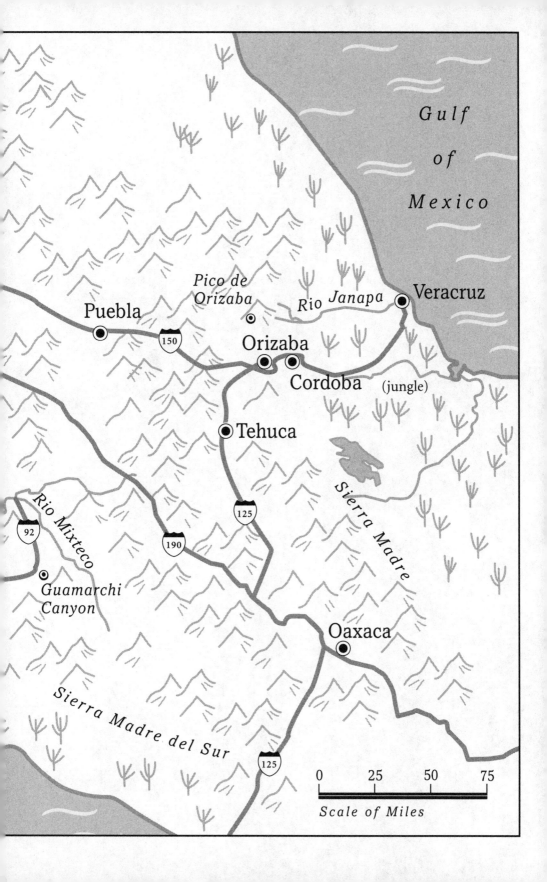

Introduction

SERIAL KILLERS TERRORIZE WOMEN IN MEXICO

By Matt Augustine, *The New York Times*
May 3, 2003

JUAREZ, Mexico—Juarez is a massive factory town plopped across the Rio Grande from El Paso. It is mostly women who work the manufacturing lines for American subsidiaries, earning wages well below the American minimum. But as dangerous as some of the industrial jobs are during the day, the Juarez night is far more terrifying. For a decade now a serial murderer has preyed on the Juarez populace, leaving a trail of mutilated bodies that have been uncovered from the surrounding desert to back alleys in the city itself.

Since 1991 over 150 women and 20 men have been murdered by a knife-wielding killer the locals have nicknamed *El Monstruo Carnicero*—the Monster Butcher—because of the horrifying way the corpses were defiled. It is not known whether the mutilation occurred before or after death. Hundreds of other people have vanished altogether. For some, the sheer numbers indicate at least some level of complicity from the government, if not direct involvement.

"Look at the number of victims and tell me the police know nothing," says Valerie Hernandez, whose daughter disappeared in 1995 and was found dead last year, buried under a foot of sand with her heart excised. "This psycho is running free and nobody is doing anything about it. No woman walks alone without terror in her heart. You want to fight terrorism? Come to Juarez. Just don't go out at night."

In 1999, Mexican authorities arrested an Egyptian-born chemist and declared that *El Monstruo Carnicero* had been caught. Indeed, the doctor confessed to several of the murders and led the police to two bodies. But a month later the killings resumed their frenetic pace, leaving the Mexican authorities to a new theory. "The Monster is behind bars," says Esteban Manber, Juarez's district attorney, "but we cannot stop his virus from spreading outside the prison. He has a copycat gang that continues the evil."

Tom Barth, a retired FBI agent, who was hired to consult on the tragedy, agrees that the killings are not the work of one person. "Look at the appalling numbers and remember that Ted Bundy killed between 30 and 40 women. I think a gang of killers is responsible for the Juarez tragedy. If I'm wrong, this is the most prolific serial killer in the history of the world."

Prologue

MOUNT COOK, NEW ZEALAND

The woman plodded forward in slow motion as if the snow were glue, gripping her feet. On the glacier less than an hour, she could already feel the cold sapping her energy through her Gore-Tex parka, chilling the flesh on her arms. She wiped the frost from her wrist barometer and shivered. Six hundred and thirty millibars and dropping—a forecast of discomfort at sea level but a harbinger of suffering at altitude.

She stepped up her pace to raise her core temperature, but backed off before breaking into a sweat. Steam wrapped her face, flowing like fog behind her as she moved, crystallizing in her black hair and breaking off as tiny icicles when her ponytail flopped against her collar.

She crested a small cornice—the overhanging lip of a breaking wave of snow, frozen as it crested two or twenty or two hundred years ago. Snow began to descend. Though it was as fluffy as down, the wind snapped up the flakes and whipped them into her face like shotgun pellets. She turned on her Petzl headlamp and allowed herself another glance at the three men chasing her.

In the narrow cone of her light, she could barely see the men through the glittering swarm of flakes, swaying there in the wind like apparitions fifty meters below. They had pursued her for five days across 300 miles of wilderness— on half-wild horses that bit and kicked, in pack rafts that overturned in the frigid rapids, on foot, hacking through slide alder vines on the valley floor, then scrambling for a day up the steep scree slope until they left all vegetation behind and reached the snow line, pushing above that to the ice edge where the air was too thin to sustain life for long. In the 142 hours since she first heard the gunshot, Kate North and the posse pursuing her had slept fewer than four.

Don't get soft on me now, she thought.

The ice beneath her was midnight blue and seemed to glow under the setting full moon, soft and peaceful. But navigation without sleep on a kiwi glacier was neither soft nor peaceful. It was a precise business. Errors meant that either the others would overtake her or she would lose trail and tumble down a thousand feet of solid ice with edges honed sharp by the Antarctic wind.

Kate pulled the laminated map out of her breathable rain pants. Fog obscured her vision for a moment, then cleared on her inhalation and fogged again. On the map, she aligned the compass along a north-south grid line, turned the map to find true north, and lifted her eyes, matching the contour lines with the terrain. She had reached Checkpoint 27 at the edge of the ice bowl ahead of schedule.

Kate twisted her body and shouted, "Let's go, guys, we're right on track! Only fifty miles to the finish!"

She didn't move back to encourage them; any step backward, however small, was a waste of energy—a waste of precious fuel—and in the toughest race in the world you guarded your calories fiercely. *Always forward.*

The three men on her Eco-Challenge team, all United States Marines, gave no sign they heard. They just pressed on, heads down, mental effort focused on following the posthole tracks of their team captain, exerting as little energy as possible by stepping in the snow pockets she had crushed for them.

The first man in the file, Gavin Kelly, halted and bent double over his ice axe. The slope seemed to be siphoning the oxygen right out of his hyperventilating lungs. He threw up all over his light hikers, his head quivering so violently as the bile rose that he actually felt warm for a moment. A thin line of purple stretched twenty feet below him where the Kool-Aid vomit that hadn't immediately frozen had rolled down the steep side before it solidified. He spat twice to clear the acid from his throat and gasped for air, shivering.

"What the hell am I doing, over?" Kelly said to a man who staggered alongside.

Major Darren Phillips, military aide to the president of the United States, removed his fleece hat, wiped the sweat from his bald scalp, and regarded his best friend. "This race is the ultimate test. Let's see what you're really made of, Marine."

"I'm not in the Marines anymore."

"Once a Marine, always a Marine."

"Amazing. The government will be happy to learn that your programming works even in freezing conditions."

Darren ignored him. The Eco-Challenge was so grueling that emotions and true character inevitably bubbled to the surface. In Kelly's case, that meant a lot of smart-ass comments. Darren had himself slipped several times during the race and revealed his own feelings, a violation that clashed with his personal code. Better to have your friends label you robotic than undisciplined or emotional.

"The nausea is normal considering the amount of sleep you've had, Kelly. Just a long day magnified."

"Yeah, five of 'em back-to-freaking-back." The exhausted racers had carried the sickness of an all-nighter with them for a hundred hours. Kelly righted himself and squinted up the hill. "Well, time to chase your goddamned girlfriend again."

"She's great, isn't she?" Darren allowed himself, feeling awkward. He hoped it did not sound like a need for confirmation.

"So the mighty Darren Phillips has finally been whipped. Tamed like a lapdog."

"Screw you, Kelly," Darren shouted over the wind, not at all angry.

Kelly clapped him on the shoulder, laughed, and started to hike. "Yeah, Kate's great, but I hope you're handy with the garden tools. Assuming she says yes, that is."

Darren grunted and pressed his hand against the inner pocket of his microfleece jacket that held the ring, checking as he had so often during the race. He planned to ask Kate to marry him in front of the Discovery Channel cameras at the finish line, a scene that might play well when he eventually ran for Congress. Assuming they reached the finish line, of course.

The men leaned into the hill again, driving their ice axes into the snow to provide support, sweat squeezing out of their heads, vaguely cognizant that *she* was prodding *them* to close the gap. The impacts of their crampons against the glacier reverberated in the ice bowl and sloshed around like waves in a tub, the left foot replaced by the right replaced by the left replaced by the right . . . hundreds of thousands of times already.

Hundreds of thousands to go.

MONDAY

This is my rifle. There are many like it, but this one is mine.

My rifle is my best friend. It is my life. I must master it as I must master my life.

My rifle, without me, is useless. Without my rifle, I am useless. I must fire my rifle true. I must shoot straighter than my enemy who is trying to kill me. I must shoot him before he shoots me. I will . . .

—United States Marine Corps Rifle Creed

– 1 –

ACAPULCO, MEXICO

Darren Phillips awoke to a splitting headache and punched the air. He often dreamed of Somali warlords with machetes come to cut him again and he took a moment to orient himself. Still alive. A hotel room. Mexico. Honeymoon. Tequila. He heard the slat of a blind clap open and felt a stab of sunlight.

In the haze, two naked women approached, both blurry and multicolored. He blinked his eyes several times and the shapes merged. She was deeply tan with the creamy white outline of a bikini painted on her body. She stood over him now, about five feet seven, unwanted fat long ago burned off her curvy frame. She was obviously athletic—he could now see the sheath of muscles that rippled her stomach. She had loose, straight dark hair wrapping an angular face, eyebrows that dipped toward a long nose, giving her a vaguely feline look.

My wife. Oh my God, my *wife*.

"Good morning, snuggle bunny," said Kate. "Not feeling so well, are we?" She hopped on the bed and straddled him, playfully bouncing him into the hotel bed. *Bounce. Bounce.*

"Leave me alone," he croaked. "And you promised to stop calling me that." The term of endearment did not seem fitting for a major of Marines, though in secret he enjoyed the moniker. Problem was, Kate liked to joust in public, often to break up a sea of testosterone. She had even dropped the S-bomb in front of the president, who had used it like a humorous cattle prod on his dogmatic aide.

"Sorry, cuddle bear. I'm just trying to roust you. It's past eight. I want to be at the cliffs by ten and I still need to get my morning loving." She planned a full day of rappelling, hiking, and sea kayaking near Acapulco's famous cliffs. Kate Phillips'—well, she was still mulling Kate *North-Phillips,* but was waiting for a time to broach it—idea of a vacation demanded adventure and *activity,* not lazing around in a beach chair. "Plus, we still have about ten shots left on the camera. I'm not sure if I got your good side."

"I'm never drinking again," moaned Darren. Before that honeymoon night, Darren had been drunk just one time in his life, the night before he flew to Saudi Arabia for Desert Storm. The night of the Crime Against Nature. After committing the Crime, he had stumbled back to the San Clemente bachelor pad and stared at himself hard in the mirror asking, *Who am I? Who am I?* before purging himself and treating his shower like a biologic decontamination drill. He detested the fact he had lost some control of his actions, however slight. His best friend and roommate, Gavin Kelly, had laughed at him and said, *Welcome to the club, I guess you're as prone to beer goggles as the rest of us.* But Darren Phillips didn't make mistakes like that. Not mistakes of judgment. Kelly might laugh at him for being wound too tight, but Kelly was too shortsighted to realize that if you have hundreds of skeletons like the Crime they'll come back to haunt you when you run for office. What if the woman sold the awful tale to the tabloids?

Darren peeked out from behind his pillow, and a flash went off.

"That'll be a good one," Kate laughed, raising the Canon Elph again. "Rated G, but our kids will have to be allowed to see something from the honeymoon."

Out of the recesses of Darren's memory came the blurred images of the couple rolling around naked and drunk, flashes occasionally lighting the room. "Oh no. What did you make me do, Kate?"

"I got you drunk and took advantage of you, that's what I did. The self-timer is a wonderful invention. You'll see the details later. Now let's finish this roll."

Darren suspected that her voracious sex drive had something to do with her athleticism, maybe boosting her estrogen level or feeding some female hormones or something. Whatever. Lately it had been off the charts. He pulled the covers up right against his chin even as she tried to snake her way under them, marveling at the role reversal. The death of sex some of his friends talked about was simply inconceivable in his marriage, he thought happily. "If you want access, you leave the camera behind. I'm too sober now. Let's expose the film. Could ruin my political career."

"Or make it. Look at Pamela Anderson." She tossed the camera on the sofa and peeled back the covers. He sat up to kiss her but she shoved him back down on the bed and leaned over him, her hair falling down and capturing his face, soft and warm.

———

An hour later they had parked their rental car by the kayak shop at Estero Beach and were carrying their K-2 down to the surf zone. Darren was irritated with his wife; the rental shop had been specific about using the ramp in the protected cove as a launching point and now Kate had convinced him to sprint across the busy street to make an ocean surf passage at Punta Pilares.

Darren believed in rules. He understood the need for conformity and excelled in bureaucracies: at Harvard, in the Marines, at CNN, and then as a Marine again where he currently served in the plum role carrying the nuclear suitcase alongside the president. The true test of a man was how well he performed within guidelines, beating others with determination and merit. If everyone made exceptions or bent those laws, he reasoned, there would be chaos.

"We're supposed to stay in the lagoon," he said.

"We'll be fine," she said as they negotiated the rookery of tourists, mostly college kids on spring break who were already digging into Pacificos. Scorched bodies littered the beach like a battlefield waged among alcohol, the sun, and common sense. To her right, a young woman with a glittering jewel embedded in her belly button removed her string-bikini top and raised her arms above her head, gyrating.

Her breasts must be three times as big as mine, Kate thought as she watched them sway. She twisted her own torso for fun, chuckling at the scant motion under her tight tank top. Too many laps in the pool. Too many paddle strokes.

Kate glanced back at her husband. Typically, he was just staring at the kayak, still grumbling. Sometimes he reminded her of one of those Wall Street types with whom she used to ride the subway, immersed in his own thoughts even as the microworld around him erupted. Still, he didn't have a wandering eye like her father, and most of the time his focus was just wonderful. A magnet.

"I'm not talking about our well-being. I'm talking about rules," Darren said, stepping between a comatose boy's legs.

"They told us where we should go. They didn't tell us where we *shouldn't* go. Besides, these dumb rules weren't made with us in mind."

Typical, thought Darren. Kate sneaked food into movie theaters, took their dog running on the beach without a leash, rappelled off the side of their apartment building. It was a spot that had been long ago rubbed raw. And a spot that was often sweet for some maddening reason. She is so right for me, he thought.

His was a rigid personality that needed to be dragged kicking and screaming toward the boundaries in life that she regularly exploded.

Kate's plan would take them on a leisurely kayak near the cliff divers, then an extended paddle south to a deserted beach surrounded by cliffs where the couple could drink beer, picnic, and get the blood up with a few rappels. And, she hoped, the fulfillment of a beach fantasy to boot. She had stuffed the camera and lunch into the waterproof pack alongside the harnesses and the climbing rope they called the Hell Bitch. The rope was slightly frayed, but she could not part with it and buy a replacement, much to Darren's chagrin. Too much history lugging it around Eco-Challenge courses.

When the kayak was at the edge of the wet sand, Kate slipped into the rear compartment and picked up her paddle, struggling to seal her spray skirt when her Eco-Challenge belt buckle caught on the lip.

"You should take that damn buckle off," said Darren when he leaned over to help. "It could get caught and prevent you from getting out if we roll. I don't know why you wear it with shorts in the first place. Like you're a rodeo chick or something."

"Yee-hah, baby." Kate had been wearing the heavy silver prize whenever she could in the nine months since they finished the Eco-Challenge, style be damned. The buckle was just a finisher's prize, so Darren refused to wear it, but of the seventy-five teams that had started in New Zealand, fewer than fifteen had finished. She was proud of eighth.

"Really. I'm worried," he said.

"I'm fine, babe. If we capsize, we'll just Eskimo-roll back up."

Darren slid into his hole and tested the rudder steering pedals with his Teva sandals. He was waiting, but Kate, behind him, wanted to taste bigger waves like those in the set just rolling in. He could feel her scooting the craft forward.

A big blue plunging wave crested white and slammed shut in a foamy froth not twenty yards from them, hissing as the bubbles burst up across the sand, turning it from white to brown. "Isn't it beautiful? Let's go!" she shouted over the roar.

A small crowd had gathered so that when Darren turned to refuse, he was staring at some college kid with bizarre facial growth in a Britney Spears T-shirt, who said, "You two aren't going out through those nasty waves, are you, dude?"

"Hell yes, we are," Darren said.

"Right on."

Darren pried the kayak forward until it was floating. He churned the water, catching hold of it and powering it past, charged by the sound of the surf zone and the squirt of adrenaline. The undertow snatched the kayak and it gathered speed. Kate joined him on the paddle and the boat shot forward, spray flying past like BBs, then the waves themselves crashing over the bow and knocking Darren back against his seat every few seconds. He bent forward on impact and pinned his paddle flat and parallel to the gunwale so it would not be stripped away by the greedy waves. The couple paddled hard when they were clear of each wave to build momentum for the next plunger, the kayak pitching wildly. The final breaker in the set sucked them up its aquamarine face and spit them out on the ocean side.

"Wahoo!" screamed Kate when they were clear. "That's what I'm talkin' about!"

The Pacific was a deep cobalt blue, and they paddled easily for several hours, taking time to admire the kindred spirits that leapt from the hundred-foot cliffs at La Quebrada before they turned north and skimmed toward the secret beach. Kate hoped that it was deserted because of the severe terrain that protected it. It lay in a long stretch of private property carefully delineated on her map. She didn't tell Darren about the redlines and the warnings, of course.

Their beach was more beautiful than she had hoped: a tiny crescent of sun-bleached sand, not more than fifty yards long, surrounded by towering cliffs that announced their presence by kicking the surf with their coral feet. She could see a crew of sandpipers working the edge of the high water line, scurrying up and down the beach like giant ants. Above them, a precarious set of steep wooden stairs led from the cove up over the cliffs.

"Wow. Isn't it perfect?" Kate asked, leaning back against the plastic seat rest and resting the paddle across the raised oval lip of her compartment. Brine from the sea and her body dripped off her nose. "Wouldn't it be great to own a property like this? Build a house up on top of that cliff? Just work out, have sex, and listen to the ocean?"

"Yeah, but I get the feeling that a Marine and a full-time adventure athlete might not be able to afford it." Darren had retired from endurance racing after Eco-Challenge New Zealand to concentrate on his military career. His new assignment to the White House didn't allow for a life, let alone hobbies that demanded three-hour daily workouts. If he was going to transition into a high government office, his spare minutes would have to be spent networking, not riding some mountain bike into the ground the way Kate seemed to do every week.

Kate had been anointed the ambassador for the fledgling sport of adventure racing. She used her notoriety to found an adventure academy for girls called You Go Girl! where she taught them what self-esteem tasted like by encouraging them to push themselves in the outdoors. She had been featured in most of the fitness magazines, including a naked shot in *Sports Illustrated*. Well, not *really* naked, she had laughed with her grumpy husband, pointing out the gray clay that covered her as she ran with a full pack, chased by a camel.

"We own the beach today, babe. And I've got plans for it that I think you'll like."

Darren had heard the fantasy several times. He paddled a little harder toward shore.

The couple pulled the kayak past the high-water mark and stretched their towels for a picnic. Kate stuck her feet into the soft sand and happily kneaded it with her toes. The sun broke free of the cliff and the sand sparkled and winked at them like glitter painted by the swiftly retreating shadow. The water turned turquoise and dazzled them.

"What'd I tell you, baby?" she said.

"You were right. It's unbelievable."

"I'm just getting warmed up." She positioned a Corona against a log, popped her hand down hard against the cap, and extended the foaming beer to her husband.

"Where'd you learn that?" he asked.

"College."

"And the salient difference between Princeton and Harvard is revealed. No wonder I pinned every tiger I ever wrestled." Kate tossed him the Corona and he continued, "*No mas.* My head is killing me, babe. No more alcohol for me ever."

"You want to cure that hangover? Drink it and see what happens."

Darren didn't think he liked the taste of beer, but in a few seconds that changed. It was really goddamn good. Careful, he thought, this is how the weak are taken prisoner.

Kate pulled off her tank top and stepped out of her shorts, then reached back and untied her silver bikini top. Darren smiled dumbly.

She smiled at him and pursed her lips, swaying her hips in a hula motion, pushing her bottoms slowly down past her strong thighs and stepping out of them. She flicked them with her right foot—still missing the big toenail she lost during the last race—and Darren caught them before they smacked his face. She tossed a tube of suntan lotion at her husband and lay down on her stomach. "Back rub," she said.

Darren glanced up around the cliffs and then back at his bride. I am truly a lucky man, he thought. He knelt beside her and squeezed the tube, lathering her firm shoulders and knotted back, kneading her neck and grinding his fingers into the dense muscles of her lats. Her build did not ruin, but accentuated her curves. "Ummmm," she hummed happily. "That's a good boy."

He was not used to alcohol and on an empty stomach he felt a buzzing warmth. When he cupped his hands and stroked her hamstrings and calves he had the urge to drink a second beer. And a much, much stronger urge, as well. She started a slow hum and the vibration in his hands felt like a purring cat. When he reached her ankles, Kate spun around and stretched her arms behind her head, sighed slowly, almost a coo, and arched her back. Her breasts and pelvis were vanilla except for her nipples and the slick black rectangle of hair. "Front," she said simply, bringing her hand up to her temple to block the peeping sun. "And get those clothes off."

"You better fix that salute when I get back, Marine."

Darren walked over to the pack and grabbed another Corona, then glanced up at the cliffs suspiciously—only blinding sun, though—and took off his clothes. He rubbed the bottle across his neck and then did the same to her, drinking some more now, pouring some in the belly button well of her flat stomach, licking it off, pouring it across her breasts, and watching her nipples grow and tighten, finishing the beer and tossing the bottle up the beach, happy and buzzed and excited, straddling her chest and dripping the lotion down on her, massaging her breasts even as she massaged him with those soft, wet hands and pulled him in tight, surrounded.

"You're so beautiful," he said.

"I want to do this in the water," she whispered. Her voice was husky and he carried her into the Pacific as quickly as he could, spooking three brown pelicans that flapped their wings until they had found their invisible cushion of air.

The water was cool. He was standing waist-deep when she wrapped her arms and legs around him and pressed herself down.

An alien voice boomed from the beach. "*Hola! Qué hace usted? Usted sabe que esto es la propiedad privada!*"

Kate pushed down on Darren's shoulders and hopped off him with a startled squeal. She hid behind her husband and peeked at the shore.

Three men were standing next to the kayak. Two of them wore white slacks and jackets like *Miami Vice* holdouts, and the third—an enormous fat man with a ponytail and square sunglasses like her grandmother wore—was dressed in an ugly purple Hawaiian shirt and long khaki shorts that were stretched wide by his tree-trunk legs.

"*Usted rompe la ley, mis amigos. Usted ensució. La natación desnuda no se permite. Entrar ilegalmente tampoco!*"

"What'd they say?" asked Darren, once again fuming at the fact his mother had pushed him into French at prep school, instead of Spanish.

"They say we're trespassing on private property. And that skinny-dipping is illegal. And that you littered on the beach with the bottle." Kate backed up until the ocean was deep enough to cover her breasts, then stepped aside of Darren and shouted, *"Arrepentido, nosotros no supimos. Nosotros no saldremos las botel-las. Hacemos nunca sucio este lugar hermoso."*

The fat man said something and the two men in jackets laughed. *"Bien en-tonces, sale del agua y me lo explica a mí!"* the fat man shouted. Kate could see the tattered triangle of sweat that darkened his shirt and matted his chest hair. His tongue was hanging out the same way her black Labrador Neptune's did after their long runs.

Kate pressed into Darren's back and whispered, "They want us up there, babe. You're probably going to have to pay them off."

"Wait one."

She pushed him forward. "Go."

He looked at her and nodded toward his waist. "I *can't* right now, baby, I've still got to calm down a little. He's still a tad excited."

Kate laughed, looked down at the water, and said in a baby voice, "Don't worry, little guy. Mommy will take care of you real soon." She laughed again and shouted to the men.

Darren began to wade forward. "How much do you think this will cost us?"

"I'm sure you'll figure out a way to pay the minimum," she said.

She watched her husband emerge from the Pacific feeling comfortable and unafraid. The ocean revealed him as he walked, his muscled form tapering sharply from his wide shoulders to his waist, eventually unveiling the big scar on his knee from the bullet that shattered his kneecap in Kuwait. He kept himself in superb shape, well-muscled but not bulky. "Lean enough to keep my jab speedy," she once heard him tell Kelly during one of their ridiculous Macho Marine Talks, "but strong enough to cave in a man's face." At six feet, Darren wasn't bigger than the men on the beach, but you couldn't see that in his confident approach, nakedness notwithstanding. She was sure the men would give a warning and send them on their way. She'd have to find another beach.

To lighten the mood, she shouted, *"Usted es agradable a mi esposo o él lo quizás golpee con su herramienta masiva!"*

The men in front of Darren broke into wild laughter. When he neared, they pointed at his groin and shouted back to Kate in Spanish, enjoying an in-joke. The chuckling fat man held his great sweaty belly as if worried it might burst. Darren knew the joke was made at his expense. His stiff nature made him an easy target for people with keen senses of humor like Kate and his buddy Kelly, so he was used to it. In fact, some part of him enjoyed the ribbing.

Darren smiled and turned back to face his wife. "What'd you tell them?"

The water was shoulder-high on his wife and her long hair was flopped back flat behind her head. She looked so beautiful. It made him nervous, given present company.

"Just that you'd do whatever they told you," she said.

Yeah, right, Darren thought.

Gil Saiz looked at the black man walking toward him and laughed again. The man's penis was shriveled and small, certainly not the "massive tool" that might flog as the lady said. It was a funny warning and Gil immediately warmed to the woman in the water. She was good-looking and had some American Indian traits, he thought, what with her severe eyebrows and jet-black hair. But even her deep tan couldn't hide her European roots. Tall and fair. Maybe Irish or Scandinavian years back but American now, a mixed breed like most of the mutts up there.

And the impurity was going to get worse. Here she was, *naked,* with a negro. A hot white woman like that with a black! It was the same unholy rap fantasy that these fucking college kids shoved in his face every spring when they took over the clubs, all the white kids dancing to spoken nonsense and acting black, baseball caps backward and pants pulled down. Confused gringos! Bad influences, too, beaming their fucking MTV violent rap crap into his house by satellite television when his son was home alone.

Still, Gil hoped the Jackrabbit might let the girl go. He glanced at her and she was smiling. Dread flooded him—he had been in similar positions too often. This woman was too striking to be ignored by Jackrabbit. Her smile would be gone soon. Gil had worked as the Jackrabbit's bodyguard for seven years, and though the soldiering never bothered him—that was business—he felt a weighty guilt when it came to all of the women who had come in contact with his equally weighty boss.

The black man came up to the three of them gesturing with his hands apologetically, speaking English like all of the spoiled tourists. It's Spanish down here, you arrogant fuck, thought Gil. At least the girl speaks it.

The black put on his shorts to cover at least part of his ugliness, pulled out a wallet, and raised his eyebrows, extending a ten-dollar bill. *Dollars, not pesos.*

"*This son of a bitch is trying to bribe me?*" said the Jackrabbit. "*With ten dollars? I could buy his woman from him right now. Get her up here. I want to see her tits.*"

Gil nodded his understanding. He slapped the wallet from the man's hand and shoved him back roughly. The black stumbled back and came up in a crouch. He has good balance, thought Gil. And no panic yet.

Gil was a big man, whose job demanded he be comfortable in a fight, relaxed enough to think even while absorbing a lucky blow. He saw in the American's face some of the same. The black looked like some little fighting dog, black eyes moving across the Jackrabbit and his fellow bodyguard, Juan, then back to

Gil. He's shifty, thought Gil. He's not afraid for himself, but he's afraid for his woman.

"*Come out of the water now, girl,*" shouted Gil in Spanish. "*Come out and get your clothes. My boss wants to speak to you.*"

"What'd he say, Kate?" Darren asked calmly. Unlike most of his generation, Darren Phillips understood real violence, both its consequences and its requirements.

"He wants me to come out of the water."

"You stay put."

Darren glared at the men and shook his head. He recognized that the fattest man wearing the shorts was in charge, and turned to him, gesturing apologetically and shaking his head. He tried to explain. "Sir. I am sorry . . ."

The Jackrabbit recoiled as if Darren had belched. "*Get this nigger out of my face.*"

Gil reached for the black man, missed his elbow but snared his wrist and yanked him backward, tripping him onto the sand. He moved in for a light kick to get the girl's attention, but the black swiveled around quickly and was on his feet, fists balled. *Fast!*

"Tell them we don't want trouble!" Darren screamed.

Darren had been an amateur pugilist in his formative years and was now a professional warrior. He had assiduously studied all manner of combat, and long ago concluded that martial conflict was not art but science with a splash of chaos. There was nothing artistic about violence.

He was stressed and he was glad for it. That meant that neurons from the cerebral cortex had already triggered the autonomic nervous system, preparing his body for action. Adrenaline prepares the body for the flight, noradrenaline prepares for the fight. In fewer than five seconds his skeletal muscles strengthened, his blood-clotting time decreased, his heart rate skyrocketed, his bladder relaxed, and his mental activity increased.

Now calm down, Darren thought, and take control.

He heard Kate yelling in Spanish. The biggest man in the white jacket moved in again. "Stay back," said Darren, but the man's hand was moving, so he flung the sand he was clenching into the man's eyes and blocked the punch, returning a sharp jab that he pulled. *Could have been much worse, amigo.* His left fist returned to its defensive position. "Stop this! We'll leave!"

Gil went to his knees, holding his head and thinking that the man must have used a blackjack. He swore loudly and rubbed his fingers across his bumpy eyelids. It felt like crushed glass. The pain was hot and his neck tingled.

When Darren turned to face the other two men he saw the pistols, both automatics and large caliber, one of them silver and reflecting the sun.

The second jacketed bodyguard in his white suit put his pistol in Darren's face. *9-mm Beretta. Thumb safety. Won't fire if the barrel's depressed.* Darren considered a grab, but when he heard Kate scream he raised his hands. *Too late now.*

Miami Vice punched him in the stomach and seemed to be trying to drill the barrel of the gun into his ear canal. "*Si usted mueve otra vez y yo fucking lo mata cabrón!*" he screamed. Darren allowed the man to pull his hands behind him and felt the sharp squeeze as flex-cuffs bound his hands tightly. Darren tried to engorge his wrists by clenching, but the man continued to yank even as the plastic handcuffs broke the skin. Darren felt blood trickle past his thumbs.

Juan pulled Darren to his feet by yanking his hands up past his shoulder blades. Darren screamed and twisted around in time to catch Gil's fist with his face. He crumpled down onto the sharp volcanic coral. A black spike drilled into his pectoral, but there was plenty of meat to keep it from penetrating more than a centimeter. His cheek was submerged in a tiny tide pool and he could taste brine with the blood.

"*Yo no hecho con usted,*" Gil said. He stepped on Darren's lower back, careful to avoid scuffing his polish on the coral.

Darren didn't speak the language, but he understood the dark underbelly of power and domination, the evil that men do. He twisted his head when he heard Kate coming out of the water, naked and vulnerable. He didn't want Kate to be within miles when men reverted to their truculent natures, let alone having her as their sole focus ten meters away on a deserted beach. He kicked Gil lightly, just to get his attention, and said, "Hey! You touch her and I'll fucking *kill you.*"

Gil slid his shoe up until it rested on Darren's neck, then twisted his shoe back and forth leisurely before turning his attention back to the naked woman. He didn't like to ogle, but she was worth the twinge of shame. Her thighs were big for a trim girl, and they hardened beneath her tanned skin each time she placed weight on a leg.

"*Stop!*" Kate shouted in Spanish when she ran up. "*Here I am. You are happy now?*"

"*He's making it bad for you,*" said the Jackrabbit.

Jackrabbit had never seen a woman with so many muscles, a mash of wicked curves. *And still somehow she is feminine,* he thought. *And long!* Her hips were wide and full but not fat. Nice dark skin that yielded to a pure cocaine-white bikini line. He stared at the black rectangle of pubic hair like it was a hundred-dollar bill or a pile of freshly cut product or a newly oiled pistol—impossible to take his eyes away.

Jackrabbit's extremities flooded with anticipation. He considered sending Gil and Juan to finish off the nigger so he could take her right there on the beach. *Scream, baby!*

"We don't want a problem," the girl told him.

He barely heard; he was watching the muscles between her hips. *"Tell him to calm down so we can have a discussion. This fighting with police makes it worse. You have enough trouble."*

"Okay. Relax. Relax."

Kate walked over to the pack and grabbed her shorts and bikini. *"You boys get a good look or do you want another second or two?"* She pulled the bikini bottoms up over her hips, followed by her shorts, and flipped the bikini top over her head. She reached into her bag for her scrunchie and tied her hair in a ponytail.

Darren was struggling to get his footing under Gil's shiny white leather shoe. Kate stroked his face. *"Darren, just let me handle them. Calm down. They're police. People have seen me naked before, you know."*

She smiled weakly, but Darren was in no mood for levity. This car was rolling downhill without brakes. *"Kate, I want you to get in the kayak and get out of here. Are you listening? Get the hell out of here. I'll take care of myself. They are not police."*

"You two talk too much," Jackrabbit interrupted. *"Did he say he was going to be a good listener now?"*

Kate stood defiant with her hands on her hips. *"Please, sir. This is my honeymoon and we wanted to . . . see the beach. Forgive us. Let us get back in the boat and we'll go."*

Jackrabbit laughed and his henchmen joined in a second later out of habit, though Gil felt increasingly guilty, especially when he heard it was the woman's honeymoon. He had never participated in the games with the women and the Jackrabbit accepted this. He would stay in the guesthouse while he and Juan delved.

"No, it's not that simple, girl," said the Jackrabbit. *"We have to take you back for some questions. Then we let you go."*

– 2 –

ACAPULCO, MEXICO

The trio escorted the couple up the zigzagging staircase, Darren in the lead with Gil's gun in his back and their backpack draped around his neck. Gil taunted him for the first few steps, but Darren, even with his hands tied behind his back, increased the pace. By the top the big bodyguard was concentrating on his breathing alone, yanking at the railing to keep up with a man powered only by Tevas.

They approached a spiked brick wall just a few yards from the cliff. Stainless-steel prongs were tastefully hidden among its ivy-covered top. Gil punched a code into a black box with one hand while roughly squeezing Darren's neck with the other. Darren noticed a surveillance camera wired to the big palm tree. A thick, heavily lacquered wooden door opened with a click, and they entered a sprawling compound with a mansion, a four-car garage, and a guesthouse with a glass roof. Palm trees dotted the compound. A pool sparkled·in the sun as the breeze rippled the surface.

"You like this? It's mine," the Jackrabbit told Kate. "Juan and Gil stay in the guesthouse. They work for me. So do hundreds of others." His roots were grounded in poverty, and he still felt it necessary to take ownership whenever he could, lest the woman think that one of the guards was in charge.

The Jackrabbit led them inside the guesthouse and waved his hand, inviting the gringos to look. The black did—in fact he looked like he was conducting a survey—but the girl just stared at him. *Is she impressed?*

The meaty deposits of fat near his knees jiggled when he moved, Kate noticed. It sickened her. The roof was part glass and the sun's rays were magnified, drying Kate's mouth—or is that just terror? she wondered. Her heart was thumping against her rib cage as if a small animal were trapped inside, and she wished it would stop so she could hear the whispers of the three men. She heard Juan ask the Jackrabbit if he could have a turn, too, and the Jackrabbit said he could do as he liked after he was finished.

Her stomach turned. She had competed in seas of men under the worst circumstances and watched them cave and quit before she did. She had been pounded and flipped by a nor'easter ten miles off Martha's Vineyard in a tiny kayak on a rainy night, she had slid down an ice slope to rescue a frozen teammate in a glacial pond, she had hiked a hundred miles across the Australian desert with one of her teammate's packs, but she had never, *never* felt the fear that was starting to infect her. She marveled at the gooseflesh on her shivering arms, struggling to regain control of her thoughts even as panic surged through her and erased all coherent processing. There was only dread and disbelief. She could not believe it was happening to her. *This is my honeymoon.*

"Stay strong, Kate," said Darren, looking around the room for a sharp edge he could use to cut the flex-cuffs. He was standing but Gil shoved him back into the couch with a force that foreshadowed future violence. The big Mexican bodyguard put his Bruno Magli into Darren's chest and pinned him to the couch, twisting the heel back and forth until he found a neat socket in Darren's breastbone. Then he kicked hard and crushed Darren's lungs, sending his air whistling out through his clenched teeth.

"*Stop! Please, stop. We'll do what you want,*" Kate stammered in Spanish. "*Just stop hurting him.*"

Jackrabbit shouted at Gil, and the bodyguard backed away. "*You remember that, girl,*" Jackrabbit said. "*That's smart, see? You listen to me and he doesn't get hurt. You come with me for the questions, now. If you tell the truth, we let you go.*"

She was crying softly now and had her head bowed. She whispered, "*Yes. I'll . . . do what you want. Just don't hurt us. Leave him alone.*"

As Jackrabbit and Juan led Kate out of the guesthouse, Darren saw something he had never seen and never expected to see: Her spirit was gone. She seemed so deflated in the men's arms, nodding and weeping, that rage filled him and he could think only of murder. "Keep your head up, baby," he said. "I'll be there soon."

Gil looked at the man sitting there helpless with his fat ape nose flaring and had a pang of regret. She wouldn't be the same woman when she came out—they never were. But that was replaced by anger when he thought about the sand in his eyes, and soon he was thinking about torturing the black man if the Jackrabbit decided to kill them instead of letting her live with the shame.

When Gil moved to shut the door behind Juan and his boss—screaming bothered his conscience—Darren grabbed the *Playboy* from the coffee table and tossed it behind him on the couch. Gil detected movement and spun around with his pistol drawn. *"Siéntese,"* he said.

Darren nodded and sat on the magazine. His bound hands found it and he began to roll it up behind his back, tightly and slowly.

———

Jackrabbit posted Juan outside his massive garage and took Kate in through the side door. Inside, there were three white Mercedes sport-utility vehicles and a black Porsche. Above them, twelve ceiling fans whirred lazily. Kate felt chilled but she was sweating freely. She stopped under a fan and leaned her head back. She tried to think but her brain seemed paralyzed.

Jackrabbit escorted her to an enclave in the corner with a teak well bar, a big screen television, and a couch. *"This is all mine,"* he said. He walked behind the bar and said, *"Drink? You drink tequila? Yes?"*

"No. What do you want, sir?" she asked in Spanish.

He pressed a button on a remote control, and the garage was painted by an eerie black light. The white SUVs glowed electric purple, and the Porsche seemed to disappear. Jackrabbit smiled; he loved the ambiance, especially because the black lights showed off his fleet. He couldn't wait to see her bikini line under the glow.

"What do you think of the black light?"

She just shrugged, staring hopelessly at his blue teeth.

"You do what I say and you two go free, yes?" The Jackrabbit filled a shot glass with Cuervo Gold and snapped the yellow liquid into his throat. It was hot when it slid fast down his gullet, warming his stomach. He filled a second glass and gulped it, too. He shuddered. The tequila was enough to stamp out the mild guilt he sometimes felt. *"Otherwise we get rough with your husband. Understand?"*

"Yes," she said weakly. *"Just don't hurt him."*

She was resigned to it and that made Jackrabbit happy. He hated the ones that fought and clawed. Still, maybe she hadn't figured it out yet. He needed her to accept the act before he performed it. It made him feel sexier when they didn't squirm in revulsion.

Jackrabbit sat on the couch. It was imported from North Carolina and built special for his load. He glanced up at the corner of the garage to confirm that his digital camera was recording. *"Dance for me. Dance and take off your clothes. Then you come sit over me, yes? Make me feel good?"* He watched her face closely for the reaction.

She started to cry again, but that was a natural and positive sign, Jackrabbit thought. Some began to fight and scream at this point, and then he had to get rough. He didn't enjoy screwing a battered woman. As much.

She nodded. *"Just . . . please don't tell my husband,"* she mumbled, almost a whisper. *"You'll never tell?"*

This was another good sign. Some of the other tourists he had met in bars— and one of the local girls—had told their husbands or fathers, and he didn't need the hassle. Of course, he was never actually charged with anything, and most of the girls kept quiet.

"No one will tell. Now dance and strip for me."

Kate began to sway her hips and tug at her tank top, exposing her stomach. The Jackrabbit saw the subtle waves of muscles and rubbed himself through his shorts.

She stopped suddenly. "I need music."

The Jackrabbit frowned, then shrugged and walked behind the bar. He returned with a set of keys and beeped open the door of the biggest Mercedes. *"This car is so expensive the stereo is better than the one in the main house."*

His fat body filled the car door and his left hip wedged into the hinge. When he turned the key and put in his Ricky Martin CD, it occurred to him that she might attack him. Or run. He spun around in a mild panic, his gut catching the steering wheel and burning a bit when some hairs were plucked, but the American girl was still standing by the bar with her head down. Defeated. Accepting. This will be a good one, he thought.

He sat back on the couch and said, *"Now dance, girlfriend."*

Ricky Martin is a good choice, thought Jackrabbit. The girls like him. Easy to dance to and how this one can dance! The girl began to shake and twist, rocking her wide hips back and forth. Ricky sang, *She'll make you take your clothes off and go dancing in the rain!* How appropriate!

Juan opened the door—the kid liked Ricky, too . . . who didn't?—and Jackrabbit waved him away, extremely annoyed with his bodyguard. Juan bowed apologetically and retreated from the garage's side door.

Ricky Martin sang, *Upside, inside out! Livin' la vida loca!*

Jackrabbit stroked his shorts.

"I want it louder!" the girl shouted over Ricky. She moved over to the car. Again Jackrabbit tensed, thinking now about the MP-5 submachine guns in the back, but again the girl showed no ulterior motive.

The music cranked. And *cranked.* And *CRANKED!*

It was too loud for him now, but she didn't try any tricks. The bass spewed from his new Boston Acoustics speakers, echoed, and shook the fat around his midsection. Jackrabbit thought briefly he might lose the nine scrambled eggs he had gorged to this horrible sonic boom. He could live with the goddamn blare for a body like hers, though, coming toward him now with erect nipples poking at her tank top. *It's not cold in here . . . is she excited?*

LIVIN' LA VIDA LOCA! Ricky Martin screamed.

"Take off your shirt!" he shouted, turgid with anticipation. *Goddamn, that's loud.*

"What?"

"TAKE OFF YOUR SHIRT!"

The girl had a different look about her and it excited Jackrabbit even more. She was dancing aggressively and her shoulders and hips seemed very, very powerful. She danced as if she was exercising. Also, she no longer seemed afraid. He could not wait to touch her now that she was going with the flow, as the gringos say.

SHE'LL MAKE YOU LIVE HER CRAZY LIFE! shouted Ricky.

The girl pulled her bikini top off and threw it in his face. Her breasts were small and creamy, jiggling like glowing flying saucers in the black light. Her stomach was rippled tan and tapered. With her belt buckle she looked like a naughty cowgirl. She moved forward and shouted, "Now, you. Take off your shorts!"

"What!"

"TAKE OFF YOUR SHORTS!"

Oh, she wants to play! She *is* excited. Little slut wants some strange now, doesn't she! The whore was unfastening her own gaudy buckle when she leaned over him and shouted, "MY NAME IS KATE NORTH! YOU HEAR ME?"

The Jackrabbit shrugged and unzipped his fly, his hairy pooch expanding like the top foil of a heated popcorn tray. What the hell did he care what her name was?

Ricky sang, *SHE'LL TAKE AWAY YOUR PAIN! LIKE A BULLET IN THE BRAIN!*

"KATE NORTH! YOU REMEMBER THAT!"

She could call herself Wonder Woman for all he cared. He tugged at his shorts and struggled to pull them over his thick thighs, leaning back to elevate his flabby backside and shoving hard with two hands even as the bad little slut moved over him, her belt pulled free and wrapped tightly around her fist now, the big Eco-Challenge buckle dangling on its weight. Her eyes were glowing a creepy electric blue. She leaned back, and the plate of metal was suddenly rocketing toward his head.

In the millisecond before the buckle struck his head there was a final thought—not tangible and recognizable, but present nevertheless. It was this: I have soldiered for twenty years for the hardest cartel in the world, I have been shot and knifed, I have taken eight lives, and *this* is how I . . .

Jackrabbit wore the thought on his face when the buckle caved his temple and came again and again, through his broken fingers. And again. The scalp tearing. And again. The skull folding. And again.

The Jackrabbit died before his body flopped down into his own pool of blood.

After the first blow Kate thought she would stop, but fear kept her recoiling from the man and anger kept the arm snapping forward.

LIVIN' LA VIDA LOCA! LIVIN' LA VIDA LOCA!

Outside, Juan was swaying happily to the music and lip-synching into the butt of his Beretta pistol. When the last note sounded, it was immediately followed by the *craack!* of a whip. He had missed eleven others.

Juan debated busting in on his boss again and decided to wait for the next song to cover his peek. *Is he whipping her?* After a few seconds, the next song blared and he reached for the handle of the garage door. When he opened it he recognized Jackrabbit's ankle pistol just before it flashed.

Juan's head snapped back and he, too, died before he hit the ground.

- 3 -

ACAPULCO, MEXICO

Darren was so totally distraught when the flat crack echoed inside the guest-house that his eyes welled and spilled over before he was even on his feet. He dug his fingernails into the rolled magazine behind his back and screamed. On this earth now thirty-three years, he was a paper tiger who had allowed his own wife to be raped and murdered while he sat on a couch.

A base rage captured him. Whether he lived no longer had meaning—with Kate gone, his only purpose was grounded in manufacturing three deaths, and it was probably best that he die, too. It was certainly better than returning home with the weighty guilt of another person martyring themselves for him, the way one of Kelly's Marines did to save him in Somalia.

The bodyguard was peeking out the window, now reaching for the door. Darren thought he would have to take a bullet or two to close the gap, but then he might be able to grab a pistol so he could shoot the bodyguards and maybe torture the fat man before he bled out. He thought of a Marine Corps T-shirt slogan: *Kill them all, let God sort 'em out.* By God if he didn't bleed out right away that was *exactly* what he was going to do. Kill every fucking person he saw.

Darren used the coffee table as a springboard. He jumped high and tucked his thighs against his chest, swinging his cuffed hands out from behind his back, underneath his legs as if jumping rope. The magazine in his hands was as hard as a metal baton and it now led the charge.

Gil had seen the girl running toward him, topless with white triangles on her breasts painted by a bikini. Juan was dead behind her, and his Hugo Boss suit was covered in blood. His mouth was open. So was his head. Gil reached for the door handle so he could shoot her when he heard a *thump!* behind him. He turned his head but his pistol was just a bit slower.

Darren swung his hands down and collapsed Gil's eye socket with the end of the magazine, then brought it back, kicked Gil in the knee, and slammed the magazine into his temple, knocking him unconscious. Darren fumbled for the pistol and found it underneath the body. The door slammed open and he rolled into a crouch, his eyes searching over the sights for the target.

She's topless. She's alive. Thank God.

Kate grabbed his trembling arm. "Let's go! Let's *go!*"

He wanted to hold her face in his hands but they were cuffed too tightly. He studied her. She was not even shaking. She had not been raped. "Are you okay? Where are the other two?"

"I killed them."

Whoa. "Watch the door." Even as Darren looked for an edge to slice himself free he was processing her statement. He wanted to hold her, but there was no time and there might be others. He sawed the plastic cuffs on the edge of a glass end table and ripped them apart. He was livid that he had allowed himself to be made impotent.

He had failed Kate just as he failed his own platoon in Desert Storm. Shot himself in the knee like a bumbling geek and then guiltily accepted a Bronze Star with a combat valor decoration when the platoon cover-up had come full circle and the higher-ups wanted to reward their golden boy.

He failed Kelly's Marine in Somalia. The young sergeant was killed fighting off a mob of gangbangers after Darren brought them into the hornet's nest on a glory quest. When his plastic knee collapsed early in that fight, he failed himself, too.

Now he had failed his own goddamn wife on their honeymoon. *What kind of man am I?*

"Any more coming?"

"No," she said, peering out. "I can see the mansion from here."

Darren moved over to Gil, fanned the unconscious man's fingers out, and smashed his foot down on each hand. By the time the second hand was pounded flat, the first had already swollen up. "In case he wakes up, Kate. Only other choice is to kill him." *And God knows he deserves dying.*

Darren flipped Gil's pistol around in his hand like a hammer and broke the man's index fingers and thumbs next. He ripped the cord from a lamp and bound the man's hands with a strangle knot, then rolled him over and searched for an extra magazine of bullets. He found a twelve-round clip and an extraordinarily large chrome cellular phone strapped onto his shoulder holster.

Kate's head was buzzing, but she was not nauseated and she had no remorse. Perhaps I'm still in shock, she thought. What happened did not make sense. She hadn't really killed two men, had she? She expected to feel sick, but nothing—not even the image of the bodyguard's head opening—could shake her feeling that she had done right by herself and by her husband. When she searched hard, the only emotion she found was a residual anger.

Darren touched her shoulder. "We need to get to the police as fast as we can. And take this one with us to get him first aid. It'll look bad if we leave him here unconscious. These people must be drug dealers or something."

"Go to the *police?* What if they *are* the police? I say we go straight to the embassy. Or get on a plane or something. I want to go home." She was able to look him in the eyes for the first time since the beach. "I want to go home, babe."

"Kate, we've killed two people. If we flee, we'll just look guilty. It's two hundred miles to Mexico City. And we sure as hell won't get on a plane! We need to get to the cops." The system would take care of them if they followed the rules, he thought.

Darren handed her the bulky silver cell phone. It was the size of a paperback novel and had a folding antenna. "This must be a satellite phone. Can you call the police station? Tell them we're on our way? I don't think it's good to hang around here."

"We can take one of the cars. It's running. I'll call on the way."

Darren handed Kate the pack, hefted Gil's body over his shoulder and followed her out past Juan's body and into the garage. Ricky Martin was still screaming and Darren noticed the blood before he saw the Jackrabbit. When he turned the corner he saw the fat man, saw his shorts pulled down around his knees and his disgusting nakedness, saw his wife glance down at him and turn her head. He fought the urge to kick the corpse. When Kate reached in the big Mercedes and shut off the music his ears rang in the silence, buzzing with hatred.

She put on her bikini top and her shirt. He saw her quaking.

"Did he touch you?"

She shook her head no and he was immediately relieved.

Darren stuffed Gil into the rear compartment. He tossed their pack in after him, and it got hung up on a black piece of metal. "Look at this!" Two MP-5 submachine guns were bolted on racks behind the driver and passenger seats. Several loaded clips of 9-mm ammunition were velcroed below. Darren examined the locks and said, "We've stumbled into a hornet's nest. Is there a small key attached to that bundle?"

Kate unclipped a red key and handed it back. "What is it?"

"Machine guns. I'm going to unlock them now, just in case."

Her face flushed. "In case what? In case *what*, Darren? Let's just drive to the embassy. This is really bad. What's happened?"

Darren rushed around and jumped into the driver's seat, searching for the garage door opener, finding it, popping the Mercedes into gear, and pressing the accelerator. The SUV jumped forward, and their heads hit the padded seats behind them. "This thing's powerful! Call the embassy and let them know what's happened, but like I said, we can't drive two hundred miles in a car stolen from a drug gang. How do I get back to town?"

The SUV roared out of the compound and approached a paved highway. "The map's in the pack," she said. "But . . . there! That's Pie de la Cuesta. Just go right, follow this all the way back up the coast. The police station is close to the Hyatt."

Kate flipped the heavy cell phone open and pressed Operator, then Send/ Talk. The button labels were in English, but she noticed Chinese or Japanese characters at the bottom near the brand logo, SpaceNet. The phone made a series of strange beeps and a man said in Spanish, *"Conductor. Three-nine-nine. Abort. Your encryption is off."*

Kate scrunched up her face, not understanding the Spanish word for "encryption." She checked to make sure she had dialed correctly, and said in Spanish, *"Hello. I need to be connected with an overseas operator, please."*

"Conductor. Three-nine-nine," the man said again.

"Is this the operator? Hello? I need a long-distance operator."

"Abort—"

Kate pressed End, growled with frustration, and waited a few minutes before pressing Operator again. The same voice said, *"Conductor. Three-nine-nine."*

"Hello. Excuse me, but I'm trying to reach the operator. I need the American embassy. Are you the operator?"

"This is Conductor. Three-nine-nine. Who is this?"

"I'm sorry, but what do I have to dial to get the operator? I keep dialing zero. I'm trying to reach the American embassy in Mexico City."

There was a long pause, and then the phone disconnected. Kate pressed End. "There's something wrong with this goddamn phone!" she yelled. "I get some strange company when I dial."

Darren was marveling at the acceleration of the car and wasn't paying attention. He was rehearsing the statement in his mind. *Attempted rape. Self-defense. I am a United States Marine and I work for the president. I need to speak with the United States consulate at once. The president himself will want to hear this.*

" . . . listening to me?"

Those three words in sequence triggered a Pavlovian response, and he snapped to attention. "Yes, I'm listening, Kate. We'll be at the police in fifteen minutes. We should probably get our story straight."

"Story? The *story* is that a man tried to rape me, and I did what I had to do to defend myself."

"I know you did, baby" he said softly. "I know you did."

————

The Mercedes moved at 200 kilometers per hour, gathering the coast highway and ripping it past them like a treadmill. The wheel was heavy with power, and Darren maneuvered the vehicle easily, passing car after car. The ocean formed the right boundary, but Darren didn't hear it . . . or anything else for that matter. The car was absolutely silent.

Three police cars came around the bend in front of them with their lights flashing. Darren braked hard and swerved to the inside lane, putting a pickup truck between their Mercedes and the police. "I don't think they saw us," Darren said when they zoomed by.

"Aren't we looking for police?"

"I want to get to town, not explain this all here. I didn't even hear their sirens. This car must be soundproof." He was very excited and some part of him was comfortable in the conundrum into which he and his wife had fallen. It was time for him to finally step up. *Take control.*

Kate was frustrated with the phone and pressed a speed dial in hopes that a third party might be able to connect her. She tapped Speed Dial and a list of code words popped up. She scrolled down to the first friendly name she saw on the LCD: Coffee. The phone made the series of strange beeps again, but this time a different man answered with a much different accent. He said in a harsh voice in Spanish, "*Jackrabbit, you've got the goddamn encryption off again. Turn it on and call me back.*" The phone clicked off.

"Shit," Kate said. "I . . . there's something wrong with this stupid thing. Or I'm so panicked I can't understand Spanish anymore."

Behind them, Gil groaned when he awoke and vomited. He began to babble.

"What's he saying?" asked Darren.

"Just gibberish. Same as the people on this phone."

"Forget the phone, Kate. When we get to the police station, I'm going to have his pistol in my back. Just in case."

"There you go again. In case. I think we should try to phone the embassy first."

"We can do it from the police station if they detain us. We'll straighten the whole thing out. Everything's gonna be fine, babe."

- 4 -

MOUNT CHAPAHUA, MEXICO

Adolfo Gomez sipped coffee as he drove up the winding road through the cloud forest to the Infestation Network's communication center. He emerged from the fog of condensation and saw the wind brushing the pines against a clean slate of azure. It was warm when he left home, but 8,000 feet of altitude acted like a wet blanket on the temperature and his mood. His throat burned the way it always did up there.

Adolfo's eight-hour shift as the acting communications officer lasted from two to ten p.m., five days a week. He was a nervous technocrat who spent his shifts worrying that some great crisis might befall the Infestation Network while he pulled duty. Deep down in the communications bunker he was a clock watcher, terrified of the red light on the secure phone. Fortunately, he hadn't seen it illuminate since his training.

Adolfo came around the last switchback and downshifted into first gear as the slope steepened. The huge satellite dish loomed over the forest. The jeep ground slowly up the hill, and he eventually saw the fences, the kennel, and the concrete roadblocks. He parked in the lot and looked outside the vehicle for any of those damn attack dogs that might have escaped before huffing his way up the last little hill, careful to stay within the white tape lines that broke the path through the minefield.

"Hello, Sergeant," he said to the soldier at the first fence. "Anything happening?"

The soldier looked bored. He nodded at the six-man detail crouched behind the firing slats in the concrete barricades. They unshouldered their weapons and half stood to watch him. "Nothing changes for us, sir. Sometimes I wish the Americans really would come down to fight. I really do."

And that's why you maintain that gun while I maintain the most secure communications network ever built, thought Adolfo, looking up at the giant DS-590 dish. He had a hand in its design specifications, and he never tired of this view. His only regret was that he could not boast about the technology in public. To his knowledge it was the only dish in the world that was built to amplify ultrawideband signals, the most revolutionary communications technology since the two-way radio.

Standard airborne communications sent radio waves on specific frequencies, which meant that no conversation was totally secure. Even the most advanced frequency hopping technologies were not impervious to eavesdropping, especially by the Americans, a persistent problem that Adolfo's new employers blamed for a vast reduction of revenue.

Ultrawideband was impenetrable. Instead of sending out radio waves, the Infestation Network's satphones sent billions of tiny pulses of electrical energy every second, not on specific frequencies but across *every frequency simultaneously*. The system Adolfo had installed with the Chinese was like the wind, everywhere and nowhere at once. Instead of communicating from relay tower to relay tower, the satphones in the Infestation Network sent their pulses into space where a satellite hovering permanently over the Americans gathered the electricity and shot it to the communications center. Adolfo's dish then amplified the energy and sent the bursts as far south as Santiago and as far north as Chicago.

The only way to communicate was to have another ultrawideband receiver or transmitter with the same embedded code, which was why the communications center on Mount Chapahua—and each satphone—required such heavy security.

"You don't really mean that. About fighting the Americans, I mean," said Adolfo.

"Yes, sir, I do. We'd chew the gringos up," said the sergeant.

"Yes, well, I hope not on my shift," Adolfo laughed.

The sergeant pressed a seven-digit code—Adolfo wasn't permitted to know any of the security measures—and the electric fence stopped buzzing. Adolfo followed the sergeant through the second fence, past the machine-gun bunkers and the dog cages, and up to the communication center's bunker door. He put his thumb on the print scanner and smiled for the camera. The big vault door hummed and popped open.

"Have a good day, sir," said the soldier.

"A boring day is a good day."

Adolfo was careful as he descended the steep staircase. The lounge was empty. That's strange, he thought, Ramon is *always* ready to go when I relieve him. Adolfo walked down the hallway into the heart of the bunker complex, no longer cognizant of the hum of the great generators beneath his feet. He entered a room filled with computers of various sizes and capabilities. A brilliant digital map of the Americas was projected on a movie screen as big as a billboard that dominated the room. The Infestation Network hubs, called hives—suppliers, customers, and protection—were depicted in a smattering of red dots scattered from Montreal to Santiago. One of the dots, which looked to be close to Acapulco, was blinking. Beside it, a series of numbers grew.

Adolfo's heart sank when he saw Ramon hunched over the two radio technicians. "Something wrong?" he asked, barely able to get the words out.

"Just one of Jackrabbit's sluts again," said Ramon, a gruff man around whom Adolfo was uncomfortable, even though they shared fewer than a few minutes together each day. Ramon wasn't recruited from telecom like Adolfo and most of the other communication experts; he had worked for the Juarez cartel for most of his life. "One of his stupid bitches got on his satphone again. He must have left it out like last time. Wait until Juarez hears. That fat bastard will be back running mules in Tijuana by nightfall."

Three months earlier, a woman had tried to use Jackrabbit's satphone to dial her brother for a ride home from the big man's mansion. Adolfo had to report it—he dare not violate protocol—and the cartel commanders had exploded.

The rules were simple: The satphones stayed locked up unless there was business—a business in which orders were rarely repeated. Even when use of the satphone was authorized, there was an elaborate checklist to ensure the encryption was operational. The Americans monitored every frequency of every airwave around them, but they were deaf to ultrawideband. Unless someone got hold of a phone, of course.

Adolfo shook his head nervously. There weren't any third chances in his new vocation, and he hoped this wouldn't reflect on him.

The four Bose speakers in the communications center started to beep as if someone were dialing. One of the radio technicians said, "Here she comes again, sir! I put her on the speakers." The technician adjusted his headset and said, "Conductor. Three-nine-nine."

"Hello. Excuse me," the woman's voice echoed in a slight American accent. "I'm trying to reach the operator. I need the American embassy. Are you the operator?"

"This is the Conductor. Three-nine-nine."

"I'm sorry, but what do I have to dial to get the operator? I keep dialing zero. I'm trying to reach the American embassy in Mexico City."

Inside his polished shoes and ironed socks, Adolfo's toes curled up.

Ramon put his hand around the technician's microphone and put his index finger up to his lips. "Don't hang up until we get a grid on her! Do we have her location yet?"

Where a Global Positioning System was accurate to a few meters, ultrawideband was accurate to within a centimeter even under a jungle canopy or in a concrete bunker.

"Just got it," the technician whispered, pointing at the map. A black arrow had suddenly appeared next to Acapulco. Ten digits popped up on the big screen.

"Enlarge the area."

The technician tapped nimbly on the keyboard, and the screen zoomed in to Acapulco proper. A cobweb of roads filled the big screen. The arrow was located about six kilometers east of the red dot indicating Jackrabbit's compound, and it was moving toward Acapulco proper. The woman clicked off, and the connection was lost.

"Sweet mother of Jesus," burst Adolfo. "Did she say the *American embassy?* Why would one of Jackrabbit's girls want the Americans?! My God! What if they get the phone?"

Ramon had the biggest breach of the Infestation Network to date on his hands, and even if his flaccid counterpart was now technically on duty, he wasn't going to let Adolfo make decisions in a crisis. Adolfo wasn't a soldier; he was a shivering geek. Ramon asked, "Did you reach Jackrabbit yet?"

"No, sir," said the technician. "No answer at his house and no answer on his civilian cell."

"Did you try his bodyguards?"

"They didn't answer the guesthouse phone, sir."

"Goddamn him. Call his brother and get some *Federales* over to the fucking house." He turned back to the first technician. "Where is the exact location of the satphone?"

The radio chief pointed at the big screen. He had enlarged a section near the coast, so it filled the twenty-foot flat screen. The black arrow was blinking, immobile. "Looks like they're on the main road back toward Acapulco."

Ramon bit his lip. Was the Jackrabbit traveling with her?

Beeps silenced the room—the woman was dialing again—and Ramon said to the technician, "Keep her on the phone this time."

"I don't think she's dialing us, sir."

They heard a digital ringing, and then a man's voice said, "Jackrabbit, you've got the encryption off again. Turn it on and call me back." *Click.*

The technician exploded. "She just used a speed dial! Sir, I'm pretty sure that was a speed dial!" Plugging preset numbers into an Infestation Network sat-phone was forbidden, though it would not have been Jackrabbit's only violation of the protocol.

"Well, who the hell did she call?" hissed Ramon.

"Too short a call for his satphone to fix his position," said the technician, "but I got the number she dialed."

On the flat screen that tracked all the phones in the network, a number came up next to Jackrabbit's phone. Ramon looked at the country code, and his stomach roiled. "Get me Deputy Attorney General Saiz. *Now.*"

When Adolfo looked at the digital map of the Americas he felt faint. South of the Mexican border one of the hives was blinking. Columbia, he thought. The woman had dialed a supplier. *A supplier in the clear!*

– 5 –

MEXICO CITY, MEXICO

Eduardo Saiz, deputy attorney general of Mexico in charge of the National Institute to Combat Drugs, typed *www.prettyyoungthings.com* into his Internet browser toolbar and glanced around the empty room out of habit. He had ten minutes before his next meeting, and he pulled his chest tight against the desk. Along with surfing free sex sites—ostensibly in search of online predators in case anyone ever asked, but who could?—Eduardo was in charge of the Federal Judicial Police, the *Federales,* the 5,000-man army of elite cops who were a ubiquitous presence in Mexico, more heavily armed than their local counterparts but just as involved.

Eduardo's intercom buzzed. "Minister Saiz, your wife just called. She wanted to make sure you knew she was feeling better. Was she sick, Minister?"

Eduardo sat bolt upright and spun around to his cabinet, reaching for his key ring. "Er, yes. She was sick last night. Nothing to worry about." But evidently there was. As a standing rule, his wife never called the office on a landline. Except, of course, when the Infestation Network wanted to talk with him. He unlocked the safe behind his chair, unlocked the steel-wrapped lead carrying case, and took out his satphone. "I'll be back in a moment," he told his secretary as he hustled outside.

The car horns never stopped blaring in Mexico City. Eduardo hoped the screeching might drown out the words he was loath to hear, but when he put the satphone to his ear they did not. The color drained from his face, and his spit was gone. He listened for five minutes, occasionally fanning his face with his hand to keep cool.

The notification left Eduardo feeling like a next of kin. He spun around to ensure no one was sneaking up on him, then he ordered the communications center to make two calls for him. The first, to the *comandante* of the Guerrero State *Federales,* ended with this sentence: "When you find the girl, get the sat-phone—that's the mission. Understood? Then interrogate her and bury her in the mountains. I don't care what Jackrabbit says. The girl dies, and it's his fault. In fact, when you find that fat son of a bitch, bring him directly to me. He gives you trouble, arrest him."

Eduardo hung up and tried to steel himself for the next conversation. But the close proximity of his own death made that hard. He half expected one of the cabs on the street to careen up into him on the sidewalk. The communication center introduced the second call with, "Stand by for *El Toro.*"

He was connected with Juarez and the leader of the largest cartel in the world.

– 6 –

MCLEAN, VIRGINIA

The black pager buzzed on the hip of Susanne Sheridan, deputy director in charge of the Crime and Narcotics Center, Directorate of Operations, Central Intelligence Agency. The Directorate of Operations was the tip of the spear for the four branches of the CIA, but with the war on terror raging she felt her area of operations was being wrongly neglected. Worse, she was now required to conduct weekly meetings for the fledgling Department of Homeland Security, where her raw intelligence was fused with that culled from other agencies like DEA, FBI, INS, and the Border Patrol. She viewed the task as well-intentioned, but also highly visible and highly disorganized. That is, necessary but ugly.

Because Homeland Security still hadn't filled the fusion billet, she had been temporarily tasked with combining all intelligence coming in from the counternarcotics nodes and the southern border. Inside the Beltway, the word "temporarily" made her shiver. At least she was able to hold the briefs on her turf.

"Woo!" she said, mistaking the pager for an errant finger. She took a karate swipe at the waistband of her skirt, then covered her mouth and giggled. "Oh, now, *darn*. There I thought it was Roger tickling me again and it was just this damn pager."

Roger Corwin of the Federal Bureau of Investigation's Latin America Division blushed deeply and raised his precisely plucked blond eyebrows. He inhaled sharply to control his anger and smelled the Aloe Lubriderm in which he had bathed his skin after his morning workout.

Corwin was not going to fall for Susanne Sheridan's ruse to play political fuck buddy. He could smell the ambition in her. Her southern accent and goofy charm masked a duplicitous harpy. She had come from the Directorate of Operations, after all, and they were incompetent glory hounds. But they *were* good liars.

Roger knew he was a good-looking man, so under ordinary circumstances flirtation from a female colleague was not an aberration. He was a quicker study than most when it came to the subtle tricks of the female species. These circumstances, however, were not ordinary. Corwin had been tapped to work closely with Sheridan in standing up these ridiculous Homeland Security briefings. For a seasoned FBI agent like Roger Corwin, helping Homeland Security was like bench pressing in the back of a garbage truck. FBI Agents were college graduates with abundant real-life experience who were trained at the most elite academy in the nation. Corwin had himself policed the freeways on his California Highway Patrol motorcycle for eleven years—and had even been granted his master's degree at night school—before he had finally been accepted into the bureau.

All manner of cats and dogs had infiltrated Homeland Security, though. Most of them were uneducated bureaucrats or military head cases. Corwin had fiercely resisted joining the traveling zoo—led by a former governor with zero security experience, to boot—but when the Christians In Action relented and strapped on their kneepads in the form of Susanne Sheridan, the FBI grudgingly forced Corwin over to do the weekly tap dance and teach the infant to crawl.

Susanne unclipped the pager from the top of her skirt and raised her hand. She said, "Excuse me, everybody. Someone is desperately waving me out. Another gentleman caller. Oh, me."

"And I thought I was the only one," said Corwin.

"You're in the lead, Roger Dodger, but the young thirtysomethings are nipping."

Corwin smiled, thinking that Sheridan had pulled the typical female ambush, using gender politics and pussy persuasion to the hilt. Here she was holding the country briefs at Langley, enemy territory in the battle between his agency and hers. Worse, she was likely going to brief the governor, who was busy across the Potomac vacillating on seniority while the new bureaucracy staffed up. He was apparently oblivious to the pronounced reputational stench the acronym CIA carried among those with "need to know," including foreign governments.

Corwin preferred to be on top. It was only a matter of time before he turned perception into reality. Homeland was the suck, but it was also the debutante in Washington. He hoped to be named a division head. When he took the reins of these intelligence wannabes, the glare would be warm and a promotion would be waiting for him behind the spotlights.

Susanne slid her chair back quietly and exited the country brief, conscious of the sharp clicks her heels made as they announced her departure. She tapped the first few bars of "Tea for Two" before she stepped out, happy to hear the room laugh. There weren't many things to smile about at the Agency lately.

Following the Aldrich Ames disaster, the head of the FBI's polygraph unit had been placed in charge of Counterintelligence to police the Agency. CIA officers resented the ensuing witch hunt. How could the Feds be crowned infallible experts in counterespionage when they allowed fruitcakes like Robert Hanssen to drag secretaries around his FBI office by their bra straps? Talk about red flags. *Helllllooo!*

This was made worse by the tit-for-tat blame game played out in the press after September 11, 2001, with both agencies leaking accusations. The blood between FBI and CIA seemed to be all bad, and Roger Corwin's ham-handed power grab ass didn't help.

Susanne smiled at her assistant, Christian Collins, when she reached the safety of the hallway. "Even if it's nothing, Christian, thanks for getting me out of that banal meeting. Regional updates are the *worst* form of torture. Next to a man with a hairy back, that is."

Susanne winked, but Christian played the straight man too well to take the bait. He had quit his Internet business two years before to work for her, but remained uncomfortable with her penchant for mixing humor into serious conversations. "This is something worthwhile, ma'am."

"Tell me someone located all the IMF money we gave the Soviets. Oops, sorry, the *Russians*."

"Oh, well, it's not that good, ma'am," Christian said. "I don't think we'll ever have hard evidence on that. But NSA *did* just hear something on the BEE-KEEPER satellite net you are just not going to believe. They just sent us the recording . . ."

She started toward Operations Center before he finished the sentence.

"Anyway, ma'am," Christian said as he hustled after his boss. "You remember when that woman came up on BEEKEEPER in the clear about three months ago? Called her brother for a ride home from Luis Calagra's—the man called Jackrabbit? Well, a woman came up on the Net fifteen minutes ago. Unencrypted. *Not* the same woman."

"So Jackrabbit is not only careless, he has not one but two stupid girlfriends." Susanne unconsciously picked up her pace. Her rapid heel strikes echoed off the polished linoleum and revealed her interest, though she tried to keep her voice neutral. The truth was, BEEKEEPER had been an obsession since the satellite rocketed into space from the Chinese launching pad in Xiangbo six months earlier and assumed a static position over central Mexico. Susanne's team suspected it had been sold to a drug cartel, but confirmation had been maddeningly elusive. BEEKEEPER was impenetrable.

"This one's different, ma'am. The girl, I mean."

"How so?"

Christian Collins cleared his throat and said, "She asked for our embassy. In the *clear*, ma'am. Then she *speed-dialed*. Some guy that was mucho pissed off to be contacted unencrypted hung up."

"The phone has stored numbers."

"That's not even the best part. I sent the recording to linguistics and they're pretty sure the woman on the phone isn't southwest Mexican like the last one. She has an unusual accent."

"Don't take this out of context, Christian, but, my God, don't stop now."

"We think she's American."

– 7 –

ACAPULCO, MEXICO

Darren parked the SUV behind the police station and tapped his lower back when he got out of the car. The pistol was tucked into the waistband of his shorts, as bulky and exciting as a wad of cash. It violated both the standard operating procedure for weapons carriage that the Corps had instilled and the need for order that had always been in his blood, but he did not have a holster. Darren reached in for the bodyguard and saw that the man was awake—not lucid, but babbling and breathing. There was a long blood stain running down his undershirt that looked like a bad power tie. He grabbed the big man by the hair and pulled him up onto his feet. The man crumpled, so Darren had to heft him onto his shoulders. He smelled like puke.

"You do the talking, Kate," Darren grunted as he took the steps two at a time.

Acapulco's chief of police, a man called Humpback, was sitting behind his desk when the American couple burst through the doors. He had been monitoring his radio closely for news of his brother, who had apparently shot someone at his estate again. The maid who reported it—some new girl on only her third week—was in custody and might have to be killed, just like last time. Some things could not be helped.

Humpback would wait for his brother's order before he did anything like that. If he killed her first, his brother might be angry and yell at him, like the time Humpback put that German tourist girl in jail after she claimed the Jackrabbit had raped her. She had gotten television cameras to come to the station a few days after her release. They had asked questions very quickly, too fast for his damaged brain to process. When they finally left, Jackrabbit was angry. That made Humpback feel bad. Jackrabbit told his big brother that he was stupid and should have just let the girl go.

For Humpback, life had been a confusing maze after a member of the Tijuana cartel clubbed him with an aluminum baseball bat, but through all the murk there was his little brother's admiration, a prize for which he competed every day. The Jackrabbit was an Important Person now, not just a soldier, and he often reminded Humpback that *he* was to thank for Humpback's job with the police. As its chief, no less. *That's* how powerful the Jackrabbit is!

When the maid's call came in, Humpback dispatched almost every single officer to Jackrabbit's mansion. He and his deputy were the only police officers in the station when the black man walked in with Gil on his back.

Gil was babbling louder, and Darren said, "Kate, tell him to shut up, will you?" He leaned over, dumped Gil into a small sofa next to Humpback's desk, and surveyed the room. The station was small, maybe the size of a Marine squad bay except not as tidy. Two cops. There was the fat man with the biggest desk and some sort of rank insignia painted on his blue shirt. He was bathing in his own sweat. Darren figured him for a desk sergeant or duty officer when he saw the other younger cop look to him for a reaction.

Locked in the holding cell behind the two cops were three college-age kids wearing American baseball caps. A map of Acapulco on the wall. A radio receiver and a loudspeaker. Both cops still sitting down. Only one police car in the parking lot, Darren remembered, but lots of civvy vehicles.

Gil began to form sentences and spoke rapidly. But he was drooling and slurring. Humpback leaned in to hear and was motioning him to slow down, slow down. Frustrated, he looked at the couple and said, *"Hable español?"*

Darren started to answer yes for her, but Kate grabbed his arm and cut him off. "No. English. Just English." She wanted the advantage. "He attacked us."

"It's . . . bitch," stammered Gil in Spanish. He was woozy and punch-drunk. He assumed the black had split his head open with a hammer. He could hear the blood roaring out. He managed to turn his head to Humpback. *"Brother. Your brother."*

Darren started to speak again but Kate whispered for him to shut up so she could listen. Had he said *hermano?*

The phone on the younger cop's desk rang and he answered it. His head jerked up, and he began to wave frantically at Humpback, on his feet now, nodding his head and answering questions a whispered word at a time, body rigid and uncomfortable. He cupped the handset and said, *"Chief. It's Comandante Rodriguez!"*

"*What does he want?*" Humpback asked, struggling to remember the chain of command.

"*He says that Jackrabbit . . .*" The deputy nodded again and began scribbling on a yellow pad. Then his mouth opened in shock. He looked right at Kate.

Next to her on the couch, Gil gasped. His hands were on fire. He brought one limply up to his mouth and licked it like a wounded cat. He started to cry. "*My fucking hands are broke. I'll kill . . . they . . . to Jackrabbit.*"

"What's the guy on the phone saying?" asked Darren, looking back and forth from the deputy to the crippled bodyguard. "And what's this jackass babbling about?"

The loudspeaker on the wall was connected to the police radio and it blared. The metallic nature of the voice could not cover its panic. "*Chief, this is Deputy Montoya. We're at your brother's house. You better come down here, Chief. Right now.*"

Kate looked into Darren's eyes and said very softly, "Do *exactly* as I say, babe."

"Something wrong?"

"They're related," she hissed.

"*Excuse me, Chief! Excuse me!*" shouted the deputy in front of Darren. He waved for Humpback to come closer, still staring at Kate. He held out the phone as if it were radioactive, but the cord would not stretch to his boss. Humpback remained at his desk, staring at the loudspeaker, wearing a mask of bewilderment. There were not enough inputs in his cracked skull to sift through the noise. After a few seconds, he was able to process this: My brother is in trouble again. My boss found out already. He wants to yell at me because of it. It is embarrassing to have the gringos here now.

Humpback dismissively waved both arms at the couple. "*You go outside now.*"

"*No, Chief,*" shouted the deputy, cupping the phone. "*Comandante Rodriguez wants us to hold these two for the Federales. He has a platoon coming. If they run . . . he said . . . he said to shoot them in the back, Chief! Some other Federales are already at the Jackrabbit's with our men. In a helicopter. I have . . . Oh, he wants to speak with you.*"

Humpback eased his chair back and stood with great effort, using the desk as a cane. "*Shoot them?*"

"*Yes, Chief. Shoot them!*"

Darren's throat tightened when he heard the inflection in the man's voice. Now his wife was digging her fingernails into his forearm. Something was terribly wrong. He eased his shooting hand behind his back.

It didn't make sense to her. The *Federales* were part of the government. Had she killed some cabinet member? How did they have her description already? She was about to whisper to Darren when the police radio blared. *"Chief! Did you read me, Chief, over."*

Gil sat up and spat blood onto the tiled floor, then he fought another wave of nausea before he regained his breath. *"Did you hear me, Humpback? These two murdered Juan, and probably your brother. The woman shot them."*

Humpback shook his head no, fumbled in the desk for his revolver, and pressed the button on his police radio microphone. *"Deputy Montoya. Put my brother on the line. That is an order. I WANT MY BROTHER!"* Rivulets of sweat popped out of his brow and his face turned a dark purple. He lived in a washing machine of sweat, but still his temperature skyrocketed, cooking his languid brain and shortening his breath. *"I'll kill them both,"* he whispered.

"Shoot him, Darren," came another whisper, this one in English.

"I'm afraid I cannot, Chief," the loudspeaker said. *"Jackrabbit is dead."*

Humpback felt for the revolver and pulled it out, fingers as meaty as stuffed sausages struggling to unclip the tiny clasp on the blue leather holster through the tears in his eyes, breathing in gasps, Darren's arm already level and rigid, shoving Kate to the ground and firing at the same time, a flash and Humpback gone from this world, now Darren swiveling his hips and shooting the deputy through the skull as well. The back of his head erupted in a fine red powder that covered the cell. The three boys inside were screaming. Darren twisted for more targets even as the blood dripped down the stainless steel bars. But there was no one left to kill.

"Chief? Are you there, Chief?" said the loudspeaker.

Darren reached over Humpback's desk and yanked the radio power cord out of the wall. His Teva sandal slid in Humpback's blood. He struggled to control the turmoil of excitement and dread that was roiling him. They had crossed the line of departure, all right. "What happened?"

"We killed that one's brother at the house!" she panted, pointing at the pile formerly known as Humpback. "*I* killed his brother. He was going to shoot us. The other one said that *Federales* are on their way. He had instructions to shoot us if we tried to flee."

"Jesus." He was going to shoot us, he thought. No question. Why? What is this? *This is combat.*

"Darren, tell me this isn't happening."

"We have to get out of here, Kate."

"Yo! Let us out!" one of the boys in the cell shouted, gripping the bleeding bars. He was wearing a navy blue Michigan T-shirt with gold lettering and had the build of a fullback or a wrestler. Dyed blond hair cropped short and spiked in the front. Dangerously tan. "Hey! Come on, man. We been here for two days. Keys are right there on that desk. We're American."

"You saw how this happened," said Darren. "Our names are Darren and Kate Phillips. We're on our honeymoon. I'm a Marine officer, and I work in the White House. My wife was almost raped; then this man tried to kill us. You need to call the embassy when you get out of here."

"You let us out and that's what we'll tell them. Get the word out, straight up."

"Can't do that," said Darren.

"Step up, man! Let us out," the boy said. The cobweb of veins in his big forehead was pulsing. His facial features were cut like a bodybuilder's, and Darren figured he must have been ingesting a pound of steroids a day. "We ain't done nothing. We're on spring break, and we get rounded up for no reason. Let us—"

The front door swung open and bounced off a wall. Kate saw a young police officer—maybe eighteen—step into the station carrying a handful of Cokes that were stacked up from his waist. His head was down, pinning the top Coke to his chest with his chin.

She and Darren ducked behind Humpback's desk. She didn't look at the body, but could smell Humpback's rusty blood. She whispered, "Did he see us?"

"Don't know. Just a little guy on a soda run." He started to thumb the hammer back, but it was a single-action pistol and the next bullet was already less than two pounds of trigger pull away. "But he's between us and freedom."

Kate grabbed his arm. "Don't kill him, Darren." She could not believe that those words were now being used in earnest, that her life had somehow shifted into some heinous caricature where her husband and she had killed two cops each. The dizzy weight of murder paralyzed her. Her mother and brother had been destroyed by the other end of a pistol like the one her own husband was now holding. Taking another life would not help anything. No more death.

Carlos "Little D" Diego froze when he saw Gil on the couch. A black man with a chrome pistol popped up from behind Humpback's desk like a devilish jack-in-the-box. Carlos dropped the Cokes and tried to run right out the door. His second step planted on a rolling can, and he was on his back trying to recover his breath before he remembered to draw his pistol. He was terrified. It smelled like puke and blood. He squirmed over behind the processing desk at the entrance, cringing when his hand knocked a can across the tile toward the cell, revealing his position.

When Little D yanked his revolver free, it quaked so violently that he knew he wouldn't be able to shoot anyone, not that he could will himself to pull the trigger in the first instance. Little D wanted to be an Olympic diver, and had joined the local force only two months earlier to support his dream, trading training time on the cliffs for a brutal duty schedule. He was bringing Cokes to the American boys, and hoped to convince Humpback to allow his gift. He felt the boys had been treated poorly and planned to lobby for their release.

Little D pressed his cheek into the metal desk and tried to hug it. He was horrified to see his boot protruding into the scuffed entranceway, and he tucked it in as fast as a mouse ducking into a hole. *"I am a police officer. Put . . . your hands up. Hands up! No, throw the gun away, first. Do it! Do it or there's trouble!"* He fought the urge to urinate.

"What'd he say?" asked Darren.

"He said to give up," she replied.

"They're here behind the desk!" shouted Gil, awake and coherent now. *"Two of them. They murdered Humpback and the oth—"*

Darren smashed the big pistol into Gil's ear, and he slumped into his own vomit.

Murdered Humpback, thought Little D, Mary, mother of Jesus! His bladder control evaporated with the words, and a dark stain spread across the lap of his blue police uniform and dripped on the tiled floor. Screw this! He was considering a run for the door when a woman shouted, *"We just want to leave in peace. It was all a mistake. We want to call the American embassy."*

"I said . . . put your . . . Throw your weapon away now! I'll shoot you!" He peeked around the desk and started to crawl toward the lockers, a meter closer to the door. It seemed an endless journey. *Please, Jesus, let me live.*

Darren extended the pistol, and it followed his eyes in the search for the cop. He whispered, "Kate, you've killed two men, probably cops. You said more are coming to kill us. *I've shot two cops in the face.* If we want to remain free, it's him or us. This is war now. Do you understand that? If we stay in here we get shot, and that's the *best* scenario. We have to get to a public place. Time's short."

Darren Phillips was indeed a man of rules, and the rules had changed.

"No. Please. Don't kill him." She thought of the Cokes and the tone in the little cop's voice. Then the bodies were in her mind. Jackrabbit's. The bodyguard. The two cops. Her mother and brother. This young cop was somebody's brother, too. So much violence in the world. Too much. *We have to stop before it gets out of control.*

Darren was flat against the floor under Humpback's desk, scanning over the pistol sights for the cop's feet. It was dark enough under the desk that the luminescent targeting dots on the sights glowed. He saw a face and a gun, centered the front sight post, and squeezed the trigger. A deep boom and a spout of fire that froze the picture of the pistol even after it jumped.

The recoil knocked the barrel of the gun into the underside of the metal desk with a clang, and it took Darren an extra moment to steady the pistol again. The cop's body was still there, but his head was no longer round. *Must be hollow tips.*

"Let's go," Darren said.

Kate silently watched the shell casing as it rolled smoking across the dirty tile. Then she put her face in her hands.

"Jesus fucking Christ, dude! Holy shit! Let us the fuck out of here, man! Seriously! You've got us involved in all this shit," the boy in the Michigan shirt screamed, still gripping the bars. "They're gonna kill us!"

Darren spun around. "You aren't involved and thank God you're not. Safest place for you is in the cell. You just tell the press we had no choice. My name is Darren Phillips. I work for the president. They tried to rape my wife."

"Fuck you," the boy said. "You think we're in position to bat for you? You don't let us out, only story we'll give is the fact you came in here and shot three people in cold blood. That's a promise. We been in here for, like, three days. Let us out and we'll do right by you. I gotta get back stateside."

"You do exactly what I say, you little punk, or—"

"Quiet, Darren," said Kate, gripping her husband's biceps. He trended toward stubbornness in conflict while she sought middle ground, which was why she was the captain of the adventure-racing teams while he played her heavy.

Kate looked at the college boy. He had huge, meaty hands that easily engulfed the vertical bars. His face was callow but sweet, a big set of teeth with a tiny purple bruise no larger than a grape under an eye. He dyed his hair like her brother used to. She pulled free of Darren's hands, grabbed the keys, and unlocked the cell. "If you're caught, you better keep your promise to me."

"We will. I swear to God we will. Thank you." His hand dwarfed hers when he took it.

Darren wanted to put a gun in the kid's face and force him and his buddies back in, but the damage was done, and he felt the squeeze of time. He glared at the Michigan boy and grabbed Kate by the wrist. "We've got to get out of here."

– 8 –

MCLEAN, VIRGINIA

The Crime and Narcotics Operations Center looked like a modern trading floor and was now just as busy. Three rows of desks were parsed into seats delineated by stacks of flat computer screens and laptops, most of them linked to the two massive Cray computers that stood guard over the rest of the smaller computers. The hum in the room was a combination of both human electricity and nearly a hundred cooling fans. The walls were soundproofed with a honeycombed foam coating that was so uneven it gave the impression that it was a series of stalactites and stalagmites. Deputy Director Susanne Sheridan coined the nickname "Bat Cave" when she took charge. It stuck.

Ten wall-mounted digital televisions were tuned to four American cable news channels and several government stations in Latin America and Russia. The Bat Cave was a combination of dark underworld and high-tech incubator, a fast-paced dance floor filled with techies and professional tricksters, overeager patriots all.

One of the baby technical analysts on loan from Science and Technology stood when Susanne entered the Bat Cave and said, "Good afternoon, ma'am." He might have been twenty-three. God, she thought, they get younger every day. And "ma'am" didn't help matters.

"Let's hear it."

The young analyst flicked his I.D. badge uncomfortably. He was about to speak when his older counterpart, an overweight man named Ted Blinky whose mannerisms put Susanne off, stood and told his subordinate, "I'll handle this."

Blinky was fifty-one, a relic for a technical analyst who still suffered acne attacks. He was a man who loved to stretch projects and, by default, patience. Susanne had once considered tasking him with constructing the correlation between his increasing age and his increasing waistline just so he would retreat into his hole for a month.

"Ma'am, there's good news and then there's *good news*." Blinky had tied his tie too short and it protruded nearly horizontally across the top of his stomach. He looked at the younger analyst and winked, nearly giggling.

The problem with techies, thought Susanne, is their bizarre sense of humor, something that must be issued with a perspicacious brain. "Shoot."

"I listened to the digital recording of the phone call NSA intercepted and guess where it was that the woman speed-dialed? In the clear, I might add."

"The White House." Susanne had a sense of humor that was dying with the old school. "Let me guess, this involves a conspiracy of the highest magnitude."

Ted Blinky was deflated. Operations bigwigs often made light of technology because they could not grasp it. They could not attack his knowledge, so they attacked his status. He hoped to change that by making a lateral move into Homeland Security operations so he could run his own team, bringing technical skill to strategic planning the same way a Dungeons & Dragons elf was both magician and warrior. "No, ma'am. We traced the call to a wealthy suburb outside Calle, Columbia. This lady called from Mexico—assuming she's in Mexico, that is—to *Columbia*. You know what he said?"

"Who?"

"Oh, sorry, the guy in Columbia who answered."

She didn't like to be baited, but Blinky held his ground of social retardation even as she stood there with her head cocked. She'd deal with it later. "What did he say, Mister Blinky?"

"He told her to turn on the encryption! See, the speed dial must have been set up by whatever guy is letting these girls use his phone. Probably the Jackrabbit. And we know he's part of the Juarez cartel and runs their Guerrero operation. And, like you said in your last narcotics brief, it's the Juarez cartel that's likely heading up this Infestation Network theory you have. All linked by BEE-KEEPER. Well, we now know the encryption code can be turned on or off in each individual phone. If we get that timing code, then BEEKEEPER is worthless. Then we're talking about a six-hundred-million-dollar piece of space junk. And this is the best, right here; what if there are *other* numbers programmed in the phone? We could nail down their whole network."

Susanne nibbled on her lower lip. "BEEKEEPER has an Achilles."

A week after the BEEKEEPER satellite took up station, Susanne tried to intercept its transmissions by moving one of the Directorate of Science and Technology's satellites below it, but the transmissions never came.

For two months BEEKEEPER just floated there, seemingly inoperative, and eventually the techies lost their patience and shifted the CIA satellite back to its normal station over Iraq. But Susanne Sheridan was now well connected—Homeland Security was the new kid at school whose big brother was the president himself.

A week after she convinced the NSA to move one of its MOUSE EARS eavesdropping satellites near BEEKEEPER, it traced a faint energy trail to a downlink in the Sierra Madre owned by a small Mexican telecommunications phone company. Susanne dispatched a clandestine service officer to survey the site, and his photographs were extraordinary—the downlink dish was a fortress protected by dogs, fences, and a platoon of soldiers.

Where the energy leaks went once they reached the mountain downlink was the salient mystery, incredibly troubling to Susanne, considering that BEE-KEEPER had been a catalyst. Five days after the satellite had taken residence, *all* of the communications—phone calls, emails, radio—from *all* of the big cartels in Latin America—not just Mexican but Columbian and Honduran as well—had ended. Just stopped cold.

The DEA and CIA were in a desperate struggle to regain the flow of chatter. American intelligence relied on two means of collection: high-tech hardware and human intelligence. CIA officers still employed some agents, but they could only be used sparingly in such treacherous waters. Recruiting agents was extremely difficult when the cartels used carrots and sticks so effectively. How could the CIA compete with million-dollar bonuses on the one hand and the promise of a family's eradication on the other? Without the eavesdropping advantage they had enjoyed for decades because of hardware, the United States was blind in the face of what Susanne called an "unholy alliance" among the cartels feeding America's insatiable appetite for drugs.

Susanne believed that an international cartel composed of local nodes had been formed around BEEKEEPER. Dozens of small cartels were gaining power and whole countries were plummeting into narco-Marxist chaos. The virus was spreading. The Abu Sayyaf in the Philippines bought weapons with kidnapping and drug money. Uzbekistanis—and what remained of the Taliban to the south—bought them with opium sales. Mexico was a more resilient ally, but Susanne believed that full regional instability south of the United States border would be a credible threat if not for one barrier: the inability of the smaller cartels to organize themselves and act as a monolithic interest. BEEKEEPER changed that, and it was the largest threat in the drug war to date.

"Play the call for me, Mister Blinky," said Susanne. "Christian, bring in the linguistics bubba."

"Should I bring in Deputy Director Corwin? I think he followed us."

"Just linguistics." She didn't want Corwin in her house while it was a mess.

Christian Collins exited the Bat Cave, and returned a moment later with a squat Korean man in tow. The digital recording of the woman's frantic voice came crisply out of the Bose 2000 speakers. The Spanish sounded flawless to Susanne. "Mister Cho, you're sure that's an American accent?"

The man from the fifth floor nodded confidently. "Positive. I've listened about a hundred times. New England, preppy, WASP. Probably New York City or Connecticut. She has an aristocratic curl in her Spanish vowels. Elite grammar school, most probably. Outside chance it's a rich suburb of Boston without the Massachusetts accent, like Wellesley, or maybe she's from D.C. Silver spoon all the way. Narrowing it further, I'd guess Upper East Side of Manhattan. Her formative years, that is. After that, I'd say she either moved around a lot—maybe a government brat—or she went away to school early. A diverse college, and maybe even high school before that, insulated from the local community where no dialect could cement."

"She must be a tourist."

Derek Cho shrugged. He didn't know what the excitement was about in the Bat Cave, but by God he wanted to. That was the thing about the fifth floor, man, you never got in on the *cool stuff.* The intelligence analysts on his side of the house just acted as bucket boys for the operators. He didn't know what BEE-KEEPER was, but he sensed it was *righteous* and had the feeling that his analysis was *important.*

Susanne was tempted to play the digital recording again, but she knew the woman might try another call, so she kept the primary speaker system dialed on the BEEKEEPER realtime channel, courtesy of the NSA. "Status of our Acapulco team?"

Christian Collins, just nine years out of Berkeley and two years out of his first startup, clicked his teeth and stood. *This* was what he had imagined when he had signed on, not the boring crap he had put up with for nearly twenty months. Susanne Sheridan had promised him responsibility in the interview, but had not told him it would be as a glorified stenographer. "We have a call in to the station chief in Mexico City. Our operations liaison just sent a case officer to Jackrabbit's location. We also have two reporters heading to the local police station to sniff around."

"Are they agents or officers?" Meaning, are they Mexican reporters on the CIA payroll or CIA officers posing as reporters.

"Agents, ma'am."

"Then we better hope the case officer running them has her shit wired. We need that phone. I mean to tell you boys, *we need that phone.* Our officer is a woman, correct? Because we don't want someone who'll spaz under pressure."

Christian Collins smiled. It was a tired joke—in truth he was tired of all her jokes, because while Ms. Sheridan could dish to her staff, she didn't like to be ribbed herself—but he enjoyed the reactions of the other men to his boss. She was the only woman around, but she ran the show. Hell, thought Christian, she had smuggled an Iraqi defector out of Lebanon on a speedboat. Pretty goddamn cool. The ancients like Blinky, to whom Deputy Director Sheridan referred as silverbacks, usually took the role reversal the hardest. Collins often pointed to the forty- and fifty-something crowd when asked what was wrong with the government. They did not know how to snatch opportunity.

Collins chuckled when he saw Twinkie King Blinky roll his eyes. "I'll call the Mexico station chief to check the gender, ma'am."

– 9 –

MEXICO CITY, MEXICO

Deputy Attorney General Eduardo Saiz slid into a bus stop and pressed the satphone into his ear, crushing out the horns and straining to hear the sounds in the Acapulco police station. The communications center had just patched him into a call between the Guerrero State *comandante* and the Acapulco station. Eduardo thought he heard pops when he first put the phone to his head.

"Deputy? Are you there, Deputy?" the *comandante* was asking someone.

"This is Octopus," interrupted Eduardo. "I am listening in to your call, *Comandante.* What is happening? Do we have the satphone yet?"

"I think that was gunshots, sir. Now the deputy does not answer. I'm sorry, let me catch you up. The Jackrabbit was found murdered at his compound. So was one of his bodyguards. An American couple—a black man and a white woman—walked into the station with Jackrabbit's surviving bodyguard. The guard was wounded, but alive."

"Tijuana hit?" The cartel run by the Sanchez brothers represented the strongest opposition to the concept of the Infestation Network. Perhaps the Americans wandered into the carnage and tried to play Good Samaritan.

"I don't think so, sir. I ordered the deputy to detain the couple until they found the phone. Then there were gunshots. I have a platoon of *Federales* speeding there as we speak, sir. In fact, they should be there now. We'll have an answer soon."

"Jesus! So the police shot the Americans?"

"I think they may have, sir. Maybe they tried to run. Those were your orders."

"Yes, well, this is going to get messy." Now my contacts here and in the United States will have to be leveraged, he thought. Perhaps *El Toro* will appreciate the fact that my control of information is a salient skill. "I want—wait, someone is speaking."

"*Stay back. Please,*" a woman pleaded in Spanish somewhere in the police station. "*We only want to go to the embassy. The man called Jackrabbit tried to rape me. Please let us go.*"

So that's it, thought Eduardo. Somehow one of Jackrabbit's victims escaped with his goddamn satphone. An American. Now there was some sort of standoff in the station. They were foolish and careless, both the Jackrabbit for his indiscretions and now these bumbling local cops who were torturing the gringos right in their own station. Jackrabbit was lucky to be dead already; *El Toro* had plans for him after this mess was cleaned.

He heard a man shouting weak warnings—sounded like a cop!—then there was a pistol shot. After a brief silence, he heard men shouting. In English. *What the hell?*

"Sir, I think they just killed a police—"

"Shut up," hissed Eduardo. "You get your *Federales* over there and tell them to shoot on sight. Send the helicopter, too. This ends in Acapulco."

– 10 –

ACAPULCO, MEXICO

Darren flung the police station doors open and vaulted the steps, sprinting toward the SUV in a crouch, Kate tucked right behind him. He did not think they could reach the embassy in Mexico City, but they didn't need to—if he attracted attention in the Hilton that would be enough to keep them alive. He opened the driver's door, found the ignition, and waited for his wife. Kate hopped in, but remained silent. He popped the clutch and slowly rolled toward the exit of the station parking lot to avoid curious eyes. He had to apply a steady brake to keep the Mercedes from moving through ten kilometers per hour.

The three college kids walked past the vehicle, and Darren watched in his rearview mirror as they shifted into a jog toward the eight-foot wall that hemmed the back of the station. The city was stitched with gutters and walls to protect its buildings from the tremendous runoff from the 3,000-foot mountains that surrounded it, though if the rain was torrential—as was the case with Hurricane Paulina—the water cascaded too quickly and too powerfully for the cobweb system to control.

The kids stopped at the wall and considered it, then jumped down into a drainage gully and disappeared. That's dumb, running that way, Darren thought. They should walk right out onto the coast highway like we're doing.

Darren put his eyes back on the main road and saw the three heavy trucks descending the hill, each of them packed with men armed with M-16 rifles and dressed in dark blue uniforms and baseball caps. Gray exhaust blurted from vertical mufflers as the trucks raced toward the station.

"Hold on," Darren said. He threw the Mercedes into reverse, spraying pieces of the gravel parking lot out onto the paved coast highway, sliding backward in an S-track until they were close to the parking lot wall, near several other civilian cars that must have belonged to the cops. "Get out!"

Kate saw one of the trucks swerve around from the other side of the police station and skid to a halt, men out and running toward the police station—*that boy didn't have to die*—rifles held high. She had a strange thought wrapped in a Talking Heads song: This is not real. This is not my beautiful house. This is not my beautiful wife.

She felt Darren's grip on her arm and followed him into a waist-high drainage ditch that ran below the wall. He had a machine gun. On her knees now, crawling behind him as fast as she could, heavy breathing, his head darting up for peeks, muck and litter all over her hands. She crinkled a Fanta grape soda can, and it sounded as loud as a church bell. Another truck roared into the parking lot, and it seemed like a hundred men were yelling. A bullhorn amplified a stream of high-pitched orders.

"Keep it coming, Kate," Darren whispered. "We can follow those kids right along the wall and out of here." He pointed and, fifty yards up the gully, she saw the three boys moving forward in hunches. Then they stopped and seemed to be arguing.

"Enemy can't see any of us in here," whispered Darren.

"Enemy? This is crazy. You hear me, Darren? Crazy. We should give ourselves up," she whispered. Isn't it funny, she thought, that I'm the one who wants to play by the rules and *he,* of all people, wants to gamble. With our lives! *Stop this madness now.*

One of the college boys had the same idea. Kate heard him yell at the others, then he started screaming. She saw his hands shoot high above his head, above the lip of the trench. He scrambled out onto the gravel parking lot. "I GIVE UP! I GIVE UP!" he screamed. "DON'T SHOOT!"

A second boy leaped up, too, and walked forward with his hands up, parallel with his friend. Ten feet into the parking lot, they got on their knees with their arms still reaching for the sun.

A wave of thunderclaps broke the air. The shots were impossibly loud, not like in the movies her husband watched all the time. Kate put her cupped hand to her mouth and could feel the reverberation in her lungs. The sharp smell of smokeless powder filled the trench. Small pieces of paper and tiny pebbles danced along the ground.

Oh my God! The world seemed to tilt and it was not as she had known it; the rules changed, horrible unleashed, a storm of ultraviolence that ripped flesh from the boys as if it were the most fragile substance in the world.

One of them folded to the ground immediately, as if a plug had been pulled out of him, but the other seemed to rattle and grabbed desperately at the red blossoms that were popping out of his shirt. All around her it sounded like acres of bubble wrap being popped, but it was ten times louder than a rock concert. Louder and louder. Can't think. Kate saw the boy's chest open in a yawn before he fell. Gray dust from the gravel floated up slowly and then danced in the hot contrails of the bullets.

Darren with his hands on her shoulders, shaking her. "Do *exactly* what I say! I'll divert them while you scoot back down the gully and take the car to the Hilton or another hotel with lots of tourists, then start screaming murder. Keys are inside. *Go, Kate.*"

"Wait. Where are you going? How do we meet?"

"I'm fine, Kate. I have a plan."

Darren turned his back on her and heard her scramble away. He wanted to tell her that he loved her, but he knew this would have set off too many alarms; she never would have left his side. He actually *did* have a plan, but survival wasn't an end state. This time he would do it right instead of watching others make the sacrifice. *I love you, baby.*

Darren popped up like a prairie dog with his hands up, surveyed his targets and got their attention, then ducked. At least twenty enemy in the open. *Standing up.* He grabbed the submachine gun and crawled forward as fast as he could, gaining distance from his wife, the men in the lot screaming now and closing in. He noticed that the Michigan boy was still in the trench with him. The kid was sobbing. *You should have stayed in your cell like I said, Blondie.*

Darren put the MP-5 to his shoulder and concentrated on keeping the sight post centered in the oval aperature. He stood from his squat. A *Federale* was standing not ten yards away, and Darren put a single bullet into him. There were two cracks—the first when the firing pin impacted the primer, igniting the gunpowder, and next when the 9-mm bullet impacted breastbone. Now a sharp swing left, and the trigger squeezed again—a spouting leg shot on a second target—and back down in the trench. Over Darren's head, 5.56-mm bullets snapped into the wall, ripping cone-shaped pieces of plaster free, chalk dust sprinkling down. His hearing was cut in half and the tone started to sing.

He waited a few seconds before he flushed and, sure enough, there were two *Federales* standing over their wounded comrades, trying to yank them from the kill zone. Darren drilled the one standing over the *Federale* with the chest wound first, and there was a loud slap when the bullet hit his abdomen. The *Federale's* legs shot out from under him and he flopped back over the other man, both of them squealing. Darren jerked left once more and sighted in on the other rescuer, who was carrying his *compañero* on his back as if he were a fireman. The wounded man watched Darren put a bullet in his savior's lower back before he crashed to the ground for the second time.

The air was filled with screams when the second wave of enemy bullets stopped. Mostly *Federales,* but he could hear over the din the kid from Michigan bellowing, "They fucking killed them! They killed my friends! What the fuck!"

"Keep moving!" Darren told him. "They're gonna be following me now." He popped his head up for good measure and ducked back down. More bullets followed. His snapshot: Some of the soldiers were crawling over toward the parked cars to get an angle. Kate was nearly at the SUV. *Please, God, let her live.*

He flipped the selector switch to automatic and cut a long burst into the group moving toward the car, holding the barrel down and left even as it kicked the other way, the hose of bullets kicking up dust. He hit one of them that he could see, and saw three others crawl back toward the station. But two of them made it to the Mercedes and were using it as cover, just on the other side of Kate as she entered through the driver's side door.

A bullet snapped by his ear, and he ducked.

The incoming fire was coming slower now, but more steadily. He could hear the miniature sonic booms as the bullets passed through the sound barrier over his head. *One of them has finally taken control,* he thought. *They're closing in.*

Darren knew the next presentation would be his last. He popped the empty magazine free and inserted another, breathing slowly and gathering himself. *Like trying to psyche yourself up to jump in front of a train,* he thought.

Darren took a brief moment to reflect, breathing deeply and ignoring the babbling Michigan boy. He saw a lizard scramble across a paper cup in the trench. It felt like twenty minutes to watch what took two seconds. He was happy with his performance in the firefight. And in the station, too, where he'd killed both men with headshots before they even squeezed off a round. He smirked. To an outsider, it would have seemed a strange thing to do at that moment, but for Darren Phillips—a Marine with hyperbolic expectations of self who had nevertheless shot himself in Desert Storm and crumbled two years later in Somalia—it was everything. *Here comes the pain!*

————

As Kate locked herself into the SUV, she heard men yelling. One of them started to pound on the passenger-side window with the butt of his rifle. Harder and harder.

She glanced out the windshield and saw others moving forward toward the ditch, rifles in their shoulders, brass casings spinning like coins flipped in the air, blue smoke washing behind them as they advanced. *Darren.*

A *Federale* jumped on the hood, pointed his rifle at her, and fired. She saw the first flash and instinctively put her hands in front of her face. *I'm so sorry.* There was a crackling eruption, but it was faint. So faint, in fact, that she assumed she had gone deaf. Nothing else happened. Kate looked up and saw that the man was still firing. The windshield had cobwebbed, lines spreading out even as the man continued to hold the trigger back. On her right, she heard another burst of gunfire that sounded like popping corn and the passenger window cobwebbed. But it, too, held its ground. *It's bulletproof glass!*

The four-hundred-thousand-dollar SUV had been designed and manufactured by Mercedes' elite custom security division. Jackrabbit's instructions to the factory manager had been simple. "I want it armored for battle," he told the German. "Like a tank."

Kate stomped on the accelerator, and the car's wheels leapt into a frenzied spin before they gripped the gravel and finally yanked the vehicle forward, gathering speed, slamming into the line of *Federales,* whose only defense against the car was to futilely raise their hands. One of them was plowed forward as if he had been shot from a cannon. Another was ripped under the vehicle and crushed by one of the huge tires. The other *Federales* scattered away from the ditch in airborne dives. Except one who dove in.

———

Darren heard the car ignite. He stood with the trigger held back against the hand grip. The submachine gun ejected brass like grass clippings cut free from a mower.

She was coming fast. One of the cops disintegrated in the wheel well. Another body came tumbling across the gravel and smacked into the wall twenty meters away. It lay there in the gully like a broken scarecrow.

Using his left hand to pull down on the machine gun, he controlled the recoil and steered the barrel. Many of the targets had turned to look at the car, not him, and his bullets were striking them in the backs of their legs and torsos. It was hard to follow the shots without tracers, so he guided the stream of bullets by the dust clouds, spraying them across his front like a squirt gun. He knew he should limit himself to single shots for accuracy, but this was round fifteen; why save them? His only duty—and it was a duty—was to spring Kate. But instead of making for the exit like she was told, she headed right at him. *Right into the kill zone.* His heart sank. He waved and shouted, "GET AWAY FROM ME!" *They'll cut her to pieces.*

A *Federale* dove away from the car and rolled into the trench next to him. Darren squeezed the trigger, but he was dry and closed with the man. The *Federale* tried to raise his M-16, but Darren grabbed the barrel and shoved it skyward, the heat scorching his hand like a hot frying pan, and wrestled the man onto his back. He almost had control of the rifle, when the Michigan boy stomped the life out of the man's face and pointed over his shoulder. "Let's get the fuck out of here, man!"

Darren spun around, and a wave of dirt from her skid washed over him like a wave. He closed his eyes and coughed. When he opened them he saw his wife.

"*Let's go!*" Kate screamed. Bullets were already clanging off the passenger doors. A ricochet screeched across the hood.

Darren pulled himself out of the ditch and slid behind the wheel. He could hear the *plinks* and the ricochets whining angrily, and he raised his eyebrows. There were impact sparks all over the thing, but no bullets were penetrating.

"It's an armored car!" Kate screamed.

"I'll say!"

Behind them, another door slammed, and Michigan Boy screamed, "GO! GO! GO!" from the backseat.

The SUV fishtailed, but Darren soon gained control. It rocketed toward the pickup truck that was blocking the exit to the street. He saw muzzle flashes all around it. The windshield began to buckle under the torrent of steel, but as they ran the gauntlet a different order was given by a *Federale,* and the tires were targeted. The only change the passengers sensed was a lull in the firing; protective foam flooded the air cavities when the first rounds penetrated the steel radials, and the SUV didn't lose any speed. Gaining it now. "Hold on!" someone yelled, the pickup growing larger and filling the cracked windshield with a dazzling puzzle of parts.

Darren rammed the truck, and the Mercedes bounced back like a cue ball. Airbags popped and snapped back their heads as if they were in a pillow fight. The truck blew into Calzada de la Cuesta, tumbled over, and collided with a city bus. The bus swerved and flipped, skidded toward the beach, and smashed into a news truck parked against the curb.

The impact shortened the Mercedes by a foot but its engines still gunned. It gained traction again and ripped out onto the main road, a sidewall clanking on the asphalt. The passage into town was now blocked by the bus wreck so Darren headed south toward the midpoint of the Acapulco crescent, crumpling the image of the bodies next to the bus and throwing it away.

"My God! Stop, Darren!" screamed Kate, shoving the deflated airbag aside so she could see. "We hit a bus! There are people . . ."

Darren shook his head. This was war. Guilt was simply an inefficiency right now, and to keep it gone—to keep it stamped out of his thoughts—he said, *"Those dead cops back there killed those people, not us! And they best stay the fuck away from us or I'll kill them all."* He tasted the bloodlust and stuffed that away, too, but he did not expunge it. He'd need it later.

"Get the map," he said, trying not to sound crazy.

Kate was badly shaken, but her brain was still functioning clearly in the sea of insanity. She was the captain of their adventure races, but she was in his world now. And she loathed it. Kate twisted around and pointed at the backpack on the seat next to the Michigan boy. "Hand me that pack. And hand up that other gun, too."

"They shot my friends," the boy said in a dead voice when he handed her the submachine gun.

"I'm so sorry," she said. *Darren was right. I never should have let them out of jail. This is madness.*

"I'll kill them," he said simply.

Darren looked into the rearview mirror, and his eyes met the Michigan boy's. The kid's were baby blue, but intense. Perhaps they were not so different after all. He nodded slightly, but the boy looked away.

The car raced south along the coast highway, with the Pacific on their right. Soon they gained altitude and the beach border gave way to a growing cliff.

"We're going to have to ditch this car now. Get out and try to hide in the forest somewhere until night," said Darren.

Kate folded the map and said, "And then what? Everyone will be hunting us."

"Still better at night."

Even at 150 kilometers per hour, the Mercedes had a smooth ride and she was able to study the map. It was quiet. "No. We need to get somewhere that's uninhabited. Then get to the embassy." She put her thumb up to the scale and pressed it out along the fold. "It's two hundred miles to Mexico City . . ."

Darren shook his head. "Kate, every police officer . . . hell, everyone in the whole fucking *country* is going to be checking every car on every . . ."

"I didn't say 'drive.' We go northeast for about ten miles, and there's nothing but forests and the Sierra Madre. Steep terrain. Deserted. No roads at all on this map. We'll ditch the car, and we can hoof it from there. Be in Mexico City in three days."

"Wait a fucking second," the Michigan boy said. "Two hundred *miles . . .* and we're gonna *walk?* That ain't happening."

The roof over the Michigan boy's head opened. Two bullets streaked past him and smashed through the glass window, trailing contrails of dusty sunlight that remained in place like laser beams. Darren felt the impacts when the

SUV shuddered, and he swerved violently, throwing Michigan Boy across the backseat.

Kate craned her head around and saw the shadow. "Helicopter!"

"I thought this was bulletproof!" shouted Michigan Boy.

"Not against big-caliber rounds," said Darren. *One of those things hits us and it'll rip us apart.* "Hold the wheel and hand me the gun."

But Kate's passenger window was already sliding down. The sound of the rotor blades compressing the thick air filled the cab with such an overwhelming power that the three Americans at once felt their lives were over, as if they were on an airliner plummeting toward the sea. *Whump-whump-whump-whump!*

"Is the safety off?" Kate screamed.

The Mercedes shuddered again as three heavy fifty-caliber bullets tore through the trunk. Chunks of carpeting cycled around the cab. The Michigan boy curled into a ball and concentrated on shrinking his big body. Darren spun the wheel hard, and the SUV fishtailed in a cloud of dust, clawing its way toward a cluster of houses across the road. "YES!" he screamed, reaching over to flip the selector switch to full automatic. "Point about fifty yards in front of the helicopter, hold down the trigger, and sweep it across!"

Kate leaned out of the window and saw the helicopter rotating into a level, hovering position. She could feel the booming of the blade slices in her stomach. A man in the open cargo door who was standing behind a black machine gun turned his head and yelled something toward the pilots. She pointed out in front of its nose and pulled the trigger, fighting and then controlling the bucking recoil as if it were a struggling animal, pulling her MP-5 across the length of the helicopter, unsure if she was even close.

The man's big gun flashed orange. She felt the sonic booms slap her ears as two bullets cracked just over her head. Then the whole helicopter lurched backward and tipped on its side, the man in the cargo door falling out and dangling on some sort of safety harness, struggling to grasp one of the skids even as the machine gun spun on its own axis and stitched the inside of the bird.

The dangling man was jerked up and into the rotor blades before the helicopter disappeared behind the cliff. Half of his body landed on the road. Two seconds later, Kate heard the growl of thunder over the Mercedes' revving engine. A thin snake of oily smoke slithered out from behind the cliff and headed toward the sky.

She sat back in her seat and pressed the button on her armrest. The window shut out the world again. She sat fiddling with the machine gun's magazine. It was silent.

Darren maneuvered between two small houses, and drove up a dirt road that was covered by a broad leaf canopy. "Where?"

"She shot 'em down!" shouted Michigan Boy. "I swear to God. I looked out the back window and the whole thing was tipping over. She must have hit the pilot 'cause next thing I know it disappears off the cliff!"

Silence again.

Kate finally found the magazine release button and popped the empty clip free of the MP-5. She felt oddly triumphant. In fact, she thought she might have a giggle fit. "Give me another set of bullets back there, Michigan Man." She took the magazine and tried to jam it into the machine gun, but her arms were shaking like a sewing machine's needle. Darren reached over to guide it, but she shook him off and eventually slapped it in and racked the bolt to chamber a round. "Still think women can't be in combat, Darren?" She felt ridiculous and punch-drunk to be saying such stupid things. She also felt good. And terrible. And then nothing at all.

Strange time to be joking. Darren thought, until he remembered the rush he had felt in Desert Storm when he had fired those LAW rockets. He hadn't hit the Iraqi vehicles, but he was shouting and whooping, nevertheless, the power in it, the adrenaline surge when the rocket streaked toward the sandborne enemy and changed the landscape. And I didn't even hit them, he thought, but Kate shot down a helicopter! *My wife!*

"Where do we go?" Darren asked.

She stared at him for a moment, then unrolled the map. "About five miles from here we head north up Highway 95D for the mountains. We'll exit and ditch the car there where the forest is thickest."

"Then we start the hike?"

Kate couldn't answer him because her throat was closing and her cheek muscles were going rigid. She thought about the man in the rotor blades. She thought about the Jackrabbit's bleeding head. *Am I going to faint?* There suddenly seemed to be a gallon of acid in her stomach. *Am I losing it?*

"My God. Kate, are you okay?"

She managed to nod before she burst into tears.

– 11 –

MEXICO CITY, MEXICO

Deputy Attorney General Eduardo Saiz dashed across the street and tried to find peace in a Catholic school playground. The pilot's transmission was garbled enough without the honking.

A whistle sounded and a recess was called. A tiny boy wearing plaid shorts and tie was the first to reach him. He bounced an inflatable red ball at Eduardo, who kicked it across the chalked foursquare court. He might as well have thrown a bone away from a retriever. The screaming children were as terrible a blight as the traffic, screeching and crying out, circling him like tiny whirlwinds in hopes he'd throw it again. When he left the government, he planned to get a place in a fishing vilage. A *quiet* place.

"Octopus, did you copy that?"

Eduardo spun and walked quickly under the monkey bars. He was pretty sure it was the *comandante,* not the pilot. The kids followed like a swarm of locusts. "No, say it again!"

"I said we have a *major* situation."

"I *know* we have a goddamned major situation!" He kicked the ball into the street, but the kids just stared after it, perplexed. It bounced off a cab, and the bastard stopped his car and shook his fist, then tossed it back into the playground. Eduardo wanted to have him killed. No, that's the pressure talking, he told himself. *I'm a man of Jesus.*

"Sir. My lieutenant was ambushed as he entered the police parking lot. Many gringos opened up with automatic weapons. He says at least one was black. His platoon managed to kill two of them—big white soldiers, clearly trained servicemen, he says—before the others fled in an armored car."

What the hell is going on? wondered Eduardo. A gang of gringos, mixed races. An armored car. Maybe this *is* drug related. But what about the girl being raped? Quite suddenly it was clear to him: This was a DEA sting operation that he did not know about. *Jackrabbit raped an undercover DEA officer!*

Eduardo's heart dropped and he sagged against a tetherball pole. If they were DEA, he'd never get the satphone. They had planted some female operative as bait, but she had been raped by Jackrabbit before the takedown. Then their whole operation had gone to shit. Still, why would DEA go to the police station? Why would they flee Acapulco?

"We have some casualties, sir."

The pilot had already told Eduardo about the fleeing car, and he knew there had been some shooting, but the prospect of friendly casualties surprised him. Eduardo welcomed the news. It meant he could kill the assassins without conjured justification, DEA or not. "Casualties?"

"They murdered . . . murdered seventeen people, Octopus. The Jackrabbit and his bodyguard, three Acapulco police officers, nine *Federales*, and three passengers on a public bus. Thirty more are injured."

"Christ! If they are American DEA they have stepped in a coyote trap. Patch me back through to the helicopter. He's shadowing the car."

"That's what I was telling you earlier, Octopus. There was some sort of rotor malfunction, and the helicopter crashed . . ."

"Oh, don't tell me this madness."

" . . . and we're trying to locate the car. I'm sealing off the city as we speak but I have only a platoon on site. Can I request help from the Army?"

Eduardo bit his lip clean through. He made a squealing, grunting noise that tickled the children and evoked delighted laughter. He snaked his tongue across the rectangular slit. The blood was warm and he spat it all over the blacktop.

Eduardo cocked the satphone back, but he did not toss it at one of the children. He knew that if he broke it over one of their heads he'd be in trouble. Hell, he'd be *killed*. He half expected a Juarez soldier to waste him right then. Why not make the run for Belize? He had two hundred thousand American dollars waiting. He would buy a boat and spend his days catching *mero* off the reefs. No, everyone close to him would be killed. Eduardo contemplated the two methods of suicide—he had narrowed his selection but had not yet chosen between the stash of pills and the rope.

He trotted back to the ministry office pinching his bleeding lip. He hoped it would not retard his speech now that information flow had become paramount, the tiller by which he would gain control over the mess. If he was to live, he knew it would be because of precise control of communication, proving to *El Toro* that he was much more valuable alive where he could leverage his contacts with the *yanquis* and his own press and government.

" . . . there, Octopus?"

"Yes, I'm here, *Comandante*. The answer is no. Do *not* involve the Army. We need to keep this contained to units we trust. All my contacts in the Army are running from the new president or totally enamored. They'd love the chance to make a name. This is a *Federale* operation alone until we find that phone. You want to use them for roadblocks, fine. But keep them away from this gang of gringos."

Eduardo was approaching the ministry guards in their khaki fatigues and green helmets. If the assassins really were Americans, the curtain was about to be raised for all the world to see, and he did not have much time. The story would have to be closely controlled. It was a growling lion and he held the whip. Perhaps he could trade American embarrassment for the phone.

Eduardo pulled out the encrypted BlackBerry pager his friend in the American FBI had given him and paged its donor.

– 12 –

MCLEAN, VIRGINIA

Roger "Dodger" Corwin tapped his manicured fingernail on Christian Collins's desk in the Bat Cave, signaling his irritation. It was a puerile message, but he needed some way to communicate the fact that there was indeed a new sheriff in town. When Sheridan had rudely departed the country brief twenty minutes earlier, Corwin had followed. She had locked herself in her little cave and her prettyboy flak, Collins, had kept him waiting outside while she greedily devoured intel that directly impacted his new area of responsibility. This after he had meticulously schooled her in his clearances and need-to-know! The FBI had superior contacts in Mexico. Corwin himself was so well networked that he could blow the CIA's petty Rolodex right to hell.

Corwin leaned close to Christian Collins and whispered, "You remember one thing, jocko, this is an interagency task force. Your boss today may be gone tomorrow. Next time I tell you I want in, you best open the goddamn door. Do I get a roger on that?"

"Yessir," said Christian Collins, wondering why he had been targeted.

"You play this thing right and I'll get you a shot, Collins. I've been watching you for a few weeks now. Unless of course you want to play her piss boy forever. Because that's all you'll get out of her. You know it and I know it."

Corwin removed his Polo blazer and stretched as tall as his five-foot, seven-inch frame would allow, as much to show his build as to let everyone know he intended to stay put. He hadn't done a triceps superset that morning for nothing. He walked to where Queen Bitch had gathered her worker bees and set the jacket over a chair in front of an occupied desk, hoping it was Sheridan's. He knew from his years of stopping careless motorists on the highway that small pinpricks of intimidation helped lever mouths open. "Let's hear this little phone call of yours."

Sheridan smiled at Corwin. She had invited him inside the Bat Cave as a goodwill courtesy and here he was throwing it in her face. Dodger was holding in his gut and swelling his chest, she was sure of it. He looked like a desperate peacock. *Just my luck, one male jackass replaced by another.* She nodded at Blinky, who played the phone call recordings again.

Corwin tapped Ted Blinky on the shoulder when the playback finished. "That girl sounds desperate all right. Hey, sports fan, can you print out the complete English translation for me? Nice job on the recordings, by the by. Good to go."

Before Sheridan could interrupt, Blinky nodded and said, "Right away, sir." She was not sure which was worse, Corwin's petty power politics or the fact that one of her own subordinates warmed to his touch like a puppy that needed a stroke.

After ejecting her roving husband, Sheridan had instituted a standing rule: Don't trust blond men with mustaches. Now here was Roger Dodger Corwin proving her right, even though his follicular hue might be credited to peroxide or lemon juice.

"How'd you get the call? Wiretap?" Corwin asked Blinky.

"Roger, you know better than to ask that question," Susanne said sweetly. "What are we if we don't protect sources and methods? The intelligence is in the call, not the source. Play nice in the sandbox, now."

Corwin's BlackBerry encrypted phonetic pager buzzed and he whipped it free of its plastic holster. He often practiced the motion. Corwin owned several handguns and though he had never fired one in anger he practiced his quick draw each shooting weekend, often in front of a mirror. He wore a concealed belt-carried holster for his Glock behind his hip, like a gunfighter, but when he went for the familiar brush he remembered the CIA's overbearing policy: no firearms within the office building.

Corwin tapped the backlight on the pager.

DODGER—GANG OF AMERICANS HAVE JUST MURDERED DOZEN MEXICAN CITIZENS AND POLICE IN ACAPULCO. DRUG RELATED. WE KILLED TWO, ARE CHASING OTHERS. THEY APPEAR TO BE PROFESSIONAL. DEA? NEED YOUR HELP. KEEP QUIET FOR NOW. I WILL SEND ALL INFORMATION. FISHERMAN.

Sheridan watched Corwin read the message. His pampered face seemed to melt. "Anything good, Roger?"

"Not really," Corwin said, ensuring the screen was clear before placing it back in its holster. You never knew what gadgets the Christians In Action wasted funds on. The fact that Eduardo Saiz had used his call sign signaled something serious—perhaps requiring an *international coalition.* Joint operational experience was an intoxicant for promotion boards.

Corwin wondered if DEA was running a big undercover operation without his knowledge. He thought about asking Jimmy Contreras, the DEA rep standing not four feet from him, but he did not want to tip his hand until there were serious chips to be harvested from his extraordinary contact.

Christian Collins stood up at his desk with a phone in one ear. He blurted, "Ma'am! Excuse me, ma'am, but I have the agent from Acapulco on the line, patched through by his case officer. He arrived at the police station to check around and found himself in the middle of a huge gunfight."

"*What?*"

"Should we ask them to leave?" Christian whispered, indicating Contreras and Corwin.

She considered it. "No. Brief all of us, but filter anything that reveals the source." It would be the last carrot for Corwin, she decided.

Christian Collins turned to face the others. "There has been a massive gunfight at the Acapulco police station."

"How do you know?" demanded Corwin.

"I can't say, sir, but there were bullets firing everywhere. *Federales* were shooting at a Mercedes pleasure truck right outside the police station. The truck escaped, but he . . . a helicopter is chasing it. Some *Federales* are dead." Christian knew the translation was not precise, but the agent was speaking very rapidly.

"Did you say there were dead *Federales?* You're sure they weren't local cops?" asked Corwin, taking the reins. Fact is, he thought, women are good in teams because they can't make the hard calls to which men grow accustomed from the moment they pick sides in the first grade.

"Yessir. *Federales.* Many others are dead. Civilians, too. A bus crashed."

"Who shot them?"

Christian Collins shrugged and held up an index finger. "Caucasian men with army haircuts. No, wait, a black man, too. Ten of them, maybe more. *Federales* killed two. Said they were soldiers. The others fled in the truck. They think it was armored."

Corwin wheeled to face the DEA, Jimmy Contreras. The fact that he was tall could not cover for his cheap taste. Contreras was wearing loose-fitting Dockers and white athletic socks that were stuffed into Wal-Mart Top-Siders. "Soldiers? You have any men operating down there, Agent Contreras?" He tried to keep his strong voice toned properly, but it had erupted in accusation.

Contreras, the DEA representative to Crime and Narcotics, towered over Corwin. He squinted down intensely like an eagle would the surface of a stream, searching for something coherent in the white noise. "Not shooting Mexican federal police officers, I don't."

Dodger Corwin squinted right back. He called the glare his B.S. detector and now it fully illuminated Contreras. The big prick loved to emphasize his Vietnam service in debate, but he would always be the simple soldier, unable to think as nimbly as the Dodger. After establishing the fact that he would not be intimidated, Corwin turned to Susanne Sheridan and said, "Do you?"

"Think about that question, Roger."

"I don't know what source you're using in Acapulco and I do not care to know. That's your business."

"Why, how thoughtful of you, Roger," she said.

He brushed it off. "Point being, this is some kind of drug hit that has escalated to the federal level. I know the Mexican deputy attorney general in charge of the *Federales*. I mean, I know him *personally.* Worked a two-year counter-narc tour side by side with the man."

"I know that lying prick, too," Contreras interrupted. "Eduardo Saiz. He's a fucking snake and quite possibly an accessory to murder. I should know. I lost a man to him and his."

I finally get a rise out of the quiet Tex-Mex, thought Corwin, and all he can bring is another outdated story from the bush. "Personal issues aside, Contreras, we can *all* agree this shoot-up ain't a goddamn coincidence." Corwin used slang when someone else tried to pull workingman-hero bullshit on him. Did he think slinging a rifle and smoking dope in Vietnam was any tougher than slinging a pistol and staying alert on a 300-CC motorcycle? "Whoever grabbed that phone has shot Mexican federal judicial police officers. That, Susanne, bumps it up to my level."

Susanne understood what Roger Corwin was, but she wanted to hear him say it. "Your level? Roger, your connection, along with all this intel, will be discussed in a Homeland Security brief where it will be fused. Then the director of Homeland Security will choose the action officer, not you. That's the role of Homeland to begin with."

Corwin's pager buzzed again and gave him a second to think. He had overstepped; when he made his power play it would be done unannounced. He focused on the message.

DODGER—ONCE I GET THEIR IDENTITIES, WILL NEED YOUR
HELP, MY FRIEND, FOR BACKGROUND INFORMATION. AS
SOON AS I KNOW ANYTHING, YOU WILL KNOW TOO. CAN

*YOU PROMISE THE REVERSE? WE WILL HELP EACH OTHER
LIKE BEFORE. FISHERMAN.*

It was going to be easy now, thought Corwin. I'm perfectly positioned. The phone was insignificant now. The only question was how to inform the director of the FBI and ultimately the president himself that something stunk south of the border.

"What does it say, Roger?" Sheridan asked.

"Only that I'm wanted back in D.C. If you'll excuse me, will you promise to update me as the calls come in to NSA or wherever it is you're getting them?"

She nodded only slightly, but Corwin knew that was about all the promise he was going to get. He strode out the Bat Cave door as if walking down the carpet to his coronation ceremony. He knew the spooks would try to scoop the higher-ups, so he toggled his speed-dial directory as he walked, wondering if his first call should be to the director of the FBI, the director of Homeland Security, or the White House chief of staff.

When Corwin left, Contreras whispered in her ear, "What an asshole."

Susanne smelled his cologne—nice—and really *noticed* Jimmy Contreras for the first time in six months. She had always considered his manner somewhat abrupt, but he spoke so rarely she had written him off as the brooding type who lacked social skill and was somehow embarrassed by it, a token donated by the DEA to tow the line with both CIA and Homeland. Looking at him now in his dark blue DEA golf shirt that stretched across his big frame, she thought differently. "Big-time."

Her focus had to be internal for the moment, happily dismissing the blond body nazi Corwin and his clumsy machinations and then turning away from Contreras with significantly less enthusiasm. "Can we get some footage?"

Christian Collins motioned to Contreras. "May I speak freely?"

"Yes, Jimmy's cleared hot."

"The agent is posing as a reporter. His news truck is on fire."

"Tell him to put it out."

"Wait a minute. *Puede usted conseguir en su carro?* Oh. He says his truck is totally destroyed, ma'am."

"Find another."

"*Email el archivo a mí.* I'm trying to get him to take about ten seconds of his digital video and convert it into an MPEG, ma'am. Then he can just send it by email. He's got a handheld that's connected to the Net but he's pretty panicked. The *Federales* are shouting at him."

"They wanted the satphone and somehow a fight started. It's the only thing that makes sense. But who would steal the phone? Anyway, he does *not* hand over his footage."

"I told him, ma'am," said Christian Collins. "He's not thinking too coherently." And who could blame the agent for losing his nerve, thought Collins, after having walked into a gun battle that destroyed his new truck along with a satellite dish. He could hear the screaming sirens two thousand miles away.

"Here she comes again, ma'am!" shouted Ted Blinky, who was monitoring the BEEKEEPER net in real time. He increased the volume on the Bat Cave speaker system even as the room hushed. Soon there came crisp tones of a Touch-Tone phone being dialed. Blinky had already set the recognition feature and numbers popped up on the movie screen as they were pressed in Acapulco:

0112123679919

"That's the number she dialed," whispered Blinky.

The phone clicked twice before the dial tone screeched again.

"She's trying to dial the states, but they cut her off before the call went through," said Susanne. "Zero-one-one is our country code. Two-one-two is New York City. Wow, linguistics was right. Christian, get me everything you can on that phone number. And see if DCI is available. Corwin just dragged us into a race with FBI."

"Yes, ma'am," said Christian. "I've received the MPEG, but the asset thinks the gringos are dead by now. He said there are about ten dead *Federales* and that it's over now for whoever did this. He saw a helicopter move to intercept them. He thinks the criminals are dying or already dead."

Susanne walked over the rubber-coated floor and stood behind Christian Collins's desk. The floor was ridged in places to absorb sound and she caught a heel, reached down when she recovered, and removed her shoes. She set them next to her assistant's computer screen and waited for the RealPlayer to run the digital video. Other men squeezed in behind Susanne, careful not to bump against her as they jockeyed for a view, though she wouldn't have minded if Jimmy Contreras lost his balance.

The video showed uniformed men standing behind a pickup truck firing M-16s at an unseen enemy. Suddenly a white sport-utility vehicle plowed into them. The silence of the replay did not dampen the impact. The pickup shot out of the field of view. A baseball cap seemed to hold its position, suspended in the air, though its owner disappeared offscreen. The camera panned, and now a bus skidded across the screen. In the background the SUV snaked away down the hill.

Susanne Sheridan whistled softly and said, "She's not dead yet."

– 13 –

40 MILES NORTHEAST OF

ACAPULCO, MEXICO

The Mercedes limped up the wooded mountainside on an overgrown switch-back that bore no signs of recent trespass. Firebreaks had disappeared ten miles ago and vines snaked across the covered trail. The deciduous forest around the sedan was so thick that branches scraped over the hood and dragged up over the broken windshield, leaving clumps of bark and splashes of chlorophyll behind where the edges caught. The ground was littered with light green prehistoric cactus and kelly green shrubs that brushed roughly against the underbelly of the Mercedes as it climbed. The evergreens up higher on the mountainside were un-molested, free to sway in the wind.

"Did it work?" asked Darren.

Kate shook her head and folded the cell phone closed. "No. I tried my dad twice, but I can't get through. Maybe the car's interfering."

The great oak trees around them had been squeezing the tunnel closed for five miles and now the two vague tracks forged years ago by tires disappeared al-together in waist-high scrub and grass. Darren slowed to a stop. "This is our stop anyway. You two get out here, check the back for any salvageable items, and hurry away from the car."

Kate didn't find anything else. They had their waterproof pack with the Hell Bitch still wrapped in a tight coil, two climbing harnesses with Figure 8 rap-pelling devices and carabiners, two bottles of beer, four chicken fajitas, suntan lotion, a 35-mm camera, a road map of Mexico, and two towels. From Jackrabbit's car she removed a Sig Sauer 10-mm automatic pistol with eight rounds, the cell phone, and two MP-5 submachine guns with only thirty rounds between them.

Darren checked the edge of the switchback. It wasn't a cliff, but it was a steep enough drop. He pointed the car through a gap in the trees and ran alongside, gripping the wheel to give the SUV guidance as it gained speed. When it was clear of the first few trees, Darren rolled free and the car careened down the slope, knocking down some small oaks and bouncing off others before it began to tumble. He didn't stay to watch the rest.

"Well, what's the farthest you've ever run?" his wife was asking the college kid when Darren jogged up alongside, slowing just a bit to adjust to their fast hiking pace. Kate had the map out and was leading the group higher instead of contouring around the hill, a decision Darren knew better than to question. The hillside was covered in knee-high scrub grass, the brittle stalks breaking underfoot and carving three narrow paths. Pacific orange-tipped butterflies flapped ahead of the intruders and settled back onto their perches when the trio passed.

"I ran a marathon once for fun," the blond kid said. "Did eight-minute miles the whole way, no problem. It's not exactly a football workout, know what I'm sayin'?" He was bug-eyed and Darren took it for nerves, the way he was swiveling his blond head around on his enormous neck as if warming up for a boxing match. He wore camouflage Billabong surfing shorts and Nike crosstrainers that looked to be around size 14. Darren and Kate were wearing Teva sandals. He grimaced at the thought of the coming blisters.

"Anything longer?" Kate asked the kid.

"Longer? Hell no. I mean, you understand that two-a-day workouts at Michigan are a helluva lot tougher than a marathon, right? No disrespect, but if you can hack it, I can hack it. Besides, I'm not certain I want to run with you two, anyhow. I may just sit up 'top the hill here, wait for the motherfuckers who did my friends; I'll kill them. You saw it. Just shot them for nothin'!"

"You stay with us if you want to live," said Darren. "Give me the pack."

"Like I need you to carry this pack? I'm about to go to the NFL, bro. You'll be leanin' on *me* soon. I been training for the draft combine. I'm rated to go in the first round. No shit. My forty is close to four-five. My vertical is thirty-seven inches. That's hops for a white boy, know what I'm sayin'? I'm the Eminem of the defensive backfield."

He winked at Darren, but the message was not understood. Darren was contemplating ways to get the pack with the weapons without offending the kid, wrestling against a martial instinct to bark at him. A chorus of chirps from hummingbirds and thrushes filled the silence and made it hard to concentrate on a delicate sentence.

Kate said, "Neck says he has good feet."

"Oh most def, most def," panted the kid.

"He'll need them. Neck?" asked Darren.

The boy stuck out his hand and Darren took it, annoyed when the kid over-did the squeeze, the pack straps accentuating his huge chest. He had diamond studs glinting prominently in each ear lobe. His bleached hair was spiked in dried clumps of gel that looked as if he had just dried his wet head with a towel. "I'm Neck Cappucco. Guess I shoulda stayed in that cell like you said."

"Well, that's past. I'm Major Darren Phillips. What's your real name?"

"Major?"

"In the Marine Corps."

"That's weird, bro. Maybe I should call myself Strong Safety Neck Cappucco when I meet people. What happens when you ain't a major no more? Don't peo-ple get confused?"

Darren thought about saying, the only person around here that's perma-nently confused is you, but instead said, "No."

"Anyway, my name's Vinny, but everyone on the team calls me Neck, yo. On account of me having this big neck." He grabbed his enormous throat.

Indeed, Darren thought his neck was as wide as his head. In a turtleneck he would look like he was hiding a whiplash collar. "What team?"

"Yo, man, can't you read?" Neck pointed to the Michigan T-shirt and smirked. "I played strong safety for the Wolverines. Started for three years. I'm gonna be a high draft choice on April tenth. Did you see the Rose Bowl? I'm the one that made the goal line hit on Andrew Brenner, dude. UCLA fullback. Knocked him stone-cold. I had six sacks this year and five picks."

"I'll take that pack now, Neck," said Darren as he popped the strap clips from the kid's humongous shoulders. The kid was well built, but fast twitch muscles required commensurate fuel consumption and grew heavier with each step. He'd quit in twenty miles. Besides, Darren thought, the kid is a braggart. Big mouths were usually inversely proportional to fortitude in endurance sports. Except in the case of his wife, of course.

"I'm bigger than you, yo," said Neck.

Darren continued to hike, removing the submachine guns and redistribut-ing the ammunition between clips. "Kate and I do this for a living. Or, she does. I used to."

"So *I'm* the only one that does this for a living."

The kid's smile was enormous and his teeth were as large as dominos. His bravado suddenly grated on Darren, noticing the thorny barbed wire tattoos that encircled Neck's biceps for the first time. He decided not to give the kid the satisfaction his nickname apparently provided, remembering that fraternizing

with subordinates led to trouble. And on this trip they would need a rank structure. Kate would guide, he would be both tactician and protector, the kid would
do whatever the hell he was told to.

"Here, carry an MP-5, Cappucco. Each of us has fifteen rounds. Make sure
the safety is on at all times and watch the muzzle. Don't fire unless I say. Single
shot only."

The threesome leaned into the hill and began to hike away from the trail,
Kate in the lead setting a wicked pace. She didn't run but her long legs bent,
swung toward higher ground, planted and extended as fluidly as if she were on a
stair machine. She felt good moving away from Acapulco with its bodies and
madness. The clean air and the scent of tropical scrub forest helped her forget
the past hour. Coconut palms acted as levers for both climb and spirit. Eventually the familiar sounds of her sandals crunching, her lungs working, her heart
pumping blood past her eardrum, insects chirping, and her bare knees scratch-
ing through the thatch allowed her to think of a future again.

Those without a future kept popping into her mind.

Kate thought about her brother, gone four years now, and turned around to
watch Neck labor up from below. He and her brother were so alike, she thought,
sharing a brash but harmless lust for both sport and self at a time in their lives
when she could find neither. She shuddered when she thought about college and
turned back to the hill, using the anger as fuel.

She had fought so hard to change herself. Hiking up that Mexican mountainside, Kate was a long way from third grade's "Fatso" North, a long way from
the girl who was bigger and taller than every classmate at Spence, a long way
from the cunning and cruel Princeton jackasses who had called her "NOT"
North at the height of her freshman fifteen struggle—a nickname that remained
mysterious for two years until she realized it was an acronym for Nanook Of The.

Her father arranged a banking analyst position for her on Wall Street after
graduation that she accepted out of inertia, joking bitterly that a fat whale may
stop swimming but still pushes water. She hated the job. The long hours made
her more lonely and the free meals made her more rotund. Then one night at
the office at around ten p.m.—still two hours away from an ice cream snack and
a car home to repeat the misery when she awoke—she saw the Eco-Challenge on
television and was mesmerized.

It was a brutal competition that pushed its racers to the edges of their
emotional and physical limits—then shoved them past. Teams of four paddled,
hiked, rappelled, kayaked, climbed, mountain-biked, and ran toward a finish
line that was over 350 miles away, foraging for their own water and food and
navigating by map and compass. It was a grueling expedition in which the clock
never stopped. The competitors became increasingly disoriented, balancing

sleepless nausea and incoherence with decision-making, speed, and ultimately teamwork. The teams had to be co-ed, and Kate saw that the women were respected leaders, relied upon for what they brought to the team instead of the unspoken criteria upon which Kate believed she was judged every day at the office and on the streets.

Kate left New York for California and started the long walk into adventure. She was not a gifted athlete—she couldn't put a ball through a hoop, cradle one in a webbed pouch, or kick one into the corner of a goal. That didn't matter. In adventure racing the only requirement was a fierce, relentless willpower. When she tasted the change she was immediately addicted and fed the habit of exercise daily. Her excess weight retreated, revealing a shape she was overjoyed to discover, and, more than that, a garrulous personality that had been beaten down for so long. Every mile run and weight lifted built both body and self-esteem, which probably explained her soaring confidence.

Most people walk the equivalent of once around the globe in seventy-five years. Kate North had done that in the last two years alone.

———

Two hours passed and Neck's calves were burning. Initially, when the chiquita started so fast, he presumed that she was just getting distance from the trail, or maybe even trying to prove herself since it was clear that of the three of them, he was in the best shape. But the chick was still moving like a robot. Hell yeah, some kind of *hot* billy goat robot with legs that scientists should clone or something. Why waste time on sheep when you could reverberate or resuscitate or whatever a pleasure machine like Kate, who was driving up so fast that it was hard for Neck to watch her tight ass if he wanted to keep up.

A bevy of Monarch butterflies came fluttering out of a section of the broadleaf forest. Neck bounded away from them with his hands over his head. Last thing he needed was to get stung, especially by a swarm of exotic bugs. He'd seen the Discovery Channel often enough to know that every insect in the Third World would kill you dead.

His muscles were awash in lactic acid. It was a nice burn, but goddamn, he just needed to rest them so they could repair the tears and come back even bigger. Worse, the air was so thick here his lungs ached. His breathing had grown louder than the plants swishing across his big thighs. Maybe all the plants were stealing his oxygen! That was it, all right. Greedy bastards.

To take his mind off the workout, Neck reverted to his tricks, either fantasizing about heroism or concentrating on complex football problems like coverage responsibilities when facing hurry-up offenses. That was why he was so highly rated, after all. He was a thinker out there in the arena, a fucking war god who was also, according to *College Football Weekly,* a football genius. Goddamn right!

Now he was Russell Crowe in *Gladiator* climbing high in an attack to rescue some hot Egyptian princess—preferably a blonde—wearing those Arabian-style clothes, maybe loose silk pants that gave way to rock hard abs and a see-through top with big nipples and a veil and all that good shit.

His submachine gun was a broad sword . . . no, actually a submachine gun was good-to-go in the first place, so maybe he'd pick another fantasy. How about an army one where he was like his dad in Viet-fucking-nam and this—

His bare shin brushed a prickly pear cactus. Neck hopped back in pain and bent over to rub out the trickle of blood. Two thin barbs were imbedded in his shaved leg and he pulled them out one by one. Little fuckers! He wanted to alert the couple but decided it was cooler to tell them later, the way he didn't tell his team his hand was fractured until *after* the Notre Dame game two years ago. Talk about balls-to-the-wall tough. Dried blood would help his point, so he left the tiny wound alone and started to hike again.

With the draft just a month away, Neck convinced himself that the hike was doing him good. He'd done well in the preliminary scout combines—well enough that his agent told him a low first-round selection was likely—and what a story this would be. Tossed in jail because he stuck up for his friends during the Hot Body contest at the *Drunken Marlin.* Shot at by Mexicans. Hiking to Mexico City. Here was the character factor the NFL representative had talked about!

Then Neck thought about his dead friends, and his mood plummeted. He would have cried if he were allowed to. He was so tired. His thighs were on fire. He looked up and the chick—Kate—had gained another two steps on him. *Goddamn.* He glanced back and her humorless husband was just humming right along, too. Neck couldn't bring himself to ask her to slow down—she was just a girl—so he exhaled loudly. Maybe he was sick or something. Fucking Mexicans hadn't fed him well enough. Hell yeah, that was it. Hershel Walker said his body was an army, and so was Neck's, and just like his old man used to tell him, an army had to be *fed!*

"Woooo," he said again to get her attention.

Kate stopped when she heard him. He was asking for a break. Granted, he didn't actually *say* anything, but after six years of racing with men, she knew their egos squashed cries for help into not-so-subtle signals.

Kate checked her direction with her Suunto wristwatch while she waited for the guys. She watched Neck climb up to her with his hands on his knees the way her little brother did when she took him on hikes. She smiled. She was happy that the big kid had kept up the pace for so long. "Use full sole contact as you ascend, not just the balls of your feet. Plant your heels and use that football ass of yours."

Neck nodded and put his head between his knees, too tired to speak yet. He rotated around so it would look like he was watching Darren climb, but he really wanted to give her a better view. He had been told more than once by chicks that he had a nice ass, the primary power source in football, and he was happy Kate had noticed it, too.

Hell, she was married to a black dude so he really wasn't surprised. His teammates said he had a ghetto booty, after all. Too bad Kate hadn't seen it during a game; girls always commented on the way it looked in the tight pants, even better than the butts of the ten other defensive starters, all black. He would have won the Hot Body contest at *Drunken Marlin* if he hadn't passed out. Then the guys had drawn all over his face. Man, was he pissed. Of course, that's what started the whole thing and he suddenly felt guilty and sad. They were dead.

"Are you okay, Neck?" she asked.

He turned to face her, hoping she would notice his bloody shin. "I'm just starving, is all. Know what I'm sayin'? They didn't feed us for two days. Running on empty here, and that's tough for a big baller. Hard to be a playa when I ain't got the grub, yo." It was a half lie—they had been given three meals of tortillas, chicken, and eggs a day, and Little D had even smuggled in some fish tacos, which Neck considered to be just a fucked-up way of doing business, but they *did* taste good. But even with lunch just three hours old, he was famished. His body consumed food at an incredible burn rate.

Kate saw his shin but she did not make mention. Endurance racing was a war of attrition between mind and body. Injuries were inevitable. They had to be minimized and even ignored lest the mind inflate them exponentially with each mile trod. She walked behind Darren and rummaged around in the pack. "You better eat these, then," she said, tossing the package of aluminum foil at Neck. "Chicken fajitas I packed for lunch. We were going to picnic . . ." Her mind drifted back to the beach and she shook her head. That was then, this is now. In an hour, the life she had worked so hard to build had evaporated.

Her father had tried to push her into a world dominated by a doomed and vapid upper-class social network, which was being steadily replaced on the leading edge, reduced to haughty charity balls often organized by people who had no idea what their charities actually did—inconsequential considering the salient goals were to get a listing on the invite as "sponsors" and a picture in "Sunday Styles" in the *Times*.

But now Kate North was her own person and there was power in it. She understood why men like her father lusted for words like "status" and "respect," as if they were great treasures. That's where he was on the night of the murders of her brother and mother—working for those words.

She felt her throat begin to close again and was struck by the drastic shift in her emotions her daydream had sparked, tears just a thought away, the wild and raw Mexican terrain pushing them closer and closer. She looked at her husband, fighting for control, walked up to him, and hugged him. He looked into her eyes and pushed her head gently into his chest. He was so comforting that her breathing slowed. The squall was gone.

Kate patted her husband's neck and nuzzled once more before she turned to Neck. "Neck, this is going to be the most painful experience you've ever had, but you can make it if you believe."

"I already believe," grumbled Neck between bites of his chicken burrito. "If you can make it, I can make it. Besides, all you got is sandals and I have the newest Nike crosstrainers. Starbursts, see? I'm sponsored already." He lifted up his leg and swiveled his ankle so both his pristine sneaker and his bloody shin were showcased.

"No, Neck, we've done this distance before and our bodies know what to expect. You'll be taken by surprise and in about sixteen hours your body will start to shut down."

"You got the wrong white boy."

"Listen to me. Ultra-endurance sports are different. You'll be nauseated because of lack of blood flow to your stomach and sleep deprivation. In sixteen hours you'll feel sick—I mean *really* sick—and you'll hear a voice telling you to stop. A day later your body will have consumed its fuel and it will cannibalize itself. The following day your body will be so stressed that your immune system will be squashed, and you will not be able to rally. The little voice will tell you that you are going to die. Don't give in."

Neck shook his head slowly as a form of communication because his mouth was full of guacamole, chicken, and tortilla. He chomped happily. "Look, Kate, you don't understand something. I play Division One football for Michigan. I'm a modern-day gladiator and my body is *always* at war with something. I work out twice a day. All I'm saying is, don't worry about me. Where you two go, I go. Question is, how we gonna get to Mexico City if we can't use the roads? Are we going the right way?"

Kate pointed at her wrist compass. "We'll use the road map and cross over roads at night, using them as limiting features, sticking to streambeds and thicker, unpopulated terrain. We'll move fastest at night when we can go out in the open. We'll get there. *I* do *this* for a living."

"No *problemo*, then."

"We'll see," said Darren, eyeing the remaining fajitas.

Kate poked her husband gently in the ribs. "Anyway, eat all of them, Neck. You'll need the fuel. We'll rest here for a few minutes until you finish. I know you can make it."

"Hell yeah, I can."

Darren let the pack drop. Kate snaked her hand in behind the Hell Bitch and unzipped the waterproof pouch where she had stashed the cell phone. She wanted to call home. The cell phone beeped after she pressed 0 and a man said, *"Conductor. Seven-three-nine."*

"Excuse me," said Kate. *"I called half an hour ago. I need to get an outside operator."*

"Hold on, please."

She was encouraged and waved Darren over, whispering that she might be connected, but after a few seconds she heard it click and the connection was lost. "Shit! I think I almost had them. I lost the connection."

"Try dialing the States direct."

"I tried before, and it just beeped. Here, watch." She dialed her father's home and the phone beeped rapidly and clicked off.

"We may be too far out of town for the international traffic already," said Darren. "I don't think we should waste any more of the battery. Not until we can see a city or maybe some relay towers." He pulled the towels and the beers from the pack and buried them in a trench he had been digging with his bare heel.

"Wait. We need that beer," said Kate.

"It'll just dehydrate you."

Kate pulled a bottle from the tomb and shattered it over a rock. The beer didn't flow downhill for more than a few feet before the thirsty dirt absorbed it completely, drying as they watched. She held the bottle up by its neck, admiring the shard as it glinted, and stuffed it back in the pack, careful to keep it in a pouch separated from the Hell Bitch. "We'll need a knife."

Neck walked over and handed them the remaining fajitas. He had planned to eat only one, but greed had won out and he had guiltily scarfed down another as the couple talked. "Here," he said. "For you two."

Darren extended his hand—he thought the boy was lying about the starvation, otherwise he would have mentioned it while he was bitching from inside his cell—but Kate playfully slapped it away and said, "Nope. You eat it, Neck. Believe me, you'll need the energy."

Neck shook his head, but when the pair turned away to consult the road map, he took a nibble, a larger bite, looked at their backs again, then gobbled up the rest. He tossed the ball of foil on the ground. It rolled downhill and was arrested by a low cactus.

"Kick that in the trench and cover it up, youngster," said Darren.

Neck felt guiltier still and tapped the ball into the morgue with the towels and the beers. "Youngster? How old are you?"

"Thirty-three," said Darren.

"Well, I ain't that much younger. I'm twenty-two."

Darren studied the kid. Perhaps eleven years *wasn't* a big gap, but he looked a world apart with his earrings and tattoos. There was something about Neck's generation that made him feel old. And wise. Were American children getting stupider? Then again, he resented the Baby Boomers for their attitude toward his gang of Generation Xers. Maybe he was just keeping the shit rolling downhill.

"I could be, like, dating Kate now and it wouldn't be no big deal," Neck said. "Or you could be dating my sister, man. Not now, 'cause she's only fourteen, but if she was my age, I mean. Let's say we were twins."

"That's hard for me to imagine."

"Not you and me, dude. Me and my sister. Then you'd be dating her, right?"

No, thought Darren, there *is* something I don't like about this generation. "Not if she looks like you, Cappucco. Tan in a bottle plus steroids equals serious depreciation in the brain-housing group." He wasn't as good with one-liners as his wife but he chuckled at this one. It was pretty good.

Neck frowned. He held his breath so the big Schwarzenegger vein in his forehead would throb. He didn't like strangers making fun of him and it was a stupid joke anyway and the guy was so high and mighty and just so totally fucking anal and white-bread and his own *wife* liked Neck's ass so he could just fuck *off,* as far as Neck was concerned.

Still, Neck understood the rules of the locker room and the guy was probably just joking. Dumbass. He would let it slide, but it *was* a dangerous thing to say to a Wolverine who was about to join the NFL. In two years he'd be able to steal Kate right away from him. Take her out on the big city in a limo, cut the line at Moomba, slap down the professional plastic, order up the Cristal and some of that fancy fish-egg dip and . . . BuddaBing Baby! Neck Cappucco, all-pro, king of the motherfucking bling!

When he stepped off behind Kate, Neck wished she had packed *five* fajitas so he could have eaten *all* of them.

– 14 –

MEXICO CITY, MEXICO

Deputy Attorney General Eduardo Saiz had just returned from briefing his president and was feeling neutrally buoyant, not quite comfortable sitting on the edge of his desk, but still exponentially happier than he had been while expecting that an *El Toro* assassin might immediately transform his existence into a bloody history. In fact, his paranoia had proved useful. He wanted a global nickname for the gringo murderers that would resonate and *Los Asesinos* was silently accepted by the president himself. It bore close enough resemblance to the English term, so that surely even the average gringo would figure it out. It was but one example of his gift for crisis management, and *El Toro* had congratulated him for it—and for convincing the president to let Eduardo head the search for *Los Asesinos*—while hustling back to his office.

Now Eduardo was facing his staff in his hot office in the ministry. He was sitting awkwardly, trying to cover his ripped lip with the Evian water bottle while pinning his arms against his sides in hopes of containing the fecund droplets that were trying to flee his soaked armpits. A fan whirred overhead.

His military aide, a fifty-year-old man in an army uniform, stood and said, "Sir, General Childama would like to offer you any support you need."

"Thank you, Victor," said Eduardo. "I spoke with the general in the president's office and he told me the same. It is most gracious of you. We will pull together after this loss. But I'll tell you what I told him. *Los Asesinos* killed my men, now my men want—and deserve—the mission. But I have taken the general up on his offer for roadblock assistance." Containment was the key: both in keeping *Los Asesinos* corralled and in keeping the army on the periphery. The Network could just as easily be exposed by a bumbling Mexican soldier snatching the sat-phone as by American DEAs who had started all this murder to begin with.

"Yes, sir. I understand the need for payback as well as any. If we see *Los Asesinos,* your men will execute the takedown. On that I give you a guarantee."

"I am obliged. And so are my men."

The soldier added, "We have already begun to deploy on the highways, sir."

Eduardo nodded graciously, staring at the manila folder his judicial police aide-de-camp was using as a personal air conditioner. It was thick. That meant the young man had information on *Los Asesinos.* And if he had information, they were not DEA at all. Eduardo had already attached the glorious English phrase "drug-related" to the gringos during his initial call to his contact in the Reuters news service, and now he allowed himself a sliver of hope that *Los Asesinos* really *were* civilian dealers executing a side deal with Jackrabbit.

He extended his hand, palm up. "Looks like you've already found a great deal, Morales. Tell me they are not DEA."

Jorge Morales took one more swipe at the air and handed his boss the folder. "No, sir. American civilians."

Eduardo pounded the desk with his fist. "Good news!"

"I'm afraid the news is not good, sir."

Eduardo took the folder with him as he circled the desk in deep despair. He sat heavily in his cushioned chair, staring at the photograph of his wife. How did it come to this insanity? He opened the folder as deliberately as he did his mail-box, terrified that *El Toro* had made good on his promise to put a diamondback rattler inside. But that was years ago.

On top of the stack of printouts was a color Xerox of a woman wearing only a backpack running along a beach next to a camel. *What the hell?* It was apparently copied from *Sports Illustrated.* He looked at the next picture in the pile and a black United States Marine Corps officer looking severe in his dress blue uniform was staring back at him.

"*Los Asesinos?*"

"Yes, sir," said Morales. "Darren Phillips and Kate North. Americans vacationing in Acapulco."

"*Vacationing?*"

"Yes, sir. Our detectives found a rental kayak at Jackrabbit's compound. They traced them back to the Estero Beach rental shop, found their hotel, and ultimately found passports and other evidence. Then I did a Lexis-Nexis and a Google search on the names and came up with all that."

Eduardo thumbed the stack of printouts as if shuffling a deck of cards. "Quite a lot. Well done. So the indication is that they were meeting this despicable Jackrabbit character to buy drugs. Any indication of past offenses?"

Jorge Morales chided himself for having thrown Jackrabbit's name out so casually. The colonel was not *on payroll,* but his boss had covered well for the slip. He would be more careful when there were outsiders present. "It is an open question, sir. That's clearly what they were up to, as you stated in your brief to the press, but I think the Americans may doubt our theory. The woman is some sort of sports hero. Her husband, as you can see, is a Marine. Worse, he is a military aide to the president of the United States."

"You're joking. Military aide?"

"Yes. I think he carries the nuclear codes."

It grew very quiet in the office of the deputy attorney general. The overhead fan pressed down on Eduardo's head like a great weight. It seemed to be blowing the hot air down on him like a hair dryer. Eduardo watched a photocopy of a *Los Angeles Times* article about the woman slowly rotate under the breeze. He asked very deliberately, "Where are the others?"

"Others, sir?"

"Yes, damn it. Who were the other gringos involved? Initial word from the site was that our platoon fought many soldiers and killed two."

"The dead are two American college students who had been locked in the Acapulco jail for fighting and drunkenness two nights before. The detectives believe *Los Asesinos* freed them as hostages. It's unclear who killed them. A third, an American football player for the University of Michigan named Vincent Cappucco, is still missing. We assume he's traveling with *Los Asesinos.*"

"That makes no sense. What about the others? I was told there were many."

"That's what the *Federale* lieutenant thought, sir. But it appears it was just those five. They were mistaken for soldiers because they were fit."

"Nineteen murders of Mexican citizens and two dead American university students, and you are telling me a couple of *tourists* are responsible?" Morales did not answer, just stood there staring like an imbecile. No, Eduardo decided, I'll have to do this myself. It will be difficult, and the setup has to be perfect, but there is a chance. "Will you all excuse me for about thirty minutes? As you can see, I need to think."

As his staff shuffled out, Eduardo grabbed his aide by the elbow and said, "One more thing, Morales. See if you can come up with some darker pictures of *Los Asesinos.* These are not sinister enough to feed to the press. If you cannot, we'll use their passport photos. No one takes good passport photos. Look how fat the girl looks in hers. Huge. And the black looks like a rapist without his uniform."

Alone at last in the big oven, Eduardo hurried over to his wall safe and removed the satphone, careful to keep it out of his leaky forehead's line of fire. There was one missed call, from the Guerrero State *comandante.* Eduardo ordered the communications center to patch him through, unwilling to believe that there was good news waiting but hopeful nevertheless. Killing *Los Asesinos* was now only half of the problem anyway. The sell would be tougher.

"Good news, Octopus!" the *comandante* said.

Thank Christ. "You killed them?"

"Well, we have them, sir. Their location, I mean. Conductor has traced another call on Jackrabbit's phone."

"Where?"

"About sixty kilometers outside Acapulco. Very rugged wilderness at the edge of the mountains along Highway ninety-five."

"Are more helicopters going there?" Eduardo asked, sitting now.

"We only have two more choppers ourselves and they are down for maintenance. Anyway it's too mountainous to land a bird, Octopus, so I have requested four army helicopters to circle overhead where they cannot interfere."

"The army? They'll take hours to get organized."

"Yes, sir. That's why I have dispatched both of my dog teams. These are the elite teams you inspected during your last visit, sir. They are on site. We will have their track in a few minutes, and an hour or so later we'll have them."

"How can we be sure they'll find the track?"

"If I may interrupt, Octopus. This is Conductor at the communications center," a metallic voice said. "We have differential location systems on all the satphones. We kept the American girl on the phone long enough to get an exact location. Looks like they're seventeen kilometers from a firebreak off Highway ninety-five on a steep hill, fifty-seven kilometers north of Acapulco just below Highway ninety-two near a town called Zocoalpta."

"Lots of people around?"

"No, Octopus. Entire area is pretty deserted, which is good. We'll guide the dog teams right to the centimeter."

"You better," said Eduardo. "Let me be clear—all federal Guerrero and Oaxaca police assets are to aid however they can. The recovery of our satphone takes top priority. *Comandante,* if you wish to involve the army, do it only sparingly. And let me repeat Toro's instructions that this . . . *incident* not be disseminated to our friends south of the border. Keep me appraised."

Eduardo Saiz flittered his tongue into the ragged slash cut by his big front teeth and tasted the tangy hot copper, thinking he might need stitches. Then he picked up his BlackBerry and started typing.

DODGER—HAVE IDENTIFIED ASSASSINS. AMERICAN DRUG DEALERS WITH WHITE HOUSE CONNECTION. WILL NEED YOUR HELP IN BRINGING THIS PUBLIC. NAMES WILL FOLLOW WHEN I CONFIRM. FISHERMAN.

- 15 -

MCLEAN, VIRGINIA

The Bat Cave was silent as the calls were played again. Susanne Sheridan said, "What is that tone before the calls? Different from the dial tone. Did you guys hear it?"

"It's not actually a *tone*, ma'am," Ted Blinky said. He was just about to bring up the data burst he had discovered and was disappointed she heard it, too. It was just a faint beep in the background. Perhaps she had been looking over his shoulder while he was breaking it down on his monitor. He hated the race for credit because he rarely won. "And it's not exactly *before* the calls, ma'am. It actually happens about ten seconds into the call. What's interesting is the signature. It's layered. In a normal tone, say, when a piano hits a key . . ."

"Did you figure it out or not, Mister Blinky?" Susanne interrupted, noticing a particle of potato chip clinging to the lower reaches of the tech analyst's beard.

"Well, not yet, ma'am. That's what I was getting at. I'm going to have to use a radical new technology called a digitally enhanced breakout, or DEB."

"The DEB isn't *new*," said Christian Collins.

"Quiet, Christian," Susanne said. "Mister Blinky, get at it."

"Excuse me, ma'am?"

"You said you were getting at something. Well, Mister Blinky, you're already there. What did you find?"

Blinky paused, unsure if her smile was meant to soften or sharpen the prod. He decided that she thickened her southern accent on purpose to condescend. It was so annoying. Now she was rushing him because she simply was not capable of understanding the DEB. She was covering up for embarrassment by pulling rank, just like all the other operations glory hounds. "I figured out they're digits. Numbers. The tone, I mean. Ten digits crushed together. I assume that they came up in the clear only because she had no encryption. Once I program the proper DEB, I'll have the numbers themselves. But what's *really* interesting is that this tone is only present on a couple of the phone calls. The shorter hang-ups have none."

Blinky felt important and glanced at the audience to solidify the feeling. He wasn't an operations officer but he would be soon. "My hunch is, the satphone is secretly dialing phone numbers so others can listen in. Ten digits. That's a phone call, all right."

Susanne put a pencil in her mouth and chewed on it. Then her eyebrows rose and she asked her assistant, "What do you think, ye man of the hair gel?"

Christian Collins studied the numbers, irritated at the rib. He used hair gel to appear neat and professional. Her timing stank. In two years this was the first time he could remember Deputy Director Sheridan having solicited his opinion. It was about time, all right, but he was victim of a brain freeze—even though he was sure he had ten theories just a second ago!—while that hairy fucking geek Blinky smirked at him.

Susanne asked, "Well, is he right, Christian?"

Absent even a single thought—under the pressure he doubted if he could recognize his own number if he saw it—Christian Collins relented and croaked, "Yes, ma'am. I think he is. Ten digits is a phone number."

"Now come on, Christian . . ."

Hearing her harsh opening, Collins immediately knew he was wrong. And he had sold his nuts to Blinky to boot. Why did she ambush him in public?

She continued, "Why would this phone automatically connect to a third party? Think about how these phone calls are transmitted. Everything runs through BEEKEEPER. That means that a third party does not have to eavesdrop; by definition, they are already privy. We believe these communications are ultra-wideband. So why ten digits? And why does it take a certain number of seconds before this burst is sent?"

The men remained silent. Susanne was only looking at Christian Collins and Blinky felt slighted. The kid claimed to be high-tech but he was just a callow political wannabe. Any asshole could have found venture funding in the late nineties.

Blinky said, "What you're saying is, ma'am, that this is specific to ultrawide-band. So we should focus on its properties. It can't be jammed. It does not use frequencies, so we can't listen to the calls, and because these bursts of electrical energy are sailing around the air, maybe the ten digits are some form of timing code."

"What else?" she asked, still staring at Christian. She wanted him to get it, but this was a real-time event. Training could come later.

She was about to speak when Jimmy Contreras practically growled, "It's some kind of beacon sending out a ten-digit-grid coordinate."

A young intelligence analyst walked briskly from the rear of the Bat Cave and whispered in Susanne's ear. Susanne said, "Just so our colleagues don't think you were whispering sweet nothings, please tell them what you told me."

The analyst blushed and said, "I traced the New York call to a William North and got a housekeeper. His daughter, Kate North, is currently vacationing in Acapulco on her honeymoon. There's stuff all over the Web about her. She grew up on the Upper East Side, went to Princeton, now is a professional adventure athlete or something. Get this: Her new husband is a Marine who works in the White House."

Susanne stood but did not immediately speak to give weight to the last sentence. "Christian, please raise Mexico City again. We need confirmation on their identities before we alert the White House." She started toward the Bat Cave entrance, mentally running through her new chain of command in an effort to figure out whom should be notified first. With the DCI—the Director of Central Intelligence—in Israel and Corwin on the loose somewhere vying for ownership, it was far from clear.

"Oh, and Christian," she said over her shoulder. "Be a sweetheart and whip together a hard-copy set of talking points to show DHS. You're my guy, Christian."

– 16 –

MOUNT EL FRESNO

44 MILES EAST OF ACAPULCO, MEXICO

The dog team sergeant leaned back against Apollo's weight and let the big hound drag him up the hill. His sore wrist was throbbing and chafed, his shoulder socket stretched by the leather leash. "Good boy! We must be close," he gasped.

"We have chased them now for two hours up this mountain, sir. And still nothing yet," said one of the men in the posse, a young corporal next to him. "Is it possible that we have lost the scent?"

The team sergeant shook his head. "Look at the way Apollo and the other dogs strain. You think they like the climb? No, they certainly have the scent."

Finding the towels and the beer bottles had been easy for the dogs once they were given the location, and they had towed the team up the slope at a crushing pace ever since. The team sergeant looked behind him and saw that his stragglers had fallen even farther behind. He started the hunt from the road with fifty-three men: eight hounds and their handlers, five German shepherds and their attack trainers, and a forty-man platoon of *Federales*. Every man without the benefit of a dog had fallen off the pace, and even then, six of his Dog Team members were scattered below him. He did not want to face the murderers with just seven men, but the commander—not just his company commander but the *Guerrero comandante!*—had ordered him to push ahead of the setting sun. They had even given him helicopter support from the army. Every fifteen minutes they droned over his head.

"Dog, this is Hawk, over," his Motorola radio buzzed.

The team sergeant halted his detail. "This is Dog," he panted. "No sign of them. It's not possible that they had only thirty minutes' head start. Impossible, impossible. More like a few hours, I'm telling you! We must have gained a full hour on them by now. Probably more. I am down to seven men with dogs. The others are way down the slope."

"I understand, Dog. I am told to relay a message. You said before that if you had to, you could set the dogs free and they could find and damage the Americans. Stop them or at least slow them down, yes?"

Now they're listening to me. "Well, yes. I believe the dogs can *kill* them. That's why we have the German shepherds. The hounds will halt or tree them, the shepherds shred them. I think the murderers must have had three hours on us, but even so the dogs will catch them soon."

"Yes, Dog, we understand. You are coming up to the ridge but it is getting dark. We think we can flush the Americans before it gets too dark to spot them from the air. There are only cliffs if they continue on their path like this. You are to release the dogs now and follow on foot."

Finally, the sergeant thought. He turned to his corporal. "Tell the others in the Hound Squad to release their animals. The ones behind us release first. When the dogs get up here, we'll release our hounds."

"What about the German shepherds, sir?"

"Not yet. We wait maybe ten minutes to release them. Let the hounds find the murderers and hold their attention, then the shepherds come in and kill them." The sergeant tried to spit into the dry dirt, but the white, foamy spittle just rolled out and stuck to his lower lip like crumbs of styrofoam. I may be tired, he thought as he looked up the mountain, but my dogs are not. Somewhere up there, the Americans who murdered his *compañeros* were going to die a violent death of ripping teeth.

– 17 –

49 MILES NORTHEAST OF

ACAPULCO, MEXICO

"*You gotta be* shitting me," said Neck as he leaned over the edge. "We come all this way and run into a dead end." He sat down with a groan and propped his throbbing feet up on a rock, expecting his sneakers to bulge with every beat of his heart.

Kate looked down the cliff. It was a steep shale rock face that dove into a thickly vegetated slope about a hundred meters below. There were several ledges, but a descent would need planning. They had arrived at the top of the first range of the Sierra Madre del Sur, small compared to those farther east. She looked down the ridgeline in search of another route, but it was hard to see beyond a few meters. It was frosted with lush trees that were bursting with leaves. She petted some pink trumpet flowers and left dark streaks of dirty sweat.

"This ridgeline runs for quite a ways. I guess we can—What's that? Hear it?"

The trio turned toward the sound. On the long slope below they could hear faint barks of dogs moving up the hill. "Must be tracking us. Should have buried those towels deeper. I was lazy," said Darren. "Those dogs still can only go as fast as the men attached."

"Shhh. No, listen," whispered Kate. "Moving way too fast for humans. Must be running free. We need to descend the cliff. They'll lose the scent that way, too. Right?"

Darren unbuckled the pack and peered over the ledge to the east. It was nearly vertical with few discernable holds in the deep shadow of the setting sun. "Yeah, no one can follow us down there. Problem is, looks awfully far for the Hell Bitch." He pulled the rope free and tossed the coil over the edge. It spiraled past the crags and spilled into a pile on a small ledge eighty feet below with a thud that echoed up the wall. He pulled the rope up a few feet and grabbed the duct taped halfway mark. "That's more than seventy-five feet just to that little ledge. Too big a rappel to double up on the rope."

Neck pointed his MP-5 at the trees. "Hurry the fuck up. I hate dogs."

Kate said, "I'll rig a retrievable rappel. Get a harness on Neck."

"That's a big risk," said Darren.

"So are those dogs," said Neck.

Darren was sliding the climbing harness up over Neck's meaty thighs when the pace and volume of the barks increased dramatically. He turned to tell Kate that there was no time, but she was already moving past him, pointing at a torch pine tree with a large, low branch jutting out eight feet off the ground. "Get up on the branch!"

The dogs were close now and Darren cursed to himself for failing to judge their approach. He put the MP-5 around Kate's shoulders by the sling and cupped his hands. She stepped in the pocket and was launched up, hands around the branch, past her waist, feet finding a tenuous purchase. She grasped the trunk.

Darren could hear the dogs crashing through the brush now. Twigs snapped like firecrackers but he could not see them. The onrush of sounds reminded him of the Iraqi APCs that he felt and heard in Desert Storm before actually seeing. He boosted Neck up, and the branch bent terribly.

"Switch places," Kate said. She pulled Neck closer to the trunk, using him for balance when she was on the other side, on the thinner part of the branch. Even on the thickest piece of the branch Neck gave it a wicked bow, so he put one sneaker over the other in the socket.

"Will it support me?" Darren asked.

Kate saw the first dog appear in the forest behind her husband. It was some kind of hound dog moving low to the ground, so graceful it was almost gliding over the patch of spider lilies. Behind it, three more dogs galloped along as if they were deer. "GET UP HERE!"

Darren clamped the branch where it was thickest—next to Neck's feet—and did a pull-up, swinging his legs forward and up over the branch, coming to rest horizontally on top where he tried to balance on his abdomen like a gymnast. His muscles immediately began to twitch under the pressure. Blood squeezed into his head and his face darkened. The dogs scratched the trunk and were wild with frustration, taking vain leaps up at his face as he struggled to keep his muscular legs rigid and elevated. A Teva slipped off his foot and a hound savaged it before returning to its place on the trunk.

"SHOOT THEM!" Darren gasped, his entire head quaking with strain now.

"Hold on to me, Neck," said Kate. "I'm going to lean forward."

Neck wrapped his big hand around the back of her neck and his fingers pulled on her traps. She was able to lean out and balance well enough to unsling the MP-5. The weight of the weapon's barrel tipped the sights over a dog and she pulled the trigger. The machine gun's bark silenced the dog's. The animal bellowed terribly and skidded away on two legs, howling and crying. It rolled over on its side before it got twenty feet and struggled to draw breath. The others winced and retreated when they heard the gunshot, but soon four more hounds raced past them and the growing group returned to attack the tree. Kate fired one bullet at a time until the yelps of pain drowned the shots.

Darren pivoted and dropped to the ground. "Toss me the weapon!"

Kate handed it down carefully and pointed at a howling dog. "Put that one out of its misery, Darren."

"Don't have enough bullets for mercy," he said, putting the rifle in his shoulder, backing up against a boulder at the edge of the cliff, and scanning the trees. He pulled the magazine free for a moment, gauged its weight, and slapped it back into the submachine gun. *Two or three more bullets.* "I don't hear any more dogs. Do you two?"

The air was thick with screams from the wounded hounds. "I can't hear anything over these poor dogs," she said. "Please kill them, Darren. We don't want them to find this position anyway. Whoever's hunting us, I mean."

"Keep an eye out for others." He moved forward and began to club the surviving hounds to death. Their skulls were hard and the vibration of the MP-5 stung his hands.

Neck thought about jumping down to help, but some part of him rejected the notion. He wasn't part of this nightmare. He didn't kill anybody. Hell, he didn't even kill any dogs. "What's happening here, Kate? I mean, this is crazy. What if we was to stop here and give ourselves up?"

"Come on down," said Darren. "It's quiet now. No more dogs in the distance. We need to get down this cliff right-goddamn-now. Neck, toss me that MP-5. We need to redistribute bullets."

Darren grabbed the MP-5 in midair as it came down from the tree but tensed when he looked back up at Neck. The boy seemed to stare at him blankly for a moment before Darren saw his eyes shift over his shoulder and open wide, arm extending rigid and straight, pointing, Kate screaming something. Darren jerked around and raised the weapon, instinct forcing him on a knee. A gray blur hurtled through the air toward his face. Too fast to be human, he thought in the split second before he pulled the trigger—the same span of time it took for the small hairs on his neck and arms to electrify and snap bolt upright.

The two rounds caught the German shepherd in the face and killed it instantly. Still, the body continued to glide and seventy pounds slammed into Darren at over twenty miles per hour, crunching the machine gun into his chest and knocking him to his back, taking his wind and four more erratic bullets with it. He gasped for air, scrambled onto his knees, and was able to put a single bullet into the side of the second dog before its jaws snapped shut around his forearm. The raging dog planted its front legs into the dirt, hunched tight with its ears back and flush, trying to yank him to the ground in a savage tug-of-war.

Darren's blood mixed with foreign saliva. He swung the MP-5 around, but chose instead to empty the clip into a third shepherd that darted around a tree. It took all four bullets to put the dog down, tumbling harmlessly into the other dog like a kamikaze blown off course just in time.

All of the attacking dogs were silent save for low, guttural growls. All of the humans were screaming—also guttural.

Neck jumped from his branch and brought both legs down onto the back of the dog that had Darren. He weighed 220 pounds and ten years of squats had swelled his legs; Neck broke the dog's spine instantly. He tumbled athletically, grabbed the MP-5 that was lying on the ground, brought the barrel up and pointed at another German shepherd that was sprinting toward him. He felt oddly proud of what he had done—*leaping from a tree and crushing that dog, then rolling just like an Idaho drill.* He thought he might just blow this new dog into a thousand bits.

Neck waved his hand vaguely at the tree in an attempt to let Kate know that the guys had it covered down there, but the dog was faster than he thought and he sighted in and squeezed. The trigger fought his finger and the sick feeling of fear panicked him enough that his next move lacked sufficient aggression to beat back the dog. *The safety's on! Darren put the safety on!*

He swung the rifle out weakly, and the shepherd absorbed the blow and found his meaty calf on the way by, tearing now in a violent series of jerks like a shark that took Neck's legs out from under him.

The dog moved for his face and Neck saw the bubbling saliva—tinged red with his own blood—dripping from those black, jagged gums that dangled and flapped as the thing clawed up his stomach. Now the animal's heated, ragged breath and its claws digging into his abs as it straddled him and pinned him down, empty eyes that wrapped an otherworldly promise of nature come full circle, come to play tag with a boy who had once kicked his own dog, those ears pinned back in a serpentine shadow of want, two fangs straining for his neck—

which he no longer considered so big and powerful. Neck felt himself go weak under the animal's bloodlust and he screeched. It was an inhuman cry and he marveled at its source even as he continued to blow out his air.

Three shots from a pistol snapped into the beast's side and made it dance. Its big head curled toward the wounds as it leapt away from Neck and skidded to rest on its side, attempting to right itself like a ship in final tilt, pulled to its death by cauterized punctures and gravity.

Kate ran past Neck and put the pistol against the side of a new dog wrestling with Darren. She pulled the trigger several times. Her wrist ached from the recoil, but the pain disappeared when the dog released Darren's machine gun and turned on her. She fired the rest of her rounds wildly and none struck its mark. The slide on the pistol stayed back and the trigger went limp, so she flung it at the dog and ran for the tree. The dog limped after her.

Neck put two bullets from his MP-5 into its ear. It collapsed and when the echo dissipated, the forest was quiet for the first time in five minutes. For the humans, though, the high-pitched tone of broken eardrums glazed their world.

Darren scanned the trees, but there were no more dogs. Still, Kate and Neck gathered next to him like a herd and waited. His MP-5 was out of bullets and so was the pistol he had given his wife. "Give me that weapon," he told Neck.

"Almost out, too," said the boy, swinging the MP-5 in the direction from which the dogs had come as if a hidden bullet might save him. "Holy shit. What the fuck was this? Never heard them comin'."

Darren said, "Shepherds don't bark, apparently."

"We need to get out of here," said Kate. "Darren, you play lookout while I get the harness on Neck and get him down. Oh my God! Are you badly hurt?"

Darren glanced at his forearm and saw two deep puncture wounds and a smattering of smaller cuts. The blood was still trickling free and he tested his range of motion and his grip. When he clenched his fist hard to confirm he had his strength, a squirt of blood painted Neck's Nikes. "I'm fine. Just two cuts. Gonna be sore when I wake up . . . which is to say in five days. You?"

"Not a scratch. No bullets left, though. Neck?"

Neck put a toe in the dirt to wipe off Darren's blood and twisted his knee around. "Fucker got my calf, is all. Not bad, looks like. I got lots to spare. See? That blood on the front of my shoe is actually from a cactus a few hours ago. Hurt worse than the dog bite. That dog was gonna eat me before you shot it, Kate. I swear to God he was gonna eat me! Returned the favor, though, didn't I? Little fucker's still alive. Look at it." Neck walked over to the dog that was still breathing and caved in its head with a single, savage blow of the steel machine gun.

When he looked at the couple, Neck's face was covered in dots of dog red and Darren had the feeling that the boy might make it after all.

Kate reached into the pack and held up the camera and suntan lotion. "I forgot about the waterproof pouch under the lid. So I guess we ditch the camera and the empty guns? They'll be no use on the hike. I'll carry the road map. Darren, you can carry the gun with the bullets."

Neck managed to free the magazine. "Only three bullets left."

Kate nodded. "Okay. I say we keep the suntan lotion just in case we cross some desert. And we'll probably need the Hell Bitch even after this rappel, so we'll keep the harnesses after this descent."

Darren grabbed the camera. "We have a use for this camera. We can send a message to the world with it. Neck, do me a favor and drag a few of those carcasses into a pile here."

"Why, bro?"

"Just do it." Darren hated it when orders were not immediately followed.

"Real original," Neck said, and walked over to one of the dogs.

Darren took off his shirt and turned to his wife. "Kate, take the suntan lotion and get a small twig. You're going to write a message on my back, snap some pictures of it, then we'll leave the camera for them to find and develop."

She shook her head. "Two problems, babe. One, I'm not sure if we need the outside world glancing at what's in this camera. Our first night . . . remember?" Darren groaned at the hazy memory of the photo session and shrugged sheepishly. "Second, the drug dealers or the cops or *whoever* finds this are *not* going to release a message from us to the outside world."

"You all took some porno shots on that camera?" asked Neck. "Cool."

Darren was irritated with the boy, but his wife said, "Some damn good ones, too."

Darren whispered, "You're exactly right, Kate. We need to get the *Federales* to *want* to release the photos once they develop them. Trust me on this—they will." He tossed her the lotion.

———

Kate leaned back on the Hell Bitch and watched her retrievable anchor bite down on itself, the tension of the rope clamping the single-wrap loop tight to the tree. A friction hold instead of a knot protected her from a two-hundred-foot fall. It would have been safer to wrap it twice around the tree atop the cliff, but then she ran the risk of not being able to free the rope for the second pitch.

Below her, Darren and Neck stood perched on a tiny ledge on the cliff face. She took a last glimpse at the pile of dead dogs and folded herself into an "L" position with her legs perpendicular to the rock and her torso parallel with it. Her right hand acted as a brake just beyond her right hip as she smoothly descended the face. Bounding—pushing away from the face in giant bounces like the rappels in Hollywood—was poor form anyway, she thought, but on a retrievable, the sudden movement would prove fatal. The rope was not, after all, tied off.

She felt the burn of the Hell Bitch as it snaked through Darren's tank top, wrapped around her brake hand, and eventually her husband's hands were on her hips. Darren guided her to the ledge and pulled her in tight. There on a three-foot ledge a hundred feet above Mexican terra she felt secure. Kate unclipped her Figure 8 descender, took the tension off the Hell Bitch, and snapped her like a whip. The wave she created in the rope glided up the cliff, where it disappeared at the top.

"Stand by for rope," she said.

"What's that mean?" Neck looked up and pulled himself tight against a crag when he saw the ribbons of rope coming down toward him. "What the hell! Jesus! It came untied!"

"My weight was keeping it tied," Kate said, holding tight as the Hell Bitch spilled over them and continued its fall. She was pulled forward, but Neck encircled her arm and yanked her back in tight. She could feel him trembling.

"Ho. Now wait a fucking second. I ain't goin' down without this thing tied off. I mean, no way." He glanced down and his stomach tried to ascend to his eyes.

"Guess you'll just be staying on this ledge, then," said Darren, helping Kate bind the rope to a short but thick spire of rock. "I'll get my sister to help you down in a week."

Kate was about to soften her husband's line of argument—he was not blessed in the tact department—but she saw Neck quickly nod his acceptance. "I'll go," Neck whispered.

Darren often used classic third-grade machismo tactics like questioning bravery when he debated other men. She thought them absurd, and knew that her own leadership blend of setting the example, humor, and pep worked better in most circumstances, but she was keenly aware of their potent effectiveness among the duller-tooled alpha males.

Kate looked east across the small valley and saw a helicopter sweeping low in the massive shadow of the ridgeline, a red running light winking at her as if keeping her secret. It's too thickly wooded for them, she thought. They'll never find us. The helicopter flew past the trio and slowed somewhere on the other side of the cliff. Mechanical sounds trailed it and then were muted by the rising wind and the clapping of leaves and needles. Tall evergreens spread out unevenly for miles, gaining two meters of altitude for every one they lost, rustling expectantly as she watched their color disappear.

She breathed the crisp air through her nose and tried to allow the purity of the oxygen calm her. She marveled at her husband's ability to put the past in its place; this was their reality now and she needed to avoid nostalgia. That would be difficult. She had spent her whole life dreaming of the moment that she had experienced only six hours before, married to both a wonderful man and a wonderful sense of self. She wrapped the memory in an embrace so fierce that a tear squeezed out of her eye. They had killed *Federales.* They were fugitives now.

The sun vanished and now the Sierra Madre del Sur loomed in the afterglow, framing the valley with their peaks. They were the daughters of Mexico's central mountain spine, boasting of an arduous test Kate would have to pass before they allowed her to test underfoot their dominant mother: the Sierra Madre.

- 18 -

WASHINGTON, D.C.

Jimmy Contreras studied the two photographs that were mounted on the wall behind George Henry's desk. He knew it was rude to stare over the director of Homeland Security's head but his curiosity was too powerful. The pictures were candid amateur photographs, but Contreras felt their authenticity was damaged by the polished crimson cedar frames in which they had been professionally mounted. Just like a politician to pound at the message of empathy with a golden hammer, Contreras thought.

In the first picture, a color shot taken when the director was the governor of Georgia, Henry was smiling broadly in front of a white colonial house, surrounded by his family. But it was the second that held Jimmy Contreras's gaze, a black-and-white photograph from Vietnam. George Henry as a young man was smiling just as broadly, posing shirtless and pale in front of a howitzer in some central highland firebase. Must have been tough as an officer, thought Contreras, who was saddened by the fact the lieutenant was alone in the picture. That war was tough enough surrounded by *compañeros*. Nobody deserved to be lonely there, not even officers.

The faces came back to him now and Contreras yearned not only for their lives but also for his youth, wasted so carelessly by a generation of men who now referred to themselves as the "greatest." He sighed because the bitterness was bubbling up. Bureaucracy drove him mad, but he was careless enough in meetings without the springboard. He was there to support Deputy Director Sheridan and their mutual cause, though while Susanne wanted to see the safe return of the honeymooning couple, Contreras did not give a damn. Their well-being meant zero after they killed innocents. Anyway, they probably would not survive the night. He decided to limit his comments to curt responses.

"Deputy Director Sheridan, thanks for coming so quickly," said Henry, standing to greet her and Contreras. He was a thick man who seemed to be constructed in blocks.

Susanne shook his hand and said, "This is Agent Jimmy Contreras, sir. He's our liaison from the DEA for counter-narcotics work, specializing in Mexico."

"Glad to meet you, Jimmy."

Contreras shook the man's hand and immediately liked him. It was more than Vietnam but he could not pinpoint it. He looked hard-core. "Likewise, sir."

"I assume you two know everybody here?"

Roger Corwin had alerted the heavyweights, as she expected. George Marsden, director of the FBI, smiled at her and nodded. Roberta "Bobby" Kennedy, White House chief of staff, was seated next to him. Welcome to the show, she thought.

Susanne smiled at Kennedy and said, "All but Ms. Kennedy. It's a pleasure to meet you, ma'am."

"We've been waiting."

So much for the Ya-Ya Sisterhood, thought Susanne. Kennedy was an austere woman whose singular focus tended to burn those on the periphery. She was dressed in an unflattering gray pantsuit that ignited regret in Susanne, who preferred skirts.

Susanne quickly walked across the room and sat next to Contreras, crossing her legs self-consciously. "I apologize, Ms. Kennedy. I know you're busy."

Susanne felt exposed. Clearly Dodger Corwin had prompted the meeting. The first step in bureaucratic success—claiming individual credit by preemption, rushing to keep the hierarchy informed—was an act that inspired cognitive dissonance in CIA officers. With the director of Central Intelligence in Israel and the deputy director in Tampa, George Henry had invited her unescorted. She had brought Contreras as her heavy.

Susanne did not plan the grand entrance but it would prove worthwhile. She had been delayed because she wanted to arrive at the knife fight with a gun—the identities and brief sheets on the couple to whom the Mexicans were referring as *Los Asesinos*. It was the ace that Corwin did not have in his rush to play Chicken Little.

"Nicely understated, Ms. Sheridan," said Bobby Kennedy. "Busy. Yes, we're busy, all right. Busy wrangling support for an international war on terror, busy holding fragile domestic and international coalitions together, busy bailing out a sinking economy, busy keeping our southern border secure by leveraging the president's close relationship with Mexico. And now we have a first-class embarrassment on our hands. A military aide to the president of the United States, someone supposedly screened and entrusted by us to carry nuclear codes, is about to be named the prime suspect in that awful mess in Acapulco that has tied up the news wires since this afternoon."

"How did you identify him, ma'am?" Susanne asked a second before her deduction overrode her surprise. *Did one of my people leak it? Ted Blinky? No, Corwin has someone on the inside down south.*

"Sorry, Susanne," said Roger Corwin evenly. "I found the identities, but we don't reveal sources and methods."

Corwin smiled slightly and she suspected they were either caps or LaserBrite. In fact, staring at his manufactured tan and manicured eyebrows, Susanne decided that searching for something genuine in the man's face would be like sitting on the edge of Loch Ness with a camera.

"Yes, well, however you got the information, we are indebted to you, Roger," Kennedy said. "The president was able to call the president of Mexico before they went public down south. They agreed to reveal the identities of *Los Asesinos* jointly tonight in a statement to be released at ten p.m. That gives us three hours to figure out how this happened in the first place."

George Henry stood and walked around from behind his desk. Corwin shot to his feet, but Henry waved him down, choosing instead to lean against the lip of his desk. He dominated the other five, all seated on couches and chairs. "Roger, why don't you brief Susanne and Jimmy to catch them up on your findings."

Susanne was surprised at this. She had faxed a first-class set of talking points to Henry an hour earlier so he could control the meeting. But now he was deferring to Corwin of all people. Why? *To distance himself from me.*

"Well, sir, there's not much yet," said Corwin. "As I said, I have a team working on background information as we speak. I'm confident I'll have details by ten. What I've learned directly from my relationships in Mexico is that Marine Major Darren Phillips and his wife Kate were on vacation in Acapulco and tried to buy some drugs. Somehow it escalated into what everyone has seen on MSNBC. The Mexican authorities have witnesses who saw this couple shoot several Mexican federal police officers and two American college students. They may or may not have either in their custody or their care a third college student named Vincent Cappucco. He's currently missing. They also may or may not have the satellite phone I mentioned. No need to brief Susanne and Jim on that. They were in on the earlier meeting I held.

"That's the bulk of it, sir, but I would emphasize here how important the relationship we at the FBI have cultivated with the Mexican government has become. They are eager to share information. I'll turn over whatever I get to you and the White House as I get it."

"Roger's being modest," said FBI Director George Marsden. "The Mexican attorney general himself called me thirty minutes ago and asked for Roger's personal assistance. Apparently he and the man they are entrusting with the investigation down there have worked together before. My recommendation is that we place Roger in charge of the investigation on this end. He can best serve as liaison to Mexico. I don't mean to sound blunt, but I don't see what this has to do with Homeland Security. George, we're here to support you, but this is best handled by us, not elevated to your office. That only raises suspicion. We make an issue of this and the White House gets stained."

Susanne did not like the direction the meeting was taking. A backroom deal had already been cut.

"We at the White House second that," said Bobby Kennedy. "The crucial aspect here is to erect a wall between the president and this madness. That means information and a very measured, contained response. Roger seems incredibly well positioned and he's already saved us from ambush once. When this goes public tonight there are going to be a series of fires to put out, including attacks from the other side of the aisle, I'm sure, about how we hired this Marine to carry the football in the first place. This is a serious black eye and it has not even started to swell."

Roger Corwin leaned forward, spread his thick fingers, and bent them backward. It was an unconscious habit he had developed as a means of triggering questions about his large calluses, to which he would answer with a quick brief on weightlifting. "I've got people looking into Phillips's polygraph tests for clues, ma'am. And when his background information comes in you'll be informed immediately."

Susanne studied George Henry. He remained quiet and the power relationship was unveiled. Corwin had already managed to minimize the importance of the satphone. The goal here was to protect the president and keep the Mexican-American relationship on track. Why had she been invited in the first place?

With no introduction, Susanne plunged ahead herself. "I submit that this incident was not, in fact, drug-related. That's a cover the Mexican authorities are using."

"You're saying the president of Mexico is lying about this?" burst Bobby Kennedy. "That's outrageous. He's carrying out the first anti-corruption crackdown in fifty years."

"Not the president, ma'am. Someone below him. I can't explain how this couple got tangled up with a known cartel leader to begin with, but I believe the story is manufactured."

"You can't confirm that," said Roger Corwin, wondering how she knew their identities to begin with.

"No, but this couple was on their honeymoon. That isn't the time to run drugs."

"How do you know?"

"Sources and methods, Roger." She was angry and it came out without delicacy.

"At ease. At ease," said George Henry, breaking his silence. "Hate to see that what I've been reading in the papers about the love between your agencies is true."

Susanne studied George Henry. So the DHS had refused to use the talking points. But good old Christian, portrait of efficiency, had slapped together three background slides. They were rough, but they grounded her argument. "Sir, may I dim the lights? I already have some of the information Ms. Kennedy is asking for. This will take fewer than five minutes."

Susanne pulled the tiny projector from her briefcase and set it on the oak coffee table so that it shone clearly on the side wall, below an inscribed plaque with an empty 155-mm shell casing. She pressed a button on a remote control and the first slide popped up. "My assistant, Christian Collins, did a quick background check. As you see, the couple does not exactly fit the profile of murderous drug users."

Name: Kate North Phillips	**Ht./Wt.:** 5'7"/ 130 lbs (articles) 169 lbs (driver license)
DOB: 15 June, 1971	**Ethnicity:** Caucasian
Home: Washington, D.C.	**Edu:** Princeton, B.A., 1993

NOK: Darren Phillips (husband). Father is William North III of New York City, partner at Goldman, Sachs. Mother and younger brother are deceased (1997 double murder).

Prof: Former banking analyst at Goldman, Sachs. Founder and CEO of You Go Girl! an Outward Bound-type school for girls. Kate is also an "adventure racer" and competes in non-motorized, nonstop endurance races of up to 500 miles in length around the world.

Pers: Met her husband, Major Darren Phillips, USMC, while adventure racing. College roommates (note—not a single one of the three we reached thus far maintains any contact with her) call her "quiet" but two present acquaintances call her "hilarious," "gregarious," and "cocky." She has described herself in print as having the "willpower to be the last man standing" during her races. Her workout routine as quoted in some of the magazines is prodigious, to understate it. Possesses a variety of outdoors skills.

"Everyone finished reading?" asked Susanne.

"Her weight. One hundred sixty-nine or one hundred thirty, which is it?" Bobby Kennedy asked for some reason.

"Both, ma'am." Susanne flipped to the picture from *Sports Illustrated* with Kate on the cover running naked on the beach next to a camel. "She got her driver's license nine years ago, but eventually lost the weight when she turned into this."

"We know how her mother and brother died?" Marsden asked, interested.

"Not yet, sir. Her friends said she rarely talked about it. We have yet to reach her father."

"I can knock that out immediately, sir," said Corwin, devastated that he had been scooped in front of his boss. Domestic background checks were FBI turf, not CIA. Bitch.

Bobby Kennedy said, "Pull up Phillips's sheet."

Name: Darren Phillips **Ht./Wt.:** 6'0"/ 190 lbs.

DOB: 13 November, 1968 **Ethnicity:** African-American

Home: Laguna Beach, CA **Edu:** Harvard, B.A., 1990

NOK: Kate Phillips (wife). Mother is Jackie Phillips of Oakland, CA. Father, Staff Sergeant John Phillips, USMC, was KIA (Khe Sahn, Republic of Vietnam, 1968).

Prof: Major, United States Marine Corps. Just assigned as a military aide in the White House, traveling with the President. Infantry platoon commander in Gulf War, won Bronze Star and Purple Heart. Medically discharged by Marines for a broken kneecap, joined CNN as a military advisor and reported from Somalia during *Restore Hope*. Reinstated in the Marines in 1994.

Pers: Met wife Kate North while adventure racing. Prep school All-American wrestler at St. Paul's. All-Ivy wrestler at Harvard and commander of his ROTC unit. Described as "political," "stiff," "by-the-book," "strong, but he's still a kiss-ass," and "poster Marine, and that's not always good" by three peers on phone interviews. Peers respect but do not seem to admire him like seniors: Marine Fitness Reports label him "the finest junior officer I have ever seen—should be groomed for general," "thrives on responsibility and excels where others complain." Phillips was injured in a riot in Somalia in which a Marine died and another reporter was beaten severely. His Harvard roommate Gavin Kelly was sentenced to five years at The Hague for actions there.

"That's no drug dealer," said Susanne.

Corwin wanted to say, doesn't mean he's not a user, but even he felt uncertain. He'd wait for more information from Saiz before committing.

"Do you have information on the college kids?" asked Kennedy.

"Just the missing boy, ma'am," said Susanne, thankful that the Mexican agent was able to lift the information from a local cop in Acapulco. "Here it is."

Name: Vincent Cappucco	**Ht./Wt.:** 6'3"/ 220 lbs.
DOB: 5 September, 1981	**Ethnicity:** Caucasian
Home: Bergen, NJ	**Edu:** University of Michigan, B.A. expected 2003

NOK: John and Kim Cappucco (father and step-mother).

Prof: Student

Pers: Three-sport athlete at Bergen Catholic high school who chose a football scholarship over an offer to join the Yankees in the minor leagues. Three-year starting strong safety for the Wolverines, likely a top draft choice in the NFL (*Pro Football Weekly* said of his draft prospects, "An excellent run defender and a big hitter with a big mouth. Must have majored in trash talking. A total pain in the neck for offenses.) Called "loyal," "cocky," "heart of gold," "emotional," and "big, dumb, and happy" by peers, family, and coaches. Strong family ties. Speaks Italian and Spanish. Raised money for the family of a local cop who was killed on 9/11.

"That's it," Susanne said, snapping off the projector and passing out the brief packets. She watched the FBI director scribble a note to Corwin, who crumpled it and nodded. "This is not about drugs. It's about a satellite phone. Someone in the Mexican chain of command wants it, and so do we. Fact is, that American couple has it."

Bobby Kennedy glanced at her watch. "Roger already briefed us on the phone."

"Did he? Then he told you that phone represents the greatest source of counter-narcotics intelligence since we commenced the war on drugs. Director Marsden, that is why I must disagree with you, sir. This *is* a threat to our national security and should be monitored by this office. I believe that an international cartel has formed around this satellite system with the potential to destabilize countries. Their network is dependent on ultrawideband encrypted communications. We get the satphone and we shut it down."

"Is there any hyperbole in what you just said?" asked Marsden sternly.

"Let me ask it my way," George Henry interrupted. "Jimmy, is this phone like landing at Inch'on or Normandy? What I mean is, will this be a terrific success that is short-lived or a permanent turn in . . ."

"I know what you mean, sir," said Contreras. "It's not the end of the war, but it's closer to D-Day than Inch'on. Call it an Iwo Jima. It's really damn important and it could break their backs."

"Why is this Phillips involved?" Henry asked.

Contreras shrugged. He had spoken enough this meeting.

"Do you think he killed these people?"

Contreras paused. "Yes. Any Marine might do the same if pressed."

Susanne quickly added, "The profiles point to this: Darren and Kate Phillips are not drug dealers. I don't know how they ended up with the cartel's satphone. I don't know how people were killed. But I do know we need to recover that phone."

"How?" asked Decker.

"The president can offer our assistance—helicopters with thermal sights, satellite assets, radio intercepts, and spec ops. We need to be there when this couple is arrested. If the Mexicans refuse, we push back on their drug theory and begin our own leaks. Life gets very difficult if the bluff is called. The press is going to do that anyway. Finally, if we can pinpoint a location, we send a clandestine team to find the couple and recover the phone."

Bobby Kennedy chuckled harshly. "Not in Mexico we don't. No cowboy stuff. Politically it is not feasible. Yemen, fine. Next door, unacceptable. Is that clear?" Kennedy glanced at her watch again. "Excuse me for being so blunt, but I have to get back to reality soon. Next?"

"I asked Susanne for an opinion, not policy, and that's exactly what she gave," Henry said. He paused, then turned to the FBI director. "George, your thoughts?"

George Marsden shrugged and raised his eyebrows. "I gotta tell you, George, I don't believe they are drug dealers. Personal use, I don't know. I've seen stranger things. Why else did they contact this cartel character? We'll beat the brush tonight. See if this Marine has any priors. See what he said about past drug use. Hell, maybe it's the woman. We've got a big problem right now with pro athletes buying steroids in Mexico. Give us the lead here."

Susanne said, "With all due respect, sir, this thing's over when the sun comes up. We need to get a team on the ground now."

The director of Homeland Security stood and walked back around his desk, a theatrical move that signaled finality. "I have two observations. First, the question whether this fire should be contained by Homeland Security or handled on a less visible, personal level—say by FBI through Roger—is still open. Let's see what else comes out between now and a morning meeting at, say, zero-nine hundred."

Susanne wanted to shrink inside her chair. If Homeland was out and Corwin was in, she was over and out.

Henry continued, "Second—and at this point it is truly secondary to protecting the reputation of the president and the leadership—is the phone. Susanne, while I understand your urgency, you understand that we can't go forcing our will upon a sovereign nation representing a massive United States voting bloc. We need to shield the president from this mess. Whether we believe the Phillips are guilty or innocent is of little consequence. The Mexicans have dead police and civilians on their hands. They won't want our help in capturing whoever it was who did it and we can't do anything about that. What are we going to do—invade?"

And that's it, Susanne thought. She was first out the door, striding ahead of Contreras and Corwin to avoid the awkwardness of conversation, too disappointed to speak. Why had George Henry set her up for failure? Another politician trying to stay in the updraft. In the end it was cover-your-ass all the way.

Contreras wanted to call it a night but he followed her. DEA was too cheap to spring for a car so Sheridan was his ride home. Anyway, he sure as hell didn't want to talk with Dodger Corwin.

Corwin enjoyed watching them increase the pace. Contreras looked like a big faithful dog trailing after that queen bitch. He wondered if they were going to go screw their tears away. Director Marsden had been called by Mexico requesting his services. What a coup! He could not wait to pump out a superset on his bench.

Well, almost, Corwin thought. Two more plays. First, he needed a source inside the Bat Cave. Now that Sheridan had been outed, she would go cloak-and-dagger and her clam would snap shut. He was on the rise and she was crashing—he'd find a recruit.

For the second play, Corwin turned into an alcove and began to type into his encrypted BlackBerry.

FISHERMAN—BIG NAMES ARE INVOLVED. CAN'T DISCUSS THESE BRIEFS, BUT YOU NEED PROOF OF A NARCOTICS CONNECTION. PUT STRAIGHT, OLD AMIGO, THIS COUPLE MEETING A DEALER TO BUY DRUGS STINKS AND WE DO NOT BUY SHIT. GIVE ME SOLIDS. DODGER.

– 19 –

MEXICO CITY, MEXICO

Eduardo Saiz stood just outside the press briefing room while the president of Mexico delivered his prepared remarks. *Los Asesinos* had captured the world's attention. He heard the camera shutters clicking away and saw the flashes illuminating the president like lightning. It occurred to him that he might be famous after this, though that would do him little good working for the Network. Once you went *on payroll* you didn't change careers.

Eduardo grabbed his aide's arm. "Get me some water."

"Right away, sir," whispered Jorge Morales.

"Poland Springs, not Evian. I want to connect to the Americans watching."

Eduardo pulled open the door and peeked—the room was more crowded than it had been for the president's inaugural press conference. He had never seen it so packed. Those reporters lucky enough to be seated all seemed to be raising their hands at once. All of them were shouting. In the dark background, about three meters up, he saw the red lights of the cameras watching him.

During his initial brief three hours earlier, Eduardo made it clear that the murders were a derivative of a botched drug purchase. Guerrero State *Federales* had been surveilling Jackrabbit's compound for many months, noting a steady stream of drug mules on supply runs posing as vacationers. There was a shootout at the compound followed by a chase. Roadblocks funneled the couple to the Acapulco police station. When the *Federales* attempted to apprehend the buyers they were murdered in cold blood.

There were few questions at that brief. Eduardo had outed the Jackrabbit— no harm now that he was two meters deep—and the reporters were distracted enough by the volume of information. He had given them each a nice packet of information on Jackrabbit to corroborate, green-lighted directly by Juarez. But now that the president had identified the drug mules as American honeymooners, the reporters were in an absolute uproar.

Worse, *Los Asesinos* were still out in the mountains. His stomach bubbled when he thought of the dead dogs and the last message he received from the Guerrero *comandante:* Unless they jumped to their deaths they've moved along the ridgeline. Probably north along Highway 95. We're pursuing, but we'll need more dogs and sunlight before we start the search again.

"But, sir," Eduardo heard a rude reporter shout in English at the president, "why did *Los Asesinos* go to the police station after they killed the two men at the mansion?"

The president turned and glanced at Eduardo, frowned, and shook his head. He wasn't *on payroll* and that made Eduardo nervous. He had already sifted through the military ranks and uprooted years of recruitment. Was the Federal Judicial Police infrastructure next?

"As I've said, Deputy Attorney General Saiz will get into the details of the situation, including their motives, but I believe that preliminary indications are that the murderers were trapped by our *Federales* at the police station. Regardless, I just wanted to make it clear that we are working closely with the United States on this. President O'Reilly and I had a good talk and we will continue to have them."

"Is it true the Americans offered assistance?" asked a local newsman.

"Yes, President O'Reilly offered to help in the hunt for these killers, but I told him we need no help. The Federal Judicial Police have some strong leads."

"Sir, what did President O'Reilly say about Darren Phillips? Does he believe he's guilty?" asked another American.

"You can ask him yourself. We have known each other for many years and I do not reveal what is shared between friends. But I will take this opportunity to say that we will keep the United States apprised at every turn as we pursue *Los Asesinos.* President O'Reilly extended his very personal condolences to the Mexican people . . ."

Eduardo's satphone buzzed. He backed into the anteroom and eagerly toggled the power switch. *Los Asesinos* had been killed, he was sure of it.

"This is Octopus."

"Stand by for *El Toro.*"

They are just words, he told himself, so relax. Saiz leaned against the windowsill, staring out at the first stars that had managed to blink through the perpetual haze of Mexico City, but not seeing them. Instead, he saw the terrible face of the man on the other end of his satphone. Eduardo was a religious man cognizant of the fact that he was descending a staircase to hell. But he also loved his wife and two children. To climb back up at this point was to lose them.

Please, God, let me recover the stolen satphone. If You help me, I will give up this nonsense forever. This is the last thing I will ask for.

"I am watching that fool on television. *Los Asesinos* still have my phone?"

"We will have them tomorrow, *Toro,*" Saiz said. "At first light, probably. Earlier if they try to use the satphone again. Then we can reacquire the scent."

"Not good enough, your word. What else?"

I will die tomorrow, Eduardo thought, if I cannot prove my value to the Network. "I control most of the policing infrastructure, sir. I have been appointed to lead the investigation, as you know. The president trusts me. I have worked hard to win that trust. Many hours, many dinners, many private talks. He is a tough one. Very scrupulous. Asks many questions. But I have his ear. I have convinced him to commit all available assets—"

"You're wasting my time. We can always buy another you."

"Another me?"

"Another you."

And there it is. "*Toro,* I . . . have done much more. I would fully brief you but I have to go brief the press soon."

"Now. The politician can wait."

"I have enlarged our surveillance circle around the city and am throwing up roadblocks everywhere from here to Oaxaca and Acapulco. That is only the beginning, *Toro!* I have a top special forces team from my elite Rapid Response Unit fully outfitted and waiting with their helicopter at a nearby base. These are very tough men. To accompany them, I have hired the best tracker in the nation and his prized bloodhound. Have you heard of Felix? He's so good he uses only one name."

Only silence.

"This man Felix," Eduardo continued, "he's supposed to be incredible, *Toro.* He's world renowned. Tracks wild game in the jungle. Does not need sleep. Tracked a large jaguar for three days in Costa Rica! We have talked to some who used Felix before and he's extraordinary. When we find *Los Asesinos*—if one of our many checkpoints or even some farmer doesn't kill them immediately—I'll drop off the tracker and four of the best soldiers we have. You should see these men, *Toro.* Incredible!"

"I want *El Monstruo Carnicero* to go along. Activate him."

Eduardo paused. Did he hear *Toro* correctly? The visions came faster than the words and they muted him. Knives and blood. FBI Most Wanted List. As tenuous as the situation was, the idea of introducing *El Monstruo Carnicero* into the mess was so troubling that Eduardo felt he should object, a near suicidal course of action given his position but one he was compelled to take. Activating that thing *El Monstruo Carnicero* would be like using dynamite to extinguish a small fire, he thought. Eduardo's path had been heinous since going *on payroll,* but now he could see the Devil itself. *It will stop here.*

"*Toro,* the tracker Felix and the four soldiers will be more than sufficient. Additionally, I have trucks and transport helicopters full of *Federales* if you wish who—"

"I wish," came the gravelly response.

"Excuse me, sir?"

"I only say things once. I do not ask opinions, Octopus. I give orders. *Los Asesinos* have ground through your pathetic men, your pathetic dogs . . . *a god-damned helicopter* . . . and they are laughing. Well, I am not laughing. Are you?"

"God help me, no, sir."

"*El Monstruo Carnicero* goes."

"Sir, he's on the American FBI Most Wanted List. This could attract most unwanted attention if something went wrong," Eduardo practically whined.

"Something already *is* wrong, you fool. If that satphone is not in my hands soon, you and your seed will meet *El Monstruo Carnicero* under different circumstances. Read the papers about Juarez and you'll get the picture."

"I'll activate him, *Toro.*"

"You have the procedure?"

"Yes. Hidden for fifteen years now. I will activate him tomorrow."

"Do it tonight. But before you do, I want you to relay this message to the team you've assembled: After *Los Asesinos* are killed, I want them to kill *El Monstruo Carnicero* as well. The little Aztec has become a real problem for us up here. You've heard?"

"No, sir," Saiz lied.

"He's building a small cult. Recruiting addicts to participate in his . . . *extracurriculars.* There are bodies without hearts turning up all over the place."

"Right away, sir."

"Oh, and I assume you're going to kill the tracker, Felix, as well."

"As you wish, *Toro.*"

Eduardo turned his phone off and sat down heavily in a green plastic chair next to the door. He wanted to wriggle into the fetal position, but he had to speak soon and besides he was wearing his new Armani suit. It was because of *El Monstruo Carnicero* that Eduardo had been baptized in evil in the first place, when he was young and with soul. Now the cycle was repeating. Can I be cleansed in confession if I stop the killings right now? he wondered. I can take Elsie and the kids to Belize. I have the plan in place. But our parents, our cousins, our friends will be executed. Are their lives worth more than *Los As-*

esinos? Of course they are. *But no good Christian can be involved with a thing like* El Monstruo Carnicero.

It was cool in the anteroom but Eduardo felt the sweat spread across his back, chilling him and causing him to tremble. He had been taking bribes for most of his government career, of course, but they were low-level payments from businessmen and politicians with extracurricular interests, not the fat plus-up he was granted fifteen years before when his star suddenly rose.

El Toro had given him no choice anyway. As a deputy attorney general, he made a salary equivalent to fifteen thousand U.S. dollars. Small bribes moved his income to mid-five figures. When he was placed *on payroll,* though, he made half a million. And he had his life. Simple choice, really—work with us, the cartel had told him, or we'll butcher your family. Most of his superiors were *on payroll* as well, so Eduardo quickly accepted.

The cartel desperately needed him. Eduardo had just been assigned as Mexico's liaison to the Americans in their search for Luis Gonzalez's killer. Gonzalez was a young American DEA agent who had somehow managed to penetrate the Tijuana Cartel, Mexico's most notorious. This feat was so incredible—apparently the gringos had planted the boy scout four years earlier—that the Americans didn't even want to inform the Mexican government for fear of a leak. So it was kept strictly need to know: the president and vice president of Mexico, and their attorney general.

Three weeks after the information was swapped, Gonzalez's mutilated and decapitated corpse was dumped near the border checkpoint. The Americans exploded. Their ancient President Reagan threatened economic penalties if the killer wasn't brought to justice and their supercilious Congress passed a bill subjecting Mexico to a yearly drug certification process that reduced his own country to groveling. The pressure sparked a witch hunt.

Eduardo was appointed chief investigator because he was young and untainted; his record was clean. Within a week, he was on the cartel payroll with a clear mission: Nudge the Americans off track and slow their progress.

But the Americans were good—too good given the information Eduardo had provided in piecemeal—and it was obvious they had many sources and drew from an inexhaustible pot of money second only to the cartel's. By month's end, they had the identities of the snitches who had leaked Gonzalez's penetration and the killer himself, but not before Eduardo was able to warn the cartel.

The snitches—the Mexican attorney general and the vice president's brother-in-law—fled to France and still resided there. The killer himself, a tiny Indian who claimed he was pureblood Aztec, was rushed underground by the cartel and vanished. Some in the cartel argued that he be eradicated, but the big boss wanted him around because he had a penchant for torture that few enjoyed. His location is need-to-know only, a cartel lieutenant told Eduardo before handing him a background folder and an official activation procedure.

Before he locked the file away, Eduardo studied the scant information on the torture expert. The murderer's real name was never revealed for security reasons. He came from an impoverished Indian family that earned money by dressing in authentic Aztec clothing—feather headdresses, face paint, calf plumes, broadleaf skirts—and dancing for tourists in Oaxaca, as the previous three generations had done.

The boy deeply resented the performances and tried to enlist in the Army after filling his pockets with stones to make the weight minimum. The recruiting sergeant laughed at him, saying he was still too small and that the Army didn't take Indians anyway. Then the boy insulted the sergeant and found himself in full gear the next morning, carrying a heavy rucksack packed with rocks next to two hardy drill instructors, who flanked him for the entire foot march. They screamed profanities during the first twenty-five kilometers and encouragement during the last twenty-five.

Notwithstanding his heavy load, the boy was the fastest hiker the recruit training staff in Oaxaca had ever seen. His fitness was so impressive that a tryout with the Olympic walking team was arranged once the boy completed training. But the boy never made it. He was by far and away the smallest recruit in the battalion and one of the poorest. To earn money, he performed magic tricks for the other recruits, incredible sleight-of-hand maneuvers, whereby foam balls would disappear, cards would shuffle themselves and, most importantly in a battalion formed for violence, knives would zip around with the precision of hornets.

There was another recruit in the squad bay who claimed to be good with a blade, however, and one night the Indian spilled his guts all over the deck. His recruit sergeant made a rushed phone call and the cartel had him in its possession the following day. They expected to use him for a contract murder or two, then eliminate him, but the young monster was too skilled; he did things that nauseated even the cartel's hardest soldiers.

When an enemy was captured, the Indian usually arrived hours later with his knives and a grin, as was the case with the DEA traitor the government exposed. He filleted Luis Gonzalez's skin, cutting the webbing from between his fingers and toes as a "warm up," a cartel soldier later told Eduardo. And when it was clear that Gonzalez had told all he knew, when he screamed and begged to be shot, invoking the Virgin Mother—causing even the cruelest soldiers to glance at each other and pull their pistols—the Indian said only, "I'd like some earplugs please, sir, because it's going to get a lot louder before I'm done here."

The Indian boy was eighteen years old.

The Americans raged for close to a decade in an effort to find the killer, but the Indian simply vanished. Eduardo, however, believed he was still in the country. Starting a few years after the cartel had hidden him, over a hundred women in Juarez had been found mutilated and raped, and another *two hundred* had gone missing, body counts that were simply off the charts. This Juarez killer, nicknamed *El Monstruo Carnicero* by the terrified residents, had murdered three hundred innocents, slow-cut victims of an evil so pure it needed a new category.

Now *El Toro* had confirmed that *El Monstruo Carnicero* was never officially retired. Juarez had continued to use the godless Indian beast as a torturer of the cartel's enemies, Eduardo suspected, and in return turned a blind eye to its sadistic addiction. It had grown increasingly reckless every year. Sometimes there were bodies left on the streets for the police to dispose of, especially dangerous considering the American obsession with finding his identity.

El Monstruo Carnicero confirmed Eduardo's belief in God. Here was an unexplainable evil unless you believed in the Devil, and if there was a Devil then there was a Lord. In world without personal responsibility, a world where sin was supposed to be rationalized if you dug deeply into the sinner's background, *El Monstruo Carnicero* was an aberration. The darkness in the Monster Butcher didn't come from his parents. Or his surroundings. *It just was.*

———

Eduardo's aide tapped him on the shoulder with the Poland Springs bottle and put it into his hands. "Sir! Are you all right? You're almost on."

"Fine." He was the lead actor in this play.

"The president is getting a lot of questions about motive. He's deferring to you."

Eduardo waved him away. He placed the bottle against his forehead and felt the cool trickle of condensation mix with his own sweat. Perhaps his connection to *El Monstruo Carnicero* could be used for some good after all. It was lusty trade bait.

After a decade, the deaths in Juarez were starting to attract the attention of the American press. Most of the dead girls worked in the massive American exploitation plants the gringos had erected in Juarez on the cheap. Television exposés, *New York Times* stories, and even a documentary film eventually paved the way for investigators.

The detectives didn't solve the murders, of course, but their conclusions were troublesome for the cartel at a time when they were consolidating the cartels on the continent into the Network. The final FBI report was simple: The torture marks on the bodies they found in the desert indicated the precise work of a serial murderer, but the staggering numbers meant that others were involved, or at least complacent. Additionally, the few male bodies they were able to study had large patches of skin missing, while the females had had their hearts removed, evidence of different motives.

Before they were forced out by the local governor, the FBI agents added the unidentified killer to a short International Most Wanted List that contained just one other Mexican citizen—the anonymous murderer of DEA agent Luis Gonzalez.

Eduardo could hear the president winding down but he wanted to get a shot across the American bow. He tapped the backlight on his BlackBerry and started to type.

> *DODGER—YOU SAID YOU CAN'T DISCUSS YOUR BRIEFS BUT I AM TELLING YOU ALL. WE NEED AN OPEN LINE. I AM ABOUT TO BE GRILLED BY YOUR PRESS . . . TURN ON YOUR TV. I NEED YOUR FULL SUPPORT, OLD FRIEND, TO LIFT THIS UNWARRANTED PRESSURE. YOUR REPORTERS DOUBT WHAT IS FACT. SO I OFFER THIS IN CONFIDENCE: YOU BACK MY THEORIES—THEY ARE ROCK TIGHT—AND I WILL DELIVER ONE OF FBI MOST WANTED TO YOU PERSONALLY. WE WILL SHARE CREDIT. FISHERMAN.*

– 20 –

CAMBRIDGE, MASSACHUSETTS

Gavin Kelly studied the classmates in his Entrepreneurial Finance study group and sighed. It was almost eleven p.m. in the classroom—twenty-three hundred hours in his former incarnation—and all of the wonks were still eagerly *tap-tap-tapping* into their personal laptops. The classroom was shaped like a miniature horseshoe and his study group sat spread out in rows that gained height as they receded. The assiduous students that sat in front called it the fishbowl. Kelly and his fellow misfits—regular consumption of kegged beer was sufficient for qualification—sat in the far row and called it the toilet bowl.

Kelly was too cheap to own his own laptop, so he was seated behind a large school desktop, which allowed him to monitor the Red Sox Gamecast on ESPN.com piped in on the school's Ethernet while his peers flailed at correlations. He cringed when he saw the plump middle reliever on the mound.

"May I make an observation here?" he asked the group.

"At least we've trained him to ask for permission now," said a woman without raising her head. It got a low chuckle.

Absent a mathematics background, Kelly—like the rest of his fellow "poets" sprinkled around Harvard Business School—had been placed in a study group full of former Web entrepreneurs, banking analysts, and corporate consultants, Excel spreadsheet superheroes all. The poets were relegated to lost arts like human resource management and integrity, but even on the latter subject Kelly was compelled to defer. After all, while other poets hailed from professional sports or entertainment ventures, Kelly was fresh out of jail on an obstruction of justice charge in a murder case. Not exactly what the application meant by "real world" experience.

"The relative value of a sudsy draft is rising exponentially with each minute, while the utility of this problem set is being devalued," continued Kelly. "If I make a beer run, will you loveless bastards drink with me?"

None answered. Millionaires were blossoming all around him and the words Startup, Valuation, Funded, IPO, Branding, First Mover, Biz Dev, and the hated Synergy were slung around school 24/7, rapid-fire, *rat-a-tat-tat,* the banal billboards of the dot-com age. Kelly remembered his former life where Waste, Ding, Erase, Plug, Nail, Light 'em Up, End, Shoot, Kill, Fuck Them Up, and other *cool* words—phrases that promised adventure and wild and *real tests*—were pieces of his vernacular. He remembered the day when he was completing an infiltration swim with his Marine reconnaissance platoon off the California coast, just 500 meters away from the traffic that was already clogging Interstate 5. His gunnery sergeant pointed up at the red taillights and said, "Coulda been you, sir." Kelly pulled the plastic wrap from his M-16 and said, "Poor bastards. That'll never be me, Gunny. NFW." He remembered the Leadership Failure—the dead Somali and the goddamn cover-up that had landed him a court martial and a swift discharge from the Corps.

Now I've become what I most despised. I aspire to stare at computers for a living.

Kelly glanced at the screen in time to see a hanging curve ball die a violent death. He chose a short walk instead of a foot through the computer. He wandered away from his study group toward the computer lab where he saw that his friend Gary Partoyan—a former squid but not a total car wreck of an individual—had been cast off as well.

"Adding value to your group, I see."

"Hey, Kelly. Check out Drudge. Looks like another jarhead's in a shit sandwich."

"Worse than the one who cut the cable car?" whispered Kelly, already typing the URL into the computer connected to the adjacent desk.

"Yup. Even worse than the one who killed an innocent Somali virgin male on a beach and covered up that heinous crime." Partoyan watched Kelly's face to make sure he hadn't stepped over the line with so personal a jab, but Kelly was still wearing his cocky smirk.

"Virgin? Oh yeah, the Navy wasn't on deck yet."

"Fuck off. Anyway, this jarhead shot, like, *fifty* people on some drug rampage in Mexico. Killed twenty. This was after he toked all night with his wife."

"Right." *Mexico.*

"I'm telling you, dude. Check it out. He worked in the White House. Best part is, he was on his goddamn honeymoon. Kelly, when a jarhead screws the pooch he really gets it, doesn't he!"

"Marines don't do anything half-ass." *White House. Honeymoon.*

When Drudge's Web page dropped across his screen, Kelly whispered, "Holy shit," and sucked in a breath of air that he did not release for a full minute. He devoured the story, his heart hammering even as his principled world ceased to exist. He fought the urge to stand, gripping the table. When he finished, he sighed and whispered, "There's no way in hell."

"It's all there in HTML, dude," said Partoyan.

"No. I know this guy. This is fucking bullshit," he hissed.

Partoyan had never seen Kelly flush like that. His face was a deep crimson. Partoyan whispered halfheartedly, "How do you know him?"

"He's my best friend."

Kelly surfed to two other news sites and carefully read their accounts. They were the same. They were insane. He bolted from the lab and ran across the parking lot, avoiding the glows of the tall lamps for some reason that he did not understand but enjoyed nevertheless. Early springtime and a splash of humidity for the first time in months. What's the weather like in those Mexican mountains? he wondered.

He clambered over the chain-link fence surrounding Soldiers Field Stadium, where Darren had corralled him into many a workout when they were undergraduate roommates. The lunatic is free from the asylum, he thought. How can I get to Acapulco with a weapon? Running now along a sideline of faded chalk that was illuminated by moonlight, Kelly hurdled a bench and headed up the stadium's cement steps to the top row. The scrapes of his soles and the gusts of his lungs as they devoured the night air were amplified by the stadium, and he sounded like a tiny steam engine.

At the top Kelly looked out at the boathouse and the Charles River, then up at the splash of stars. As an infantry Marine he had spent his formative years living like a vampire, catching catnaps under camouflage tarps during the day and rising to hunt at night, walking the hills of Camp Pendleton with a rifle in his shoulder and his creature comforts stuffed into a backpack, propelled forward by the adventure lust with which he and his mates were both cursed and blessed. He had come to associate the night with the dangerous promises of the great game, and now the stars brought back all the old feelings of purpose and loyalty in a mad rush. Kelly was driven right up to berserk, filled with the anticipation that danger and responsibility wrought in a man who had lost his moral azimuth in Somalia at the exact moment when he finally felt he belonged to that wicked and marvelous cult, the United States Marine Corps.

– 21 –

JUAREZ, MEXICO

Her eyes dried when there were no tears left in her ducts and they began to ache, slowly at first, dull throbs that were everywhere and nowhere, then more sharply with every beat of her heart, a horrible itch that she could not scratch, piercing pain radiating from her eyeballs back behind her head. Her purpose in life seemed to narrow on the ability to blink. Of course, that was impossible now that her eyelids had been removed.

"Don't cry, girl," the little man with the painted face told her. "You're going to die an Aztec death tonight, and there is honor in it. When I spill your *chalchiuh-atl* it will feed the earth. The sun will rise tomorrow."

The devil had a high, squeaking voice that cracked in her ears. She groaned and let the tears come up from her throat but there were none left. He wore a thin, scraggly beard that squiggled out from the tip of his otherwise bare chin. There were only a few strands. He traced her face with them and it was a tickle of fire.

She turned her head. Like most women in Juarez, she had lived in fear of the Monster Butcher for several years, and now that she had been captured she did not want to see his face, terrified that it would be worse than the one that chased her in nightmares. All she could see was that he was smaller than her fourteen-year-old brother and that blue face paint had been smeared on his tiny face. He was wearing a turquoise necklace. A bright blue tattoo was stitched into his chest.

How did he catch me? He's so small.

She remembered drinking. Remembered the police questioning her . . .

"Huitzilopochtli killed his four hundred brothers and sisters when he escaped the womb. Know how many I've killed? One hundred ninety-four. That's including you, dog. The warriors I'm raising have killed another hundred."

He snatched a jagged stone blade from the chair that propped up the full-length mirror into which he stared when he fought the girls. He twisted the crude knife slowly in front of her face. "Know what this is? It's a razor of *itztli*, volcanic rock that my ancestors used on their sacrifices. It's hard as flint. Feel it." He stabbed the blade into the soft flesh below her chin.

She started to pray. "Hail Mary, full of . . ."

He covered her mouth. "That's the Spanish in you talking. You're ten cunts removed from pure-blood Mexica and now your mind is weak. My people been killing you and yours for seven hundred years. When the great temple of Huitzilopochtli was built, the bravest soldiers performed their sacrifices at the top so the blood could spill down the steps. And do you know what they did with the *itztli* razor?"

She thought about her dog, Palm Tree. She hoped her sister would remember to feed him tomorrow. Palm Tree liked to sleep at the foot of her bed and her sister was jealous because of it. She sometimes neglected him.

El Monstruo Carnicero leaned close to her ear and whispered, "They cut out their hearts while they were still beating."

———

He rolled the corpse up in the plastic sheets and mulled over a dumping spot—the topsoil in his backyard concealed over sixty bodies and he had lost track of their plots. He decided it was too much trouble and went inside to call one of his gang. He had recruited a group of indigenous youngsters from the cartel and was schooling them in the ancient art. They were wild when they were high, yipping like coyotes during each festival, but they were also lazy and had taken to dumping the bodies out in the desert, often uncovered. What did he care? It only added to his legend.

The phone rang before he arrived. "Hello."

"Hello. Is Mister Rivera home?"

"Wrong number."

"Oh. Luis Rivera?"

"Wrong number, I told you."

"Excuse me."

El Monstruo Carnicero moved quickly to his bedroom and reached into his sock drawer. Thin, delicate fingers danced across the two throwing knives he kept hidden—there were over fifty knives scattered throughout the apartment—and found a thick packet of photographs. He shuffled through the stack of the crimson girls until he found the picture he had taken of himself with his war paint and Aztec warrior outfit. On the back, he had scrawled "Luis Rivera" so he would remember the code.

He had been activated again. Granted, *El Toro* had been feeding him low-level interrogations and intimidation work for years in exchange for protection from all the mongrels who resented him, but this phone call was different. Now mother Mexica herself needed his skills, sharpened on the bones of hundreds since she last sponsored his employment.

El Monstruo Carnicero gathered his clothing and personals in fewer than fifteen minutes, but he took nearly an hour to choose his blades from the arsenal he had built over the years. He kept his best knives in the cellar as if they were fine wines, displayed on a hand-crafted oak rack between the gas-fired kiln he used to heat-treat his blades and the cryogenic deep freezer that was used for hardening. After a delicious deliberation, he chose his newest throwing knives, Falcon and Eagle, a heavy chopping parang he called Bear Claw, and the most experienced of the bunch, a pliable filet knife called Barracuda. He fit them snugly in their homes in his leather belt and howled.

He took the cellar steps in bounds and stood straddling the corpse with his kit bag in his hand. He was so excited that he made his warrior face in the mirror and danced around his kill, carefully avoiding the offering while he practiced his footwork. It had been, what, *fifteen years* since Mexica last used his services, and he was eager to serve again in the open. In front of an audience. Writing the activation code down had been forbidden, of course, but he was terrified that the call might come one night and find itself dismissed. Over the last decade, he had listened to many wrong-number calls, and each time he had run excitedly to the sock drawer, only to close it a few moments later, disappointed.

Why was Mexica's finest warrior called? Another meddling American DEA agent? Certainly to hunt and interrogate someone important. Welcomed into the arms of the powerful again because they *needed his skills.* Aztecs valued the warrior class above all others for they were a warrior people, a culture that kindled violence; when the Europeans arrived the whole country had gone soft, but there was still a need for the fast knife, wasn't there!

But first this thing at his feet. He kicked the corpse and spat, his saliva sliding down the plastic as slowly as a snail, giving him time to fetch his shovel, smash the dead girl-dog in the head again just to be sure, and drag it out past the porch next to the garden. *El Monstruo Carnicero* normally would have probed the soil gently—he didn't like it when he stabbed into old corpses—but he was concentrating on the activation, the precise actions that were required to avoid the Americans. *El Toro* told him they were waiting for his reemergence each day. *That's* how important he was. Well, no more wait!

TUESDAY

There is one activity for which the Aztecs were notorious: the large-scale killing of humans in ritual sacrifices. The killings were not remote top-of-the-pyramid affairs. If only the high priests and rulers killed, they carried out most of their butchers' work en plein air, and not only in the main temple precinct, but in the neighborhood temples and on the streets.

—Inga Clendinnen, *Aztecs*

– 22 –

SIERRA MADRE DEL SUR, MEXICO

Kate seemed to glide down the long finger of earth, legs gobbling up the moon-lit scrub brush on their way into the valley. After a series of long climbs over the last five hours, she was loath to surrender the altitude she had gained, but happy to rest her legs on the downhill. She kept them loose and rubbery en route to the dark valley ahead, trying to break up the pockets of lactic acid.

She stubbed an unprotected toe for the hundredth time. It was a welcome distraction from the friction blisters that had formed under her feet over the last twenty miles. She was so used to them they were like annoying in-laws. Blisters form when the epidermis separates, leaving painful pockets of fluid to be pressure-crunched right into exposed nerve endings.

Stubbed toes were more intense but brief. She did not yell but sighed, one measure of pain outdoing another for her attention. She knelt and parted the soft tangle grass to inspect her toenails. One was two-months gone, the other floated on a pad of dry blood. She would lose it tonight, the third of the young year. This sucks, she thought. She had visited an Acapulco nail salon the morning before for a pedicure and a young girl had painted the most beautiful yellow daisy on top of a shiny coat of pink polish. She opened herself to tiny feelings of regret—she considered herself a girly-girl in spite of a reputation that cornered her—but realized that, given her circumstances, sadness was a currency better spent elsewhere.

She glanced up and in the darkness the crest of the ridge was bright black against the midnight blue sky. Eel weeds shimmered on the crest until Darren's bald silhouette unmasked itself. It rose like the moon, a steaming oval and then a sudden jag out the width of his wide shoulders, tapering as he neared the top of the climb. When he was atop, she saw the shadow wave its arm in recognition and she was comforted. When they were racing, Kate took the lead as the navigator and captain, often moving out just ahead of the team to set the pace. But as the days wore on and tempers wore thin she traveled with her husband. She could make difficult decisions under stress but did not like to play the hammer when it came to implementing them. Darren did that.

"It's gonna be a few," her husband whispered when he was at her side. "Kid's hurting. He's still plodding up to that crest."

"He's strong."

"Yeah, but how's his willpower?"

"He's got sneakers. We have sandals."

Her husband grunted and put his hands on his hips. He was not prone to pontification and exhaustion further narrowed his expression.

Five minutes later, the husky outline of Neck Cappucco appeared with its hands on its head. "Goddamn," he gasped when he eventually stumbled down. "That was a bitch, yo."

"Well, we have to keep moving, I'm afraid. We can't keep tracing Highway ninety-two when the sun comes up."

She waited for his next sentence, but when the boy didn't ask for a break she smiled to herself. *He's determined.* Since the dog attack, Kate had led them on a five-hour, twenty-mile speed hike moving parallel to an east running highway. Including the drive and the long, ten-mile climb up to the first cliff, that put them about seventy miles out of Acapulco. Mexico City is fewer than 125 miles from here, she thought, two days away.

But Darren doesn't want to go to Mexico City.

She agreed that they had to avoid the roads and take a more difficult route over the mountains, but it took some talking before he convinced her that Mexico City would be an impenetrable fortress. She sighed. Two hundred fifty miles to go. Another sleepless journey into pain. The more things change, the more things stay the same. You know, she thought, that was the topic of the Advanced Placement exam in high school. Constructing an essay should take my mind off the hump for an hour . . .

"I'll meet you two down there," whispered Neck. "I gotta do the doo, know what I'm sayin'? Not feeling too good."

Neck limped behind a desert palm tree whose vertical dry leaves looked like a crown in silhouette. Thinking about it, Kate hadn't seen a coconut palm in a while, which meant that they must have moved out of the tropical band of flora that edged the Sierra Madre del Sur.

"I have to make a head call, too," said Darren.

"Head call? Try using 'bathroom' . . . you seem to be reverting to Marine form."

"I never left."

Kate sat down on a pad of cardinal sage and watched her husband gimp away. She first met him during the grueling four-day tryout for her adventure team, six months after the deaths of her brother and mother. She had assembled most of the guys simply by putting word out through her normal channels to the quasi-insane—triathletes, ultramarathoners, and anyone else willing to spend all of their free time training for a race that offered no recognition and no prize money, only a hyperbolic experience with pain that they would have to pay for to encounter. But she was in California, not the Upper East Side, and the tryout was crowded.

Darren was the only military guy in a sea of semiprofessional athletes. He toted a Marine-issue metal-framed rucksack to their lightweight, cushioned backpacks, and was dead last after the first fourteen hours. But professional athletes trained scientifically and were unprepared for the absence of food and recovery time that Kate had designed. Three days later Darren was one of only four left standing, just trudging along in silence while the others tried to win her favor by chatting nonstop.

On the last terrible asphalt hike back to the Newport Beach parking lot where she had gathered them 100 hours before, they limped past a grocery store where a trucker was weighing a sack of vegetables on a large scale. It occured to Kate that although she had given specific instructions on pack weight, she had never actually weighed them. She set hers down and it came in at 28 pounds, 3 over the minimum. Then the excuses started when the next three men plunked their loads, weighing in at 20, 17, and 13 pounds.

"Most of mine was water weight at the start and I drank it all."

"I thought twenty-five pounds was just a guideline."

"I'm pretty sure this scale is off."

Darren was last and his needle balanced on thirty. If he was upset at the others he never complained—the only reaction Kate registered was a cocked eyebrow.

In the parking lot, the four survivors congratulated one another and took private lobbying turns with Kate for spots on the team. The other men had been shocked by the tryout's severity but Darren told her that while it was the hardest fitness event he'd endured it did not surprise him.

"In the Marines," he had said, "misery and starvation are not surprising."

"So you're a miserable person?" she had asked him jokingly.

"Only when I fail," he had said evenly. Then he extended his hand—no hug like the rest of the guys—thanked her for the opportunity, and walked over to his car.

"Hey, Darren," she had called after him. "Don't I get a hug after that?"

He had dropped his pack behind his polished ivory Ford Mustang and practically marched over to her, smiling for the first time, his teeth so white against his deep, black skin, easily the most confident person she had ever met even though she had heard him speak perhaps ten or twenty times in four days. He had wrapped her in his arms, and she felt a marked tingle of warmth and nervous excitement that she had never before experienced. Then he had leaned in close against her cheek and whispered, "You can have anything you want. You're the captain."

Now, watching him stagger back toward her through the cauliflower bushes, she felt a fierce love for him. When they had first started dating, she had questioned her own motives. The rumor among her friends was that she had transformed her own body and wanted an Adonis as a reward, a supremely disciplined Marine to boot, whose personality verified that the lush they knew in college as Kate North had vanished. The whisper among the New York social circle was that she had married a black man to get back at her father. Neither was true. Darren's relentless drive was coupled with a loyalty that she had immediately savored. He was her first and she had fallen hard. The fact that he was a stone fox did not hurt, either.

But early on she would lie next to him in bed and watch him as he slept, wondering if she was there with him in the dark as a delayed reaction to the deaths of her mother and brother. Was she simply testing the liberal views on race with which she had been instilled? She had chafed at the thought. Even now the very existence of the question deeply bothered her. Of course not. She had loved him then just as she loved him now. He was never a means to assuage guilt. Even her father had joined the sometimes overbearing chorus that told her Darren Phillips was the catch of a lifetime.

Still, she remembered that there was a brief time when her subconscious feelings toward black men troubled her. When she was back in the city for the funeral, a black man had approached her on Lexington Avenue and she fought the strong urge to flee across the street, struggling to stand still all the way up to the point where he asked where the subway for the number 4 or 5 train was. She was so upset with the irrational fear that she had burst into tears right there under the Hunter College pedestrian overpass.

The strange feelings continued, caught in a maddening cyclone in which she questioned and dismissed the origin of the feelings themselves, which gave rise to more intense fear, which sparked more and more guilt. She did not judge skin color and the thought of even irrational, subconscious bias deeply disappointed her.

Her mother was supposed to have retired the year before, but with her husband gone all the time the high school students dampened the loneliness. And the special-needs kids, by definition, best assuaged her emptiness. Her brother was back home for Thanksgiving with a strained Achilles and permission from his football coaches at Penn. Her father was working late, or with a mistress, who knew or cared? Kate was in California, having told her mother she could not miss two training days in a row. A student asked to come inside the brownstone for extra help. He and three friends tied up her brother and mother, robbed them, and murdered them.

They were black kids, but they could have been any race. The fact that she had screamed at three black kids with do-rags who were horsing around on the subway that Christmas was just a coincidence. They could have been any race. The fact that she had convinced her father that night to raise a scholarship fund in her mother's memory specifically benefiting black high school students was just a coincidence.

The fact that she had pursued and then fallen in love with a black man six months later was just a coincidence.

Kate saw a pine needle stuck to Darren's scalp when he drew close. She peeled it off and then hugged him hard, melting into his chest. "Do you think Neck will make it?" she asked.

"Mile thirty of three hundred, baby, and that's too early to tell." He had known hundreds like Neck Cappucco, and most of them yielded to pressure, *real* pressure, when they tasted it for the first time. The kid was on the clock.

"I think we should tell him the plan. He deserves to know," she whispered.

He shook his head. "No. We do *not* reveal the destination. It's for his own good. If he finds out we're crossing the continent he'll fold. When they catch him, he'll blab away the real plan. And if he *does* make it, think of the fog that will roll into that thick head of his when he sees the Bay of Campeche."

"That's harsh."

"Look, you aren't the one stuck listening to him. I bet he thinks he's in Asia."

"You're on," whispered Kate. "Let's wager a fat, juicy steak dinner at Outback—"

"Stop it. You know the rules." On the Eco-Challenge, all talk about food was prohibited, lest the famished racers drive themselves mad.

" . . . or a thick, piping hot pizza with mushrooms and pepperoni . . ."

Darren's stomach growled and he grabbed her playfully, pinning her arms to her sides and pulling her in close, smiling. "Stop it . . ."

" . . . or," she whispered, "the loser can be sex slave for a day. The day we make it home. Bet you miss those Kate specials, don't you, sweetie?" She tugged him in close.

"Mind if I watch?" asked Neck.

Darren spun around quickly, embarrassed and angry that he hadn't heard the kid, angrier still when he saw Neck's stupid grin. He had a big mouth and there were teeth everywhere. "Now *this* is the kind of spring break I was hopin' for," the football player said. Hands rubbing together now as if warming himself. No, pleasuring himself, thought Darren, who believed that sex and bathroom humor should remain locked in their respective vaults. Oversized pervert.

Darren studied the boy in the moonlight. His diamond earrings were winking at him in the moonlight, mocking Darren's traditionalist attitude. Only eleven years but an ocean of difference, thought Darren, lamenting the downfall of American culture in his generation. Well, *his* form of culture, where MLK, Clint Eastwood, Teddy Roosevelt, Abraham Lincoln, Winston Churchill, Jackie Robinson, Bruce Springsteen, and Colin Powell (whom he had met several times!) stood watch on the walls against all comers.

He started to speak, but his wife touched his arm and cut him off. "Well, Neck, it *is* my honeymoon, you know. Woman's gotta do what a woman's gotta do, and that includes her husband. You want to watch, fine. Just stay out of the way."

"Ohhh, snap. I been watching your legs, too, Kate. Like when you mentioned my ass, right, that you been watching? Anyway, I told Darren here that I shoulda written my *thesis* on those legs, yo! Too bad you left that camera; I could take some more shots for you all. Work it! Work it, girlfriend!" said Neck.

Darren watched them laugh, grinding his jaw. It was 0300 and his tenuous sense of humor had vanished long before. He held up the compass that was glued to his watch and checked his position with the stars, aligning the Southern Cross, then pointed farther down the draw. "We best get going," he said when his wife stopped giggling to draw breath. "There's bound to be water down there. If not, we need to push as far as we can while it's cool and dark. They'll be looking for us come daylight."

"Hold it up, dude," said Neck. "My dogs are barking. We've gone like, what, forty miles by now on foot without a break?"

"About thirty, tough guy," Darren said, pissed that he was still calling him "dude." He knew he should stop prodding but he was tired and angry. Kate would fix it. "But we have to move as far as we can at night, so try a little harder, Frappuccino."

Frappuccino! Vinny Cappuco had once knocked a man's teeth deep into his throat for calling him Cappuccino, but *Frappuccino! That was a chick drink, wasn't it?* Neck was confused and angry, and he was having trouble stringing coherent thoughts anyway, so he raised his fists, dropping them just as quickly when Kate moved up to him, as beautiful as she was. He was tired.

"I'm takin' a break and you don't have no say, Darren. Not taking another . . . fucking . . . *step*. And you stop disrespecting me, or I'll throw down when this is over. I'm not kidding, neither."

"Yes, you are."

Neck wasn't sure if he'd heard correctly. Did Darren just stand up to him without a care in the world? "I'll bust your ass up right here in front of your girl, you little bitch."

"Darren!" hissed Kate. "Go down the hill and wait for us. Stop being a jerk. I want to talk to Neck. *Alone.*"

Darren grumbled and headed down the hill, irritated that he had slipped up and received a familial rebuke for it, *irate* that the kid had the gall to call him a bitch. A serious disagreement was coming. When they approached, Cappucco was wearing a smile and chugged right along, even winked at him as he passed, somehow eager to hike.

Kate walked up next and said, "I'll endure Neck's company up front. You take tail end, Charlie."

"How'd you convince him?" he whispered.

"Easy," she laughed, striding away from him again. "I promised I'd fuck him if he managed to get to Mexico City."

Kate moved forward quickly, giggling to herself, and was soon overcome by a wave of laughter that escaped her in the form of tears. She knew it really wasn't that funny, but she was sleep-deprived and the pressure of the whole situation just pulled the giggles out of her, as unconscious as a sneeze. Besides, it was never the joke with Darren; the real zinger came in his reaction. She loved to laugh and she loved to trade barbs, especially with her husband, a by-the-book man who was a tractor beam for sarcasm.

Darren put his hands on his hips and gritted his teeth. Why did she have to use "fuck" instead of "sleep with"? he thought hazily. She didn't really say that to Cappucco, did she? Of course not. He was sleepless enough to bite so she baited him. *Stop being so gullible.* Fifteen years with Kelly should have prepared him for Kate. *Relax, it was a joke.*

When he finally stepped out his vision closed in, his scalp tingled, and he nearly passed out. He realized that he had been holding his breath, so he opened his mouth. It took him a few seconds before he was able to step out again.

He carried the images with him for another three miles, rolling the word "fuck" across his tongue like a bitter lozenge, using it as a source of fuel to keep his mind off the pounds on his back and the cavorting couple in front.

– 23 –

MCLEAN, VIRGINIA

Deputy Director Susanne Sheridan yawned and rotated her head slowly, stretching her neck. It was almost four in the morning and except for Contreras and the duty officer the Bat Cave was deserted, but she was more excited than tired. Given her belief that the American couple was still alive somewhere in the Mexican mountains carrying an ultrawideband satellite telephone that would unlock the cartel's communications network, this was not wholly surprising. The fact that Jimmy Contreras had sounded so urgent over the phone didn't hurt, either.

She extended Contreras a steaming cup of coffee. Food was prohibited in the Bat Cave, but Susanne had issued herself a pass. The air was rich with a Starbucks delivery that had been X-rayed four times before it hit their lips.

Susanne took a deep sip and brought her ear slowly to her shoulder, working out a kink. Her identification badge shifted on its chain necklace and disappeared inside her blouse. She thought about asking the tall Drug Enforcement Agency agent to fish it out for her and then chuckled to herself. Boy she *was* tired.

Contreras was a nice rest stop for her eyes, even with his frazzled hair. Whatever it was that woke him was important enough to send an impeccably groomed man out the door without a shower. He had changed back into his cotton golf shirt and wore it well for his age. Too bad he didn't like to speak, she thought. He seemed to prefer brooding to real communication, but then again he was male.

"You were saying, ma'am?" Jimmy said.

"Please call me Susanne, Special Agent Contreras. Oh, I'm sorry, you guys are just *regular agents,* aren't you? Pity the FBI got the jump on the superlative."

Contreras stared at her quizzically.

"Look, it's four in the morning," she continued. "So call me Susanne. Why'd you bring that iron?" She pointed to his camouflage gym bag, then noticed the sharp crease in his pants and the shine on his black loafers. "Were you in the military, Agent Contreras?"

"No. I was a Marine."

"Well, I'm not going to be the one to break the bit of news about the Marines being part of what civilians believe to be the military."

She knew all about him from the rigorous background check before joining Narcotics and Organized Crime, of course. He was born in the tiny fishing village of Xcalac, Mexico, on the Yucatán. According to his uncle, Jimmy and his mother made the thousand-mile journey when he was ten, crossing into California with a coyote who tried to rape his mother. The immigrants beat the man to death and rolled him into a gully south of Calexico before they made their dash to the border.

A month later, a kid stabbed Jimmy over a Popsicle in East Los Angeles, then stole the change in his pocket. Jimmy had earned the money for that red, white, and blue Bomb Pop from his new paper route, but had gained the taste for vengeance in that Calexico gully. Two years later, the young thief got his arm broken by a fourteen-year-old in a Little League uniform wielding a shiny pine bat. Jimmy had saved his tips for several months and spit-polished the bat for the special occasion.

Jimmy chased The Dream by sorting mail for a quarter an hour until a Marine recruiter in dress-blue deltas told him about The Chance in 1967. Many young immigrants were pulling a year of duty in country in exchange for citizenship. Two tours later, the young American didn't like the country to which he returned, and he joined the L.A.P.D. to help right the ship.

Jimmy Contreras was self-righteous and it was a perfect marriage considering the environment in late 1960s California. He built a high arrest record for a flatfoot but came home each night convinced he had not done enough. So when he was given the chance to join a new organization that was about to wage full-scale *war* against those who threatened both of his countries—the Drug Enforcement Agency—he leapt at the chance.

Jimmy was assigned to undercover work and was one of the DEA's rising stars until 1988, when his partner was murdered in Tijuana. Too angry and distracted for undercover work, his field career was eventually terminated after a series of complaints filed by the Mexicans. He had only recently landed his sunset tour in D.C.

To Susanne, Jimmy Contreras appeared to be a very lonely man who should have left the frustratingly ineffective world of international drug policing long ago.

"So what do you have, Jimmy? I've got zippo to report from the satellites."

Jimmy nodded gravely and Susanne saw his face darken, if that was possible. He had natural circles under his eyes, but under the fluorescent lights they seemed purple. His features tightened and for a moment she was afraid he might cry, until she recognized the look as anger. He handed her a videodisk. "Hope you have a strong stomach."

She smiled and said, "It's a job requirement with all the bureaucratic crap I put up with. Let her rip." She inserted the disk and tilted her head to make sense of the image on the big screen. When she realized that the pulpy red mess on the screen was a *human being,* she could not stop her hand from cupping her mouth.

"That is—was—my best friend. Luis Gonzalez. You've heard of him?"

Susanne nodded. It was a terrible story that had preceded Contreras's arrival at CIA with whispers about obsession. "What does this have to do with us, Jimmy?"

"The thing that carved Luis up like that is a full-blooded Aztec Indian. He's small, has tattoos of hummingbirds on his chest, and used to wear a necklace. The rest is sketchy. I made a promise to Rita Gonzalez—and myself—fifteen years ago and I aim to keep it. You ever make a promise like that?"

"Yes. Not to marry a philistine again," she said, trying to keep it light for trepidation's sake, not humor's. She was wary of his mood. He was shifty and agitated.

"Then I started reading about that serial killer in Juarez—the Monster Butcher. You remember the brief I gave last November on *El Monstruo Carnicero,* the murderer on the FBI Most Wanted List? I pushed to get down there. I had it from a solid source that the Butcher had done Luis. My request was denied."

"If you're asking me to transfer . . ."

"Most of the dead women were missing their hearts. Some men had their skins removed, just like Luis. The women had zero drug connection, but *every single one of the men did.* See? The Juarez cartel was still employing this animal, but he was killing women on the side. Our source had no idea."

"Our source?"

Contreras nodded impatiently. "Yes. Yes. We purchased the activation code for *El Monstruo Carnicero* ten years ago—if the government ever called him again. They never did. Info from inside the cartels themselves is sparse. It costs too much money to buy them, the best sources are too well paid, and it's too dangerous. They kill on *suspicion*. We can't get the good information because of the terror that protects him. The government is different. People can be bought. I knew there was a connection, so I applied some serious pressure. Hell, I almost lost my badge in the months after I lost Luis."

"Well, don't get close to losing it again. FBI Most Wanted is Corwin's bag."

He shrugged it off. "*El Monstruo Carnicero*'s location was deeply compartmentalized within the government and I couldn't get at it, but I did buy just a slice of the code they would use to contact him. Not the entire chain so I could trace him, but just the knowledge that he had been activated. For over a decade I've waited for that phone call. We got it just after midnight."

"This is not a coincidence?"

"I don't believe in coincidence." He was keyed up and it sounded harsh. "Do you?"

Now here I am at the culmination of this man's professional life, Susanne thought. Just my luck, playing nanny to a midlife crisis. "This monster was enlisted to torture Darren and Kate Phillips?"

Susanne glanced up at the body and thought about that happy couple experiencing death the same way. She realized that she was developing a bond with the newlyweds, though in truth the phone was most important.

"If they haven't already been killed, yes. He's their torture agent."

"So you think they've been captured?"

"I don't know. They may be using *El Monstruo Carnicero* to find the couple. If he's the same *puta* who did Luis, then he's strong on his feet. A racewalker. I think Juarez is pulling out all the stops, and come sunup, *El Monstruo Carnicero* will be looking for the Americans."

"The whole country is looking."

"No, I don't think so. The cartel will keep the posse narrow, so they can control it. My guess is that Eduardo Saiz is their contact."

He was starting to make her nervous. Not for what he might do, but what he might say in a few hours. They had word that the president himself was going to visit the morning brief. Could she risk taking Jimmy along? The CIA had a cowboy reputation as it was. "There's no proof of that, Jimmy."

"I worked with the man years ago. That's all the proof I need. He's a leech. So if I'm Saiz, I don't involve the army because I can't control them. I keep it nice and tight to my vest. Which is exactly what we need to do."

Susanne set her coffee down and stretched again. Here it comes, she thought. I'm just too tired to deal with it right now. She could hear the computer cooling fans blowing away the silence. "What are you suggesting, Jimmy?"

"We know the satphone automatically gives up its location, right?"

"After a few seconds, yes. There are S and T folks working on it as we speak."

"The cartel is waiting for their next call. We can do the same thing if we crack that location burst. I'll head down south and organize a team. You clear it with Tampa. We have several Army surveillance–sniper teams in country doing counter-narc missions and I know the mission commander. When you give me the satphone location, I'll take a small team there as fast as possible. I need to get to them before *El Monstruo Carnicero* does. You want the phone, I want the butcher. That's why I'm asking for your support."

"They'll never approve a hard extract, Jimmy," Susanne said firmly. "This is one notch above General Justicz in Tampa. This needs the stamp of SecDef and DCI, and that means hardass Bobby Kennedy and that means no. So let's short-cut the process and *just say no.*"

Contreras sighed. "I'm not asking for approval. I will do it myself, with just a bit of help from you. Just information and some money. The DEA slush fund sucks."

She expected something that pushed the envelope. This exploded it. He was fully willing to risk his career for a chance at revenge, a poorly conceived plot that circumvented the law and would devastate anyone on the periphery, let alone on the inside. She felt a pang of regret; what she would say next had to be strong enough to quash his rogue wants, and to do it she had to be harsh. "I'm sorry, but no. What you're proposing could land us both in jail. Frankly, it's asinine. Best we can do is pitch this information to the DCI or DHS. I'm not going outside of the chain of command, and neither are you. Not on my watch."

Contreras was furious. He ejected the videodisk and threw it in his bag. He tried to pull the zipper past the iron but it stuck, so he ripped it up and over. "Your watch? Let me tell you something. After this morning, you ain't gonna *have* a watch. Feds'll take the whole thing under their wing." He strode across the Bat Cave and struggled with the reinforced bar latch. "Two hundred dead women for your place in the food chain. Now will you let me the hell out of here, please?"

– 24 –

ZAMPEDRO ARMY BASE, MEXICO

Felix stroked the head of his best friend and rubbed his belly. Sniff-Sniff warmed to his touch and rubbed his floppy ears against his master's palm. The dog's freshly shampooed hairs felt like silk. Sniff-Sniff nuzzled his hand and Felix felt his breath snorting hot and cold in his palm, the dog's million-peso nose idling like an overpowered muscle car at a stoplight.

Of the thousands of dogs Felix had bred for his business, Sniff-Sniff was his greatest achievement, the finest hunting dog in all the world. The bloodhound had taken second place in the ESPN Outdoor Games World Championships in Los Angeles to a hound from Alabama, and would have won had the Americans not decided the prize should go to one of their own.

Felix was proud of his record as a tracker, proud that he took clients on *real* hunts that required *real* stalking and *real* marksmanship. And patience. He had once pursued a stubborn ram for three days, following it even when his client quit the hunt. What kind of example would he have set for Sniff-Sniff if he had bagged, too? No, when the dog put nose to ground, something was going to be shot.

Finding these murderers won't be as difficult as the ram fiasco, he thought, not if Sniff-Sniff acquires the scent. Tracking human beings was simple. They were slow and they smelled worse as the chase progressed. *Hunting* human beings, however, seemed an outlandish prospect before Felix heard how *Los Asesinos* had murdered all his people. Like most of his countrymen, he was driven mad by the television pictures of the sobbing relatives of the honorable men and women who had been murdered by two drug-addicted gringos. It was a righteous hunt.

He looked at the four soldiers sitting across the briefing table from him, squinting to block out the bright overhead lights. Around them, the Army base was in deep slumber. The echo of some anonymous soldier's snores filled the hangar. It was 0430 and the government briefing agent had just told the team that it should get another two hours' sleep to prepare for the hunt. Felix tapped his finger on the map. "Terrain may be hard."

"Not as hard as we are, old man," said Sergeant Oscar Pena, Mexican Special Police Forces. He balled his fists so the twenty-three-year-old veins on his arms flushed.

"Yes, well, we'll see," said Felix, stroking his gray stubble absentmindedly. He had twenty years on the youngsters but was curious to see how they moved in the bush. "Even if you and your *compañeros* fall back, young man, I have a rifle and I'll complete the hunt. It will be a pleasure to kill these murderers."

Sergeant Pena nodded and spat some flaky tobacco juice on the cement floor of the hangar. He liked to catch a buzz when he awoke each morning the same as another might drink coffee. "Fall back? In your dreams, daddy. I'll drop you after five k."

"Even so, I'm quite a shot."

"Listen, old man. I have the best eyesight. And if I see them, I'll kill them."

Felix studied the youngster. He hoped the hunt was quick. "Who is in charge here, anyway?"

"I am," said the little Indian at the end of the table in a high, effeminate voice.

Pena could not stand to look at him. His shoulders barely cleared the table in the sitting position. He wore a thin beard that squirted out of the end of his chin like the whiskers below a catfish's lower lip. His ruddy cheeks were as oily as his long black hair, pulled back in a ponytail that snaked into his shirt and made his abnormally large forehead seem even more grotesque. To top off the carnival show, he wore an aqua necklace like a girl.

"Sir, is that right?" Pena asked his lieutenant. "This puppet is in charge?"

When Lieutenant Garza, the officer in charge of the four-man special-forces detachment, nodded, Pena opened his mouth and stared at the Indian. The first thing he thought, besides snickering at how tiny the nasty runt was, was that the Indian must have been retarded or at least deformed, given his massive head. His giant brow looked to Sergeant Pena like the prow of a battleship, just not as clean.

The idea that the Indian weasel was in charge of the posse clashed with his world view. He had not even paid attention to the brief! He just sat there looking at the photographs of *Los Asesinos* the entire time, stroking the one where the woman was posing in her bikini on the beach. Well, it *was* a hot picture, Pena thought, but killing the gringos was the most important task of their lives and the Indian was thumbing his nose at the briefer. And here Pena was, in peak athletic form, won the smoker box-off for all the special forces police in his weight class, expert rifleman, and he had to deal with a cockroach like *that!*

"How you gonna lead from the rear, little friend?" Pena asked the Indian. "These gringos do that long race, Eco-Challenge. You would have heard that if you listened to the brief. They're tired, yes, but I bet they still move fast and definitely put up a fight. What you gonna do then? Call your big brother? Who is this guy, anyway?"

"Quiet, Sergeant Pena," said Lieutenant Garza. "If the *comandante* says he's in charge, then he's in charge. Still, I must ask, sir, what are your qualifications?"

The Indian with the oiled hair just stared back. His eyes were black and lifeless. His nose hooked out from his head like an enormous broken beak, savagely broken at its midpoint so that its lower half drooped vertically below his upper lip like an elephant's trunk. He was wearing a black silk shirt with a collar that had gone out of style in 1979.

"That's not your concern. Don't talk to me. You five—and the goddamn dog—just stay out of my way once we land in the helicopter and find them."

His lieutenant was offended, so Pena knew his right to speak had been reinstated. "You watch how you talk to my lieutenant, you little Indian maggot," he said, though he really didn't give a damn what the waif said about his lieutenant. He just wanted to vent. "You exercise some manners or I'll teach you some. Maybe I'll pound that fucked-up head of yours back into shape so you aren't so ugly."

The Indian blew him a kiss. "My head is tall because I am wise. When I was born, my father crushed my skull and flattened it with boards, as is Aztec custom. You don't know this because you are impure. And stupid."

Pena was unsettled by the kiss. He had been in several fistfights and was comfortable with stare-downs like the one he entered with the Indian. He prided himself on his ability to gauge the potential for a fight in another man's eyes, and they almost always backed down. If they looked stout, Pena hit them right then.

"Say that again and I put a fist through your freaky head."

Pena watched for the greasy little thing's reaction and it surprised him. Scared him a little, even, with those black eyes reflecting little squares from the fluorescent lights, the hint of a smile. It was not show, not bluff, almost a *private* flush at the corners of his feminine lips. No, Pena shook his head, that's not possible. I'm overreacting. Still, when the man stood and slinked off, he gave Pena a quick wink that turned his stomach.

"Fucking freak," Pena hissed. "Stay away from me, you tiny Indian piglet."

When Sniff-Sniff ambled by minutes later, the bloodhound brushed Pena's leg. The young sergeant was so startled, he hit his knee on the table and swore fiercely.

———

El Monstruo Carnicero spread a towel across his bunk and set his weapons down next to his sharpening stone and granular oil. He picked up his two newest throwing blades, Falcon and Eagle, and stroked their razor curves before giving them a final taste of the stone for the night. Both were forged with cold rolled stainless steel and covered with a black titanium nitrate coating. They were given disproportional weight in their heads because of his throwing style. Starting with their sharp points, the heavy darts bowed wide like a spade, then tapered sleekly back along two blood grooves that had been high-speed buff-polished and could burrow through skin and flesh with the smallest burst of momentum. He had drilled tiny holes from their midsections to clear out their rectangular tails more as ornaments than for mechanics; what the tiny tunnels gained in aerodynamic stability they lost in speed. No matter—*El Monstruo Carnicero* had a lightning fast arm for someone so small and the loss of a few kilometers per hour was a tiny price to pay for that whistle of death the knives made as they screamed toward their targets.

"What you doing, Indian?" asked Sergeant Pena, who was bunking across from him.

"I'm Aztec, but you'll learn that, gringo."

"Gringo? What the fuck you saying, *puta?*"

El Monstruo Carnicero cocked his long head. He selected the heavy chopping blade next. Weighing close to a kilogram, Bear Claw was more parang than machete because of its heavy, bulbous tip. Retreating from its round lollipop head, Bear Claw tapered suddenly to its long slicing edge before reaching its saw-toothed cutting edge, a six-centimeter section of twin-peaked jags that could cut through bone.

"What you got there?" asked Pena.

El Monstruo Carnicero held up Bear Claw. "This blade was forged of high chromium, fine-grained steel. I built it fat at the top to seize momentum early in the swipe. See? That way it builds through the length of the slash so that the strike is destroying at the finish." He cut the air in front of the *Federale.*

Pena did not like the sound of the air parting. He backed up against his bunk and reached for his M-4. "Oh yeah? This is an air-cooled, gas-operated 5.56-mm carbine with an infrared scope. I can shoot you eight hundred meters away. Don't know what your knife can do that far."

El Monstruo Carnicero snatched Barracuda from its rightful place at the head of his collection. He whirled the blade with his spindly fingers, then sheathed it with a simple promise: "Next time you come out, the first person you see you get to taste." The long, flexible filet blade was *El Monstruo Carnicero's* weapon of choice. He had crafted it over the course of a week when he worked for that butterfly knife manufacturer, just prior to entering the army, and it had been at his side ever since—from the first interrogation of the gringo DEA in 1987 to the latest question and answer sessions at the cartel's new Juarez ranch. And, of course, his own private sessions.

"Let me see that one," said Pena.

"You don't want to see it. Barracuda is made of the finest, softest steel. It was heat-injected with carbon for maximum sharpness. If it so much as rested on your thumb its teeth would part your skin. With some speed, I push it in up to its hilt, bending around bones and cartilage so it can taste morsels like tendons, arteries, and organs."

"That's a lot of talk," said Pena, tapping the underslung black thermoplastic grenade launcher. "This forty-millimeter cannon can fire high explosive rounds or beehives. Know what that is? It's a shotgun blast of two hundred pellets in your ass."

El Monstruo Carnicero was puzzled. He wasn't used to his conversational partners being able to speak at will, let alone engage in verbal jousts. "Barracuda is like a precision scalpel. I can peel a grape for nearly two hundred centimeters."

"That's good, Indian. Peel your foreskin with it so you can suck your own dick."

———

Pena awoke at dawn to assemble his pack and clean his weapon again. The black gringo Phillips was a United States Marine and Pena wanted to be ready for a firefight, should it come to that, please Mary. It would be an honor to plug him with a bullet. He glanced at his war gear—M-4 assault rifle, 145 rounds of ammunition (he had another 300 rounds stored in a crate but he didn't want to hump the weight), two high explosive grenades, five 40-mm grenades, a 9-mm Beretta pistol, a new set of night-vision goggles, and an engraved bowie knife affectionately named War Dog he liked to show off, dangling it prominently on his gear belt so it bounced against his right hip.

Pena pulled out his cleaning kit and punched his rifle bore with several patches—all clean—then coated his weapon with another bath of lubricant and set it gently on the rack. He checked his mountain pack for the fifth time in a day, extracting and then repacking each waterproofed piece of kit. Satisfied, he glanced at his sleeping *compañeros,* grabbed his cleaning kit, slipped into his flip-flops, and rubbed his head. There was something wrong.

He rushed to the barracks bathroom and grabbed at his hair in front of the mirror. Tufts of it fell spinning in lazy circles on their way to the tile, whole patches—perfect squares—coming loose, his head a geometrical patchwork of hair and stubble now. *That fucker cut pieces of my hair!*

Pena wheeled around in a fury and there he was, not even 150 centimeters tall, naked except for skivvies that dangled desperately from his narrow hips and his turquoise necklace that looked like it could snap his turkey neck. His chest had almost no meat on it, nearly concave. In the center of his breastbone was a tattoo of a blue hummingbird holding a little knife. There was another near his belly button. I have a tat of a skull, Pena thought, and this fag chooses little birds. This Peter Pan Indian is a fucking fairy but he has some big balls. *Payback time!*

"You gonna pay now, *puta,*" said Pena.

"You want me?" the little Indian hissed. He stood in front of one of the exits, blocking it. His thin little beard danced when he spoke, and Pena looked at those terrible, opaque eyes. He was a disgusting excuse for a human being.

Pena licked his lips and noticed that one of the man's hands was hidden behind his back. Probably a gun, he reasoned. No way the little cockroach would fight on even terms. "Not right now I don't," he said, adding, "but I will later, you Indian maggot," to save some pride.

Pena walked toward the man but something stopped him before he gained closure. It wasn't right, the man's fierce look, almost lusty. After all, it was *Pena* who should be the angry one, the aggressor. That man had cut little symbols into his hair and yet *the Indian* was still confrontational. It shouldn't play like that. He should back down. Pena was *allowed* to be pissed. Something in the mano-a-mano world was not right.

"What do you have behind your back?"

"Knife. You want to find out what kind?"

"You gonna use it if I do?" Pena was nervous now, but he didn't want to lose face and walk out the other exit.

"Yes. An Aztec warrior must feed the earth with blood. It's best to kill another warrior, like you. I'll cut you deep in your gut, then fuck you and ride you while you bleed, holding your precious Spanish stomach and crying. Then maybe I come in your mouth before I rip out your heart, little boy. Come here for a taste."

Pena was stunned. He felt pinpricks radiate from his fingers up the back of his neck. He heard the hum of the fluorescent lights above him. He could hear the man breathing, could hear himself, could feel the acid roil his stomach and weaken his legs, could taste the tension in the air. The glands in his cheeks robbed his mouth of its saliva and his lips cracked when he opened his mouth. He froze.

What did he just say?

When *El Monstruo Carnicero* smiled, Pena sprinted out the second exit and back to his hooch, flip-flops slapping the cement floor in full retreat.

– 25 –

WASHINGTON, D.C.

President Scott O'Reilly was taller than he appeared on television. Susanne was flustered enough to begin with, having been hastily ushered into the Oval Office. Now she quietly cleared her throat to prepare for the introduction as his big hand came gliding toward hers and engulfed it. He was a year younger than Susanne, but she immediately felt like a freshman being approached by a senior.

"You must be the lone dissenter I'm hearing about."

"Susanne Sheridan, sir. Deputy director for Organized Crime and Narcotics. Also the CIA rep to Homeland. Actually, the DEA rep on my team shares my view but he's stuck on the Beltway."

"Right, well, have a seat."

He pointed toward the antique sofa on which Roger Corwin sat smiling like an overripe piece of fruit. Chief of Staff Kennedy, FBI Director Marsden, and Homeland Security Director Henry had snagged the private rest stops. She nodded at Corwin and tucked herself into the corner of the couch, careful to stretch her skirt over her knees.

"You know everyone, I presume?" the president asked politely.

Corwin cut his smile off, noticing the green fluorescent backlight on his BlackBerry was flashing. He had set it on "meeting" mode so it would not bring unwanted attention, tucking it behind his freshly pumped quadriceps out of the president's view. He tilted the pager and shifted his eyes just slightly to read the text.

DODGER—JUST CONFIRMED IRREFUTABLE EVIDENCE. THEY USE DRUGS. PRESS IN FRENZY NOW. I HAVE KEPT THEM WAITING FOR HALF AN HOUR. CAN I START MY BRIEF?—FISHERMAN

Corwin tackled the difficult chore of typing with the thumb of his weak hand. It did not deter him. He hadn't been squeezing the gripper all these years for nothing.

NEED FEW MORE MINUYTES. WAIT.

The president glanced out the window where Marine One was idling on the lawn. "Ms. Sheridan, I have a decision to make and I understand you carry a fresh point of view. My advisors think it's cut and dry, but Major Phillips worked for me. Understand?" He squinted at her and her heart increased in cadence. He was a former Ivy League basketball player and sitting on the edge of his desk he looked like the Washington Monument.

"Yes, sir. It's an embarrassing position for the White House to find itself in."

"No, you don't understand," O'Reilly said curtly. "What I meant was, I *know* Darren Phillips. Or at least I thought I did. Simple question: Did he do this?"

She was surprised to be so nervous. She tried to soothe her quavering voice by imagining he was naked. It did not work. The only image that came for some reason was silver chest hair to match his head. "The violence? I think he may have, sir—"

"No, not the violence. Did he go to Mexico on his honeymoon and attempt to purchase drugs?"

She had always prided herself for being direct. *Don't start qualifying now.* "No, sir." There was texture in her risky position and she felt articulate again. "The drug connection was manufactured. Darren and his wife grabbed . . ."

"Kate. I know her. Terrific young woman."

"Yessir, Kate . . . grabbed a satellite phone that threatens the encryption of a drug cartel's entire communications network. Why they grabbed it, I don't know. But it had zero to do with drugs."

"Sir," said Roger Corwin, "may I brief her on the polygraph results?"

Corwin opened a red folder stamped "Roger Corwin's Eyes Only" and removed a sheet of paper as if he were young Arthur pulling the sword from the stone. He set it on her lap. "What you have in front of you is taken from Major Darren Phillips's polygraph screen before becoming a military aide to the president. You can see that he failed the question 'Would you ever consider taking drugs?' As for his wife, Kate North, she was once rushed to the infirmary for an overdose at Princeton."

And here we go, she thought, still surprised he was willing to fight her at the very end of the limb. In the government, battles were fought quietly where risk could be managed. Why was he so convinced?

"If I were Darren Phillips I'd argue that question, too. 'Would you consider' is a hypothetical and it has no place in a poly. Just by virtue of being asked the question Phillips was 'considering.' "

"I'm just stating facts so the president can make a decision. That Phillips failed that question is, in the opinion of this polygrapher, a fact. That his wife overdosed in college is a fact."

"What drug?" asked Susanne.

Corwin hesitated. "Alcohol. But binge drinking might point to something else."

"Now come on, Roger," Susanne said sweetly. "What's the college experience without a good stomach pump? We've all been there."

She saw the president smirk, but Roberta Kennedy interjected before Susanne was able to leverage the joke. "No, Ms. Sheridan, I most certainly have *never* been there. Leave your own indiscretions out of this. You don't seem to understand the gravity here. It seems one of the president's military aides has murdered twenty Mexican citizens and two Americans. He may have taken a third American hostage. All indications are that this was drug related. It started at a drug lord's house. Roger tells us that some marijuana residue was found in their hotel room. Wait until *that* goes public this morning."

"Marijuana residue can be days or even months old. They can't prove it belongs to the Phillipses," Susanne said and immediately wanted to rescind.

Kennedy said, "You don't get it, do you? This is both a human tragedy and a public relations disaster. This Marine officer was entrusted by us to carry the football. And we blame the Russians for being lax with their nukes! All dealings with Mexico—be they NAFTA or devaluation—have the guilty undercurrent of narcotics. Now a member of our staff goes down there to *purchase* narcotics.

"If it were not for the president's close relationship with the president of Mexico, this incident would explode. The press corps is going to swarm him in five minutes. We need to issue a brief statement of sorrow and regret that supports the Mexicans in their effort to find Major Phillips. Then it's dismissed. We're trying to fight a global war, not deal with personal failings. What's your opinion?"

The president remained silent.

Susanne took it as a sign that he was pushing back on the recommendation of the big three. "I apologize for being flip. I view this incident gravely as well. I think the president should not only express sorrow, but also express veiled support for this couple."

"Ms. Sheridan, I'm from Montana," said Bobby Kennedy, an introduction she used prolifically though she had worked on the Hill since graduating college. Everyone inside the Beltway either clung to withered roots or invented them. "In Montana, you may think you're doing the birds a favor by filling the feeder. But often you attract a bear. Well, we don't want to attract that bear."

Susanne turned to George Henry and decided to take the risk. "Sir, did you bring up *El Monstruo Carnicero?*"

Henry frowned at her and said sharply, "No. As we discussed on the phone, it has zero relevance in this meeting."

Roger Corwin unconsciously straightened his spine and sat up. His eyes went from Sheridan to Henry and back again. He was so totally focused on this new vein of conversation that for a moment he did not breathe. What the hell does Sheridan know about *El Monstruo Carnicero?* he wondered. And why did they keep this from me? That's clearly FBI turf.

The fog began to lift and Corwin edged forward to the lip of the couch. As a CHP officer he had been an exceptional interrogator. He often unraveled the lies right there in the middle of the goddamned accident scene with the tires still spinning and the ambulatory still weeping. His first trick was to split up the parties so he could attack the truth in piecemeal.

Now Sheridan was on one side of a car wreck and Eduardo Saiz was on the other. The serial murderer *El Monstruo Carnicero* was between them. That's who Saiz is talking about, he concluded. It wasn't Mullah Omar, as he had allowed himself to hope, but it was still pretty goddamned succulent. *I'm going to get credit for collaring a fucking serial killer.*

Roger Corwin's deduction had taken fewer than two seconds. He edged out and leaned forward enough so that Sheridan's view of the president was half blocked.

"Who is this now?" asked the president.

Roger Corwin boomed, "It's Spanish for 'the monster butcher,' a serial murderer who's been on the FBI Most Wanted List for three years. We believe he may have killed over a hundred people in Juarez, right across the Rio from El Paso." He quickly turned to his boss, George Marsden, and said, "Sir, he's the one I was talking about on our way over here."

Marsden nodded vaguely and said, "Oh, right."

"Mister President, I've been working with the Mexicans for some time on this bastard. Over the past few weeks the Mexican investigators have unearthed some tangible clues. They've been coming to me for cuts on my thoughts. I believe we're close to a collar. Maybe even late this week."

Susanne thought her lower jaw might drop right through the couch like an anvil.

"What does this have to do with Major Phillips?" asked the president.

Corwin shrugged. "I don't know, sir." He eased back into the couch, hoping he hadn't jumped the gun. He needed whatever information she had. He turned to Sheridan and rotated his extended hand as if turning a door knob to say, your turn now. "Susanne?"

Susanne shook her head. She had been trumped, badly, in front of the president of the United States and the director of Homeland Security. This was the second time that Corwin had either intercepted or found a different source for similar information. Contreras himself? Of course not. Well, not impossible. Ted Blinky? Christian Collins?

"Nothing, sir," she said. "I just thought it was important you know about this murderer. There are three hundred missing right across the border."

The president scratched his ear absentmindedly. "Yes, well, that's horrible, but one thing at a time. I've got to get to New York. Recommendations? George?"

George Henry said, "It's pretty clear that this isn't Homeland Security real estate. The phone's important, yes, but this squall became a hurricane when Mexican citizens started dying. I recommend this be handled by FBI. All we can do is hope this does not get more bloody. The press is going to have a field day as it is with the nuclear angle."

George Marsden said, "Sir, Roger is incredibly well positioned on this. Not only with the Mexicans but also in taking the lead on the investigation here at home. He's already come up with something called the 'digital breakout' that may be able to track the Phillipses if they use the phone again. I recommend he hold daily press conferences at the FBI to feed the reporters. Best if you stay out of this one."

Susanne was rocked by the FBI director's statement. If Corwin knew about the digital tracking method Ted Blinky was working on, then someone within her own organization *was* leaking information. Had Jimmy Contreras turned on her that quickly?

The president turned to his chief of staff. "Bobby?"

"Sir, I could not agree more. Go with the statement we discussed: 'I was horrified to learn about the senseless tragedy in Mexico yesterday. My thoughts and prayers are with the victims' families.' Don't mention Phillips."

"What do you think of him, sir?" Susanne interrupted. Spontaneous speech from the Eisenhower couch was a rarity, and Bobby Kennedy looked angry enough to set her on fire.

"Major Phillips is . . ." The president seemed to be debating further speech, not his opinion. Finally he said, "A good man."

"Then that's exactly what you should say if asked, sir."

Roger Corwin raised his hand as if he were in elementary school, hedging the bet that Sheridan had made so boldly. She had her chips on the table as he had hoped and he needed to participate. My professional reputation will be sealed with the next sentence, he thought. *Saiz sure as hell better be right.*

"Having worked with Susanne these past weeks, I understand her position. But it's wrong. It is really a question of truth, isn't it? Were there drugs in *Los Asesinos*' hotel room? Were they meeting with a cartel operative? I believe drugs have everything to do with this."

The president stood and the other five were up in an instant. He escorted them out into the hall and said, "Well, you'll have my decision in about three minutes. Thank you." With two secret service bodyguards in the lead, he walked outside and started across the lawn to Marine One.

Susanne followed the others into a conference room where several televisions were blaring. George Henry glanced her way and slowly moved alongside. "I want to see you alone when this is finished," he hissed.

"Yes, sir," she said softly.

She caught Corwin winking at her.

On the screen now on all the American cable networks, the president walked up to the cameras. The cropped green grass behind him fanned out in wind streaks. Questions were screamed so they could be heard over the whirling rotor blades of Marine One, but there were so many of them the president just squinted and waved his hands. "I was horrified to learn about the tragedy in Mexico yesterday. My thoughts and prayers are with the victims' families this morning."

"Thank God," said Bobby Kennedy. "He can get stubborn when it comes to judging someone's character. Once he bets on a horse he sometimes doubles down instead of walking away."

Susanne expected little else. The president was, after all, a politician. Her thoughts shifted to her next task, apologizing to George Henry and asking to keep her job at Homeland. But as she watched the president step toward Marine One on television, she saw him wheel around in response to a question.

"Major Phillips?" the president said. The rotor wash lifted his tie and he snagged it, pinning it to his chest. "Of course I know him. And the Darren Phillips I know is a good man. I'm as eager to get to the bottom of this as anyone else."

– 26 –

MEXICO CITY, MEXICO

A thick pillar of sunlight was plunging into the anteroom and Eduardo backed into a corner to avoid it. It was hot enough in the dark. He had ordered his aide, Jorge Morales, to kill the air-conditioning in preparation for the press briefing in order to contain the number of questions—he wanted the media uncomfortable and irritated when he presented the evidence of marijuana residue found in the hotel room of *Los Asesinos*—but that was forty-five minutes ago, before Dodger requested the delay. Now the temperature was soaring. Still, the delay had proved incredibly beneficial. So propitious, in fact, that Eduardo wondered if he even needed Dodger Corwin anymore.

When Morales had returned from building services, he handed Eduardo a stack of photographs. "Wait until you see these, sir. The film from *Los Asesinos'* camera that we found near the dead dogs has been developed. Incredible! You were right, sir."

Eduardo had put his face against the wall and thumbed through the pile of pictures as if counting one hundred large. Oh, thank Christ, he thought. His theory was too good to be true, but it *was* true. The Americans *were* buyers. He had pumped his fist and smiled, careful not to pop the stitches in his lip. "I want these enlarged immediately," he had hissed. "Blow them up big so everyone can see. The whole goddamn world. Everyone gets a copy. Hurry!"

"Already done, sir. I took the liberty of ordering a color copy packet for each reporter. Well, the first hundred reporters, at least. I included the pornographic shots, sir. I thought that might help show what *Los Asesinos* really are. God-damned murdering drug addicts," Morales had hissed.

The BlackBerry tittered and jarred Eduardo into the present. He unclipped it and read.

GO NOW!

"Jorge?"

"Yes, sir?" Morales called from the press room, startled.

"I'm coming in. Are the photographs ready?"

"Two minutes, sir. I'll set them up behind you while you're speaking."

"Let's do this thing."

Eduardo faced the window again and retucked his dark blue shirt. He was dressed in a charcoal Polo suit and a Hermès tie that had taken his wife twenty minutes to fix. His image was about to go worldwide.

He smelled the sweatbox before he entered the room. Seeing him, the reporters fought for his attention like crazed groupies. He saw polka dots of sweat on all the light-colored shirts in the room.

"Good morning, ladies and gentlemen," Eduardo said in Spanish. *"I am going to conduct this brief in English. It seems we have many Americans here this morning and I've been told they are, how shall I say, language handicapped."* This allowed Eduardo to accomplish three things—widen the gulf of resentment, speak directly to the world, and show off his command of English.

"I apologize for the heat. I'll give a short statement and then take questions. At the end of the brief, you will get photographs which will confirm the guilt of *Los Asesinos.*

"This morning we have confirmed that marijuana residue was found in the hotel room of *Los Asesinos,* along with some distasteful items that shall remain private. I won't take questions on these . . . *quirks* because they may not be relevant to this murder case. I deal only in facts.

"Fact: *Los Asesinos* rented a kayak and paddled to the hidden beach owned by a drug dealer we have come to know as Jackrabbit Calagra. A federal police task force had been watching Jackrabbit for several months and we believe he was using the beach as a dealing point to avoid detection. There was a gunfight at his house. He and a bodyguard were shot dead.

"Fact: Cornered at the Acapulco police station, *Los Asesinos* shot three police to death, then used three American college students as hostages to make their escape. *Los Asesinos* were armed with machine guns and over twenty Mexican citizens were murdered. Two of the hostages were killed and a third is still missing.

"Finally, fact: This morning we have uncovered additional evidence in

Los Asesinos' own words that they were trying to buy drugs. It is *irrefutable.* Questions?"

Eduardo struggled to hear what the American woman was shouting at him. It was louder than that goddamned playground yesterday. Something about *Los Asesinos'* motive again, and he hoped he might use some of his prepared sound bites. He didn't want anything about the murderers to get lost in the translation, especially these stingers.

"I don't know what was in *Los Asesinos'* minds, *señorita,* but Darren Phillips shot the three Acapulco police officers in *cold blood,* as you say. Their names, just to remind you, were Carlos Diego, Francisco Ordonez, and Juan Calagra. All murdered in cold blood. Carlos Diego was on our Olympic diving team."

Eduardo was happy that he remembered to hammer on the names of the deceased so the victims would not be faceless.

"When these *asesinos* heard the Federal Judicial Police Force arrive outside, they forced the three American boys from the University of Michigan out of the cell and used them as hostages. Actually, they were *human shields,* according to the *Federales* that survived. My men were naturally reluctant to open fire on *human shields.* It was then that two of the American boys tried to run, and *Los Asesinos* shot them in the backs. I cannot explain why, *señorita.* I don't pretend to understand the mind of murderers." I should have said "minds," he thought.

"But what about the third boy? Vinny Cappucco? He's a football player, you said?" she asked.

"Yes, and he is our main concern. He is the reason why our helicopter did not simply shoot *Los Asesinos.* This office still hopes . . . Ah, here, ladies and gentlemen, are the photographs I have mentioned."

Eduardo waved Morales toward the podium and pointed at the easel. The posterboard pictures were five feet long and it took a moment for the young aide to balance them. The photostats were still warm and Eduardo could smell the ink. Touching one of them was like grabbing a mug of warm coffee in the morning. Morales covered the easel with a sheet.

Eduardo stared at the audience and paused for dramatic effect—and to allow the cameras to focus—until the murmur faded. "Many in the United States have questioned our preliminary theory of robbery and drugs. I submit to you that perhaps you do not know what these people are really like. Well, I do. I've dedicated the last ten years fighting this virus with my friends in the American FBI and DEA. Drugs ruin lives. It is a *scourge* that does not discriminate for background or borders. Shame on those of you who have implied that it was Mexicans who brought this on themselves, that *Los Asesinos* are somehow innocent. But if you won't respect my word, here is what *Los Asesinos* say for themselves."

Eduardo yanked the cover away from the first display—a portrait of the naked and entangled couple in a hotel room—and there was an audible gasp in the room. The crackling of camera shutters sounded like rain plunking on his porch, cool and soothing.

"These pictures were found in the *asesinos'* camera that they dumped in the woods. My intention is not to make this a pornographic show. I submit these to show that there was a different and quite reckless side to this couple, contrary to our early belief."

Eduardo shared a solemn look with Morales and waited for the buzz to fade. He was so totally buoyed he fought the urge to shout for joy. Since he was placed *on payroll,* he had done terrible things, God forgive him. When he had ordered *Los Asesinos'* deaths only eighteen hours earlier, the concomitant guilt of murdering innocents had flooded him again. But it was righteous this time! Eduardo had not one milligram of regret.

He nodded at Morales and the next poster was placed on the easel. Even now the photograph seemed divine to him. The sun block message was white and chalky running across the undulating muscles of Darren Phillips's big back. "Read the message from *Los Asesinos,* ladies and gentlemen, because they are talking to you. I am quite sure that you will reach the same conclusion we did."

The rumble in the room grew to a roar. Hands and then reporters themselves shot up. Everyone was yelling. He heard an American reporter say, "My God, are you reading this?"

– 27 –

WASHINGTON, D.C.

Susanne Sheridan stared at the photograph of Darren Phillips's back that dominated every television screen in the White House conference room. Satellite relays and microwave transmissions meant that the television junkie in Oshkosh, Wisconsin, often received intelligence directly relevant to the national interest at the exact moment that the intelligence services did.

DHS George Henry walked up close to one of the screens and slowly shook his head as if he were punch-drunk. Written in white suntan lotion on Phillips's back:

> *GOD FORGIVE US!*
> *JUST WANTED TO BUY COKE.*
> *WE GO MEX CITY*
> *FOR FAIR TRIAL!*

"This is *exactly* what I was afraid of," said Bobby Kennedy. Her cell phone rang and she looked at the interface. "My God, it's the president already. Well, I warned him, didn't I? We all did." She put the phone in her ear and glared at Susanne as she walked out the door. "Except you," she added.

George Henry was the senior person in the room and the others waited for his response. Finally he said, "Is this genuine?"

Corwin stayed quiet. This was Sheridan's tar baby.

"I think it is, sir. No way they'd stage this and send it worldwide," Susanne offered. "Hara-kiri seems like a good option for me right now."

The director of Homeland Security pounded the desk with a clenched fist. A banker's lamp tipped over and its bright green plastic shade cracked. He tried to kick a chair over but it had wheels and went spinning across the room. Susanne knew him to be a calm man under pressure, but this was not panic but raw anger. She caught a flash in his eyes, the potential for interpersonal violence, but it abated. "I should have known better, goddamn it. I just sent the president into a *fucking* ambush."

Susanne said, "Sir, it was me who . . ."

"You stay quiet," he said, pointing at her. Then he wheeled toward Corwin and asked, "Did you know this was coming? You've got all the goddamned contacts."

"No, sir," Corwin said evenly. "I knew about the marijuana residue—as I mentioned—but my source did not get me this information."

"Yeah, well, the timing sucks. Did that Mexican deputy attorney general wait for the president to speak before he dropped this bomb?"

"Eduardo Saiz? Oh, I doubt it sir. Just a bad coincidence."

Henry looked Corwin over carefully before turning to FBI Director Marsden. "George, this is now squarely in your court. Darren Phillips says so himself. I'll get on the horn to the president and insist on FBI jurisdiction. The Homeland team has dumped enough fuel on this P.R. fire, now you guys will have to put it out. The president's comments will make it harder. He came off as totally skeptical, and I doubt Bobby will want him to publicly wipe all that egg off his face."

"Well, it's our fault, too," Marsden said. "I should have emphasized the FBI's relationship with the Mexicans. Especially all of Roger's contacts."

"Roger's contacts. Yes, well, I'm sure you'll be able to leverage them better than we did," he said carefully, turning to Corwin with an extended hand. "Well, Roger, looks like we'll need a new liaison to Homeland. You'll be too busy with your big case."

"It's been a pleasure, sir," Corwin said, shaking his hand vigorously. "But I'll be back soon. I have the feeling this one will wrap up quickly. Oh, and I'd like to add that Susanne has been terrific to work with. This isn't on her; we just had different opinions. Could have gone either way."

"Noted."

Corwin smiled and turned to Susanne. "I'd like to follow up with you on the digitally enhanced breakout this afternoon. Have your technology folks located the couple yet? Last I checked, they were working on it."

Susanne was not surprised to have her snitch thrown back into her own face. She was too weakened to respond with anything but a nod.

The FBI men exited and Susanne was left alone with the director of Homeland Security. "You and I need to have a long talk before your hara-kiri," he said. "So stop eyeballing that window."

– 28 –

SIERRA MADRE DEL SUR, MEXICO

Neck tried to think about the hot coed from UCSD he had hooked three nights earlier, but it was tough given the bursa sac that was expanding in his knee and the creeping drag of sleeplessness that was spreading in his head. Neck was over thirty hours without sleep, and coherent thought had become elusive.

After twenty-four hours without rest, a human being's capacity for mental work and physical reaction is equivalent to having a .1 percent blood alcohol level, above the legal limit for operating an automobile in the fifty U.S. states. With each subsequent sleepless night, mental faculties are further degraded by twenty-five percent so that by the fourth day, simple decisions become emotionally wrenching, exponentially draining puzzles—and this is for *sedentary* insomniacs.

Neck remembered that she was talkative. The little California hottie had said some cool things about his body, but he struggled to remember exactly *what* she said. In fact, apart from the purple bikini top and the little red devil tattoo on her lower back, he could not remember what she looked like. Every time the image started to form he took another step, his knee fired up, he cringed, and she was gone.

She had a hard little body, didn't she? Must have. After all, Neck Cappucco didn't slum. Especially when he himself was just so ripped up that day. His own body was the bomb, just totally fucking whack, and he had studied every inch of it in pinpoint detail as an architect would a precisely drafted sketch. Neck performed a yearly assessment of his back and ass with the simple use of a tripod and a digital video camera. He wished he had narrower hips so his glutes looked rounder, and the mole on his spine enraged him, but, my God, he *was* an army! Everywhere he went he studied the bodies of other men before even women did, not that he was gay or anything.

Don't even go there, dude!

For several steps he watched his right sneaker pulling the savannah underfoot as if he were on a giant treadmill, careful to avoid the barrel cactuses that had the annoying habit of ruining his daydreams. He tried to think about how big his feet were and how far he was going so he could back into some kind of time-distance equation, but he might as well have explained time travel while he was at it.

No way he was gay! When he was showering with the guys he was looking at lats and traps and tris and hammies, not cranks. Hell, Neck was a reterosexual love machine that was gonna roar out of the gates on Draft Day, a cold pimp daddy who knew how to handle both fame and breasts with real class, like Don Juan or Don Trump or the Rock.

Neck thought about the purple bikini top. She must have been smoking hot to have the balls, or ogaries or whatever, to approach him. He remembered he had ignored his thirst that parched morning. In fact, he had purposely burned his breakfast toast, then scraped off the black char so as not to ingest any residual water that might bloat him. On the beach he liked his muscles to *pop.*

Still, did she have blond hair, dirty blond hair, or bleached blond hair? Forgetful, he substituted Kate into his fantasy, brunette or not, which gave him a guilty kind of pleasure in the microsecond before his right foot struck the earth again.

"Yo. My knee is *killing* me. And my feet . . . they're just *all* fucked up. I need to stop. And *eat.* Shit, I feel like I'm starving. Maybe I *am* starving."

Darren assumed Neck Cappucco was talking to his wife. The kid hadn't spoken to him since they crossed the river fifteen miles back. Sure enough, Kate walked over to him and rubbed his back maternally. Microcosm of the United States, Darren thought. Complain loudly enough and someone will rush to take care of you. Personal responsibility was headed right out the window if the Boomers hadn't already torched it.

"Have you thought of stories to take your mind off the pain?" Kate asked Neck.

"I been doin' that pretty well for, like, five hours, Kate. I even been thinking of you, no offense, yo. But I'm sick."

"We're all hurting," said Darren. "Fight through it and suck it up."

"The hunger is perfectly normal, Neck," cooed Kate, her smoky voice a contrast to Darren's deep bark. She knew when a man had to be mothered and when he had to be scolded. "Think about it. We started the hike yesterday afternoon. It's . . . eleven o'clock now. You've been hiking for twenty-one hours straight, burning a minimum of five hundred fifty calories an hour. That's . . . what?"

"Eleven thousand five hundred fifty calories," Darren said quickly. He prided himself on his ability to cut through the sleepless chaos and make decisions under pressure. "Just break it down like this. Twenty-one is ten plus ten plus one . . ."

"*Anyway,*" interrupted Kate, "that's ten thousand at a minimum, more like twelve. You've been doing so well, Neck. The fact is, our bodies ate our glycogen stores hours ago and now they're almost finished devouring the fat. Muscles are next. We need to find some food."

"The fruit back there," mumbled Neck, trying to remember how long it had been since she fed him those bean pods. His mind had blended all the memories of the last day into the same foggy hour. How long did she say they'd been going?

Kate said, "The tamarinds, yes. In a survival situation we would have eaten the whole tree. I mean, this *is* survival's essence—what we're doing—but the fruit flesh was sour. That's why we just drank a little juice. Those pods would have wreaked havoc on our stomachs. Possibly immobilized us. No calories are worth that."

"Food and rest," gasped Neck, wiping his big face. "My ten-million-dollar knee is dog meat."

"I think a break here is appropriate," said Kate. "We all need a rest. Darren, can you find us a protected place to rest? I'll help Neck to his feet."

Darren glared at Cappucco's Nike Air Starbursts for a long second, grumbled his agreement, and headed downhill to inspect a small depression where the fir and juniper forest gave way to a large clearing. His own toes were mangled and three toenails were already blackened by dry blood at their roots. His left heel carried a blister the size of a golf ball. The Teva sandals offered his feet about fifty percent of the protection Cappucco's sneakers would have given him, yet the kid was still bitching.

But maybe he was just being too hard on Cappucco, letting his own pain color his view of the kid. He needed to focus on helping his wife and Cappucco, not make it harder on the boy. After all, for an adventure-racing virgin he had showed extraordinary strength. *Long way to go, though, young stud.*

The depression was a perfect rest stop. Thanks to a thick ring of thorny scrub that encircled the shallow hole, it provided them concealment, a mental rest from the helicopters that had been buzzing all morning. Darren watched a bumblebee hover next to one of the hundreds of white orchids on the bush. He considered eating it, but could not remember whether it had a stinger.

Neck crunched through the bushes and sat back hard against a root. He struggled to pull the sneakers from his feet, but they were turgid with blood from the walk. He eventually popped his left shoe off, but his right leg refused to bend.

Kate noticed Neck's knee for the first time. It was as large as a grapefruit. "Looks like you have some fluid in your knee. That happens when your kneecap rubs . . ."

"I know what it is. There's a pouch of fluid between the kneecap and the skin to give it some padding, and all this rubbing has irritated it." Neck could not explain the difference between a mammal and an amphibian, but he understood the intricate details of sports medicine related to his body. "Now there's some bloody water that's flooding my bursa sac. It's called patellar bursitis or housemaid's knee, but the team calls it slave's knee 'cause it can happen if you're on your knees a bunch. Defensive lineman get Slave's. No offense, Darren, it was the brothers who came up with it in the first place."

Darren heard his name and looked at Neck blankly before setting his head back onto a pillow of vines he had fluffed up. What the hell did slavery have to do with him? He was a United States Marine major from Harvard. Do bee wings have protein? Is a bumblebee hairy?

"We may have to drain it," Kate said. "It's just normal wear and tear."

"Normal? None of this shit here is normal. I don't see your knees swollen."

"Your muscles are stronger than ours, but they haven't been trained for slow twitch work and your tendons are not used to the constant stress. No matter how strong your muscles, your tendons still have to connect them to bone, and they're stressed."

"Yeah, the tendon is a softer tissue. Harder to build up."

"That's right. But your muscles are your engines. You'll be fine." She pulled the shoe off as gently as she could, and a stream of blood drained past the ankle pad and turned a limestone dark purple. When she stripped off his sock, Kate winced at the odor and laughed. "Smells like something died in here, Neck. Wow, that's one hell of a blister! I think Darren has a rival. I'm going to have to pop that."

Darren tossed the pack and Kate retrieved the broken Corona bottle, grabbed Neck's foot, and stabbed a thin jag into the blood blister. In her experience, it was best not to debate such hasty field operations. A popped blister was excruciating at first, but far better in the long run. Or walk.

Neck wore a grave face. He's in his first serious valley, she thought. The inward focus was natural and, in this case, beneficial. He's hurting so much I bet he doesn't know who he's running from, she thought. Indeed, she was so tired that the phantom pursuers were secondary.

"Look, Kate, I'm supposed to be drafted in a month. And I'm losing all this fucking weight and my knee is stiff as hell. I have a scouting combine in *two weeks.* I'm trying not to give myself all these props and shit but, like, in a year you will know who Neck Cappucco is, and everything. My agent says I should be able to get an action figure of me, too. Know what I'm sayin'? Darren, you down, bro?"

Down? thought Darren. What the hell is that and why the hell is he asking me? He equated slang with laziness. Worse, he equated ghetto babble with weakness and sadness, and could not understand how a college kid from the Jersey suburbs had embraced it while others were trying to erase it.

Now he remembered the slave's knee comment and realized that Neck Cappucco felt badly for *him* because he was *black.* It was almost as infuriating as Belafonte's empty-headed comments about Colin Powell. Moron. Colin did not want to enter the intrarace war but I will someday, Darren thought, and I'll wipe the notion of "authentic black" from the earth. Victimology and anti-intellectualism is killing us.

"No, Neck, I do not understand you."

Neck considered giving up right there. Staying back and taking his chances with the authorities. He didn't do anything wrong, so why was he jeopardizing his career?

Then he remembered his friends, especially the way Tom Hershenson had died. It seemed so long ago, like another person's life. He exhaled and his face, which had tightened, expanded again. "I guess I'm just tired, is all. We're about a hundred miles down, right?"

Kate shot Darren a glance—you had to balance news of navigational progress in delicate concert with the team's psyche during long races, stretching the truth, using fictional miles as both carrots and sticks. Neck needed a carrot. "More," she said. "About forty miles driving and we've humped probably seventy-five miles."

"Wow. Over halfway to Mexico City, huh? You both think I'm soft, don't you? I know he does." Neck pointed at Darren accusatorily. "Well, I'm not. Pop my knee, Kate. Drain it so we can get going again."

She didn't even hesitate, raising the bloody Corona shard by its neck. He reached for something—anything—to take his mind off the dripping bottle. Look at her legs, he thought, staring at the stringy muscles barely corralled by her sweaty skin, oozing strength but yet, somehow, feminine and wondrous, the length of them lined with white streaks of dried salt, which seemed to flow down from her shorts, a hidden . . .

"Oowww," he hissed, fiercely clenching the ground. "Fuck *me.*"

Kate dropped the bottle and grabbed his knee around the slit, squeezing bloody pulp out like juice from an orange until her fingers could feel the kneecap again.

Watching him, Darren felt guilty that he had called Cappucco out the night before. He *was* tough. More than that, Darren was ashamed that he had lost his cool; it violated his belief that he was consummately even keeled. Tact was a Marine Corps leadership trait, after all.

When the boy thanked his wife, Darren said, "Thanks for driving on, Neck. You'll make a good wife for somebody someday." It was as close to an apology as he could come.

Cappucco looked at him and nodded. "And you make a good wife for someone right now. Right, Kate?" "Frappuccino" had hit Cappucco hard, and for the previous seven hours he could think of nothing else.

She blushed and laughed. "Yeah. I'm still trying to teach him how I like my shirts ironed, though. Now before we charge on, I suggest a nap. Watch what a difference it makes."

———

Darren turned the beeping Oakley Explorer watch off forty minutes later. During the Eco-Challenge, he was the lightest sleeper and when Kate called for rest the four team watches were strapped together in a bundle and placed next to his ear, all the alarms synchronized. Without Darren, the exhausted teams would have slept for twenty hours. Of course, no one was trying to kill you in the Eco-Challenge—Darren had not slept.

Five minutes later they were on their feet, jumping up and down to extinguish the fires that had ignited when the blood poured back into their sore muscles, fighting the lactic acid for space.

"Feels like summer two-a-days," said Neck. "Let's find some grub." Kate was right, he thought, I'm my old me again! Neck Cappucco—train wrecker! *I just needed a little sleep.* He felt impossibly stiff but also impossibly rested. He noticed Darren struggling to get his right arm into a shoulder strap of the pack, so he limped forward to help. He felt as if he were walking on coals. Actually, he had done that on a dare when he was in Hawaii watching the Pro Bowl and this was much worse.

"Turn around."

"What for?" asked Darren, who was bent double, facing him.

"I'm not gonna fuck you in the ass, dude, so relax. This isn't the Marine Corps."

Kate and Neck giggled but Darren did not. Didn't even fake it. He had taken a thorn under the nail of his big toe hours ago and now it was throbbing horribly. He bit his lip. *Boom . . . Boom . . . BOOM* as the blood filled his feet and electrified them, amping up with each heartbeat.

A dog barked and the three of them went to ground. Another bark, Darren with a finger to his lips, raising the submachine gun and flicking the safety to single shot. *Only three bullets left.* He crawled to the edge of the depression and peered through the dense brush. A sheepdog was sniffing and growling right on the other side of the scrub. A hundred meters behind it, a man on a horse was ambling cautiously up the arroyo. No, Darren realized, he's just a boy, about fifteen years old, wearing a cowboy hat and blue jeans. *That's a rifle in his scabbard.*

The dog smelled Darren's rank scent and barked furiously, a machine-gun rattle of warning, inching closer, sticking his head into the shrub now. He was mangy and had streaks of yellow in his dark coat. The boy called for his dog and the canine's ears stood erect. It twisted its head toward its owner, then continued the alarm.

"Got a boy on a horse back there behind it," Darren whispered. "He's got a gun."

"Anyone else?" asked Neck.

Behind the boy, Darren could see nothing but oak trees and overgrown bushes. He was coming up a dry riverbed and the horse was kicking stones as it hoofed the sand. "Negative. Just him."

The dog found an opening in the brush and squeezed down on its elbows, squiggled forward, and stopped at the lip of the hole. It yelped wildly when it finally sourced the smell.

Darren lunged forward, snatched the animal by the scruff of its neck, and yanked it into the hole. It twisted violently and shook loose of his grasp, running back toward the circle of brush. But Neck was too fast. The football player snared a leg, hefted the small dog over his head, and slammed it down onto a rock. It was lifeless when he wiped his hands.

"He's coming back," whispered Kate, who had moved up to the brush. "He's still calling, but . . . he really *is* a boy. Don't hurt him, Darren."

Me? thought Darren. He's got a weapon, too.

"Think he'll give us food?" gasped Neck, the dead dog at his feet. He figured it'd be okay if they cooked it. Hell, the Japanese ate dogs like it was cool. *Wait . . . did he say the boy had a gun?* Neck dropped to his stomach and scrambled behind the couple. A bullet hole could take several weeks to heal.

Kate saw her husband's hands on the gun, saw the face that had scared her so badly in the police station, the same underlying message it always wore, but heightened and dangerous now. Altered ever so slightly. She had noticed the determination on his face from the moment she first saw it four years before, but now there was *something else* that had bubbled up and colored his look, a wildness that she couldn't quite interpret. Is he *enjoying* this? she wondered. *Does he like violence and war?*

"I'm going to do what I have to do," was all he told her.

– 29 –

SIERRA MADRE DEL SUR, MEXICO

Pedro Cruz watched his dog bound over to the thicket and for a moment his heart raced. Stop it, he commanded himself, embarrassed that he had let the stupid dog scare him again. *Los Asesinos* are *not* hiding in the bushes. The dog is just chasing another rabbit. I did not know I had a daughter, is what father would say, look at her sweat.

Pedro was thankful his father let him hunt for *Los Asesinos* alone, otherwise he'd be ashamed. Twice before on hunting trips, he'd crept up behind his barking dog, safety on the 20-gauge clicking back and forth, using the skills his father had taught him, circling downwind and trying to flush the birds into open ground. He wasn't hunting grouse this time. He was hunting people! And not just any old stupid people. He was hunting *Los Asesinos,* the most ruthless murderers Mexico had ever known, for *ten million pesos!* After he bought his parents a new house in Oaxaca, he would buy himself a fine pony and a new shotgun— maybe even a 12-gauge. The kind that had hurt his shoulder. His *father* used a 12-gauge and so would Mexico's finest bounty hunter.

Pedro had asked for permission at dinner, after he heard the state radio broadcast. His mother hadn't wanted him to go alone, but his father said, "Nonsense, boy's fourteen years old. He's ready for an adventure, aren't you, Pedro? I tell you, Mother, *Los Asesinos* may have escaped the *Federales* but they do not have a chance against our son, do they, Pedro?" Then his father had laughed and clapped him on the shoulder. It was wonderful.

After he had excused himself to pack and rest—Pedro wanted a good sleep for his holy quest—he heard his parents arguing and it angered him. Not the hoarse whispers but the argument itself, his father's words: Relax, Maria, he's not going to find *anybody* out there, they've just been in Acapulco and they're heading *north* for Mexico City, and even if they *were* to come this far south, they'd take three days to get here, so if it makes you feel better we'll have him home by five."

When his mother came to kiss him good night she had packed three days' rations—just in case, she told him—and when she leaned over him, he saw her eyes glinting. "Don't worry, Mom," he said, "when I catch them I'm buying you a house. Nothing is going to happen to me."

Pedro called for his stupid dog once more and turned Tumbleweed around, heading back home to the horse pen. That dumb dog's good around the cows and horses, he thought, but it *sucks* as a hunting dog. Now maybe he'll learn his lesson when Tumbleweed and I leave him.

But Pedro didn't have the stomach to leave his favorite dog. He soon glanced back to check if it was following. He saw it burrowing into the thicket after the rabbit; then it just vanished. His dog disappeared as if sucked into an invisible vacuum cleaner. Gone! He heard a howl, then a terrible crunch. Did he capture a rabbit?

Pedro licked his lips and steadied Tumbleweed, fighting the urge to reach for his shotgun. He called his dog again and his voice cracked. Tumbleweed whinnied and Pedro stroked his long neck. "Shhh, boy," he said. "Shhhhhh." Pedro listened, but there was nothing but Tumbleweed's hooves scraping across the pebbles and the low brush. He could feel Tumbleweed's muscles rippling anxiously beneath his hand. He wanted to ride away right then—gallop home with a story about *Los Asesinos*—but his father could spot a lie and he would be whipped for leaving the stupid dog.

Pedro trotted Tumbleweed up to a cluster of desert pine trees and tied him loosely—he might need a quick getaway. He pulled the shotgun from the scabbard and crept forward, trying to get an angle where he could see into the small thicket, toes testing the ground for careful sole placement, just like his father had taught him, silent, moving upwind and keeping his distance, eyes straining at the few pieces of light that managed to penetrate the patch of brush, thumb clicking the safety off, breathing tempo increasing, muscles taut and rigid. *If this is another rabbit, I'm going to* kill *that stupid dog.*

Pedro moved toward the scrub after a five-minute wait, when fear of his imagination finally overwhelmed his fear of the thicket. He brought the shotgun up to his shoulder and the barrel moved with his eyes. He kicked one of the bushes to roust his dog, but still only the silence and his breathing. He saw a glint—almost metallic—and as he swung the shotgun, a firecracker exploded and his gun was gone.

His hands stung worse than the time his father made him bat fastballs without gloves. Blood squirted out of his hand as he sprinted toward Tumbleweed, something horrible crashing through the thicket behind him. Chasing him. As big as a bear. *It wants to eat me!*

When he reached Tumbleweed, Pedro glanced back and saw that it *was* a bear—no, wait, a big black man with a machine gun. One of *Los Asesinos!* Pedro grabbed his pommel and realized he was missing a finger. Blood was shooting out of the ragged stub with every beat of his heart, over three times a second. His horse whinnied and reared back. Pedro dug his heels into Tumbleweed's sides and screamed, wheeling him around with a savage tug on the right rein.

Tumbleweed's big head slammed into the black bear and knocked him down. He fell into the streambed trying to catch his breath. A blond man appeared as Pedro started forward—*the captive boy from the American football team wants me to rescue him!* He yanked back on Tumbleweed's reins, screaming, "*Subida encendido!*"

The blond man looked angry. *He's trying to kill me, too!* Pedro pulled himself flat to his big horse's back and yanked him right, steering Tumbleweed like a rocket, kicking his horse into a gallop, streaking for a clearing. Tumbleweed's eyeball burst all over him before he heard the first bullet, but the second one slammed into his horse's head. He heard a whip crack when it shattered the horse's skull. Tumbleweed just dropped out from under him and he was flying, his arms pinwheeling just before he skidded into the gravel. Then the black bear's hand was on him, clawing up his back to his neck.

Pedro spun and tried to bite the man, but his forearm was so big he could not get his teeth around it properly. It felt like an oak log. He felt the man's thumb in his neck, pushing harder as he struggled to breathe, then he felt fuzzy and warm and sleepy.

Kate soothed the boy so Darren could finish the knot. "You shot his finger off," she said. She stroked his thick hair and whispered to him. The boy was crying softly.

"I was aiming for the shotgun and at the last moment he shifted it."

"That was nice shooting, Darren," breathed Neck. "Killed that fucking horse *dead*, dude. Otherwise he was gettin' away. Getting away with this gold mine, dude." He held up the saddlebag and set the food items side by side on a rock. A tall stack of corn tortillas, a kilogram of beef jerky, four steak sandwiches, a gallon plastic bag filled with a thick mixture of Spanish rice and chicken, five oranges, four cans of dog food, three mangos, and three papayas. "Little man's got a appetite. We ain't gonna kill him, are we?"

Darren finished tying the boy's wrists together behind his back, a thin strip of rawhide holding them in place connected to a noose around the boy's neck. "No. I'll take a bullet before I kill a boy."

Neck said, "Can we eat? I got cramps like . . . I don't know. Like a Somalian."

"A Somalian?" asked Darren.

"Yeah, dude. They're, like, starving their asses off. You been there?"

"Yes."

"That's real, yo."

Darren did not like Neck's vernacular, but in this case it seemed to fit. "Yes. It's real." He stared at the food. His relentless hunger came from somewhere deep inside, a fractious want that he wrestled with. But his wife was still whispering to the Mexican boy and he would not eat before she did, a habit he formed in the Marines where the officers ate last. He would wait until she finished her questions, even while Cappucco chomped happily on a steak sandwich.

When she was five minutes into her interrogation, Neck's big head jerked up. "*What?!* You hear what he said, Kate? Everyone thinks you two took me hostage! That you two executed Eric and Jimmy outside the station!"

"You speak Spanish, Neck? Why didn't you say anything?" Kate asked.

"Yeah. Pretty good, actually. You were getting on with him so well I figured I wouldn't interrupt, see what I'm sayin'?" Neck felt guilty. The truth was that he had wanted to eat so badly that he kept quiet to avoid interpretation duty.

Kate looked at Darren. "The television is saying we killed Neck's friends. They say we're holding Neck hostage. They say we've killed over *twenty* people, Darren, and they're offering a huge reward. They call us 'The Assassins.' "

Darren shrugged. It was not a bad nickname, all in all. As for the wild story, well, propaganda was a part of warfare. Witness his father's Vietnam: The press eagerly gobbled up the nonsense the North Viets spewed. "Yeah, well, get some chow and we can discuss what to do about him."

She shook her head. "They've got all the roads to Mexico City staked out. Roadblocks everywhere."

"Did they release the photographs?"

"Yes. Pedro here said his parents sent him out of the room when the naked shots came out, even though they blacked us out."

"Great. And my back?"

"*Yes.* The message was released, too. Pedro says he thinks we're on drugs."

Darren pumped his fist. "We need to hide the horse and tie the boy up. Someone will come along to pick him up. No need for the submachine gun now that I'm out of bullets, and this shotgun's ruined." He picked up the broken

20-gauge and tossed it in the bushes. "We need to get moving. Kelly will be on his way."

"Who's Kelly?" Neck managed to sneak past the steak and bread. A trickle of juice ran down his chin and he caught it with his finger and swathed his tongue with it.

"Darren, Pedro says he's more than a full day's walk from his home. Maybe we can just let him go. Walk home, I mean," said Kate.

"Nope." He looked down and the boy turned his head. "Tell you what, I'll tie him to a tree next to that stream—so he can drink—and I'll keep it so that he can escape after a few hours if he gets desperate. Walk from there."

"Kelly the guy who's gonna pick us up in Mexico City?" asked Neck.

"If we get there."

"How do you know he got the message, dude?"

"Well, I know the guy pretty well."

Kate pulled out the satellite phone. "We should try a call, even if it means using some batteries. Maybe Kelly's answering machine? Or your mom? If this is a satellite phone, it might work out here."

She dialed Darren's mother's phone number and waited for the connection. After a few seconds, she heard a *click* and the phone began to ring. Then the connection was lost.

"Shit. I got disconnected, just like last time. Should I try again?"

Darren shook his head. "Like I said, we need to wait until we're close to a city. A satellite feed drains the battery and it's probably trying to switch to land relays. We need to get a move on. And, Cappucco, save some of that chow for us, young stud, or you pop your own blisters next time."

– 30 –

ZAMPEDRO ARMY BASE, MEXICO

Felix was taking a brush to Sniff-Sniff's fine coat when the lieutenant jogged over to him. "We've got them! Just got the location of *Los Asesinos,* about a thirty-minute flight. My men are already moving to the helicopter. Have you seen the Indian?"

"Not since breakfast. He's probably behind the barracks throwing his knives. That or looking at the nudie pictures of the woman again. I'll see you at the helicopter."

Felix clucked his tongue—he viewed the whistle as a classless signal—and Sniff-Sniff followed him over to his bunk, the dog's manicured nails clicking across the tiled floor of the hangar. He grabbed his well-provisioned pack and stuck *Los Asesinos'* towels into his hound's nose again, not that his pride and joy would need any help tracking a couple of sweaty, stinking gringos. Hell, *he* could probably find their trail alone, assuming the *comandante*'s assertion about finding their exact location was correct. He slung the pack over his shoulder and grabbed his weapon—a .30-06 hunting rifle with which he had once plugged a bighorn sheep from 900 meters.

Felix and Sniff-Sniff dashed across the tarmac toward the waiting helicopter where the brash young sergeant helped them into the troop hold. Pebbles washed across Felix's chest as he hefted his forty-kilogram canine inside. Sniff-Sniff ambled into a corner, circled once, and sat down. The lieutenant remained standing outside the bird in a hunch, scanning the compound.

"Any sign of the freak who's running the show?" Sergeant Pena screamed over the rotor wash, his eyes darting around. "The lieutenant is getting nervous. Not that that's anything new."

"Haven't seen him, son!" yelled Felix, strapping into a seat.

"You're packed for war! This is as heavy as mine is! Between us—us four soldiers and you and your dog, I mean—we don't need that little Indian grease-ball anyhow! I say we leave without him! *Los Asesinos* are getting a head start as we speak!"

The lieutenant overheard and shook his head dismissively, still bent over as if the rotor might chop off his head. He pointed toward the hangar and swung himself up into the Huey. "Here he comes now."

Sergeant Pena looked out the cargo door and saw *El Monstruo Carnicero* walking casually across the tarmac, dressed in white running sneakers, black pants that were too tight and outlined the man's stick legs, and, what, a *silk* shirt?! *Pussy.*

Then Pena saw the handle of a machete flushing on either side of the man's slick hair as he walked. Saw a wide leather belt with a few knives that caught the sun and turned them sparkling white. But where was his pack? What about water and food and spare clothes? After all, *Los Asesinos* would be in the high mountains soon, where the temperature varied by twenty degrees Celsius! Pena unveiled all of his observations for his lieutenant and then crawled across his *compañeros* so he could be seated as far away from the freak as possible. "He ain't drinking my water," he mumbled to no one in particular.

When *El Monstruo Carnicero* hopped into the Huey, it began to vibrate as it powered up. The men in its belly felt the charge of anticipation as they leaned into the bulkhead and meshed with the machine.

"Siir," said the lieutenant, "Arrre you ssuure you have pacckked enoughh?"

The Indian ran his fingers through his hair, then grasped his skinny beard and stroked it from his chin to where it ended ten centimeters later. He unbuttoned his breast pocket and snatched the photographs, buttoning it just as quickly and smoothing his shirt. The lieutenant marveled at how quickly and deftly he had managed it, almost as if the man was showing off his hand speed, like a card trick.

"I told you not to talk to me," the Indian said simply. He smiled wide. His teeth were very white and his lips, when they stretched taut, were sinewy and ruddy. The lieutenant turned his head and focused on his M-16. The Indian made him uncomfortable.

El Monstruo Carnicero went back to his pictures, worried that imagined details of the sacrifice might bring him bad luck. Huitzilopochtli deserved a surprise. But it was hard not to look at the girl Kate North. He controlled his breathing so as not to fog the Polaroids and delved into the honeymoon shots, *soaked* in her tan lines, the curves and such a bad, bad girl, aren't you, with those little smiles and that head thrown back and your wild hair and biting that little lip. I'll show you how to bite a lip!

El Monstruo Carnicero's head began to buzz again, and it was a struggle not to stand and scream out, or dance and punch the air, or reach for a blade and slice one of the men sitting across from him, just to see what would happen. He looked at the sergeant with the loud mouth and thought about filleting the mutt's throat with Barracuda.

El Monstruo Carnicero sighed and flipped to the next shot. This one made him angry, what with the black man in it, looking back at him. He studied the man's body again and decided that he'd have to kill him slowly to show him what real power was, maybe even laugh when he carved him up. The man so proud of himself, so vain with his big muscles, flexing them on purpose. Better yet, he'd love to take the girl Kate North and play with her in front of this man.

No, *El Monstruo Carnicero* decided. Better to kill the man first and be sure about it. He was a soldier and probably could fight well. It will be fun. *El Monstruo Carnicero* wanted his time with the girl Kate North to be his alone. He wanted to be able to concentrate solely on his bounty while he watched her last hours play out.

Alone with the girl Kate North.

– 31 –

MCLEAN, VIRGINIA

Susanne Sheridan wanted to go home and sleep, but she still had an intelligence center to run, her sense of duty holding a fading lead in a race against creeping professional devastation. George Henry had made it quite clear: She had encouraged the president to go out on a limb, it broke with a crack heard around the world, and the president would not be the only one with his face smudged. It wasn't personal, he told her, but risks carry penalties as well as rewards.

Henry hadn't relieved her of command because she did not officially work for him. But it was a matter of hours. Henry had arranged for an emergency meeting with the director of Central Intelligence—when DCI touched down at Langley Air Force Base that night from his visit to the West Bank, she and Henry would be waiting in a hangar conference room. All those years spent undercover in the world's shit-holes working two jobs—most often as a State Department wonk during the day before transforming into a case officer at night—and for what? A failed marriage and two children who joked that their childhoods had been robbed.

She looked around the Bat Cave. The image of Philips's back glowed on the digital theater screen and seemed to be squelching the normal energy of the place. Word had leaked ahead of her arrival—no doubt originating at Corwin and distributed by the snitch—and the only sounds she heard were clicks of keyboard keys being tapped and the relentless hum of the computer banks. She caught Jimmy Contreras staring at her, but he was quick to turn his head before she made eye contact. Here I sit, she thought, lame-duck leader of a lame-duck organization.

Her deputy, Christian Collins, broke the silence for her. "Ma'am, I enlarged the images if you want to take a closer look. They look suspicious."

Good old Christian, she thought, always one to kick the tires. DHS would never have to worry about Christian taking a risk or speaking out of turn. "FBI has this case now. Or didn't you get that word?"

"Yes, ma'am, Agent Contreras told us."

Susanne glanced at Contreras again, but he was typing.

"Ma'am, I think I want to raise the possibility that the Mexican government set this up," said Collins. "I'm just saying it's a possibility."

"Well, there's conviction for you, gentlemen," she said, immediately regretting it. She was just trying to toughen Christian up.

Ted Blinky chuckled. Both of them had blood in the water but he couldn't exactly pile on the deputy director. She had rank—for now—so he chose the dot-com superhero. "Absurd and illogical. That photograph has to be genuine."

Susanne shot Blinky a sinister look, but she should have thanked the Science and Technology analyst. She had been looking for a means to reassert control, and now Blinky was handing her the conch. "One moment alone please, Mister Blinky."

She walked over to the two Cray computers with Blinky and started whispering. Blinky pulled on his big earlobe as a signal he could not hear, further grating her. There were long stands of white hair growing from his ear that she had the urge to pluck. Slowly.

"Mister Blinky, I am allowing you, a technology analyst, the luxury of spoken expression so that you feel you are part of the intelligence team. That's the second time you've been condescending to Christian in public and there will not be a third. Violate the social contract again and your only form of interpersonal communication will come on a chat-room screen."

What a hypocrite, Ted Blinky thought. She condescended all the time, albeit with a Cheshire cat's smile. If he had tits he might be able to get away with it, too.

"I want to clarify, ma'am," said Christian Collins when the two returned to the screen. He was both embarrassed and elated that his boss had slapped Blinky's pee-pee. "The photograph is likely real. Way too risky for their government to set it up knowing it will be scrutinized the world over. But after having researched and written the quick profiles of the couple, I do not believe they were in any way involved in a drug deal."

"Welcome to the club. Unfortunately, we're already on double secret probation."

"Yes, but see those irregularities in the writing?" Christian said after the laugh died down. "Plus, look at his arm."

Everyone in the Cave turned and studied the message.

GOD FORGIVE US!
ONLY WANTED TO BUY COKE.
WE GO MEX CITY
FOR A FAIR TRIAL!

"The Mexican government may have killed them already," Christian continued. "Maybe they put the lotion on Phillips's corpse and snapped the picture. Or they forced them to take the picture at gunpoint, then killed them. See these puncture wounds on his arm, here?" He pulled out a laser pointer and shined it on Phillips's left forearm, making small circles around several tiny puncture wounds as a means to cover his unsteady hand. "I think these cuts on his forearm are signs of torture."

Susanne did not agree, but just listening to the young man deliberate gave her a boost. Maybe she was not crazy after all. "Can we enlarge those please, Mister Blinky?"

Now the forearm filled the screen like a giant black baseball bat, veins running its length like ridges in wood. Several bright red holes were visible. "Wow. Good catch," Susanne said, taking the pointer. "I wouldn't say torture, though. It's symmetrical, almost like a bite mark. Two punctures . . . there and there . . . then smaller nicks in that crescent shape. I'd guess it's a dog bite. Implications?"

"If they were caught by dogs and tortured, then these two are likely dead and the satellite phone has been recovered, ma'am. They'll probably present the bodies in a day or so—maybe even tonight—after a fake gun battle in the mountains."

"Good, but I don't believe it," said Susanne. "This here is the real deal, folks. If we are to believe the good Deputy Attorney General Saiz . . ."

"Don't," Jimmy Contreras interrupted. He was standing behind her now with his interest piqued but did not add anything else.

"Either way, not only did these two have a great tumble in the sack—I assume all you boys feasted on those photos before I got back here—but they rolled around with some attack dogs, too. My, what a honeymoon."

"You're saying Phillips willingly wrote this, ma'am," said Christian before the silence got awkward. His boss had a bawdy wit that made some uncomfortable, including himself. Best to keep things moving. "That may explain the irregularities in the writing."

"What irregularities?" Susanne asked.

Christian reached for another laser pointer. His hand trembled so he flickered the red dot around wildly. "Can we pan back up to the message and enlarge the 'G'?"

G

"Again, please."

"See these little jags in the lettering?" Christian asked. "There are little tick marks on either side of the letters. Little slashes that look like wires."

Susanne walked right up close to the screen. The letters looked like they had sprouted hairs. *My God, it's so obvious.* She spun around and boomed, "If we can read this, then anyone with a computer screen can. Which is exactly what Darren Phillips must want. Christian, call our media liaison officer and see if he can cap this story for a few hours. Dozens of reporters will already have seen this. Who knows Morse code?"

Jimmy Contreras stepped forward.

———

An hour later, a jumble of letters appeared on the theater screen. Contreras had deciphered the Morse in fifteen minutes, but further progress had proved elusive.

"What's the status from encryption?" asked Susanne.

Ted Blinky said, "They're not hopeful, ma'am. It's a crude code but it's quite effective. Phillips never repeats an instruction, so we can't nail down any letters. Encryption is attempting to crack the message in reverse, churning it through the mainframe with locations in Mexico and dates, but Phillips was smart enough to skip around to throw us. Plus, I think he's sprinkled in bogus letters."

"Our best bet is finding this Gavin Kelly that the message is meant for, ma'am," Christian Collins chimed in. "That's who 'GK' is. He's the key to the whole thing."

"Why Kelly?" Susanne asked.

Christian shrugged. "He's his best friend. Presumably only he understands the reference. They were in the Marines together. They were roommates. I still have the brief I typed up yesterday. It's not complete . . ."

"Put it up."

Name: Gavin Kelly   **Ht./Wt.:** 6'2"/200 lbs.

DOB: 29 October, 1968   **Ethnicity:** Caucasian

Home: Cambridge, MA   **Edu:** Harvard, B.A., 1990. Harvard M.B.A. (current)

NOK: Tom and Alexandra Kelly

Prof: Marine infantry officer in Desert Storm and Restore Hope. In Somalia, Kelly covered up a murder committed by one of his men and was court-martialed. Served a five-year term in The Hague. Currently a business student.

Pers: Involved in two serious firefights—one in Somalia, one in Kuwait—that were used as positive character references by his defense attorney. Marine fitness reports describe him as having "unlimited potential that he periodically jeopardizes," and "needs to work on discipline to become a 'whole Marine officer.' "

"When were these pictures broadcast by Mexico?" Jimmy Contreras asked.

"Two hours ago, sir," said Christian Collins.

"This thing'll spread like the Santa Anas. Where's Kelly now?"

"I guess he's at Harvard, sir, if you can believe it."

"No. I mean, what's his address?" Contreras was agitated, checking his watch and then his cell phone. "Well?"

"I . . . don't know, sir," said Collins.

Contreras walked over to his desk, snatched his coat and his gym bag, and headed toward the exit. Susanne had to half run to intercept him. She grabbed him roughly by the crook of his arm and spun him. "Where are you going? Let's crack this thing."

He sighed and whispered, "I'm sorry, but I'll be honest with you. I'm informing Corwin so he can put in a request for FBI surveillance. Kelly is the key and when he figures this message he'll be gone. I need to be part of the snatch team."

"When did this happen?"

"What?"

"You and Corwin as fuck buddies, that's what."

Contreras was struck by her vehemence. He had written off Sheridan's relentless sense of humor as insecurity, a forced means by which she could relate to all the men who surrounded her. By feigning a cool mask of nonchalance, she had garnered the reputation of being cool under fire. This was the first time he had seen her really angry and it put him off. Worse, she was questioning his loyalty, the very propellant that drove him.

"He called me an hour ago and offered a give-and-take," he said. The fact Dodger Corwin had the key to *El Monstruo Carnicero* sickened him, but there was no other way now. "He's worried no information from the Cave will reach him. Look, we have to inform FBI anyway. You said it yourself. This allows me to get what I need, too."

"What you need? A lesson in these two words, Jimmy: semper fidelis."

His head tingled and the muscles in his sunken cheeks went rigid. If the Bat Cave door was not made of reinforced steel he would have smashed it with his fist. He expected her to turn away on so personal a dig, but she stood full force in the confrontation. Her hair was still pulled back in a tight bun—he remembered he had awoken her at three in the morning and she probably had not considered it since—giving her a severe but attractive look. Now Contreras was surprised to feel guilty for having let her down.

"I'm no good at this political bullshit, so let me break it down for you," Contreras said. "He's in, you're out, and I need to get to Mexico one way or another."

Susanne put her rigid finger an inch from his nose. "You're no good at politics, Jimmy, because you have let an obsession override your senses. You think Corwin is going to let you snare *El Monstruo Carnicero* in return for selling me out? *Please.*"

"I'm not selling you out. I'm getting mine."

"Then don't feed me a line about him contacting you an hour ago. You've been leaking to him the whole time, including the digital breakout we're working to track the Phillipses." Susanne toggled the exit interface on the titanium bar and opened the door to the Bat Cave so he could leave. "Good luck, Jimmy, and don't forget to write. You still work here, you know. I'll refer you to a good proctologist when you get back."

Contreras stormed out, but spun around before she was able to shut the door. He was strong enough to hold it open with one hand even as she leaned her body in. "I'll swallow most of that, Susanne, but what I said about communicating with Corwin is true. I ain't the snitch you're looking for. If it's not in your imagination, then your problem is still inside that door. Don't ever question my integrity again."

– 32 –

CAMBRIDGE, MASSACHUSETTS

Gavin Kelly left his undergraduate girlfriend's Eliot House room just after one o'clock. Noon classes had just finished and a group of women was giggling its way up the stone steps toward him. Their chatter fluttered all around the stairwell. He had hoped to avoid the youngsters. Crossing the minefields into Kuwait had been easier than infiltrating and exfiltrating from his girlfriend's hooch whenever she didn't feel like napping in his Central Square apartment. It was bad enough to be called a "cradle robber" by business school geeks, but the quizzical stares of coeds could make a guy feel downright guilty.

One of the women saw him standing on a landing and her silence was infectious. His reputation in the dorm was dual pronged—former felon turned graduate school predator—so he winked and continued down.

"You women need any tutoring in finance, you let me know, you hear?"

"As if," said one when he was safely outside.

He stepped out into the courtyard and stood there staring at his girlfriend's window to see what her surprise was going to be. She blew him a kiss and flashed her breasts, pressing them against her window. Kelly laughed, pulled up his T-shirt, and exposed his big hairy chest.

"That's pretty rude," said a woman walking past him with a pile of books. "Rude and indecent. That what they teach you across the river?" Kelly was pretty sure she was a grad student like him, a proctor from the law school getting free room and board in exchange for cracking the undergraduate whip.

"Naw. Over there they just teach us exploitation and malfeasance."

"Figures. Maybe one day they'll teach you how to get a life, asshole."

"Hey," he called after her. "That's hate speech. What's your student I.D. number?"

Another glorious afternoon at Harvard College!

Kelly took a final glance up at his girlfriend and waved. As a veteran of Marine Corps deployments—fleet Marines went overseas for six months every year and a half—Kelly knew that mission creep was often accompanied by another type of dull ache. He was elated when his girlfriend had insisted he swing by for a visit before his little vacation. *Ah, the sacrifices I make for you, Phillips.*

Kelly trotted up Holyoke Street and stepped up between the white pillars of the Owl Club front porch. When he stepped into the foyer, a tiny undergraduate named Nguyen Nguyen shouted his name and rushed over. Undergraduate members associated their notorious alumnus with free beer and reacted to his appearance like Pavlovian dogs.

"You're late, Gavin," said Nguyen.

"Sorry, Winster. Got no keg with me today. Just cash."

"Finished the Web site for you. Whaddaya need the I.D. for? Probably for your underage girlfriend, right, dude?" laughed Nguyen. He lifted his crimson crew T-shirt and coughed into it. Nguyen spent most of his time inside the club in a dank room he had converted into a technology incubator. It seemed to Kelly that he was sick all the time.

"You should get out more, Nguyen. You're pale for a Vietnamese."

"Yeah, well, I used to be tan until your old man dumped all that Agent Orange on my ass," Nguyen laughed, leading Kelly up the winding staircase below the photographs of the club's distinguished graduates. Phillips's picture hung there among the senators and actors, the youngest alumnus ever inducted. Nguyen pointed at it and said, "This is about Darren Phillips, isn't it?"

Kelly grabbed Nguyen around the neck and pushed him back against the stuffed snow owl. "I told you to keep this between you and me. Now shut it down, stud, or you'll be doing me and mine a massive disservice."

Kelly feigned anger as Nguyen continued his trudge upstairs, but in truth he felt sanguine and relaxed. Part of being a Marine officer was acting angry. He could turn it on when he had to, but he did not take small failures of other people personally. That required an element of self-righteousness and while his Marine Corps roommate Darren Phillips had it, Kelly was far too conflicted and far too fearful of hypocrisy to really dish out a convincing ass-chewing.

At the third floor Kelly pulled a wad of one-hundred-dollar bills as thick as an ice cream sandwich out of his jeans pocket. His entire savings account—$23,800, including the ten grand from the student loan with which he was supposed to pay spring tuition in a few days—was stashed between his pockets and a waist belt, starched packets he had withdrawn that morning in preparation for the adventure. With the new identification the Winster would provide him, Kelly only needed to find weapons and he was cleared hot for Mexico. Assuming the phone call from Phillips came, that is. Kelly figured the odds were it'd come from jail, but he hoped it might originate from some village in the middle of an escape and evasion.

When Kelly walked into the bootstrapped graphic design studio, Nguyen was sitting behind a blue iMac plopped on some faded red milk crates. Behind him, there was a six-megapixel professional digital camera on a tripod. Behind that there was a poster of Anna Kournikova in a Catholic schoolgirl's uniform. She carried a dripping red lollipop.

Kelly pointed at the poster. "I don't want to know what goes on between you and her in your mind, Winster."

"Don't need imagination, Gavin. They got her head superimposed in porn movies now. Wanna check it out before we start? I hacked an adult passkey for free."

Kelly knew better than to go head-to-head with a twenty-year-old on anything to do with sex. The thought of Nguyen in his den alone with the Internet made him cringe. "God no. Just set me up with that I.D."

Nguyen pointed at a stool and positioned the camera. "I'm giving you a Texas driver's license. Your name's Harold Callahan, like you asked for. The Web site's done, too. Added all the text you gave me. Got pictures from spring break and everything. Look into the red light and smile pretty."

Kelly smiled at the flash. "What's it called?"

" 'Springbreaktexasadventures.com.' Sorry but 'springbreakadventures' was taken. Anyway, that's it. My normal fee is a hundred bucks, but since you bought us so much beer this year . . ."

"Nonsense, Winster," said Kelly, handing him a hundred. "Hell, I'm using all of you when I come calling with my kegs. My youth was robbed and I hate to drink alone." It was said in jest but it was true. The Hague had embedded a fear of being alone.

Nguyen had him put on some thick glasses that reminded Kelly of Marine Corps birth-control glasses. He ran the digital image through a heated lamination machine and tucked it into a white envelope. "We got to wait a few minutes for them to cool down or you'll mess up the holograms. So, my clients mostly want to drink or rent a car. Whaddaya want this for, Gavin?"

"Why do you keep a box of tissues and Vaseline in that milk crate, sports fan?" Kelly smiled. "Some things are better left unsaid."

Nguyen grimaced. "So what do you think about Darren Phillips's confession?"

"Confession? They caught him?"

"No. I mean that message on his back."

Kelly walked around behind the iMac and stood over Nguyen. "Show me. *Now.*"

"Okay, okay. Relax, dude. You're all red. It's creepy."

Nguyen's fingers nimbly crushed out a digital sentence and CNN.com appeared on the monitor. He pushed his cheap rolling chair back so Kelly could lean in. "See what I mean. Looks like . . ."

"Quiet, Winster. Can you enlarge the picture?"

Nguyen opened a photography application and placed his pointer on the photograph of Darren's back, enlarging and then refining the image so it was crisp.

Kelly was so intent he thought that he might miss something if he blinked. The message was written with finger paint. No, sunscreen. Either Phillips was dead already or it was a code. No way it was legit. Cocaine? Please. Phillips did not even drink. Hell, he had refused to pop ibuprofen in the Eco-Challenge when he cut his foot open.

Kelly concentrated on the words first. Failing to find anything, he said to Nguyen, "Winster, can you magnify a few of the letters?"

Nguyen exhaled as if he had been insulted. It took just two enlargements before they saw the small series of jags in each letter, some drawn left and some to the right, tiny lines no more than a quarter of an inch long radiating from the letters themselves, nearly imperceptible. The thin lines came in bunches of twos, threes, and fours.

"I need some time alone, Winster," said Kelly.

"Hey, man, this is my shop."

Kelly stood and lifted Nguyen and his chair in the air, walking him to the door like a bouncer. "Don't worry, Winster, I brought my own hand lotion."

Nguyen considered an argument, then remembered the computer in the library below. He could probably hack the message faster than Gavin himself. He walked out the door and bounced down the stairs.

Kelly locked the door and opened another Explorer window when he was seated behind the iMac. He navigated to the Google homepage and typed "Morse Code." Just like Phillips to actually *remember* the code, thought Kelly. *In the year 2003, the government's first Terminator got in trouble with the Mexicans.*

He started by assuming a left hash mark was a dash and a right jag a dot, but after ten letters he had translated:

LSHGUWSJHF

When Kelly tried the opposite interpretation his own initials came up first and his body jerked as if he had stuck his finger into a socket.

GKHELPUSEMTSTLASTNAME2D15U73U32U61D7 . . .

Kelly glanced up nervously to make sure no one was watching. He peered out the window and surveyed the street. It was an odd thing to do, he thought, but he was overcome by the power of a secret code. Phillips's message was being read by millions of eyes, but it had been sent specifically to *him*. With the paranoia came the sweet rush of adrenaline. *I'm back in the game.* He added slashes to separate the words.

GK/HELP/USE/MTST/LAST/NAME/2D1/5U7/3U3/2U6/1D7 . . .

Kelly stared at the four letters "MTST" for ten full minutes. Montana State? Motor Transport? Most? No, he thought, this simple Morse code will eventually be discovered by the entire world. How long ago did this picture go public? Probably a few hours. Hell, it's *already* been discovered. "MTST" is an acronym for my eyeballs alone, Kelly thought. Some secret we shared. *Think.*

"Mount Saint!" burst Kelly. The very mention of Helen whatshername was enough to get Phillips to raise his fists, knowledge Kelly gleefully leveraged as a form of entertainment. If the Crime Against Nature was not the worst skeleton in Phillips's closet, she was certainly the biggest.

Kelly struggled to think of the Mount Saint's last name and then remembered that she had worked in Orange County animal control. That's why Phillips bristled whenever he heard "lap" and "dog" used in the same sentence; Kelly had hit him with the label just before Phillips committed the Crime, when he curled up in Helen's lap on the lounge chair next to the pool table, just before she pressed his head into her bosom and lured him out of the bar. When he found her name online—Helen Stoyakavich—Kelly translated the code following Phillips's instructions in fewer than ten minutes, writing on his hand so he left neither a paper nor electronic trail.

They're not going to Mexico City, suckers, Kelly thought. *Good on you, Phillips.* He searched in Google for "Map of Mexico" and, finding the city to which Phillips had pointed him, typed "Brownsville, Texas, and charter boat." Before he spat into his palm, he read the message once more.

BEACH XTRCT FRI 0600 12 MI N OF VCRUZ

Kelly was jogging toward his apartment on Metz Street to get his packed duffel bag when he saw the burly blond man. He was sitting on the steps of his apartment building dressed in blue-and-red striped MC Hammer weight-lifting pants and a gray Harvard sweatshirt. Looking at him, Kelly understood just how out of place he himself must have looked in Somalia, a crocodile trying to blend with the swimmers in the pool. The man glanced at him, coughed harshly, then bent down to tie his sneaker.

"Good morning," he said to Kelly. He was wearing one of those Euro waist pouches that Kelly detested and had a Magnum P.I. mustache. Farther down the sidewalk, Kelly saw two men in suits carrying briefcases, odd, considering that Cambridge was filled with either techies or liberals, both of whom eschewed formal wear as a form of silent protest.

The jogger extended his hand. "I'm Roger Edwards. Just moved into the building."

"Phillip Glass," said Kelly quickly. "I actually don't live here, though. Visiting my girlfriend."

The man's mouth opened, and he suddenly stretched his hands over his head, an awkward movement that made Kelly uneasy. *A poor man's signal.* The two men in the suits stopped their approach and set their briefcases on the hood of a parked car. One was a Hispanic guy as tall as he was, about six-two, who pulled out a glossy sheet and studied it.

"You run often, Roger? I'm a member of the Hash House Harriers if you're interested."

"Every day, man."

Kelly didn't believe it. He was too bulky for a runner. "How far you going?"

"Just ten today."

Kelly glanced at the blond man's shoes. Nike Air Max IIs. Discontinued three years ago. Not a scratch on them. "Nice meeting you, Roger," he said, stepping into the foyer.

Kelly noticed but did not look at the two men standing at the top of the stairs by his apartment. He walked quickly to his landlady's residence down the main hall and rapped on the door. The woman cracked it open, then smiled at Kelly and welcomed him in.

Kelly jumped inside and shut the door as someone screamed, "That was him!"

"My God, what is it, Gavin?" his landlady asked.

Kelly locked the door and jammed a chair under the doorknob. "I caught a gang of men raping a woman on the landing, Mrs. Shea. They're posing as federal agents."

"Oh Lord!" she said, stumbling backward. Kelly grabbed her arm to keep her upright and escorted her to the kitchen.

"Listen, they have guns. You call the cops, I'm going back to help her. Whatever you do, don't open that door! They'll lie to get in here!"

Kelly pried the back kitchen window open and slithered out onto the patio. He sprinted for the wall in the backyard and climbed up, absorbing a wire barb with the palm of his hand when he flipped himself over. He landed on Brattle Street between two parked cars and duck-walked until a group of students stopped to stare—Kelly looked out of synch even to the most jaded eyes.

A Lincoln Town Car roared free of the curb and swerved out behind him, the only American car in a sea of Saabs. Kelly darted up a busy one-way road, thankful for the Volkswagen Bug that was coming toward him. He dodged it, but the Lincoln sedan did not. He heard the screech of brakes and a mild collision.

Kelly slowed to a jog and gathered his breath, then turned around and headed back parallel to the accident site on Foster Street, several blocks closer to the river. He was sure the Feds would radio his last direction of movement. Sure enough, he heard horns, but no sirens. Either the cops were late to the party or they had not been invited.

Kelly approached the Charles River at a brisk walk, trailing closely behind a group of rowers walking down JFK Street on their way to crew practice. He was almost past Kirkland House when he heard the *clip-clop* of dress shoes coming up fast behind him.

The Hispanic man in the suit was running downhill, pistol drawn and badge flopping around his chest, radio in one hand. "Gavin Kelly, this is the DEA! If you want your friend to live, you stop right there! Otherwise he's a dead man!"

Kelly sprinted down Memorial Drive and the tall man followed, yelling at him at first and then just resigned to the chase. The man was fast for his age and Kelly was forced to increase his pace. He's just a cop pushing fifty, Kelly thought. He'll tire.

Kelly raced along the Cambridge side of the river until he noticed a woman riding a silver mountain bike along the river path on the opposite side. He cut sharply up and over the bricks of Weeks footbridge, then sprinted downhill to intercept her.

"Stop! Stop right there!" Kelly shouted. "I'm a police officer!"

The woman shrieked and skidded to a halt. Kelly grabbed her handlebars and she screamed, "Somebody help me!"

"Police! Let go of your bike, ma'am!"

"No, you're not. Help!"

Kelly grabbed her wrist and bent it until her body followed, flipping her from the bike and onto her back. He was pushing the bike away from her when a Good Samaritan wearing a tight red, white, and blue U.S. Post Office Lycra racing unisuit and riding a beautiful, full suspension Gary Fisher racing bike cut him off and grabbed Kelly's new ride by the seat post. "You hold it right there, dude. Let go of her bike!"

Kelly glanced at the man's feet—basket clips, good thing he's a wannabe—and said, "Okay, relax, man." Then he slammed his fist into the man's face, pulling his punch. The man's clear Oakley glasses snapped in half against Kelly's middle knuckle. He fell off his bike holding his face.

As Kelly rode away on the light aluminum bike, weaving through the traffic on Soldiers Field Road crammed bumper to bumper to the Mass Pike tollbooth, he glanced back. The DEA agent was struggling with the screaming woman over her bike. The Samaritan seemed a bit more sheepish in his tight outfit, choosing to wave a fist at Kelly instead of intervening again. His gut struggled against his polymer skin like an enwombed baby. *Man had it coming wearing an outfit like that.*

– 33 –

SIERRA MADRE DEL SUR, MEXICO

The posse labored up the arroyo, the clipped nails of the hound snicking across rocks, rubber soles of the men that followed behind crushing dry balls of dirt into dust that was sucked downhill. They had been hiking for five hours across the savage terrain, and the lush valley where they had found the injured boy and his dead horse was twenty-five kilometers west. They were gaining height. The land was stitched with steep incisions where ancient rivers once flowed but had been tapped for irrigation or blown dry. A stale wind was roaring down the gully and slowly splitting their dehydrated lips. It was as if they were walking into the mouth of a giant hair dryer.

The waning sun was dragging the temperature with it. Felix shuddered, watching the green grow dark with the shadows, the forest tightening in on them. He emerged from the riverbed behind Sniff-Sniff and smelled the fresh pine needles that blanketed the path. He worried that his friend might lose the scent, but the hound plodded along, head down and tail wagging. Felix halted Sniff-Sniff to catch his breath. He was a big hound, and Felix could wrap his incredible ears all the way around his waist. He wanted to bury his face in the softness for warmth.

"I'm going to put on my warm gear. *Los Asesinos* are very fast hikers. Incredible. Heading almost due east. Must be lost."

"You sure the dog hasn't lost the scent, old man?" said Sergeant Pena.

"Yes" was the only sentence Felix wasted on such a stupid question.

The thick odor had initially acted as a detergent for his own scent when they entered the pine zone, but as they penetrated deeper Pena became convinced it was a noxious poison that was twisting his stomach. He pulled his undershirt back over his mouth and nose. "We shouldn't have wasted so much time with that boy. We wasted an hour talking to him, finding the horse, waiting for the rescue chopper. That was dumb."

"Would you have just left the boy?"

"No. Well, yes. I would have told the chopper where to pick him up and hiked from there right away. Fucking Lieutenant Garza, man. It was his call. This dog had the scent right away, remember?"

Of course Sniff-Sniff got it quickly, you ass, thought Felix. He is only the finest hunting dog in the world. And it was true—not ten minutes had gone by after the helicopter insert when Sniff-Sniff began to bark. But then the little boy had cried out. The lieutenant debriefed him excitedly and made a long radio report. And the man who held the rank—the little Indian—had just sat there atop the dead horse near the thicket, looking at his pictures. Hadn't said a word all trip.

"We should stop for a brief rest. Eat and recharge," panted Lieutenant Garza when he reached the two men who had walked point for the duration of the hike. "Lopez and Camdera are falling back. Pena, I can relieve you from point duty. Replace you with Camdera. Maybe that will spark him."

"Camdera is a weak sister," said Pena. "No, sir. I prefer it up here."

The lieutenant stared at his young hard-charger, marveling at the boy's self-lessness. After all, if *Los Asesinos* were waiting in ambush, the point would likely be slaughtered. He didn't care about the hunter or the dog but in fairness to Pena, he shouldn't walk the point forever. Not that Garza was going to take the lead as an officer, but he had two other subordinates to rotate up there.

"Your sacrifice is noted, but you deserve a rest."

"No, sir. I have to stay up here." Pena wasn't worried about an ambush. Well, okay, a *little,* but as far as he was concerned, the most dangerous man in those woods was the Indian who trailed the file, occasionally launching a throwing blade into a tree, never saying a word. He peered downslope and saw him moving easily behind his exhausted *compañeros,* almost *strolling.* The Indian walked up to a thin pine and yanked a piece of his steel arsenal free, spinning and sticking it back in his belt. Camdera and Lopez better step it up, he thought, or that crazy fucker might throw a knife at them. The pace had been hard, but with freaky bighead behind them they should find the energy to sprint!

"I want to stay here on point, sir."

"Fine," said the lieutenant, sitting to untie his boot. "Camdera and Lopez need to rest so we stop now, but you tell me when you want off the point."

A few minutes after the soldiers had removed their boots to dry their feet, *El Monstruo Carnicero* ambled up, chewing on a wad of tobacco halfheartedly, some of it dribbling off the tip of his beard. Pena was digging into his pack for a fresh pair of socks when he heard the Indian's falsetto song. It sounded as light and jittery as wind skidding through the needles. He is a gifted hiker, thought Pena, probably because he is some kind of altitude village freak. While the soldiers had gasped their way up into the mountains, the oily rat just walked along, looking almost bored any time Pena snuck a glance. He was careful to turn his head away when the Indian approached.

Pena saw the man's white running sneakers—Reebok with red racing stripes—gliding toward him. He reached for his pistol, but didn't dare look up, angry for not setting down on the uphill side of his fellow soldiers, as far away from freaky as possible.

"Why you stopped?" asked the Indian.

"Been five hours," said Lieutenant Garza. "We need a sock change and a listening halt. We're closing in."

"Only thing you're closing in on is your own death," said the Indian. The sunset glowed behind him and in the split second before the final sliver of the day was sucked behind a small peak, the orange fulminated, outlining the man's delicate figure, turning the clouds a deep pink and the man's face into a featureless shadow. Pena turned away before he was caught staring.

The Indian pointed at Lopez and Camdera. "Those two *putas* are slowing us down. I'm going to sharpen my knives. When I'm done, you five better be moving. And if they fall off the pace again we leave them to die in their own shame. *Los Asesinos* are laughing at all of you sons of bitches."

Pena watched his lieutenant closely, watched the greenhorn just sitting there like a child, stunned and thunderstruck. Wasn't he going to stick up for himself? "Okay, sir," the coward said lamely. "But we're going to have words when we return."

"We have them right now, Lieutenant," the freak hissed. "Want more?"

Why don't we kill him now? thought Pena. Circle him and gun him down! Hadn't the lieutenant hinted that loose ends might have to be tied after they wasted *Los Asesinos?* He noticed that the man's sneakers had not yet moved, though. They were still a meter in front of him. Then they slowly shifted around until the rubber toes were pointing right at him. *What the hell?*

Pena did not look up. He kept his head down and dared a glance at his team and his lieutenant. They were staring at him. He had the awful feeling that the freak was staring, too. He fidgeted in the silence and eventually looked up. The man smiled, and Pena saw that the bottom of his beard was rotten with tobacco. A milked, flaccid leaf was dangling heavily on a single wire strand of black hair.

"Wondered when you were going to snake a glance, boy," the Indian said.

"You been avoiding me all trip. You walk back with me when we start. I teach you this."

The man smiled. Pena felt flushed and tepid. The man snapped his arm down and Pena startled, unclipping his holster. As the man rotated around, a throwing blade somehow appeared in his hand. His arm cocked and the knife was a blur, the blade not tumbling but streaking flat, striking a tree twenty meters away and stopping its quiver well before Pena was able to control his own.

- 34 -

WASHINGTON, D.C.

Jimmy Contreras didn't have a seat. He was standing in the corner of Roger Corwin's FBI office under the record traffic stop plaque, scowling. Corwin couldn't figure out if he was grumpy about having botched the Gavin Kelly grab, grumpy about standing, or grumpy with his life status in general. Corwin wondered if he was really even a United States citizen. Whatever.

Corwin had called his secretary as soon as the Lear touched down at Reagan National and told her to get five seats ready for him and his four special agents. The DEA did not rate the rest. Corwin and his special agents had flushed Kelly according to plan—well, a contingency anyway—right into Contreras's arms. Yes, there were Feds with him at the post behind the fence, but as senior man Contreras was accountable. Especially after pushing so hard to join the raid to begin with.

"What have we got on this slick motherfucker Kelly?" Corwin asked. He was pissed, and he wanted his subordinates on their heels where he could control them. As a CHP officer, he had learned that profanity often startled the guilty. Well, the white ones anyway.

"Kelly withdrew twenty-three thousand dollars from his bank account this morning when it opened, sir," said one of his men, a kid named Ed Modinger fresh out of Quantico he had tapped for grunt work. "There has been no use of his credit cards except the flights we discussed. He had reservations from Logan to Mexico City tonight. One round-trip adding two one-ways back from Mexico City this Friday."

Corwin opened his desk drawer and plunked his lucky handcuffs on top.

He had a habit of spinning the bracelets through the latch system and out the other side, seeing how many clicks he could get with a single finger tap. His record was eight—almost clear through—but that was the day Agent Rita Nagle had dumped her cone of water on his head for a harmless remark about female grooming. "Cash purchases of tickets today?"

"No one named Gavin Kelly has flown today and no one has fit his description, sir. We've got a full airport lockdown Charlie alert and his picture is on the TRAP facial recognition system. Seventeen people at Logan paid cash for same-day flights to southern states and we're trying to track them. Still checking New York, Providence, and Hartford. Don't know how he could have gotten on board without identification, though, sir."

"No phone calls that we know of to any of the Phillipses' relatives?" Corwin asked.

"None, sir," said another agent, who had been tasked with communications.

"His car still in Cambridge?"

"Yes, sir," said agent Modinger.

Corwin tapped a cuff and it snapped shut around his own wrist. He could measure the efficacy of a workout pump by how many latches it took until it was snug. He checked his watch. Plenty of time for a Viagra and a lift before heading to Mexico City. "Tell you what this Ivy League punk is going to do. He's on a bus right now to Texas. Maybe a train. He'll try to slip across the border there. Modinger, alert INS and get their ports on the lookout, then pack some clothes. You'll be coming with me to Mexico tonight. I'll get Kelly's information out on the wire down there and add a nifty bounty for his arrest as some icing. He hasn't broken any laws, but he's what I will label 'a person of interest' if the press starts barking. That'll bring him in. The rest of you hit your respective assignments all goddamn night. We catch Kelly and we catch *Los Asesinos*. Get to it."

Corwin waited until Contreras was halfway out the door before he said, "Not you, Jimmy. Got something for you."

Contreras centered himself on Corwin's desk and glared at him. Corwin didn't like to play the supplicant—on the highway his rule was keep them seated, keep control—so he stood and indicated that it was Contreras who should sit. "You said I'd be accompanying you to Mexico," said Contreras. "You said you had information on *El Monstruo Carnicero*'s location."

Corwin shook his head. "No, I didn't. What I said was, as long as you keep the information coming, I keep you in the loop. Now, Jimmy, that was just a business school student that slipped you today. I defended you, but some of the guys are starting to wonder what value you're adding."

"You put me in front of *El Monstruo Carnicero* and I'll show you value."

Corwin raised both hands in mock surrender. "Tell you what. You get your ass back to Langley and come back with something. The hidden message was nice, but, hell, the media cracked that Morse code just a few hours later. Chick I'm dating even saw the marks. Sheridan's holding out on me. You go get it. You do that—you bring us to *Los Asesinos*—then, yes, I'll lead you right to the Monster Butcher's doorstep, *amigo*."

- 35 -

MCLEAN, VIRGINIA

Ted Blinky hadn't taken his eyes off his monitor for several hours and his pupils had shrunk to the size of BBs. He was prone to letting his very detail-oriented mind meander into theory unless he was specifically tasked. Deputy Director Sheridan had put him on the digital breakout and here he was, perhaps a minute away from cracking the location code on the phone. His only regret as he typed in the last bits of Java script was that he had told her it was possible to hack it in the first place. He and his fellow programmers preferred to label things impossible so their efforts might be appreciated, if only for a moment.

"Deputy Director Sheridan," he said loudly so even the attachments in the corner of the cave could hear him. "You might want to take a look at this."

When she stood, several other chairs were pushed back. Blinky smiled and tilted his head to lure her over to his computer screen. He was delighted when it worked. She leaned over his shoulder and he tried to remember where he was in the faint fog of perfume. Oh, yes. "I authored some code that slowed the digital tapes to ten percent of original speed, but the tone was still too fast, so I cut it to a tenth of one percent and that *still* didn't work. Incredible, right?"

"Incredible, Mister Blinky, considering I have to meet the director's plane at Langley Air Base in fewer than thirty minutes."

"Yes, heard about that, ma'am. Sorry. Anyway, I used the digitally enhanced breakout and wrote a new code to parse the differences in the numbers. There they are."

Blinky had retracted the digital projection screen for effect and now it descended from the ceiling and illuminated a series of numbers. All of the Bat Cave dwellers stared as if studying chess pieces.

Monday

1507 EST: 5324167999
1509 EST: 5443367845
1556 EST: 5978895677

Tuesday

1146 EST: 0885411567

"That's fantastic. It really is," she said.

Blinky smiled. "I've put the times of the calls on the left in Eastern Standard Time. Notice that while she made six phone calls, we only heard four data bursts. The shorter calls—like when she speed-dialed the Columbian and the second time she tried New York—didn't produce numbers, almost as if the phone didn't have enough time to send them. Anyway, watch this."

The numbers on the screen were replaced by a digital color map of Guerrero State, Mexico. Four tiny jpegs of the couple in their *New York Times* engagement photo popped up—two in Acapulco, one on the west side of the mountain range labeled Sierra Madre del Sur, and one far to the east in a valley.

"This is their journey so far," Blinky said, thinking the icons were a nice touch.

There was a scale on the bottom of the display. Susanne used her arm to measure a hundred map miles, then placed it along the couple's route. It bent away from Mexico City toward Oaxaca. "They're a little off course. Drifting south from Mexico City."

"Excuse me, ma'am," said Ted Blinky, rolling now, "but with this code I can also break into their calls. As long as they remain encrypted, that is."

"Wow. Can we try calling them?" she said eagerly.

"No, ma'am. But next time they come up on the Net, I've set up a back trace and we should be able to communicate."

"Well, let's hope there *is* a next time. Print those grid coordinates out so I can bring them to DCI. Won't save me, but my successor will benefit. Christian, you have the con." She did not know what the word meant but many of the former military ops officers said it and it had become habit. "It may be brief. The director will probably send my relief over in a few days."

The talking points Christian Collins had prepared almost slipped from his hands. His face drained of color and his mouth propped open slightly. Oh, cripes, Susanne thought, Christian saw himself moving up.

"Maybe you could . . ." Christian couldn't finish.

I don't have time for this, Susanne thought. "Christian, you're supercompetent. But in all honesty I could not recommend you to be in charge. Besides, a good word from me would just get you demoted," she said, patting him on the shoulder. "Gotta go. Can't be late to my own execution. We'll laugh about this someday."

Ted Blinky wanted to stand up and shout, Welcome to reality, hotshot. This isn't a dot-com—in the government seniority still counts!

But Blinky's stock was rising and he did not want to create his own friction, as he had done early in his career. He would be the teacher, and slick Silicon Valley stud was just a wide-eyed pupil. Pity that he was finally getting some traction with Sheridan when she was on the outs. "Agent Contreras is waiting outside, by the way," said Blinky.

"You didn't let him in?" asked Sheridan.

"No, ma'am, I did not."

"Well, how long has he been out there?"

Blinky smiled. "About an hour, ma'am."

When the electromagnetic locks on the Bat Cave entrance beeped open she strode briskly out into the quiet hallway. Jimmy Contreras was chatting with a janitor who was leaning on a steel floor polisher. She heard Contreras call her name before the polisher started up, masking his trot.

"We have to talk," he said loudly.

"And I have to meet my maker in the form of Homeland and DCI."

"Well, I just returned from the biggest fiasco I've ever seen. Did you hear about Cambridge? Corwin botched the Kelly snatch."

She put a finger to her lips and continued on downstairs, past the guards, past the lonely stars that had been chiseled into the wall for fallen CIA officers, and out through the glass doors. It was a warm night for April and she could see the bloom on the row of cherry blossoms that decorated the winding entrance to the new headquarters building.

"Look, I'm doing my best to get what we both want," said Contreras. "First chance I get to bust brush and snare this couple I'm taking it. If you can't accept that, that's your issue. Not mine. Without me working with Corwin, you'd be blind."

"And without you working with me, Corwin would be blind. Is that it?"

"That doesn't matter to me and you know it. I just need a sugar daddy and he's the only one who still has a job." He saw the frustrated sadness in her face and quickly added, "I'm sorry. I didn't mean it like that."

She walked over to the bronze statue of Nathan Hale, the first American to be captured for spying. In 1776, George Washington had asked for a volunteer to scout British troop strength and Hale had stepped forward, penetrating British lines disguised as a Dutch teacher. He was caught in New York after completing the mission and executed. Most fingered his cousin as the snitch, though it was never proven.

Susanne noticed that the statue's hands and feet were bound, realizing that she had never really studied Hale. Just before he was hanged, Hale had uttered the phrase: "I only regret that I have but one life to lose for my country."

He was twenty-one years old.

Susanne handed Contreras the location sheets and the corresponding brief. "You know what, Jimmy? You have nothing to apologize for. We can't break up when we haven't even started dating, can we? Those are the Phillipses' locations at the times indicated. Also, we have the ability to get a message to them if Corwin wants one delivered. If they come up on the Net again, I'll buzz you on your secure cell with their location in UTM grid coordinates. What you do from there is on you."

Contreras nodded gratefully and snorted. "What I do then? Lock and load, that's what I do. That Indian is on the clock." He held up the packet of papers and tucked them in a leather carry case that looked as if it had been freshly spit-shined. "This is my ticket to Mexico. I won't bother explaining, but thanks, Susanne. It's great. Good luck tonight."

Watching him walk down the stone steps toward the guardhouse, Susanne wondered whose future was murkier.

– 36 –

SIERRA MADRE RANGE, MEXICO

Darren Phillips was not a nurturer by nature. For two miles he flailed for some sentence that might motivate Cappucco. He knew he had the tendency to sound condescending, so he searched his tired memory for some common ground. Or at least a compliment. But watching the kid limp along, exaggerating his already labored breathing while mumbling profanities, Darren just wasn't in the coddling mood. The truly selfless were greedy with their own pain.

Cappucco didn't exactly have the market cornered when it came to exhaustion, not after thirty hours and a hundred miles without rest. Hell, Darren thought, I've been sleepless for . . . It took him ten minutes to calculate the time he awoke in his hotel room. Eventually he settled on thirty-nine hours. Why had he drifted back next to Cappucco in the first place? Why was he even *thinking* about Cappucco?

The sleep monster tugged at his eyelids and he saw a giant rabbit with bloody fangs waiting for him between two pine trees. He bit his tongue and the rabbit was instantly replaced by a cumulus cloud. When he was close enough to see it was a bush, Darren was not relieved but disappointed. He had already decided how he would kill and devour the rabbit.

Fifteen minutes later, he remembered that Kate had sent him back to encourage the kid. She had walked with Cappucco the whole day and needed some time to catch her breath. Darren decided to swallow his sense of order to placate his wife. After a struggle he had something good to say. It would certainly resonate with the kid because Darren knew so little about it.

"Tell me something, Cappucco," Darren whispered when the hulk appeared in a strip of moonlight. "What's the deal with the whole Backstreet Boys thing?"

Neck didn't look up—it was hard enough to walk during the day, and now that darkness had come once more, magnifying his already overpowering thirst for sleep, he had to concentrate on his footwork. He was so sleep-deprived that stumbling had replaced walking. The hallucinations had started an hour before, when a rocket ship blasted out of a tree, a dragon riding it. The self-righteous guy, goddamn what *was* his name, was talking . . . ohgoddamn hit that stump my fucking toe oh goddamn, this is fucking crazy we havetostoprightnowIneed-sleep.

". . . deal?" asked someone. Darren Phillips. That's his name.

"What?" asked Neck.

"I think you drifted off on me. What I was saying was, what's up with this boy bands phenomenon?"

"Dude, what the fuck are you trying to say to me?" Neck felt like he was stepping on razor blades every time he put a foot down. He had sacrificed his second layer of skin to the ground an hour earlier, so thirsty that he wanted to put his bare feet in his mouth and pop the blisters so he could get some cool water.

"What I'm talking about, youngster, is male perversion. When I was in school we had New Kids on the Block." Darren needed his full breath to ascend a boulder and he paused the speech for a second. He knew they were approaching the spine of the Sierra Madre, and guessed from the burning in his lungs and the frigid temperature that they were above 7,000 feet. The air was as fragile and brittle as his mood.

"Thing was, we all used to laugh at them as a joke, you know? But I read an article that said you college kids *like* 'N Sync and Backstreet Boys and all these other dorks."

Neck was irritated. Phillips wasn't funny and, worse, he didn't even know what he was talking about. He planned to ambush Phillips about hip-hop music later; he bet Phillips didn't know a single rap star. Fucking Eskimo Pie. "First of all, I said I liked the Backstreet Boys. I'm not into 'N Sync. Half of them are, like, Disney Mouseketeers. The Backstreet Boys rock. What's it to you?"

Darren felt fully awake for the first time in hours. Cappucco *differentiated* among the bands. Perhaps it is the lure of vigorous debate that revived me, he thought, or maybe it's just this kid's whole generation's perverted freak worship, but I feel awake. "But they're just manufactured, earringed airheads. All of them are the same. Cookie-cut geeks with their cheesy goatees and their wanna-be bad-boy piercings."

"What the fuck do earrings have to do with anything? You're just afraid of free expression, dude. I mean, listen to you. You're, what, only eleven years older? All military and shit? It's free expression, you fucking nazi! What do you care about what band I like? Or if I wear earrings?" Neck tugged at his ears, fingering his diamond studs, then reached for a ponderosa tree to help him up through the softwood forest.

"Just making conversation. Besides," Darren said, "you look like a pirate or something with those things. I just never knew a pirate who wore a bottled tan quite as well as you."

"Shut up or I'll break you in half, Eskimo."

Eskimo? Darren tried to interpret. Was the kid stupid enough to think he was from the Aleutian Islands? Perhaps. "Watch those hallucinations, double-half-caf-cappuccino. Twenty miles from here your testicles might actually descend and you might actually follow through."

"Come any closer and I'll put my fist through your head," said Neck.

"Darren! Neck!" Kate hissed. She hobbled down and put her hands on her husband's pectorals. He took several steps back, immediately regretful. "In case you two can't figure it out for yourselves, we're on the same side. You assholes are *teammates*."

Kate was as shocked as she was angry. What was it with men that made the concept of teamwork take a backseat to hubris? Was it so hard just to encourage each other instead of exchanging venomous prattle for pride? To stuff their petty differences for the greater good? For *necessity*? Because their *lives* were at stake?!

"We need to keep moving while it's dark. We should be approaching the Guamuchil Canyon soon, according to the stupid map. Neck, why don't you take the lead with me. Darren, you just walk in back, as much as you're helping."

- 37 -

MEXICO CITY, MEXICO

Deputy Attorney General Saiz greeted Roger Corwin with a hug and a few slaps on the back that were sufficient in interval and force to burp a baby. Corwin had seen the open arms coming and inflated his lungs to harden his lats. He enjoyed hugs from males. Not only did he consider it an expression of worldliness—outside the United States cheek kisses often hastened diplomacy—but also he relished the grope itself, however brief. It gave him a benchmark.

Sometimes men hid their sloth in expensive suits that fooled the eyes, but they could not fool Corwin's hands. Jimmy Contreras, for instance, looked okay in a suit because he was tall and broad, but Corwin had studied him carefully on the Lear flight. The DEA had been removing his jacket when Corwin saw the telltale pouches on his hips. Now he could not wait for the transition to casual wear the following day to show his team a thing or two about symmetry and sculpture.

"Good to see you, Roger," said Saiz. He was dressed in a hound's-tooth double-breasted Armani suit centered on a red power tie with a dimple.

"Thanks for inviting us," said Corwin.

Saiz laughed heartily and winked at the five-man American FBI entourage. "But I did not invite you, old friend. You invited yourself!"

Corwin joined in the laughter, but the remark irritated him. There was truth in the jab, and Saiz knew better than to run his mouth when there were reporters around the corner. He'd known Saiz for many years and had never seen him so keyed up. "Eduardo, I want to introduce you to Jim Contreras. He's my liaison to DEA. One of your Mexican *compadres*."

"Ah, yes? Nice to meet you, James. When did you go AWOL?" Saiz asked in Spanish, extending his hand with a smile.

Contreras wanted to rip the man's arm off and was mildly disappointed in himself when he actually shook his hand. *"AWOL?"*

"When did you flee to the north?"

"You know, Deputy Attorney General, we've met before. Almost fifteen years ago before you reached this lofty position. I used to work with Luis Gonzalez."

"Aquí? Who?" Saiz asked, switching to English.

"Agent Luis Gonzalez, sir. He was captured by the Rodriguez brothers and murdered. I worked some of the case with you in eighty-eight and eighty-nine. We never did find the killer once we flushed the attorney general."

"Oh, yes, of course. Tragic case. I think I remember you now, Jimmy." Saiz turned and spoke to all five Americans. "What a mess. Well, I can tell you that times have changed. My president tolerates exactly zero corruption. But he's also a real . . . *ball-buster* and I appreciate the show of support today. Roger, will Jimmy be joining us with the boy and Cappucco's parents onstage?"

Contreras recoiled at the thought of appearing within fifty meters of Eduardo Saiz on worldwide television. "I . . ."

Corwin recoiled at the possible publicity drain. "No. Just me and you, amigo."

"Okay, good. Let's go. *Amigo.*" Saiz escorted Corwin from the anteroom, leaving Contreras and the three Feds to watch the teleplay on the closed circuit monitors. As they approached the stage, Corwin saw a small boy wearing an arm cast sitting behind the curtain, eating a bowl of chocolate ice cream while his parents watched. Seeing the men, the boy stood and his parents put a comb through his hair.

"That the kid?" asked Corwin.

"Yes. Hey, I have a request, old friend," Saiz said, grabbing Corwin by the arm to stop his advance. "How does one join your witness protection program?"

"Witness protection? In the States? Who for?"

Saiz smiled weakly. "For my family, old friend. For me and my family."

"Come on."

"I'm deathly serious, Roger. I released the pictures of *Los Asesinos* before I studied them. Embarrassing. The code in the sun lotion is going to get me killed. I sent my wife and girls to Cancún. They think they're on vacation."

Corwin concentrated on Saiz's facial tells—the corners of his mouth, his glistening eyebrows, the lines in his forehead. He'd listened to enough stories in the breakdown lane to sense the stress. What the hell was he talking about? Releasing the photos without scouring them was careless, yes, but they had served their purpose. Who was going to kill Saiz and, more importantly, had Saiz somehow dragged him into a bog?

Corwin touched his own mustache as a signal. Saiz wiped four tiny rivulets of sweat from his upper lip. "What are you into, Eduardo?"

"Me? Jesus and Mary, Roger. What am I into?"

"What are you into?"

"I'll tell you what the fuck I'm into. I fucking ransacked the Jackrabbit's compound for clues and entered the belly of the shark. I've got evidence tying a serial killer to a drug cartel, and now my life is at risk."

Now Corwin's personal radar was fully illuminated. He synched up with Saiz. *So that's how DEA knows that Monster Butcher has been activated. Some government snitch leaked it. But is Saiz clean? It's key that he is.* "You're talking about *El Monstruo Carnicero?* He's my Most Wanted prize, right?"

Corwin saw Saiz's lips part just enough to conclude his shock was genuine. "How did you know? Is that why you brought Contreras?"

Corwin waved dismissively. What did that have to do with Contreras? The boy was walking over so he whispered, "Listen to me. Contreras is a piss boy and he has nothing to do with this. He just doesn't realize it. You bring me the Monster Butcher—me alone and, yeah, I think I can work something out. If not protection, then enough money from the reward to set you up in Spain or wherever."

"Reward? How much?"

Hearing him say it, Corwin wondered what FBI policy was on finding sunken treasure. Was he entitled to any of it? After all, he'd set it up. Was there a way around the red tape? "Five hundred grand from some women's organization, another five hundred or so from the U.S. government."

"How much for the murderer your man Contreras mentioned?"

"Guy who killed the DEA agent? That was over ten years ago. Must be well over a million, I'd imagine. Maybe more. Why? You have a lead on that guy, too?"

"Maybe they're not so different." Saiz winked and turned away from Corwin. It was time to raise the curtain on the boy.

————

Saiz was impressed with the boy Pedro's reading skills. For a peasant, he had some real gumption. It was going so well that he even allowed the boy to field some questions. His sling and his puffy face were turning the tide against *Los Asesinos* again, Saiz could feel it. When the boy was asked if *Los Asesinos* had been kind to him, Saiz smoothly pulled the microphone away from the boy, thanked him for his bravery, and told the crowd that he was a shining example of

Mexico's pride. He held up the plaque and the medal for the cameras once more, then handed them to Pedro. He was careful to place the plaque in the boy's damaged hand. It clattered to the floor. Saiz patted the young hero on the back and handed it back to him.

"Sir! Sir!" the woman from Fox News shouted down the others. Of all the reporters jammed into the conference room, Eduardo thought that the Americans were the rudest. They shouted all the time. "Can we ask Pedro a few more questions? Please?"

"I'm sorry, no, he's tired. And he's scheduled for his second surgery tomorrow."

"Well, did he say if the Phillipses said anything to him?"

"Before or after they shot his finger off, *señora?*"

"I'm sorry?"

"The point is, *señora,* that I'm quite sure Pedro had other things to worry about when *Los Asesinos* ambushed him, like escaping with his life." The crowd gave a chuckle that admonished the questioner. "His dog and his horse weren't so lucky. And let me again say this, Pedro did see Mister Vinny Cappucco alive, and that brings me the greatest hope.

"Ladies and gentlemen, I am sure you have been wondering who these people are who have just arrived behind me. I would like to introduce Mr. and Mrs. John Cappucco, Vinny's parents, and three of his teammates from the University of Michigan. We have flown them here as guests of the government while Mexico's finest endeavor to recover their son from the *clutches of terror.*"

Saiz had rehearsed the last line in front of a mirror. He was quite happy with the way it had rolled out of his mouth. He waved his hand grandly and a heavy-set man in a suit with dark hair and sunken eyes approached the microphone. Behind him, three young men in Wolverine letter jackets bowed their heads solemnly.

"Uhh, hello, my name is Johnny Cappucco and I'm Neck's—Neck is Vinny's nickname—um, I'm Neck's father. The first people we have to thank are Attorney General Saiz and all the folks in the Mexican government who've been keeping us informed. They flew me and my wife and Neck's teammates down here. I want to thank them for keeping us up to date on Vinny's hostage status and for doing all they can to liberate him from these animals. I also want to thank Mister Corwin and the rest of the FBI folks we just met. Our deepest sympathies are with the families of Tom Hershenson and Ben Nemo—and all the people who were murdered, not just Neck's friends."

John Cappucco made the sign of the cross and Eduardo nearly clapped. *El Toro* had called in a rage after the media reported the Morse code message and there had been talk of a funeral. But Eduardo had recovered nicely and was as well positioned as he had ever been to recover the satphone. *Am I winning my life back here?*

"Neck's a tough kid and we know he'll make it," Cappucco said. He looked back at the football players and nodded. They returned the salute, one with a clenched fist. "I just want to say to Neck's kidnappers, you best let my boy go, 'cause he's a helluva lot better 'n you are. Please . . . boy, this is tough. I don't wish this on anyone."

John Cappucco exhaled loudly. His eyes welled and spilled over. "And so help me God, if you harm him, me and the guys behind me, we'll make the rest of your lives a living hell. I swear to God."

———

Contreras felt filthy just standing there watching it unfold on the closed circuit. He had the urge to burst in on the press conference, grab John Cappucco by the shoulders, and shake the truth into him. No way his son was a kidnap victim. Either he was already dead—and being used as motivation for the press—or he was traveling willfully.

That was the truth, but Contreras had long ago learned that everyone had their own truth. That he and his mates could have saved the South Vietnamese was the truth, but those who had sent him in country to begin with had their own version, a weak-kneed supplicant to careerism and paranoia. That *El Monstruo Carnicero* had extinguished Luis courtesy of a government leak was the truth. That Saiz was somehow involved was the truth.

What the fuck am I doing here? Be a man and finish this thing.

The bitterness rose up in Contreras's throat like a steam engine roaring out of a tunnel. He wanted to smash his fist into one of the televisions. He stormed out of the anteroom, tucking himself into a pillar of velvet curtains that had been drawn for the show. His .40 automatic pistol was in his hand now, its usual place of refuge during these episodes. Contreras leaned back so he was totally concealed, closed his left eye, slowed his breathing and raised his arm until the luminous beads on his rear sight straddled the unfocused mass that was Deputy Attorney General Eduardo Saiz. His pupil widened just before the front sight post came up and level. The path to righteousness was clear, two pounds of trigger pull away. *What is the truth, pendejo?*

Contreras holstered his pistol and exhaled, then walked back into the room with the FBI dicks. The flag of Mexico was stretched out on the wall above him. Contreras felt an intense mixture of pride and sadness that was hard to parse. Then again, he had not felt an uninterrupted emotion except the pungent lust for revenge since he had received the word of the monster. Frustration maybe.

The young agent, Modinger, had been writing for some time while keeping a cell phone pressed to his ear. He seemed like a good kid. Contreras leaned over to see, but Modinger shifted and blocked his view.

"What you got there?" Contreras asked nicely.

"We should probably wait for Agent Corwin to finish up, sir."

In an instant, Contreras decided the kid was like all the others, though some part of him knew the agent was just being loyal. "Don't make me repeat myself."

The other three agents gathered around him and Modinger shrugged. What the hell, he thought. The guy looks like he's about to crack. Talk about needing a chill pill.

"I figured Gavin Kelly would buy a weapon and to do it he'd need a valid driver's license. Even in Texas. But if he knew the loopholes, he'd go to a gun show and pay cash. That way his name wouldn't go national on the purchase and there would be no waiting period. So I sent out agents to all the big border towns and we got lucky. Private dealer named Buckley in Brownsville sold him a match grade .30-06 Winchester hunting rifle with a Bushnell 20X scope. Kelly spent twenty minutes zeroing the thing in a field behind the show. Also bought an AR-15—familiar territory for a guy who spent his formative years carrying the M-16—and a Beretta 9-mm pistol, also a familiar toy. We got agents canvassing the border."

"Brownsville?" said Contreras. "That's a fast bus."

Modinger nodded. "I thought the same. So I narrowed our search of airline passengers who paid cash to south Texas and came up with this." Modinger handed Contreras a grainy black-and-white fax of a man wearing large glasses, holding what looked like a balloon with his teeth moving through an airline security checkpoint. It was Gavin Kelly. "He flew under the alias Harold Callahan. I presume he had a fake I.D."

"T. F. Green in Providence? Damn time stamp says it was only three hours after we lost him. How'd he slip through the facial recognition TRAP alert?"

Modinger pointed at the picture. "See the bubble he's blowing with gum and the glasses worn on the tip of his nose? They screwed up the imager by adding artificial dimensions and angles to his face. Anyway, I launched a search to match the weapon purchase with ammo and a local Brownsville sporting goods store called Marple's had a big purchase. Hundred rounds for the Winchester, two hundred for the pistol, over a *thousand* .223 rounds for the AR-15. This kid's loaded for bear, sir."

"Are the ports on the border notified?"

"Yessir, but they won't nab him. I figure he'll slip across the border around Brownsville and some local Mexican will call it in. We're posting a hundred-thousand-dollar reward all along the border. Only a matter of time before his white ass is in its rightful sling."

– 38 –

GULF OF MEXICO

Gavin Kelly throttled back from 4,000 rpm and brought the metal stick into neutral. The following wake took the Mako, lifted its tail, and pitched it forward, not a small feat considering the presence of the two 100-gallon fuel bladders and all the ammunition. The full moon had risen above the cliffs of Mexico and Kelly wanted to check his gear before continuing.

He stumbled aft—he was tall and had suspect agility—and opened the enormous Igloo cooler he had purchased in Brownsville. Inside, the rifles and all the ammunition were carefully wrapped and waterproofed in plastic. He removed the pistol and three 9-mm magazines, then duct-taped the fish box shut and tied the 100-foot fluorescent float line to one of the handles. If the Mexican Navy attempted an inspection, he planned to dump the entire arsenal overboard, hoping to record its GPS location and recover it later. As for the pistol, well, he should probably have stowed that, too, but the fact was that he just felt *better* with a pistol.

Kelly thought about his mission and regret filled him so suddenly that he thought he might cry right there in the serene Bay of Campeche on a beautiful night. This happened every time he thought about combat. He hated war partly because the wrong people died, and partly because he was unsure if he was really built for it. He was responsible for two dead Marines in Somalia and Kuwait. Infantry casualties seemed to have been exclusive to his watch and his men. And for what? So their lieutenant could write a lonely letter steeped with words like "honorable" and "sacrifice" and "quick"? Fuck that. Fuck the whole goddamn backward world. You'd think civilization would have advanced enough to relish humanity, and yet there was a persistent evil that could only be contained by a combat boot on its throat and a gun in its mouth.

The thought of Darren and Kate fighting for their lives to escape this madness made him curse out loud. Kelly wondered if they were even alive. And how was Kate holding up now that the base brutality of life had sprouted up around her? Kelly was attracted to Kate. Her vibrancy and sense of humor seemed to mesh better with him than with Phillips, but of course Phillips beat him in everything and getting the perfect girl in the end was the coup de grâce in their competitive relationship. Kelly knew that some part of him had been robbed in Somalia and at The Hague. He would have to drift along, searching for something or someone who might provide solace.

Kelly recovered quickly, now tasting that side of him that craved the electricity of war. Adventure had been so elusive since the Corps divorced him—all the mountains had been climbed, all continents conquered, all races run, over and over. Of course, it was hard to get out and about while in the brig. He belonged in the Marine Corps, the last of the true professions.

His business school classmates would have disagreed, but they had different daydreams. Where they fantasized about equity—visions of *Fortune* cover stories dancing in their heads—Kelly dreamed of terrorists taking over the school, muggers coming at him from the Cambridge alleys, China attacking Taiwan and *forcing* the Corps to take him back. As his father and grandfather both told him, they'd never seen a crowded battlefield.

He checked the chamber of the Beretta by tugging on the slide. The brass sheath of the bullet looked blue in the moonlight. He placed the pistol in the radio box below the steering console. Then he illuminated his Magellan GPS and added some power to the throttle to find his track: fifty miles on heading 193 magnetic—taking him south in international waters—then a slithering course for two hundred fifty miles following the contour of the coast, then thirty miles on course 270, straight into Veracruz harbor.

WEDNESDAY

Finally the victim, the slow-carved object lesson of Mexica supremacy, exhausted by exertion and loss of blood, would falter and fall, to be dispatched by the usual heart excision . . . What is notable about this system, apart from its glamour, is how very little cooperative it was. The great warriors were solitary hunters.

—INGA CLENDINNEN, *AZTECS*

- 39 -

GUAMUCHIL CANYON, MEXICO

The three of them stood gawking for several minutes before anyone spoke. The canyon was a majestic force—a jagged gorge with walls more than 400 feet deep, a plunging series of thin ridges and yawning cracks that jutted in and out of the earth in an explosion of angles. To Kate, it seemed as if a flash flood had carved the earth and polished its walls, then receded just as quickly. The cliffs reflected a blue glow and the river itself glittered as it churned in the captured moonlight.

A huge, frothy waterfall spilled into the river just west of them, its white noise filling the gorge like the avalanche she saw in the Alps, echoes intertwined with and indiscernible from the original sounds. The silence of the night seemed to boost its roar. The river had a wicked slope and the white-water rapids looked like phosphorescent offspring of natural power. She was taken in by the beauty. Looking was one thing, but to cross it . . .

"I hate to be the consistent dude of negativity here, but how the fuck we gonna get across that thing?" asked Neck, wincing as he shifted his weight from one swollen foot to another.

"Hard to tell from this stupid road map," said Kate, "but this canyon runs for quite a while. And we have to cross it somewhere. I think we can make it down in three pitches. Down those little ledges." *Always forward.*

"Christ."

"Look on the other side. We can climb that." She pointed across the gorge. The far side was thickly dotted with evergreens and the slope wasn't as severe. "We'll be up on the high plain moving out in no time."

"What about the river? We'll be swept down the rapids."

Kate said, "Well, I'm probably the strong swimmer here. I'll tie the Hell Bitch around my waist and then I can pull you two across the river when I'm over."

"She can do it, Neck," said Darren, using the kid's nickname as an olive branch.

"I didn't say she couldn't," said Neck.

———

Marooned on a thin strip of pebble beach an hour later, Kate glanced up at the canyon wall and was pleased that she had selected the route properly. They had almost cliffed out 200 feet above the river, balancing on a thin crag until she down-climbed a narrow crack and set up the retrievable.

Darren was stuffing the harnesses into the waterproof pack when she said, "Leave that open, babe."

"Yeah, I'm crawlin' inside," said Neck. "I almost died up there. I'm still a little freaked. Seriously, Kate, I ain't a strong swimmer and I'm not sure if I can get across, even with the rope." He sat down hard and the pebbles crunched.

"You just float. I'll pull you."

"Not at night over those rapids you won't," Neck said. "We sleep here."

"Neck, we have to cross now."

"No fucking way. I've given in a lot but now. We can cross in the morning."

Kate stripped off her tank top, reached behind her back, and unclasped her silver bikini. She tossed them in Neck's starstruck face. She was unbuttoning her shorts when Darren grabbed her arm. "What're you doing?" he asked. "Put your shirt back on."

"We need to keep our clothes dry. Especially now that we're at altitude. You guys strip down, too. We'll put them back on when we're across." The beach was cramped and when she stepped back her left foot splashed into the river. It was like licking the top of a nine volt battery. "OOOOh! That's cold!"

Kate tugged her shorts past her waist and stood tall and naked, goose bumps covering her body, tightening the skin and flushing her muscles. She tossed her clothes at Darren and said, "Let's go, guys. Strip. I'm going to see you naked on the other side, anyway." Her teeth snapped together. She grabbed the Hell Bitch from her stunned husband's hand, fastened a tight bowline around her waist, and covered her breasts with her arms not for embarrassment's sake but for her body heat's.

You've come a long way baby, she thought.

"I'm going upriver as far as I can. If I don't make it across, the rope will swing me back over to this side anyway. And, Neck, don't tell me you've gone shy on me. I think reciprocity is in order. I see you gawking." She smiled and when he flashed his toothy grin she knew that she had bolstered his spirits once again.

Neck giggled. "Can you take a rain check? You know how cold I am right now?"

She took the bait happily. "How cold?"

He pinched his fingers but stopped when they were an inch apart. "I'm, like, *that* cold. I'll get naked when Jake's warm again to show him off."

"Don't tell me you're one of those cheesy guys who still names his penis. I broke Darren of that habit a year ago."

"No shit! Well, what'd he call it?" Neck laughed.

"Mini-Me," she said and turned her back on them for effect.

It was a masterful management of the situation with Cappucco, Darren thought, as he watched the kid who had complained for the last hour about the river crossing laugh again and nod his fat head.

"She's lying," Darren said lamely. "It was Mega-Me."

"Yeah. Right, bro."

Kate walked upstream trailing the lifeline. When she found a platform she windmilled her arms, trying to warm herself before the plunge, but they were too sore. I'll get warm quickly, she thought, *if* I can make it across the first time. She waded in up to her thighs and began to hyperventilate, sucking oxygen deep into her stomach first, as if she was eating the air itself, then swelling her lungs, inflating them until they crushed against her ribs. She wanted to minimize the shock of the frigidity. At first there was a sharp stab of painful cold, but soon her legs were numb and tingling and her lungs could hold oxygen longer than a few seconds. "Okay, boys. Don't let go."

She crouched and sprang forward, pointing upriver into the torrent, and when her face hit the frigid water her scalp tightened and her big swallow of air was gone. She shot across the river at a diagonal, her arms extended with her hands flush on top of each other, head down for hydrodynamics, kicking furiously and tilting to the right. In river running there are two types of swimming: defensive, when you're riding the rapids in survival mode, and aggressive, when you have somewhere you need to go.

The flow caught her flank as if she had been hit by a blimp, sweeping her down into a small set of rapids. Her arms pinwheeled, hands cupped, grabbing the water and snapping it past her chest and hips. A rock scraped a strip of skin from her thigh like a cheese grater but still she churned, a desperate torpedo of muscle fighting an indifferent and relentless current that had not changed for two centuries.

Kate was halfway across when a funnel sucked her between two rocks. She quickly tucked into a cannonball, tumbling across rocks as it disgorged her. She oriented herself after the somersault and churned for the protected flat water behind a large boulder twenty yards downriver, aiming for a point well above the rock. Rushing toward it, she sprinted furiously upriver for five exhausting strokes, then glided into the placid water of the eddy. The water was moving so fast past both sides of the boulder that, directly behind it, the river was actually flowing upstream in an effort to fill the shadow space.

Her breath was ragged and labored. She was careful to keep her sandaled feet off the bottom. She tried to grip the boulder but her fingers were too numb so she kicked steadily and easily, her hands balled up, trying to generate friction on the stone. Her eyes followed the rope upstream. Darren and Neck were standing about 70 feet upriver; when she had started, they were 100 feet downriver.

"You okay, Kate?!" Darren screamed.

"Yes!"

"I've only got about twenty feet of slack left! If you can't make it on this try, I'll tow you back and give it a shot myself!"

She nodded and looked at the shore, fewer than ten feet away. If she tried to swim, the current would drag her downriver and the rope would snap taut and swing her back to the other side. She kicked hard and managed to claw her way on top of the rock, flopping up like a dolphin out of water. "Give me all the slack!" she screamed.

Kate crouched and her left calf tightened and cramped. She moaned and sat back hard on the boulder, working at the tight ball with her fingers, trying to knead out the cramp. When she stood again, her lower leg felt wooden and weak, and she favored it. So it was her right leg that powered the leap. She landed with a *splash!* just shy of the shore and her Teva wedged into a small crevice, holding her leg in place and twisting it when the current found her again and tried to pull her downstream. She snatched a log branch and yanked her foot out, her body swinging around, legs downstream, one pull-up and a grunt. She rolled onto the grassy bank. She allowed herself a few seconds of rest before she acknowledged the cheers of her teammates. *Anytime, baby!*

Darren, who had been angry at her naked and immodest display in front of Cappucco—*couldn't she have asked the jerk to turn his head?*—stared across the river and whispered, "That's my girl."

He didn't think Cheeseball heard him over the roaring waterfall but Cappucco said, "And it's a fucking crime, too."

– 40 –

GUAMUCHIL CANYON, MEXICO

Felix centered the crosshairs of his 40X scope on the naked woman and slipped off the safety with a smooth flick of his thumb. From the size of her form in his sight, he estimated the distance at about 200 meters. No adjustments would be needed. The patches of white painted over her pleasure zones were magnets in the low light. He moved the crosshairs from her tan belly up to her head, went through his breathing routine, waited for his heart rate to drop, held his breath, and simulated a shot just after he felt his heart thump. "Bang," he whispered. "Should I kill her?"

"You'll do nothing," said the little Indian. "We kill the men first. Then we go down to the girl Kate North and get the phone."

Felix scanned the opposite bank with his scope. "I don't see the men. They must be right below us, tucked against the cliff. And you mean kill just the black one, yes? The other one's a hostage."

"The phone is most important."

"So where is it? She's naked and I don't see the phone."

"They must have a waterproof bag. That's why she's naked, you old fool. You just do as I say. No more questions."

El Monstruo Carnicero gave the tracker a hard look, then did the same to the lieutenant and his three soldiers, all of whom were flat on their bellies at the top edge of the gorge, peering down at the girl, Kate North, rifles in their shoulders. The dog growled softly and the tracker hushed him and patted his belly.

El Monstruo Carnicero took the pair of binoculars from the old man and focused on his girl, Kate North. She was resting after that hard swim. And what a feat, naked! His urge swelled as he watched her stomach go up and down, the beads of water rolling past her navel. Like she is all sweaty, he thought. Even though she is freezing. He looked at her pelvis and ground his own into the dirt, careful to keep the binoculars steady.

His eyelid began to twitch. *Not long now, girl.* But how was he going to get down there after her? The stupid lieutenant didn't bring a rope! He'd have to shoot Kate North's man to hold her in place until he could figure out how to get down to the river.

El Monstruo Carnicero watched her stand and remove the rope from her waist, her hair glistening as she walked back upstream towing the rope across the water like a child would a heavy wagon. She tossed her head and grabbed the end of her hair, then squeezed out some water, naked but unconcerned. No, he thought, *proud.* She shouted across the river and wrapped the rope around a tree.

El Monstruo Carnicero turned to the posse and whispered, "She's going to tie the rope off and drag the two men across. I think they'll be tied to the rope. If they are, I want the old man to shoot the black man in the water. In the lower back or the legs, not the head. Then we probably shoot the other one in a leg. Lieutenant, you scout for a way down there, otherwise we call for a helicopter and I make sure to tell the *comandante* you're too stupid to bring a rope. *Los Asesinos* didn't forget."

"I suggest we call now then, sir. It's too steep for us."

"I told you not to speak to me unless I want." Doesn't matter if it takes me an hour, he thought, she'll stay with her dying husband and I will play with her soon.

One of the soldiers whispered and *El Monstruo Carnicero* leaned over the edge and looked down; the two men were naked and wading into the water with a backpack. They were tied to the rope, about thirty feet apart, just as he had expected. He glanced right and nodded at the tracker, who took his hand from his damn dog—he was always touching the dog and *El Monstruo Carnicero* was troubled by it—and brought the big hunting rifle up into his shoulder.

"Shoot them."

The men jumped into the water. *El Monstruo Carnicero* watched the girl Kate North pulling them across even as the river pulled them downstream. The dog barked suddenly, and barked again and again when the echo bounced back from the opposite canyon wall and scared it. The whole goddamn canyon was yelping now. The girl Kate North snapped her head up and the rope was suddenly free from the tree. She ran holding it and leapt into the stream, disappearing in the white water. The tracker fired his cannon but the bullet disappeared into froth. Three heads bobbed just a few times before being swept around the corner out of sight. The echo of the shot cracked back.

When *El Monstruo Carnicero* looked, there was only the empty river.

"Bad dog," growled Felix. "I pulled that shot."

Sniff-Sniff must have been confused by the cliff, Felix thought, so it's not his fault. After all, we had the chance to kill the woman right away, but the Indian didn't want that. You *always* took the shots you were given when hunting because you never knew what the next opportunity would be.

Felix swatted Sniff-Sniff on the nose—more for the other five men than himself—and the blood hound reeled back and skittered over next to the Indian, who was livid. Felix saw the man make a quick move with his hands, too fast to follow even with his trained eyes. Sniff-Sniff squealed and sprinted into the woods howling.

"What did you do to him?!" demanded Felix. He held his rifle menacingly.

The Indian walked over with a smile that stretched his greasy face. His head was shaped like an enormous turnip and his grin reminded Felix of the Dr. Seuss character Grinch. He placed something warm in Felix's hand and said, "Next time I hand you his heart."

When the tracker looked at the gift, he saw one of Sniff-Sniff's big floppy ears, the hair still smooth from its last brushing.

– 41 –

GUAMUCHIL CANYON, MEXICO

When Darren saw Kate jump into the river, any thoughts he had as to *why* she had done it were quickly obfuscated by a survival instinct that had been honed over the past five years trailing her in the wild. The tug of the rope was immediately replaced by the crushing weight of the flood. The roaring chaos snapped him up and sucked him downstream. Waves crashed and dunked his head underwater. He struggled to free himself from the Hell Bitch to gain maneuverability. Before his hands found the knot, he slid roughly across a rock and was dunked into a frothy hole just beyond it. The water was freezing but his mind focused on oxygen, not warmth. He tried to catch a breath but the cycle of water just pushed him back under, keeping him pinned against the back side of the rock. *Washing-machine rapid!*

Darren had seen Kate extricate herself from a similarly vicious hydraulic during a kayak trip two years before. He tried to remember what she had done to free herself from the turmoil. Then the rope stretched tight and popped him free of the hole—Cappucco was tied in 30 feet downstream and, 70 feet beyond him, Kate was probably still holding on. Their body weights had yanked him out.

He surfaced and saw Cappucco's panicked face. He was all eyeballs and teeth in the moonlight. "Keep your feet downstream so you can push off the rocks! Roll onto your back!" Darren screamed.

The angle of the river tipped and the men gathered speed. They raced past rocks hidden beneath the resplendent stream that revealed themselves only when the violent hydro ricochets encased the air and sprayed skyward, aerated and white. Darren and Neck whipped around a sudden turn in the canyon's wall.

Darren saw a thick fallen tree jutting out from the shore ten meters into the river.

"Get your arms in front and get around it!" Darren shouted to Cappucco, but the kid was closer to the middle of the river and missed the fallen tree. Darren rolled onto his stomach and swam as hard as he could. Of all the dangers in white water, strainers were the worst. If you weren't able to get up and over them, hidden branches sometimes lurked underneath, acting as sieves that trapped the unwary and the unlucky, holding them underwater and drowning them.

The water sloshed into the tree and was carved up by its branches. Lips of water hissed and squirted. The river was seething in its rush to get to the Pacific, and the patch that had melted somewhere high in the Sierra Madre and was now carrying Darren Phillips was no different. It slammed his chest against the tree and folded him in half. He wrapped the log, his naked testicles crushed against the bark, the dull tingle creeping up through his stomach to his Adam's apple. He reached across and tried to get on top of the tree but the force of the water and now the tug of the rope began to drag him under.

His feet found branches—*big* branches. He kicked and when they did not yield he panicked. The flow was relentless and he felt as if a bus was on his shoulders. His journey under the log became inevitable and he sucked in a last breath and prayed for an opening in the branches below.

Water buried him. The current twisted him sideways and pinned him tight against three thick branches. He shifted his hands from an attempt at escape to waging an attack below the surface, bending a branch back and forth. It barely moved. He twisted up for the surface, but the backpack caught on something and his head stopped a foot from the surface. One minute, he thought as he pushed and pulled, hands and feet searching for a weakness in the net of timber.

———

Thirty feet downstream, Neck's wild ride jerked to a halt and water shot up his nose and came spurting out of his mouth in a fit of coughs. Kate's weight loaded on his waist next and he was caught stretched between the couple, eyes closed and struggling to draw a dry breath. He heard Kate screaming, "What's wrong, What's wrong?" and squinted upstream for Darren. Nothing but . . . *the log.*

"I can't . . ." A quart of water invaded his mouth and he coughed and coughed.

She was screaming her head off.

Neck reached out, grabbed the rope, and tried to pull himself upstream against the current toward Darren. His large chest created a plow and water sprayed into his face, impacting like gravel. Kate's weight was too much for his tired arms and they straightened. But when he heard her terrible scream again he galvanized himself and grabbed the Hell Bitch for another try, feeling the adrenaline this time—the familiar rage—dragging the two of them forward now, a foot at a time, absolutely determined to reach the tree, his round shoulders creating a bow wave.

Halfway to Darren, Neck decided that he wasn't strong enough to make it—*fucking river's too fast!* His arms quivered and he was about to let go of his gain when he conjured up his chief, primo, number-fucking-one motivation: his sister being assaulted.

The next ten feet came easily.

When Neck reached the tree he was spent. His forearms were thick and tight and his fingers ached. The rope disappeared under the log. Beneath the surface he saw Darren tangled in a mess of branches. *Holy shit!*

Neck corkscrewed his left arm around the rope. When he cocked his wrist the wrap held and he had a free arm. He took a deep breath and dunked his head under as if he was bobbing for apples. He snaked his right hand under the surface and found a pack strap, followed it to Darren's ribs, then snatched one of the branches that was holding him under. His teammate.

He felt Darren's hands touch his little fingers and he jerked back his hand in shock, grabbed a breath, and reached back for the branch, nearly wrapping both of Darren's hands in his big paw. *He's alive!* He pulled against the fat branch and felt it bend, felt Darren pushing as well, but it refused to snap. He let his arm extend, rested, hyperventilated, held his breath—*just like the 225 test, come on Neckyoucandothisdude*—and pulled as hard as he could. He strained so hard his head vibrated and his face turned beet red and then purple. The branch snapped with a *Pop!* that muted his shout.

Neck helped Darren claw up past his waist to his chest. He was on the wild ride again, but he managed to turn his back upstream, cradling Darren, holding his head above the surface as they accelerated. The man was weak in his arms, gasping in great heaves and gripping Neck's shoulders, well, kind of like a koala bear, he thought, wondering how the image popped into his head while shooting a set of freezing rapids. Neck heard Darren say, *I got it, I'm good, I'm good . . .* but his head rolled back and he lacked the strength to keep himself afloat. So Neck ignored his protests and kept him propped up, even as the raging water slide dunked him every few seconds.

When the sparkle of stars finally cleared and the black tunnel opened, Darren saw the Somali standing over him with those nasty potato-chip teeth and the machete. He tried to scramble backward but his arms would not move. Then he realized that it was a dream, though Cappucco's toothy grin was not.

"What happened?" He twisted his head and oriented himself: lying on a grassy bank, Kate with her hand on his head, she's naked, Neck staring at him, also naked, the white water, the log, the kid on the horse, the dogs, the helicopter, the *chase*.

My God, someone shot at us!

"You blacked out, dude. Right when I broke that branch and dragged you out from under there. You got all woozy on me. Happens a lot to women when they get in my arms, you know?" The kid laughed and slapped his shoulder.

"Oh, thank God. Are you okay, babe?" Kate asked him, tears in her eyes.

"I'm good. What happened before? Why did you cut us loose?"

"I heard a dog barking."

"I thought I heard a gunshot. Did either of you?"

They nodded their heads. Kate said, "Let's get off the riverbank and back up on the plain. It wasn't smooth, but we made it across."

She rummaged in the pack and produced her shorts and T-shirt. When she stood tall and dressed, Darren noticed that Neck turned his back and averted his eyes. Maybe I've misjudged him, thought Darren, taking Neck's hand and allowing himself to be yanked to his feet.

"Did you see anybody?" Darren asked Kate, catching his clothes in midair.

"No. I didn't. Maybe it was just a dog walking along the ridge."

"You did the righ . . ." Darren said. He experienced a head rush but his fall was broken by the kid's big arms. Collapsed against and reliant on the boy, Darren was miserable in the few seconds it took for the blood to flow back into his head.

"Now kindly turn your back, Kate," said Neck when Darren was upright again. He placed a hand over his crotch.

Kate laughed and spun around, stretching her calves and inspecting the large scrape on her thigh. "I hope I recover from this, Neck. Deprived of viewing those buns of steel."

"Yeah, well, I'll give you a peek if we make it out of here alive. You, too, Darren. We better go while my feet are still too numb to know I'm torturing them again." Neck felt quite proud of himself and his sneakers came on more easily this time.

Darren coiled the Hell Bitch, stuffed it into the pack, and stepped out toward the hinterland, ascending the wooded slope just behind the other two. His mind was full but the pain in his body permeated every thought. He felt as if he had been beaten with baseball bats. Ten minutes passed before he managed to say, "If I get out of here, Neck, it's because of you."

Neck was still thinking about the nice compliment Kate had given his ass.

His legs were burning already and his knee was swelling, but Kate had a good point. His ass would power him through. "What?"

"You saved my life," said Darren.

I can't believe it's happened again. Why are other people always rescuing me? The old feeling of fraudulence came rushing up in a man whose life was propelled by paper pedigree. Darren patted Neck on the back and extended his fingers in a high-five.

Neck looked at Phillips quizzically. He hadn't seen a high-five since the fifth grade, let alone from a brother. He slapped Phillips's hand, feeling like a girl or a computer nerd or something, and when the Marine tried to give him some kind of dorky handshake it was so awkward that Neck had to work to keep quiet. *I'm blacker than he is.*

"That was a prodigious show of strength. I'm just grateful you used it for me," Darren said. It was the strongest thanks he knew how to give, as awkward as it was.

Darren added another person to his list of benefactors. In Somalia, warlords descended on his CNN news crew in a Mogadishu intersection. When he entered the crucible, his knee buckled and his co-worker was dragged away and beaten by a mob while he crawled helplessly in the dust. A warlord hefting a machete came to put him out of his misery, but one of Kelly's Marines stuck his arm out and took the brunt of the blade that was rocketing toward his neck. Darren remembered the sound of the sergeant's biceps hitting the sand. Remembered that Marine dying.

The incident with his wife on the secluded beach was the worst, though. He could not even bring himself to think about how he had let those men drag Kate out of his arms.

And how poorly he had treated Neck Cappucco! He replayed the past forty hours and was ashamed of his supercilious conduct. Yet Neck had still pulled himself against that flood and broken that branch to save *him.* After he had threatened to fight the kid!

Darren realized Cappucco was speaking to him and asked Neck to repeat it.

"I was just saying that I owe my life to you, too, Darren. You and Kate both. I mean, the decision to leave the cell was mine, and you all have got me through since. I just hope I don't up and quit on you all. I mean, my body's giving out on me."

"You'll make it, Neck," said Darren. "I swear to you that you'll make it."

And there it was. Darren had a method of repayment. He snatched it out of the air and burned it into his psyche. Neck Cappucco would be a professional football player after all. Darren would see to it.

The trio leaned into the hill and plodded east.

– 42 –

GULF OF MEXICO

The sun brought color back into his world. Gavin Kelly warily watched the ocean turn from a black slick into a deluge of blue, the umbrella of the night folding up and exposing him. Kelly was a nocturnal creature. He sneered at the arrival of what would clearly be a beautiful day. He would have preferred serious rain and a rough sea.

He opened his storage cabinet, checked out of habit to ensure that a round was still chambered in the Beretta, and scanned the horizon for enemy ships.

Of course, much of this was just paranoia. He had been meticulous in keeping to international waters, skirting the Mexican coast all the way south, but if the coastal radar alerted the Mexican Navy he didn't stand a chance—his Mako's engine had been struggling for the last thirty minutes.

Kelly had rented it from a Brownsville marina boat-rental employee who had insisted on a $7,500 cash down payment to ensure against damage and vomit stains. Kelly had told him he was just going to be taking college kids water-skiing at South Padre Island—as he did every year—but the moment the word "break" followed the word "spring" the man had thrown up his arms and raised the price. It was a good cover story, but it was also expensive.

He checked his GPS and saw that he was fifteen miles east of Tampico, the only major coastal city between Brownsville and Veracruz. He'd traveled nearly 200 miles, about halfway to Veracruz, and was on track to arrive at Phillips's beach extract site more than two days ahead of schedule before the engine started to sputter. He'd ridden the Mercury 225 outboard too aggressively and now he could make no better than eight knots. He planned a refueling stop in

Tampico, but now he might need to find a mechanic as well, a problem considering he didn't speak any Spanish.

Why the hell did I take French in high school anyway? he wondered. What a useless fucking language. Spanish was where the leverage was. Except for the tasty French au pair he had corralled on Newport Beach, he remembered, now deciding that he had been prescient after all. Kelly convinced the giggling group of nannies to play topless volleyball with his Marine buddies. Like a gender-reversed *Top Gun* scene!

Kelly blinked and turned his attention to the motor. Five years in The Hague had made him prone to daydreams, and loneliness sparked their further proliferation. The engine was trailing a thin wisp of black smoke and the rpms were erratic. He reasoned that there was an obstruction in a fuel line somewhere, but he had no mechanical ability and placed the cover back on the outboard.

He thought of Darren Phillips, a man who used to insist that they leave their San Clemente bachelor pad for Camp Pendleton a full *hour* before morning formation in case they got a flat tire. *Do you want to be one of those lieutenants that shows up late? In front of his men! Is that leading by example?* Phillips had had an austere lust for timeliness for as long as Kelly had known him. Called it a *lack of professionalism.* What would his best friend say if he showed up late to extract him from Mexico while on the run from the *entire country!*

No, he'd get the engine fixed and be on his way. And even if it didn't improve, he'd still be there early making eight lousy knots. Maybe he should have recruited a good-looking college chick to round out the cover story. Arizona State was supposed to have some hotties. Why in the world did I waste my years at Harvard? he wondered.

Kelly snapped his head around, vowing to suspend the fantasies and concentrate only on the course to Tampico, but the habit he'd developed in prison was entrenched and soon his eyes blurred the waves and the whine of the engine became white noise. Over the next hour he thought about the bizarre downfall of Mike Tyson, the Somali sergeant Armstrong had killed on the beach, adjustable breast implants, the absurd democratic pep rally that followed Clinton's impeachment trial, setting up a steadying block to fire the AR-15 from the gunwales, Elle McPherson, Claudia Schiffer, Stephanie Seymour, Heidi Klum, and their befuddling mating preferences, whether he would wilt under fire, what a terrific woman Kate was, the ridiculous patriotic speech Phillips had delivered at his wedding, and what Kelly would say when he saw the couple next.

Kelly paused for a moment on the last one, then decided on: *Phillips, you look as ugly as six dicks tied in a knot, but it's still better than that "love me, watch me, look-at-me" face you wore for your porno shots. By the way, folks, I took the liberty of setting up a Web site and you guys have just surpassed John Wayne Bobbit's site for downloads. So don't worry about paying me back for this little extract.*

———

A mile out of Tampico, three fishing boats and a string of pangas passed him in formation. Two of the smaller wakes melded into a larger one and pitched the Mako sideways, not more than a ten-degree roll, but enough to stall the beleaguered engine. Kelly turned the key twice, pushing in for some choke, but the outboard just whirred softly. "Damn it," he whispered, walking aft to toss the anchor.

It was fifteen minutes before another boat exited the inlet and headed for the open ocean. Kelly was able to flag it down using his T-shirt. Two dark men in baseball caps pulled their panga alongside and leaned over so they could see if he had been fishing.

Kelly said, "*Hola!* My boat . . . no good. Dead. Finito. Habla anglaise?"

"*No*," said the men. One of them glanced at the Mako and whispered to the other.

Don't get paranoid. Kelly made a series of hand gestures and asked for a tow. The men shrugged and turned their palms skyward, then one of them brightened and pulled out a radio. The man nodded his head and waved as if to say, don't worry, I understand now. He keyed the radio several times and finally got an answer. He spoke very rapidly and smiled at Kelly when he was finished. "*Hay el venir del barco.*"

"You called for tow? Boat? Another boat?"

"*Sí,*" said the man as he untied from the Mako and pushed off. "*Policía.*"

Shit. Kelly watched the men wheel their boat around. When their backs were to him he rushed to the depth finder—seventy feet—and recorded his position as a waypoint on his GPS. He measured sixty feet of line and attached the buoy to one end and the fish box to the other, then dumped the armory overboard. The line whipped out and the foam buoy popped out of the stern and disappeared underwater.

Kelly heard the whine of an engine and spotted a thick, black boat—metal hull—coming toward him from the inlet. *Policía.* He grabbed the Beretta, thought about the wasted $500, and tossed it into the Atlantic with its extra magazines.

When the sailor on the Mexican Coast Guard cutter tossed him a line, Kelly smiled and waved. "*Gracias,*" he said, eyeing the crew. Four men, four M-16s. Rusty barrels. "My boat is finito. *Gracias.*"

A well-built man wearing an officer's insignia jumped into Kelly's Mako and looked him over. *"Está usted fuera de gas,"* he said.

"No habla español."

The man shouted over his shoulder and a second sailor hopped into the boat. The younger man smiled awkwardly, but it was clear that he was there to guard against any sudden moves. Kelly kept his hands out from his sides and sat on the gunwale.

The senior sailor emerged from the cockpit and looked Kelly over again. *"De dónde es usted? Es usted americano? Dónde está su forma de costumbres?"* he asked.

"No habla español." Kelly shrugged and gave his best stupid American smile.

The man grimaced and waved him up onto the cutter. Then two sailors rigged tow lines and they made their way back into the harbor dragging Kelly's Mako, the sailors jabbering and one of them speaking into a radio, sneaking glances at Kelly. Eventually the officer said, *"Americano?"*

"Sí."

- 43 -

NEW YORK CITY

William T. North III signed his car service chit, grunted at the driver, and stepped out onto Broad Street. He felt the electricity of The Street immediately, just as he had for over twenty years—the determined hustle of the men (and now women, too), the smacks of their hurried heels, the blaring of horns as the Connecticut crew jockeyed for parking, the ubiquitous presence of fear and greed, the money lust prodding all the suits. Well, we *used* to be well dressed, he thought, before this "casual" virus had infected The Street.

In the Goldman, Sachs window, Bill North's grim reflection straightened its tie and tried its best to relax. The circles under his eyes were pronounced. Since his daughter disappeared in Mexico—and the *goddamn press* had started their ambush tactics—sleep had become a cornered commodity and his emotions were as volatile as the NASDAQ, trending south with the popped bubble.

"Mr. North?" said a young man in a suit who cut off his entrance route.

"Leave me alone, damn you to hell," North said. "I've answered enough questions." He tried to brush past but the rascal grabbed his elbow.

"I have some news about Kate," the man whispered, handing him an envelope. "I got this in the mail yesterday, in an envelope addressed to me from Gavin Kelly. He was a year behind me at business school. I went to your apartment this morning and couldn't find you . . . I didn't expect you to come to work, I guess."

Before North could respond, two cameras from local stations were on him and the young man was gone, walking quickly toward Wall Street. North pushed through the throng and rode the elevator up to his office, acknowledging but not responding to the stares from his colleagues. Accusatory stares, he thought, convicting him of rearing a drug-addicted murderer.

The envelope was addressed "William North's eyes only." North hustled to his office without acknowledging his secretary, make that *office manager*, in order to appear normal. He used his Princeton letter opener to carefully slice through the fold.

Mr. North,

I couldn't remember where Mrs. Phillips worked but you must relay this message to her in person. In person, Mr. North—I am sure your phones and mail are under surveillance. I am on my way to retrieve Darren and Kate. When I extract them, they'll need a place to go and plenty of money. Get a large cash sum ready. Quietly. If they are to stand trial, we may need to get them to a non-extradition country. I'll contact you by April 20. If I do not, please have someone go to the phone bank at Baggage Claim 7 in TF Green airport. I'll call the middle phone at midnight every day, starting April 21. I apologize for the Providence phone but it was the only safe number I could jot down on my way.

Thanks again for the great wedding!

Keep your chin up and Semper Fi,

Gavin Kelly

– 44 –

SIERRA MADRE OCCIDENTAL

El Monstruo Carnicero looked at the damn dog. It looked ridiculous with the bandages taped across its ear but it had learned its lesson. Next time he would slit its belly open.

Now everything in the posse hated him, which is how he preferred the world. He relished his enemies because they validated him. The more of them the better. Young Aztecs rose to power on captured enemies, not friends. And look at the old man pet the dog! It gave him the creeps, the way a man could love an animal like that. "Hey old man," hissed *El Monstruo Carnicero*. "What you gonna do to that dog next? Cry for it? Maybe use your tears to grease up its ass-hole for you?"

The Aztec laughed but nobody else said a word. He didn't feel foolish. In his life, the laughter of others had stopped cold the moment he butchered the American agent. Since then, he had to provide his own jokes to his own audience. There were never any smiles. Even his crew looked at him warily when they made a sacrifice.

Felix looked up at him with slanted eyes and stood with his hands balled up in tight, knotted fists. "I'll beat your brains in, you little Indian worm," said Felix.

"Easy friend. He'll pay for it," said Lieutenant Garza, who turned to face the little man. The *comandante* had warned him back at Zampedro that orders concerning the Indian would be forthcoming. Now he knew what they would be: the Indian was to be arrested once *Los Asesinos* were boxed. He was sure of it. "And you, sir, will have some explaining to do when we get back to the compound. I very much doubt the *comandante* will be pleased."

El Monstruo Carnicero grunted and grabbed the end of his stringy beard, popped it into his mouth, swirled his tongue around the hair until it was tight and slick, sucked some spare tobacco juice and pulled it out, straight and smooth. "The only one who's got explaining to do is you and the old fool. We just walked for three hours and couldn't find a way across the canyon. You don't bring a rope. *Los Asesinos* have one, but not you. I wanted to walk faster, you wanted breaks. We won't allow a head start next time. And we won't stop. You better hope they use that phone again, Lieutenant, because it is *you* who owes answers."

El Monstruo Carnicero was proud of his speech and he wanted to give another. It felt good to be talking with men, telling them what to do. His was a lonely life spent hissing at victims so he didn't get much practice in debate, and he thought he clearly exerted his dominance. Young Aztec warriors fought fiercely with one another before they were permitted the privilege of battle. Look at the soldier back down again!

The lieutenant bit his lip and sat down next to his men. There was no sense in bringing up the little man's order not to shoot the woman; he'd do that for the government when they returned to Mexico City, just before the Indian was placed in the brig.

- 45 -

TAMPICO, MEXICO

Kelly was seated in an office in the Tampico police station with his hands cuffed behind his back. His guard was dressed in a rumpled khaki uniform tucked into a leather gun belt. A .38 revolver dangled awkwardly on his hip. He didn't speak English and the silence made Kelly, a man who was prone to jabber when he was nervous, even more impatient.

A short man in a freshly cleaned linen suit entered and the guard came to attention and saluted. The man wore a mustache that seemed to be as thin as a toothpick. He sat across from Kelly. "Mister Callahan, yes?"

"Yes, sir. Sí."

"Sit. Sit. Don't worry, I speak English. I'm Miguel Ramos, the resident prosecutor for your kind in Tampico. And apparently the first English speaker they could locate this morning." He laughed and Kelly faked it, joining him.

Ramos had a precise manner. He was short and had a pugnacious face, ironed blue shirt with a healthy dose of starch, yellow tie complete with the Darren Phillips special ROTC dimple.

Kelly said, "Unfortunately, I learned French as my second language, sir."

"*Oh, c'est vrai? Bien. Plusiers des americains ne parlent pas des autres langues. N'est-ce pas? Préférez-vous parler en anglais ou français? J'aime les deux.*"

The words spilled over Kelly's ability to process them and he lost everything after the first phrase. He grinned and put up his hands, exaggerating an embarrassed look. This is an erudite man, he thought. I'll have to tread lightly to get out of here quickly.

"Unfortunately, like many of my countrymen, even my French is horrible. My name is Harold Callahan and I just need to get my boat fixed."

"So I hear, Mister Callahan. So I hear. We're running your driver's license through the Texas channels right now. It's not processing for some reason. You understand, I need confirmation before I may proceed." He smiled thinly and offered Kelly a cigarette.

"No, thank you, sir."

"Don't use your own product, eh?" said Ramos.

Kelly was confused.

"Look, sir, I'm sure you can clear this up. I told your deputies that I have a personal Web site they can check: www-dot-spring-break-texas-adventures-dot-com. That'll tell you all you need to know and confirm my identity. I'm heading to Cancún for spring break. I go every year to party, take kids fishing. Make a whole trip out of it. Stop along the coast. Take my time. Same as the other trip I wrote about on the Web site."

Ramos turned to the guard and made some sort of face that caused the guard to roll his eyes. He lit a cigarette and politely blew the smoke out of the corner of his mouth. "Oh, yes. We greatly enjoyed the site. Especially the women in bikinis. So let me get this cleared up, as you say. You say you're fishing but you have no fish box. Instead, you have two one-hundred-gallon fuel drums. You say you're going to Cancún, but did you check through customs yet? No. Not this year or any other. That's illegal, you know."

Kelly's stomach tingled. Invisible needles pinpricked their way up the length of his arms. *Is he looking for me or just looking for a payoff?* "I'm happy to pay a fine—"

"Don't interrupt me again. You see, I don't like to dance. Not on a sunny morning. Not with people like you. Now, we've checked your reservation at the Cancún Sheraton, but tell me, where are you docking your boat?"

"I usually grab a canceled slip reservation when I'm down there."

"Ah, of course." Ramos popped his cigarette into his mouth, replaced it in his hand with a pen, and began jotting exaggerated notes. "Can. Cel. Ation. Now, on your Web page you advertised a different boat. Why that tiny Mako outside?"

"Short on di nero this year."

"Clearly. That is why you had nine thousand dollars in your pockets."

Ramos manufactured a harsh laugh and pulled a thick manila envelope out of his carry case. He tossed it across the table and it dropped with a thud onto Kelly's lap. "That's about the lamest story I've heard yet, Mister Callahan—whatever your name is—and I've heard some pretty terrible ones. Now, I admit your Web site confused some of the deputies here, but did you really think it would hold up? Maybe behind those blue eyes there is no brain, yes? Is that your money?"

Kelly looked the man in his eyes to convey understanding. He opened his knees and when the package plopped next to his feet, he kicked it under the table toward Ramos. "It does not have to be, sir. Not all of it. Not if I can get my boat fixed."

Ramos squinted for a moment before understanding popped his eyebrows up and caused him to practically jump to his feet. He kicked his chair across the room and leaned across the table, furious. He extended his thumb and drilled it into Kelly's collarbone. "You think you can buy me with your dirt money, *cabrón?* Poisoning your own country and mine, and you think you can just *pay a fine?*"

Kelly felt his saliva evaporate. He had grown up on the same sweat sessions on *Hill Street Blues,* but the blunt reality of the moment left him mute. I don't believe this, he thought. He's not after me to get at Phillips. *He thinks I'm running drugs.*

"I only give one chance," said Ramos, waving the guard away. He picked his chair up and sat back down, then lit another cigarette. "This is not baseball or California. One strike. If you don't give me the right answers now while you can help yourself—while this is still off the record—then I'm going to lock you up and you'll be spending a long, *long* time in Tampico."

Miguel Ramos did not look like he had the ability or the inclination to bluff. Kelly tried to speak but he was enervated and his hands were clammy and his tongue was shaking and the words dribbled their way out of his mouth, lame and guilty. "I . . . I swear to you, sir, we're on the same side. I am not into drugs."

"Oh, bullshit, Mister Callahan, bull*shit.* I stopped listening to dealers long ago. The only paperwork you had was nine thousand U.S. dollars in *cash* in your pocket. I'm sure we'll find more when we tear your boat apart. So, here we go. You're up to bat. You answer three questions and your life will get a lot better. What is your real name? What is the name of your supplier? And what is the name of your distributor?"

"Callahan is my name, sir." Kelly knew that once his real name appeared on some computer network it would trigger an avalanche. "I don't have a supplier or a distributor, so I guess I'll just take my phone call."

Ramos faked another laugh, and rank structure pulled the guard into the joke. "Oh, yes, your phone call. So you can call some Mexican lawyer whore pimped out by a cartel to represent you? Fine. Bring him on. Because the moment you do, it means the trial occurs here. There's no extradition treaty now that your country has shoved these new laws down our throats, you know. You are not going home for quite a while. Especially not when I win."

Kelly steeled himself and recovered his tongue. The outcome of the exercise was already cast, the same way it was for his court-martial. A cacophony of wiseass responses sat revving below his vocal cords and he tried to restrain the nervous tic. "I'll still take that phone call. As an aside, I should warn you that Mister Cochran has not lost a case in several years. I should also warn you that I know karate."

Ramos stood and exchanged words with the guard. "Yes, well, as soon as we get the phone fixed, you may use it. You'll be comfortable in a holding cell until then, where you can use your karate skills, I'm sure."

The guard yanked Kelly to his feet and chaperoned him down a concrete hallway that bisected the darkened cell block. Kelly struggled to find an exit strategy, but he felt himself wilting under the sudden pressure of time, listening in vain to Ramos and the guard whispering even though he could not understand them. He had over two hundred miles to go. How long were they going to ice him? His head was down and he watched long shadows shrink into his feet as he passed under each bulb that lit the damp hallway.

They stopped him at the last cell. The stench of urine and decay was so powerful that Kelly thought he might be able to lean on it. When his eyes adjusted, Kelly saw a giant man asleep on a cot, naked from the waist down. His belly swelled and sagged with each great breath. Next to him, the outside of the toilet bowl was covered with dry flakes of pink vomit that nearly glowed.

The guard shoved Kelly inside and slammed the door shut. *"Wake up, Jaime! You have a visitor!"* the guard screamed in Spanish.

The naked man awoke with a grunt that would have scattered pigs from the trough. He blinked several times, then waddled over to the corner of the cell where he labored to slip his wet jeans over his bare legs. As he emerged from the cell, Kelly saw that he was as large as a Sumo wrestler. The smell of urine gave the air texture.

"You must be pledging a fraternity," Kelly said involuntarily. "I remember those glory years well. Didn't know chicks down here dug the unibrow thing, though."

The guard pulled Kelly's hands through the bars, removed the cuffs, and said, *"This cell has room for only one. When I return, the man who is standing gets a clean cell and fresh sheets."*

Kelly's cellmate smiled at him. He was missing his front teeth and his face was still puffy from the previous night's activities. Kelly winked, then said to Ramos, *"Senor,* I did not know Andre the Giant was alive. You should sell tickets for this match."

"Apparently code dictates that we only have one man per cell. So the deputy said that he'll return in a few minutes and take the last man left standing to a clean cell."

Kelly studied his cellmate—close to three hundred pounds with thick arms that jutted out of his dirty mangled tank top like torpedoes—and abruptly sat Indian-style on the floor of the cell. "Oh, well, hell, he wins. Now get him out of here already. He stinks."

The guard and the cellmate looked confused and for a moment the only sound was a strange plopping drip somewhere by the toilet. Then the guard brightened and said, *"What I meant was, last man conscious leaves."*

Ramos and the guard turned and walked back to the offices. Kelly shouted after them, "Hey, what'd he say?"

Kelly listened to their footsteps recede. The cells were windowless and trapped the echoes of their heels. He felt the menace next to him solidify, no longer a distant possibility but a promise of catastrophe. Even if Kelly *did* survive, the clock was running on his operation. He had to get going.

Kelly leapt up, grabbed the bars, and squeezed his face between them. "Mister Ramos! I'll tell you who I am!"

– 46 –

MCLEAN, VIRGINIA

Ted Blinky was confused. In two decades of CIA service he'd seen dozens of senior officers banished to distant hellholes without warning or terminated entirely, and in each case they had been immediately severed from their current duties. Desks had been cleaned out, badges removed, contact with staff discouraged. Susanne Sheridan had met with the directors of Homeland Security and Central Intelligence the night before and had been fired. This morning she had announced her retirement, but she was still hanging around the Bat Cave. Worse, her replacement was nowhere to be found, a terribly disconcerting event for a bureaucrat whose entire life depended on the temperament of the whip-cracker above him in the chain of command. Leadership turnovers drove Blinky to the edge of crazy, happy anticipation warring with dread. Would he be working 80-hour or 40-hour weeks? Would he have to deal with bad jokes or a wicked temper?

Blinky swiveled uncomfortably in his government-issued office chair and mulled it over, not unhappy that Sheridan was leaving but not quite exuberant, either. She wasn't so bad. He reached into his briefcase and delicately pulled open the seam of the Doritos bag he had smuggled into the Cave for breakfast. The chips relaxed him.

"Wipe your mouth, Ted," said Christian Collins when Blinky had finished feasting under the desk the two shared.

Blinky stared across at the Dot Bomber and coolly licked his upper lip. "Maybe the next deputy director will allow food again. Colm Callan did when he ran this place in the nineties. I've seen 'em come, and I've seen 'em go."

"Yeah, but she's still here. I think she's still working on the BEEKEEPER case. What's that about?" asked Collins.

Blinky shrugged and turned to look at Sheridan. Her regular seat was out on the floor, but since her announcement she had retreated to the soundproof room and its secure phone. The room was a glass cube the size of a studio apartment built to defeat even internal eavesdropping devices, a place nicknamed the "torture chamber" that Blinky despised, because senior officers used it to lecture subordinates in "private." A pulse speaker system pumped inaudible white noise that broke up sound waves past a foot so the higher-ups had to get in your face to deliver the news. It was a stupid place for a dressing down, thought Blinky. With its clear walls it really didn't matter if outsiders heard what was said. The body language told all.

Sheridan saw him gawking and set down the phone. "Oh, shit," said Blinky. "Here she comes."

Sheridan opened the glass door, walked over to Collins and Blinky and smiled. "It's not polite to stare, gentlemen. You two should apply for a construction job. Or was that a last, loving look?"

"We're just sorry to hear the news, ma'am," said Blinky.

"It's total bullshit," seconded Collins.

"Any word on your replacement, ma'am?" asked Blinky. "Because you still seem to be working the case hard."

Susanne Sheridan smiled. So that's what it is, she thought. They're suspicious. *I've trained them well.* "Both of you listen to me. I want you to ignore what I'm doing. Just do your jobs and you'll be fine. Understand? Questions about me will just hurt you."

She met both their eyes to drive home the point, and the intense silence was broken by the watch officer. He stood up waving a phone. "Deputy Director Sheridan, there's a Texas DEA on line seven-seven-six who's trying to find Agent Contreras. He was routed into this office. Should I pass him over to FBI?"

Susanne said, "No, I'll take it in the torture chamber." She looked at Collins and Blinky once more and said, "When someone like me is rotting, the decay is infectious. Do your jobs." She turned and walked into the torture chamber.

"Jesus, is she going rogue?" Collins whispered to Blinky. "That's illegal."

Blinky was too distracted to answer. When the watch officer had shouted out the line, he had typed in a simple circuit patch to eavesdrop. The call must be coming in unencrypted, he thought. He picked up his headset and indicated Collins should do the same. "Want to find out? This one's coming in on an open line."

The two men ducked their heads below their computer monitors to listen.

"This is Deputy Director Susanne Sheridan. How may I help?" their boss said.

"Oh, hey, ma'am," said a startled voice on the other end. "My name is Paul Montanus. I'm a DEA agent down here in Austin. I was just looking for Agent Contreras. I didn't mean to involve you, ma'am."

"What is it? I'll give him the message."

"That's okay, ma'am. No need to involve you. Well below your pay grade."

"Well, it *won't* be okay unless you give me the message."

"Yes, ma'am," the agent said. "I was just going to ask Jimmy if he was running any active informants down in Mexico. We got some white boy locked up in a Mexican prison who claims he's Agent Contreras's little brother. Says he needs to talk to him pronto. Anyway, like I said, I hate to waste your time. Likely it's some perp he busted a while back who's out now and already got himself caught."

"Does this guy have a name?" Sheridan asked.

"Yes, ma'am. It's G. K. Contreras, according to the electronic inquiry the Mexicans sent."

Blinky and Collins heard their former boss inhale sharply.

"Agent Montanus, I'm going to give you my cell number. I need you to call me back on an encrypted line."

– 47 –

SIERRA MADRE RANGE

The trio hiked for twelve hours with few rest stops, crossing Highway 190 with an armadillo that waddled faster than they ran. The stale wind was steadily grinding its pitch higher, driving the cold right through their T-shirts and into their skins. The march had pounded away their T cells and their starved bodies could no longer fight infection. Strawberry-colored inflammation surrounded the dozens of scratches and blisters each of their dying bodies incubated, wreaking havoc with their internal temperature.

All of them were injured and to watch them pass that afternoon would have been like watching the survivors of the Bataan Death March, their only focus on lifting each leg and swinging it forward through all the swelling.

None had spoken for three hours. Neck tried to take inventory of his pain but it took fifteen minutes to decide where to start, so slow was his thought process and so great was his misery. Lack of sodium and sleep had given way to confusion. He knew that his beautiful temple was redlining but could not pinpoint the bug. Aside from the 200-mile nonstop hike, of course.

Neck started with his feet. Dotted with blisters that burst periodically and sloshed around behind his heel, it felt like someone was taking a cheese grater to their undersides.

Next, both Achilles tendons were carrying tendonitis—he could feel the little rocks of inflammation grating against the sleeves of his tendons every time he stepped, and had heard them squeak like baby mice during the last ten-minute rest halt when he rotated his ankles to loosen them up like Kate told him to.

Three hours ago.

His left shin had been scraped raw in the rapids and the scab that formed was tight and red. He couldn't see it, though, not with that pesky knee all swollen and full of plasma fluid. Kate would have to cut it with the damn bottle again during the next stop. It was more sight gag than impediment—Neck had stopped bending his knee miles ago.

For all the horribles that his legs and feet endured, they weren't the root cause of his suffering. Another heat flash raced up his back and around his neck, tingling the skin on his head and closing his vision, like the time he busted Notre Dame's wedge sophomore year and had given himself a concussion. He knew it was cold—Kate had told them she was worried about her parameter or odometer dropping—but he felt clammy.

Neck Cappucco put his hands on his knees, leaned forward, and vomited. His stomach was empty. The bile rolled slowly out of his stomach, up his esophagus, and past his tongue, taking its time, starving him of air. The acid finally dripped across his lips and he spit twice and gasped for air. "Uuhhn," he sighed. "Somethin's wrong here."

"It's normal, Neck," said Darren. "The sleeplessness is piling up on top of the exhaustion and the strain and the lack of chow. The air is thin up here and we're not acclimatized. Add some acute mountain sickness and the nausea is normal."

"You keep saying that," he said weakly. He was not used to playing the group puss, but he could not stop his brain from communicating. "I am *truly* dying here."

Kate placed her hand against Neck's forehead. "You're feverish. Bad news is, that's *also* normal. Let's take a brief rest and get you better."

She helped Neck sit and then wrapped her arm around his back. He was shivering, and Kate held him tight, pulling his big head down so it could rest on her shoulder.

Neck loved her warm body. "Kate, I need more than a short stop. Can we get some shut-eye, you think? I can't *move* anymore. I'm over."

Kate shared a quick glance with her husband. She recognized the subtlety of Neck's request. She'd seen it before when teammates had cracked. Capitulation to an adventure-racing course started with tiny requests—a little sleep, a bite of a Snickers—generated by the sirens of the mind. Once the voices planted the seeds of quitting, they flourished if nobody quashed them, the prospect of a warm bed and warm food and *normal life* growing larger with each step, spreading like a disease until the racer simply stopped and refused to move.

Kate chastised herself for letting it happen again. She had to get Neck moving.

It was darker than it should have been. The white cirrus strings had given way to gray, puffy cumulus clouds. She noticed that she no longer cast a shadow. Rain at altitude would drive them straight into hypothermia. They were up on a high ridgeline that cobwebbed for miles, and she could see clouds slithering south toward them.

She was loath to halt on so exposed a slope. "I'm sorry, Neck, but we need to get off this range before the weather hits. Tell you what, big guy. We'll descend into that valley down there—see the town in the distance?—and we'll look for shelter and get some shut-eye before nightfall."

"I really need some sleep. Something's wrong."

Kate rubbed his back vigorously, warming him. "Nothing's wrong. You've done such an impressive job. You're so strong I may have to recruit you for my next race! I just hope you stay in touch when you're a millionaire, stud muffin. I'm going up ahead to scout for a route down the mountain. I'll see you two over at that lip in a few."

Neck watched Kate limp across the slate stone, once again mesmerized by her legs, a silver charm whose motion hypnotized him. His eyes lingered for a few more seconds before he asked Darren, "What about you. You hurt?"

"Yes," Darren said.

"You don't act like it, all Silent Bob and shit."

"Well." Darren had no idea who Silent Bob was.

"Kate's special. She reminds me a lot of my mom. You're a lucky mother-fucker."

Darren did not appreciate profanity, but the words made him feel good. He stood and his feet roared to life, then his calves, then his thighs, then his traps where the pack straps had eroded them. He had a tennis-ball-sized knot of torn muscle just above his shoulder blade. "Where's your mom live now?"

"Oh, she's dead. She and my kid brother, they died in a car crash when I was thirteen. My dad's remarried but, anyways, she was real special. Real athletic like Kate. That's where I get my skills from, you know, but they didn't really have girls' sports back then. She played tennis for the community league. I miss her big-time, dude."

"Well," said Darren. He was uncomfortable when the emotional ante of a conversation was raised beyond his modest stake. "I'm sure she's proud now, Neck."

"Oh, hell yes, she is. Hell yes." He raised his hand and let Darren pull him to his feet. "Kate's like that, you know? Always real positive. You all have kids planned soon?"

Darren looked across the hill for Kate—he wanted the hell out of the conversation—but she was gone. His willingness to talk surprised him, given

that he cast a critical glare at those other men who babbled about their relationships.

"That's actually a sore subject, Neck. I want to have kids right away and she
wants to race for a few more years. Her argument is that I work too hard now,
anyway, so she'd be raising the kids alone, but she doesn't understand that in
order to have a good life you have to put your head down and work for it, right?"

Part of him wanted to take back the comments immediately, snatch them
out of the sky or give a quick retraction, but the dominant twin actually felt
good, as if a demon had been exorcised high on a Mexican mountain where the
other members of the gun club could not see or hear.

I'm just tired, he thought. I mean, what is this kid, my marriage counselor?

"Kate says you want to be a senator or something, right? Go into politics?"

How could Darren be angry with her when he was bartering in secrets himself? "Maybe after the Marines," he said softly.

"So when are you going to have the time to raise kids together? I think you
should max out on the time with her, dude. That's what I'd do, a woman like
that. Kick it and live the good life with her. That's what she wants. More time
with you, yo."

"Not everyone can play professional football, Neck."

Neck chuckled and leaned on Darren's shoulder until he felt he could walk
on his own. He rotated an ankle and the tendonitis popped like a balloon. "Oh,
come on, man. She told me all about you. Harvard? Big war hero? You're set. But
you're wound too tight, bro. I've seen how you are. You need to step up the romance!"

"Last I heard, romance was dead for men like us, Neck." Darren felt like a
kid stealing cookies from the jar by entertaining the conversation. He'd end it
soon.

Neck waved his hand as if he was a gangster rapper or gangsta rappa or
whatever it was those imbeciles called themselves. Darren relied on Kate to keep
him current with odd cultural totems like Michael Jackson's racism charges and
Carrot Top's ability to find work. He found such subjects both distasteful and
wasteful, but the whole country seemed to watch *Entertainment Tonight* and he
needed the ability to relate.

"Naw, naw, dude, listen to me here. Romance is *alive*," said Neck, color
and confidence returning to his face. "When's the last time you brought Kate
flowers? See what I'm talkin' 'bout? Love is about self-sacrifice, dude. I seen
what she's willing to give up for you. Question is, what are you willing to sacrifice for her?"

The two men started forward and both of them stepped gingerly until some
numbness set in. When they moved over the hill where Kate stood, they faced a

breeze that had been at their backs and had gone unnoticed. They had to lean forward to stay upright. Wind filled their mouths and puffed their cheeks like chipmunks.

Something the kid had said irked Darren, and he was coaxing his languid brain to break it down logically. What was he willing to sacrifice? Well, a lot! But not an entire political career. Maybe he could start coming home earlier or something, he grumbled.

A gust rippled the string grass, bending it forward in smooth waves as if it were water. Neck felt a droplet of icy sweat trickle back across his freezing cheek. "You're talking to yourself, dude. You sound like me! How do you move so fast on those chicken legs, anyway? I mean, your upper body is pretty packed but you have no legs!"

Neck had been considering Darren's legs and their capabilities for over 100 miles.

"Thing is, Neck," shouted Darren when they approached Kate, "a chicken has *extremely* powerful legs. You've seen *Rocky* where he chases one, right?"

"Oh hell yeah!"

"Well, over long distances, they can outrun sled dogs! You saw the *NBC Dateline* special on the chickens of the Iditarod, right?"

"What's Iditarod?"

"The sled dog race!" Darren wondered how long it would take for Neck's response—either affirmative or negative. Kate often played the "plant-a-thought" trick on him during the Eco-Challenge, and he was happy to play on the other side for once. He lowered his head into the wind and waited.

Draft Day evaporated and Neck's head was filled with chickens and huskies. Chickens *were* fast, that was true, but could they withstand the cold? Maybe. They had feathers and everything, just like down coats and pillows. In fact, that sweet North Face parka he liked to wear on cold days was down and, man, didn't he wish he had some dead chickens on his body now! With their guts, even, so he could shove his hands inside for warmth.

But how did their short legs make it through thick snow? Maybe their claws were like snowshoes. Little fuckers were fast, that was for sure. Maybe the snow chickens were *trained* just like he was. Highly conditioned, bad motherfucking birds. Chickens that were strong. Chickens that ran dogs down.

He felt close to an opinion.

Still, it was a full mile before his brain assembled the jumble of thoughts and another mile before Darren overheard Neck ask, "Kate, do you figure a chicken could outrun a big dog? Over distances, I mean, assuming it was in shape."

– 48 –

ZAMPEDRO ARMY BASE, MEXICO

Jimmy Contreras sat on a small berm overlooking the flight line and watched the sun set by himself. The rays rippled across the heavy smog and turned the sky bright orange. He had never opened himself to a woman, so while his dominant feeling was a form of longing, it was weighted by *compañeros* of the past, not a partner for the future. He and the rest of Corwin's team had been cleared into the base as guests of Saiz, but he felt no connection to the FBI men. In fact, he had not felt connected to anyone since Luis Gonzalez was murdered.

He sat still for an hour until the crickets grew loud. Then he composed himself and walked directly across the tarmac. He was intercepted by a soldier carrying an M-16.

"May I see some identification, sir?" the soldier asked in Spanish.

Contreras pulled out his DEA badge. *"I'm here with Eduardo Saiz. Is there a noncommissioned officer's club around here?"*

"No, sir. But there's an officer's club past the hangar."

"Guess this old sergeant will have to tolerate some stupid conversation tonight, then," Contreras said. He winked at the soldier and walked toward the hangar, skirting the floodlights illuminating the media circus under the big top. Deputy Attorney General Saiz had moved his command post from Mexico City to the *Federale* training base under the auspice of rapid response, but Contreras suspected the military presence gave him two bigger things: a grand backdrop for his acting and protection from the cartels.

Contreras entered the officer's club and sat on a stool at the bar. Corwin wouldn't appreciate his thirst, but then again, what the fuck did he care what

Roger Corwin had to say? He was in a mood. He ordered a Dos Equis and a shot of tequila, then surveyed the club. He spotted a soldier in woodland camouflage fatigues scarfing down enchiladas next to the jukebox. The special forces insignia drew Contreras closer and he walked over with his drinks in his hands. *"May I join you, Lieutenant?"*

"If you like. I'm out of here quick, though."

Contreras set the drinks on the table, removed his holster, and set the heavy pistol on top for effect, as if he were trying to get comfortable. He spun it so the muzzled barrel faced him—gunfighter etiquette—then waved at the bartender for another round.

"Police special response team?" he asked the soldier.

"Can't say."

"Well, I can. I should know a hard-charger when I see one. My name is Jimmy Contrerasoropeza. This meal is on me. I was a grunt before I joined the yanqui DEA."

The bartender brought a twin set of drinks for the soldier. Contreras pushed the soldier's shot of tequila forward and raised his own. *"To Mexico."*

The soldier shook his head. *"Sorry, but I'm on stand-by for a mission. I can't."*

"Well then, here's to you finding those sons of bitches," Contreras said.

"Who?" the soldier asked, doing a poor job at deception.

"Come on, Lieutenant. Los Asesinos, that's who. What do you think I'm here for? Let's have a toast and I'll tell you more. It'll build the fire in your belly. After fifty patrols in Vietnam, I should know."

Contreras kept his shot glass at eye level and watched the soldier study his enchilada. The soldier eventually looked around the bar, then snatched the shot glass. *"Oh, hell. We ain't going out anyway. I been on stand-by for two days. To Mexico."* He tossed the liquid into his tonsils and gritted his teeth happily, then took a long swig from his beer before pounding his chest with a fist as if trying to dislodge a peanut. *"How do you like government-issued tequila?"*

The alcohol tasted like poison. Contreras nodded vigorously and blinked some tears away that had somehow escaped the earlier purge. *So the couple is still alive,* he thought, *somewhere out there.* He waved to the bartender, then smiled at the soldier. *"Just like my mother makes."*

"Yeah, where does she live?"

"Los Angeles," said Contreras. *"Took me across the river when I was just a pup."*

The soldier nodded and killed his beer. *"Yeah, well, I'm staying put. Especially if I win the reward. Everyone in the platoon has agreed to split it even, no matter who kills those fuckers first. Well, almost even. Federale who kills Darren Phillips is going to get an extra million pesos."*

Time to go fishing, Contreras thought. He leaned in conspiratorially and cocked an eyebrow. It excited the soldier, who turned up the volume on the jukebox before putting his face close enough to hear Contreras say, *"Between you and me, Lieutenant?"*

"Of course, sir."

Contreras hesitated to build the suspense. *"I know that you know why I'm here. I'm part of the FBI team come down to help Deputy Attorney General Saiz in this manhunt. You've heard about us?"*

"Yes, sir. The comandante told us you were coming," the soldier said.

"Your comandante is tight with Saiz?"

"He's afraid of him, if that's what you're asking, sir."

Contreras formed the picture. Whatever shit the Guerrero *comandante* was eating, Saiz was feeding him. *"If you know that, then you also know that the only thing we can do is get in the way. I know you have a method to track them, and I'm not going to compromise you by asking. I also know you guys have your shit wired. Last thing you need is gringos tripping over everyone's feet, check?"*

The soldier nodded emphatically. *"I got to tell you, sir, that's a relief to hear. Me and the guys are totally bent out of shape on this one. Bad enough sitting here stroking dicks while Team One hunts without having to brief all the cats and dogs. You see the fucking media bus that rolled in?"*

Contreras nodded just as the Kylie Minogue song ended. Both men sat up rigidly, raised their fresh shots, and drank them. *"To your reward,"* Contreras said when his tongue regained sensory abilities.

"To my reward!" said the soldier.

A Mexican ballad started and they leaned across the table again. When it grew loud, Contreras whispered, *"Problem is, you ain't getting your reward. Know who's after it? We think Saiz is. Why do you think he invited us? For credit. He'll wait until you find* Los Asesinos, *then he'll have one of his cronies swoop in to claim the cash. So watch your back. Hell, maybe they're already on the inside. Can you vouch for the integrity of your team?"*

The soldier's eyes widened. He hissed, *"Fucking A, yes. We're tight."*

"You mentioned another team was out in the bush. Can you vouch for them?"

The soldier started to nod dismissively, but then his head turned suddenly, as if a fish hook had snagged his cheek. He stared out the window, lost in thought. Watching him, Contreras could feel the edge coming back on. He chugged his beer and signaled for another round. He knew he would need it.

Eventually the soldier drank from his own beer and whispered, *"They got two outsiders traveling with Team One. One's a professional hunter and his dog."*

Contreras was so close now he could taste it. The bartender arrived with two more beers and two more shots, but the soldier begged his off and looked at his watch. *"I gotta get back, sir."*

Contreras drank both tequilas, then pulled the beers close to him. They were cool and wet in his palms. When the bartender left, he grabbed the lieutenant's forearm and asked, *"And the other?"*

"Some little Indian guy. Didn't even carry a rifle. Don't ask. We didn't understand it either."

A wave of electricity washed up Jimmy Contreras's lower back and spilled out along his arms. He was laughing when he grabbed his turgid holster and clipped it back on his belt. The music sounded fuzzy and thick. He said, *"Let me walk you out."*

"What's so funny, sir?"

"Must be the tequila."

Contreras felt as if he were having an out-of-body experience. He hadn't eaten dinner and the alcohol sloshed around the walls of his stomach as he jogged back toward the command post in the hangar. He did not so much feel his feet as watch them float over the ground. By the time he walked up to the soldiers guarding Saiz's makeshift office, his hands were tingling and his head felt warm. He reached to remove his hat, then remembered that he did not wear one.

A guard took it as a salute and returned it. *"I'm afraid the attorney general asked not to be disturbed, sir."*

Ed Modinger of the FBI was seated on a campstool behind the guards perusing the pictures in a Spanish *Maxim* magazine. Seeing Contreras, he smiled and stood. "Hey, sir. We missed you at dinner. Agent Corwin was a bit agitated."

"What are you doing here?" Contreras asked, enunciating as best he could before the alcohol further softened his tongue.

Modinger tilted his head and pulled Contreras aside. "We each drew a watch assignment to help guard Saiz, if you can believe it. Apparently he doesn't trust his own people. Agent Corwin gave you zero-four to zero-eight but I scratched your name off and put mine, sir. I don't mind the double duty."

Contreras clapped him on the shoulder—too roughly, he knew. *"That's mighty white of you. I'll take your shift now."*

"I don't speak Spanish, sir."

"Sorry. I'm taking your shift now. Thanks for taking the midwatch. What is this one, eighteen hundred to twenty-two hundred?"

"Uh, yessir. Are you okay? Your eyes are all bloodshot."

"Good-to-go. Been crying a bit, is all."

Modinger started to smile, but the look on the DEA's face stopped the corners of his mouth from further drift. He nodded uncomfortably and went off to find his boss, who was probably still giving interviews in the reporters' hut.

Contreras struggled to contain his excitement. He could feel his carotid arteries squirming. *"Excuse me, friend,"* he said to a guard, pushing through.

"The attorney general will not be happy, sir. Not while he's eating."

Contreras winked. *"He will be when he sees me."*

Contreras opened the door, strode across some form of waiting room, and opened a second door with his foot. Some part of him knew it was a bad idea, but the tequila blanketed it. Eduardo Saiz was so startled that he spat a piece of hamburger onto the carpet and reached for his desk drawer. Recognizing Contreras, his shoulders sagged and he studied his plate. He had dropped his hamburger onto some papers and they were covered in ketchup and mustard. "Gosh damn! What the hell are you doing, Agent . . ."

"Contrerasoropeza."

"Yes, well, why did you burst in like that? My God!"

"I have a question for you," Contreras said in Spanish.

Saiz stuck two fingers in his mouth and licked them clean. Without taking his eyes off Contreras, he systematically dried each finger and smoothed the foil that served as a place mat. *"Then ask Roger. Let's keep the command relationship in place, shall we? You are out of order coming in like this. Totally out of order."*

"I know you're using the Monster Butcher out there. You get me on a helicopter and take me to him—right now—or I'll blow the whistle so hard they'll hear me in Washington, D.C."

Saiz took a measured bite of his hamburger and chewed contentedly. He sipped a bottle of Poland Springs and said, "Imported."

Contreras reached across the table and yanked open the desk drawer Saiz had been eyeing. He snatched a small automatic pistol and slammed it on the desk, then spun it gently with a finger as if he were twirling a bottle. *"The Monster Butcher of Juarez is the same man that killed Luis Gonzalez, isn't he?"*

The barrel slowed and pointed back toward Contreras. Saiz took another swig of water and said, *"You're drunk. Leave now and I'll forget this."*

"Forget this?" Contreras opened his wallet and removed the photograph of him and Luis Gonzalez at San Ysidro. *"I'll never forget this."*

Saiz did not look at the picture. He took a long sip of water and said in careful English, "You are barking up the wrong tree, I'm afraid. Isn't that how you gringos say it? I have informed Roger of *El Monstruo Carnicero,* and we are taking care of it. You see, I have nothing to do with that animal, but it has come to my attention that he is out there hunting for *Los Asesinos* with the rest of the country. When I locate him, I will arrest him. Whether or not you are there is up to Roger."

Contreras grabbed Saiz by the throat and tipped his chair backward. The water bottle went sailing into a fan and the hamburger bounced on the rug, leaving a red snail trail of ketchup behind it. "You're a rat-fucking liar," Contreras hissed before he dropped Saiz on his back and stormed off.

He plowed smack into Roger Corwin on his way out of the office. "Jesus Christ!" said Corwin. "Where the hell have you been, Agent Contreras? We had a debrief an hour ago. What were you two discussing?"

"None of your fucking business," slurred Contreras. He left the hangar before the news crews were able to get fresh cassettes in their Betacams, then trotted over to the FBI stateroom. It was empty. He packed his kit in the darkness, stuffing everything into a green canvas duffel bag except his body armor, which he left hanging over his bunk. His secure satellite phone had an urgent message on it, but his fingers were so intoxicated that he was approaching the motor pool by the time he managed to return the call.

"Jimmy, I've been waiting for your call like a jilted prom date," said a voice.

Contreras could smell his own breath being reflected by the folding mouthpiece. It was clearing his sinuses as he breathed. "Deputy Director Sheridan?"

"It's Susanne, Jimmy. Remember? Listen—"

"I thought you hate me," he burst.

There was a long pause on the other end. Contreras took the phone away from his ear and studied the display to ensure he still had a connection. He flashed his badge to the gate guard on his way into the motor pool, then put the phone back against his ear. The guard wheeled the barbed wire wall open.

"Hello?" Contreras asked the phone.

"I'm still here, Jimmy. Are you all right?"

"Hell yes, I'm all right. I'm about to reconcile a vehicle for official government use." He pointed at one of the white Range Rover loaners the Mexicans had given the team. A motor-pool guard rushed to it like a valet, keys jingling.

"You mean 'requisition'?" she asked.

"Reconcile. Requisition. Recon daddy gonna take a little trip. Whatever."

"Yes, well, you should know one thing before you go with them, Jimmy."

"I ain't going with no one," Contreras said. The SUV boomed across the lot and skidded in front of him. Dust swirled in the floodlights and invaded the cab when he replaced the driver. He popped his backup pistol in the glove compartment and sifted around for a map. "Anyway, what should I know, Susanne?"

"You're working for me now."

– 49 –

SIERRA MADRE RANGE, MEXICO

Kate felt the thunderheads before she saw them, sustained rumbles in her gut. The separation between lightning strikes blended over the distance, becoming steady and thick, one grumble indistinguishable from another. It was strange that the storm was approaching from the east, but in the mountains she knew enough to accept chaos. She heard the crackle as the thin layer of ice covering the scree slope cracked under her sandal. The rubber insulated her foot from the frozen dirt, but not from the air.

The afternoon darkened and night came early, flashing electric white and silent high in the stratosphere, light dancing across the bodies of the trio even as the macabre cavalry assembled above. The rain started as they were descending a steep, dirty slope, blowing in gravelly sheets from the east, spraying *up* the mountain and forcing their eyelids to close up like clamshells. Soon the sky was an ocean, and they cupped their hands over their eye sockets, searching for footholds.

Kate was the first to feel the fledgling river wash over her ankles. In the haze, she saw that the slope tipped over to her front and became a moving wall of mud. "Darren! Get out the Hell Bitch! We need to rope up!"

Darren produced the rope and Kate had them tied together in a few seconds. She found her feet again and led them to a relatively flat and immobile section. "LOOKS LIKE WE'RE IN ANOTHER 'DON'T TRY THIS AT HOME' SITUATION, BABE!" she screamed into the wind. "YOU TWO STAY PUT. I'M GOING TO SCOUT A SAFE ROUTE DOWN."

Kate checked her bowline and moved forward carefully, testing her purchase with each Teva. She estimated that the slope ran another quarter-mile of mud before it yielded to large boulders and pines. Then they could seek some shelter. She went to her knees and crawled forward to the edge of the ledge. Water washed up her legs and over her back. Her hands sank deep and suddenly the lip was gone, Kate pitched forward in a dive, feet careening up and over in a flip. The slope collapsed.

The mud slide tried to bury her like an avalanche, so she swam hard and tried to levitate, but of course she could not and her heart thundered and her mind snapped through options as if it were thumbing a deck of cards.

Darren was squinting into the fuzzy black haze when lightning flashed. He saw the Hell Bitch jump off the dirt, turn into a taut wire and yank Neck from his arms as if he had been hit by an invisible car. He flew for ten feet before tumbling out of his vision, hands clawing for purchase as he went. Darren was going to ground when he heard the Hell Bitch slithering and hissing as the slack snaked out and hardened. Then the terrible weight was dragging him and his great handfuls of mud along for the ride.

The wave of mud carried her up and over a large rock at the base of the slope. Kate reached out and snagged a pine branch just as her momentum slowed, then took a wrap with the rope and bit down. Neck and Darren raced by, riding the crest of muddy water like fallen water-skiers. They disappeared into the black, then flickered alive again in the flashbulb of another lightning bolt, standing full upright and staggering toward her. "Are you okay!" she screamed.

"Fine!" Darren said. "Guess the water . . . I don't know! Flash flood. Woo."

"We're lucky!" Kate laughed and Darren saw that her white teeth were dripping brown, as if she had just bobbed for apples in a vat of chocolate sauce.

"The fuck we are!" screamed Neck. "The *fuck* we're lucky!"

Kate went forward to help him up, but he brushed her arm away and went down on all fours, the water splashing up past his wrists and knees. Black mud was dripping off the tip of his nose. He shook his head violently like a dog trying to dry itself. He groaned and retched. When Kate touched him he recoiled as if scorched by fire. "NO!"

Kate looked at Darren—who shrugged as if to say, you better than me—and kneeled next to Neck. "Listen to me, Neck."

"*You* listen to *me*. I'm stopping here."

"So are we. A nice, long rest."

"You all need a rest? You said a long rest?" he gasped, tears cleaning his cheeks.

Kate nodded firmly at her husband and Darren said, "I know I sure as hell do. I feel like I'm going to puke. I'm freezing and I can't walk. I need to get warm."

"Oh, me too, man," said Neck, buoyed by Darren's statement. "Long rest?"

"Long and *warm*," Kate said.

The rain abated as they limped into the edge of a pine forest but the wind increased, sucked up the mountainside by the west-moving clouds. By the time Kate had picked a hole under two massive boulders to use as a sheltered rest stop, Neck was shaking uncontrollably. The rockpile formed a granite tent. She replaced the smaller stones on the ground with pine boughs while Darren rubbed Neck's arms until his hands were warm with friction.

"Get his clothes off, Darren. Yours, too."

Neck swooned and Darren eased him to the ground. "Jesus, he's going hypo."

"I . . . fah . . . freeezing, duh, dude," stammered Neck.

"Strip down and we'll sandwich him in here. It's a good shelter. You want front or back?" Kate stripped off her clothes and pegged them to a tree branch launching mud drops like bullets into the wind.

"Both of us?"

"Yes. It'll warm him fast. Front or back?"

Darren considered his two options—both of them unappealing—and reluctantly said, "Front." The Marines taught him hypothermia rescue at mountain warfare school. It was a hard thing to forget: Body heat transfer was most efficient and effective with bare skin. The back position was coveted because the Marines were loath to feel the other man's balls crushed up against his lower back when they spooned naked. Of course, as an officer he had never hopped in the sleeping bag. The one time he saw a Marine go down with hypo Darren picked the most homophobic as a spooning partner to watch the fireworks. "Can I at least have back position, sir?" the devil dog had asked him.

But now he and his *wife* had to act as electric blankets. Darren didn't want Neck to have back position on Kate. After all, Neck had a serious crush and you never know what REM sleep might bring. The thought of Neck's excitement in dream state made him cringe, however, when he remembered that he would be the taker.

What am I doing, he thought. *Just get Neck warm!*

Darren uncoiled the Hell Bitch over the pine branches to use as an insulator then carried Neck into the den, sealing the shelter with the pack and several branches. The couple spooned Neck, yelping when his frigid skin smothered theirs. Ten minutes later, Neck's body began to warm up, and he found his tongue. "My hands and fingers . . . they . . . *kill*. It's like I'm on fire. I'm tingling and burning all over."

"So's your bed buddy in front of you, Neck," said Kate. "Aren't you, Darren?"

Darren grunted. "Ignore my beautiful wife. That's blood coming back. It'll pass after some pain, Neck. Now get some sleep."

"I was thinking, are those lights down there Mexico City? We're close, right?"

Kate stayed quiet—she didn't think it was fair for Neck to be kept out of the loop, but Darren was resolute. In the silence, she could hear her husband's mind racing, and she hoped the sleeplessness would cave his stubbornness. It did.

"Neck, we are not going to Mexico City. They're going to have every road, every trail, every pass covered with troops. We're going to Veracruz where a friend of mine is going to pick us up."

Neck was thoroughly confused and for a second he thought he had been dreaming. "Veracruz? Where's that?"

"Not far. Now get some sleep."

"How's he gonna get us home? Past the roadblocks?"

Darren paused for a long time. "A boat. He's coming by boat, Neck."

"*Boat?* How do we know he'll be there?"

"He'll be there."

"But how do you *know?*"

Darren sighed. He'd opened the can and now he'd have to eat all the worms. "I plan to call my mom to confirm it. He'll have left a message with her."

"When are you gonna call? I mean, why are we going so hard if he might not be there? What if he's changed the pickup point? Maybe he wanted us to hold up, like, fifty miles ago. Can't we make sure we're going the right way? We have that phone."

Darren tried to sort through all the questions to dismiss them and he stumbled when he realized that they actually contained some logic. Or was he just too tired too think? Probably a combination, he decided. "Sleep."

"He's right, Darren," said Kate. "That city down there seems pretty big, from all the lights. Try the phone."

"Fine," said Darren. He reached out for the pack. As much as he hated the idea of Neck's nakedness pressing into his backside, it was a gloriously warm blubber with which he could not bear to part. And what could another phone call hurt, if it would quiet the pair behind him so he could sleep?

Darren turned the phone on and it glowed green, lighting the little dwelling. He dialed straight through to his mother's home and heard a click. *Come on, Mom.* He heard the first ring and his eyebrows went up, all breathing and anticipation now. He pressed it into his ear.

A woman shouted in English, "PHILLIPS, DO *NOT* USE THIS PHONE AGAIN. THE PHONE IS YOUR KEY TO FREEDOM BUT GIVES YOUR POSI-

TION WHEN YOU CALL! KEEP IT WITH YOU AND MOVE AWAY FAST! A HUNTER NAMED *EL MONSTRUO CARNICERO* IS TRACKING YOU. CALL THE FOLLOWING NUMBER ON A LAND LINE: 202—"

There was a sharp click and the call was disconnected.

Darren sat bolt upright. "Hello? OhmyGod. Get your clothes on! We need to run. The phone has a GPS and they're tracking us—"

"Who, Darren? Stop it! Calm down! Slow down!" Kate yelled, terrified because she had never seen him nervous.

"I don't . . ." He took a moment to compose himself. *Orient, observe, decide, act!* He looked at his companions and whispered, "Just get your clothes on and prepare to move out in a run. We are in mortal danger every second we delay."

Neck was the first to speak. "I'll do my best, but I don't know if I can run."

"Yes, you can, Neck," said Darren, stuffing the Hell Bitch into the pack and tucking the phone into its waterproof pouch. "Your life depends on it. You hear me?"

"Yeah, man, but *listen* . . ."

"*You* listen, Neck! You are literally running for your life right now."

In less than a minute the trio was dressed in their wet uniforms. Kate took a quick bearing and with a collective groan they slipped and slid into the forest.

"What does *el monstro carnicero* mean?" huffed Darren as he gained a choppy and painfully mechanic trot.

"The monster butcher," Neck gasped when Kate didn't answer. "Why?"

"Just curious is all."

– 50 –

ZAMPEDRO ARMY BASE, MEXICO

For a moment Eduardo Saiz thought he had been shot. The Network satphone in his shirt pocket was buzzing and shaking as angrily as a wasp caught in a jar. Every muscle in his body tensed. He dropped his water bottle for the second time in two hours and grabbed at his heart. Had that psycho Contreras sniped him? Or one of *El Toro*'s henchmen?

"This is Octopus," he said meekly when realization came to him.

"This is conductor seven-one. We just had a call intercepted by the Americans."

"*What?*"

"*Los Asesinos* were attempting to call in the open and the Americans cut in. They must have nabbed the unencrypted frequency."

"Sweet Mary. The Americans are communicating with *Los Asesinos*? Is that what you are telling me?" Should I tell my wife to try to get to Miami from Cancún? he wondered. Or can she risk a final trip home for her precious mementos?

"We cut them off quickly, Octopus. I am sending a transcript by email."

"You should have cut them off *immediately!*" Eduardo said.

"But, Octopus, your standing orders demand we get their location. We had to ensure this grid coordinate came through before we cut them off. It takes a few seconds for the location to triangulate."

Eduardo thought about the new escape plan. If he could convince Corwin to get him underground in witness protection, he and his family might be in Tucson, Arizona, or Anaheim, California, or Charlotte, North Carolina, by the weekend, roasting hot dogs or gorging on fast food or whatever it was the pampered did on Saturdays besides watching Mexican migrants cut their lush grass, green and tall because water had been greedily vampired before it hit the border. But to do it he needed to deliver the monster.

"... Octopus?"

"What?" said Eduardo.

"I said, we have already deployed the team. They should be near the drop-off by now. About seventy kilometers south of Mexico City. Not that far from your base, actually. Do you want to mobilize the other teams?"

"No, no. I will organize from here. In fact, recall the team you sent in. Hear me?"

"Octopus, we already vectored the helicopter ..."

Eduardo opened his office door and stepped outside, eyes scanning the sky in vain for the telltale blinks of helicopter lights. It was already quite cold on the high desert and he blew his breath into his cupped hand. A storm was rolling in over the mountains. "Then get me the pilots. Now."

"Negative. They're on UHF and we lost them when they went over the range."

"Then connect me to the lieutenant's goddamn satphone. We gave him an unencrypted version. Hurry!"

− 51 −

PUEBLA, MEXICO

The Bell HV-250 helicopter shuddered and lurched its way toward a small ridgeline in the dark. The pilot was wearing night vision goggles and the droplets of rain splattering the windshield looked like a swarm of lightning bugs rushing headlong into death, which is how the pilot felt. The rotor blade chopped desperately in the thin air, but even at full power the *blat-blat-blat* of the blades was smothered by the scream of the wind as it soared up from the valley floor.

The pilot pulled up on the collective. "This is gonna be close," he said before clenching his teeth. "Tell them to hold on. We make it over the peak and we're going to tip coming down the other side."

"Understood," said the copilot. He swiveled his head and looked behind him in the troop hold. In the green haze of the goggles, he saw each of the soldiers gripping their canvas seats for stability, except for the old man, who was gripping his silently barking dog. The Indian was not wearing his Mickey Mouse ears, but the copilot was too distracted to signal for him to put his head protection on. He'd get the message soon enough.

The copilot keyed his intercom. "It's going to get ugly!"

The five men glared at him as if to say, it already *is* ugly, asshole.

El Monstruo Carnicero had never been in a helicopter and he was sickened by the experience. Not physically ill, but disgusted that man had invaded Huitzilopochtli's air so ineptly. Hummingbirds had grace and beauty. The helicopter wobbled just to stay aloft.

Now the machine slowed and its nose tipped over. He was lifted right out of his seat, prevented from smashing into the roof only by the seat belt. His stomach tried to leap through his throat. It was madness. He could see the other men screaming, but he could not hear them over the wind and engine. The helicopter was plummeting toward the ground, *El Monstruo Carnicero* knew that much. He also knew that if he survived, he'd have to kill something soon to feed the earth. The ground had not been watered for days.

He looked at Lieutenant Garza next to him, who was closing his eyes and gripping his seat as if he were being electrocuted. *El Monstruo Carnicero*'s eyes were drawn to a blinking red light on the *Federale*'s belt. A phone. His hand walked along the seat like a tarantula and snatched it. He turned away from Garza and pressed the phone into his ear.

"Hello!"

"Lieutenant Garza?" asked a faint voice. "Is that you? This is Octopus. Did the *comandante* tell you what my call sign means?"

"Yes!" shouted *El Monstruo Carnicero*.

"Are you on the ground?"

"Yes!"

"Okay, listen to me. There has been an immediate change of plan. You and your men put your guns on the Indian and hold him there until we arrive. You will continue the hunt after we arrest him. If he fights, kill him. Leave your phone on. We'll use it to find your exact position. Understood, Lieutenant?"

"Yes!" shouted *El Monstruo Carnicero*. He turned the phone off and stuffed it into his waist pouch, next to Falcon. The helicopter had stopped descending, but was still buffered by the wicked winds. He saw the men remove their helmets. The hot-blooded sergeant stood and careened like a drunk fighting for balance until he reached the cargo door. He pulled it open and was blown onto his ass by a gust that tossed some of the cranials around the troop hold like Ping-Pong balls.

Sergeant Pena stepped out onto the skid of the helicopter, squinting into the waves of raindrops that zipped into his face like pellets. He knew the pilot could not risk a touchdown on such sloppy terrain. The helicopter hovered ten meters over the ridge, and like all soldiers he was eager to get out of the death machine. The skid was rising and falling with the yaw. Five meters off the deck. Seven meters off the deck. Three meters off the deck. He jumped.

It was a soft impact and he was shin-deep in shifting mud. Pena whipped his rifle out in front of him, starting to slide. He tried to dig his fingers into the side of the slope, but it was difficult with his rifle. The whole mountain seemed to be moving. He slid fifty meters down the slope into a tree, then scrambled to his knees and shouldered his rifle.

What a goatfuck! *Los Asesinos* had another head start! He heard the dog Sniff-Sniff barking and saw the old man with the bloodhound on his lap sliding down in the track he had carved. The two other soldiers were coming down right behind them. Pena scrambled to his feet to get out of their way. He wasn't worried about those four crashing into him, but the prospect of interpersonal contact with the greasy Indian prodded his legs to move his torso behind a big pine tree.

Pena covered his face so the twigs and pebbles swept down by the rotors wouldn't catch an eyeball. His lieutenant hopped out next and the clumsy bastard slipped immediately and slid down the slope like a child, upside-down on his back. Pena didn't watch the greenhorn come to rest at the forest edge—he was squinting up at the chopper for a sign of the devil. He prayed that the helicopter might be forced to take off—or even smash into the side of the mountain because of the winds—but he saw a black thing leap out like a giant bat. The corners of his mouth sagged.

Unlike the others, *El Monstruo Carnicero* kept his feet on the way down the slope, leaning forward as if skiing, muddying nothing more than his Reeboks.

"You found the scent yet?" he squeaked when he strolled up to the five men.

"We are checking the GPS," replied Lieutenant Garza quickly, searching his belt for the satphone in a panic while Pena plugged the coordinates into the Garmin GPS. The rain was so thick a jet was running off of the tip of Garza's nose, and yet he quite suddenly felt very hot. The *comandante* had specifically threatened him over the loss of the phone.

"Got location, sir," said Pena. "Just a few meters downhill, near those boulders." He pointed to a cluster of rocks that seemed to form an overhang between two pine trees.

"All of you wait down there," said Lieutenant Garza. "I am going back up to scout for a moment. Pena, come with me."

"Scout?" said Pena, looking up at the muddy hill, then back at the natural roof.

"You heard me, Sergeant. Let's go."

Lieutenant Garza wiped some clumps of mud from his boots and started to scramble up the choppy path on all fours like a bear, losing a meter of height every time he gained two. His rifle was slung awkwardly along his spine and the front sight post scraped his lower back. Liters of water came up over his knuckles and into his windbreaker, drowning his forearm. The climb was hard work and he started to fatigue before he had retrieved ten meters of elevation.

"What are we doing, sir?" asked Pena, irritated and miserable.

"Just keep your eyes on the fucking ground," Garza gasped. "I lost the cell phone. You help me find it, I put you in for a meritorious promotion."

El Monstruo Carnicero watched the two men slipping their way up the slope. Then he grunted and spat a thin string of tobacco that melted into the river of mud flowing over his sneakers. When he turned, he saw the other two soldiers retreating to the thick stand of pines and boulders for shelter. But the old man was still standing there next to him with his dog.

"When this is over we're going to talk, you and me," said Felix.

"This will be over faster than you think."

Felix frowned. "If it is, it will be because of my dog, not you." He gave Sniff-Sniff two gentle but rapid tugs with the leash, and the dog immediately responded to his unspoken language, as it were an extension of the hunter's own arm.

The dog led him past the two shivering soldiers who had tucked themselves under one of the boulders, both of them hugging their own thighs. Their windbreaker hoods were drawn so tight over their heads that Felix could only see their eyes. A wide path of mud leading from their shelter down to the woods was churned up as if it had been made by a plow. A minor river was already using it as an expressway.

"Did you do that?" Felix shouted.

One of the soldiers extended his neck, but when a stream of water splattered on the back of his head he ducked back into the rocky overhang. He shook his head.

The tracker swiveled his rifle into the crook of his arm. He clucked his tongue and Sniff-Sniff plodded downhill alongside the track. Man and dog slid down until the trees thickened and the pine needles toughened the ground. Felix halted the dog on a flat expanse and knelt to study the prints that were recognizable now. They were so widely spaced that Felix knew *Los Asesinos* had been running—deep, sloppy holes had been stomped into the mud.

Felix backed off the trail about twenty meters with Sniff-Sniff so he could inspect the dog's paws and pads while he waited for the others. He stroked the dog's head and grabbed the crook of a leg, but when Sniff-Sniff's head snapped around so did his.

"What do you want?" Felix asked the grease monkey who had followed him.

"Aren't you going to sit down like the soldiers back there? Rest those old legs?" The Indian's whisper carried the same pitch as the wind. He was wearing a tight wool poncho that was melted onto his skinny frame. The water was coming down his grotesque forehead in streaks. Something in the Indian's manner unsettled him. This is it, he thought.

Felix smiled. His big rifle was slung behind his back, out of reach. But he had predicted this clash after the little freak had cut off Sniff-Sniff's ear, and his hand drifted toward the pistol hidden on his hip. He watched the little man's hands but they were up high, stroking his ratty beard as if milking a cow. Good, he thought, wondering where the second bullet might go after he crippled the maggot with the first one. Maybe in his ear!

"I don't need no rest. I just need some privacy," said Felix.

"You and your mutt need some privacy? You're a sick man."

The tracker was prepared for the knife, but not for its speed. His pistol barrel had not yet departed the leather of his holster when his neck opened and his head folded back behind his body. He was a corpse before he hit the ground. Sniff-Sniff didn't whine or growl. He simply circled twice, moving his great nose back and forth, then leaned over the stump and lapped greedily at the neck.

El Monstruo Carnicero pinched the blood from Barracuda's thin filet blade and nimbly stuck it back in his belt sheath. Then he walked back up to the rock pile and bent over the bodies of the dead soldiers, tilting them so the blood dumped more freely into the earth. Falcon was still imbedded in the collarbone of one body—he hadn't bothered to remove it before turning on the old man. *El Monstruo Carnicero* was not a strong man and it took him several minutes before he heard the faint hiss of air coming up the blood grooves. The throwing blade popped free. He cleansed it in the mud and walked around the boulders to wait for the other two.

The lieutenant was sitting at the base of the hill with his boot off. He smiled dumbly and pointed up the slope. "Pena's still up there. I just have to get this rock out of my boot. I've had it in there for maybe forty kilometers."

El Monstruo Carnicero tossed the satphone onto the lieutenant's lap. "Looking for that?"

"My God! You son of a bitch. Wait until . . ." There was a whistle and something hit the lieutenant in the chest and robbed his breath. *He threw a rock at me!* He couldn't draw air and he collapsed to his knees, dropping the boot. He clutched the handle of the throwing blade and tried to pull it free of his chest. He was so tired.

"You need to twist first, Lieutenant," the Aztec said. "Otherwise the suction is too great. That's why I cut grooves in the sides of Eagle. Watch."

The Aztec wrapped his hands around the soldier's. The lieutenant noticed how tiny and lithe they were. The Aztec turned the knife and there was a gurgling sigh when the blade slipped free, blood bubbling at the point of the sucking chest wound, no air to be had in this world, just a vacant slide toward repose, a gasping fish out of water, the cat just watching for a moment. Then its claws extended and sliced into him. The filet blade moved over him swiftly, glinting occasionally, dripping. And all the lieutenant could do was watch.

———

Sergeant Pena rotated his wrist and wiped the face of his watch. Twenty goddamn minutes wasted. Add another thirty for the flight and *Los Asesinos* had another head start. Fucking officers covering their asses! He planted his boots deep into the mud so he could stand, lifted his hand to shield his eyes from the rain, and peered down into the folds of the dark. Nothing. Where was the goddamn lieutenant?

An uneasy feeling he recognized as fear moved into his stomach and he could suddenly hear himself breathing. He rotated his M-16 up into his shoulder and powered up the thermal scope mounted on the carrying handle. The thing was a battery vampire, but fuck it, he wanted to know where the fuck everyone was at.

Now the *click-click-click* backdrop of the thermal world as he glassed the trees. The rock pile below looked pink—must be some fading heat sources in there, he thought, probably camping while I freeze my balls off—and in front of it, a white blotch he had been trained to interpret as a human was standing there next to a smaller white blotch, probably the dog.

Pena boot-skied down to the hunter. He saw the others curled up between two boulders, sleeping in a puppy pile. "What the fuck are they doing? Where's the fucking lieutenant?" Then he realized it was not the hunter at all.

The little Indian handed him the leash. "Hold the dog," came the whisper, wind sailing across an empty clothesline.

Pena's eyes were too late in connecting with his brain. The pile of humans was not stirring. He tried to withdraw his left hand but it burned hot. When he reached to cover it, the Aztec moved close and his M-16 clattered to the ground, the shoulder strap severed. Pena's right hand darted for his pistol, but it too tasted flames and he yanked it back.

"Why you carry that knife?" the Aztec said.

Pena tucked his bleeding hands under his armpits. "What knife?"

"The one you wear so proudly on your belt. Why do you carry it?"

Pena touched his knife unconsciously. His fingers throbbed. "Just in case."

"In case?"

"Yes. In case."

"That's good. In case. I like that. Well, this is the case."

The Aztec crouched and Pena saw a long, skinny blade in his hand. Pena lunged for his pistol again, and it was as if he had grabbed a heated skillet.

"You better stop that, boy. You'll lose both your arms before we start this fight."

Pena glanced at his left hand and saw that his wrist was slit. He pressed it tight against his chest to stem the bleeding and burst, "Are you fucking crazy? What are you doing!" But he knew. He'd known for two days, since he first saw the man. He took a guarded step back and urinated. The tiny part of his mind that was still coherent told him that it was strange considering he had just had a nice piss.

The Aztec wanted a *knife fight*. Pena's hand was shaking and bleeding. It took him a moment to work the fat special operations blade free of the slippery scabbard. He wanted to relax, to taste the familiar need to fight, but he felt weak and his lust for combat left him. Maybe it was never really there, he thought, looking at the man's smile. Not really.

Pena extended the knife and crouched, finding his footing and thrusting the blade into the belly of the air as a warning, the way a snake rattles. *I can kill him. I can kill him.* "I'll kill you, *cabrón!*" he screamed.

I can't kill him. I can't kill him.

El Monstruo Carnicero watched with disappointment. Knife fighting was a violent dance of anticipation, using the blade to manipulate the opponent toward a kill strike. He had hoped for a match, but now . . . *this*. A petulant boy who desecrated the art. He decided to end him quickly. The greatest knife fighter in Mexica shouldn't waste his time on a quavering mouse like this!

"You get away from me! I'll kill you!" the boy screamed.

To confirm his suspicions, *El Monstruo Carnicero* sprang forward and jabbed at the boy's ribs, careful to remain on the balls of his feet should he counter-slash. The boy sucked in his gut and threw his body away from the filet blade, impaling himself on the pig-chopping machete that was waiting on the other side. How boring.

Oscar Pena moaned softly while the Aztec finished dressing him, praying for a quick end to the madness.

He didn't get it.

When *El Monstruo Carnicero* paid his respects to Huitzilopochti, he turned on the cell phone and stuck it in the lieutenant's mouth. Then he wiped Barracuda and Bear Claw clean and walked down to get the dog. The hound was sitting on its haunches behind the pile of bodies, waiting for him. *El Monstruo Carnicero* grabbed the leash and clucked his tongue. Sniff-Sniff acquired the scent of the foreigners easily, and was able to move faster with a full belly and the new master on the leash.

– 52 –

WEST OF TEHUACÁN, MEXICO

Neck fought the tears for a quarter-mile before he succumbed. They came rolling up from his stomach, tightening the cords on his neck as they passed, quivering his cheeks and closing his throat. He sat down for the third time on the run, only this time he put his face in his hands and wept. I haven't cried in six years, he thought, not since we lost the schoolboy championship to Martin Luther King High. But he could not stop. He sobbed and shook his head. No more.

"I can't do it," he managed to spew before his lungs inflated in jerky steps. "I just *can't.*" His pain was so great—and his sickness so deeply rooted—that his mind had narrowed to a single and invincible goal: *Stop this insanity now!*

"You have to," said Darren, prepared to talk the jumper down for the third time. That's what Neck was doing: committing suicide. Darren had studied this behavior in wartime history books and survival manuals. The human body had a tipping point when it came to relentless misery. Once triggered, some people just refused to drive on, even if it meant death. The lust for life itself, a human being's salient base instinct, was supplanted by an unyielding need to end pain. It caused exhausted soldiers to take terminal risks in combat, shivering alpine climbers to drift into deadly sleeps, and adrift sailors to chug salt water. It was the responsibility of teammates to keep them out of the abyss.

Darren's responsibility.

"NO. My body is broke permanently. My leg won't bend. Can't think. *My fingers sink into my legs!*" Neck's mind turned inward and the outside world ceased to exist. He rolled onto his side, weeping hysterically.

Kate inspected Neck's shins. When she pressed his finger on one, it created a deep dimple an inch deep that remained imprinted for several seconds. "That's edema, Neck. Fluid has seeped in between your cells; that's what's making them look fat. Don't worry, it happens to me once a month."

"Is it a disease?" he grumbled.

"No. Just makes you look tubby," Kate said trying to drive home the joke.

Neck was unresponsive so Darren took a different tack. "On your feet, dog."

Neck shook his head. He had never quit anything in his life but now he ached to join the timorous rank and file he had scorned. He had let himself down. Worse, he had let the Phillipses down. No, that wasn't quite right—Darren had predicted his demise from the start. Even if he survived, there was no *way* he was going to play pro football. He could not hack it. He was a *quitter*.

"I. Can't. Do. This," Neck said. "Understand? You two go. I'll hide somewhere and make it to a road in the morning. They think I'm a hostage, remember, and I'll say I escaped. I didn't kill anybody."

"Neck, listen to me. The police or whoever is running this thing *knows* you're no hostage. They'll torture you to find the phone and find out where we're headed. Then they'll be waiting for us in Veracruz."

Neck stopped crying. "No, Darren, I'd never give you two up. *Never*. You know that, right? It's important to me that you know that."

Kate patted his shoulder and said, "We know that, Neck."

But it was a lie and Neck saw it for what it was. They hated him. All her laughs, her encouraging talks, her flattery, her whispered secrets, her inquisitions into his life . . . they'd all been tools to prod him along. She could never respect a man—a *boy*—like him. He was a faker. He was a sham. No NFL team would ever draft a loser.

Darren said, "Listen, Neck. If you stay, we stay. Simple as that."

Neck felt guilty enough slowing them down. The prospect of stopping their entire journey because of his failure made his jaw tremble. His lower lip flushed and he cried again. *"No,"* he said. *"Please leave me here."*

Kate said, "We're not leaving you behind. Why don't we take a short sleep?"

Neck wiped his face and in his personal darkness he found a way to assuage the terrible guilt. It was so easy. He exhaled and nodded his head. "Okay. Let's sleep and we'll talk when we wake up."

Kate smiled triumphantly. "Want middle position again?"

"No. I want to sleep by myself."

"Nonsense," she said. "You're shivering and your skin is practically frozen."

"I *said*, I'm fine. Can you stop mothering me, please! I know I'm fucked up, okay, and I know I'm the lame-ass, so just leave me be! Please. I just want to sleep."

Darren touched his wife's arm and motioned with his head. She watched Neck collapse into a deep and immediate sleep on an acorn-laden piece of terrain under an oak, then followed Darren a few meters down the slope where he was clearing some twigs and stones for a hasty platform. "He okay up there?"

"Fell asleep right away. You set the alarm? Let's synchronize my watch again."

When the watches were set and placed on a stone next to Darren's head, Kate rolled her body into his big arms and nuzzled her neck into the source of his hot breath. She moaned softly and recognized the distant feelings of arousal, gone just as quickly as his warmth enveloped her and lulled her consciousness. Before she let herself be consumed, she whispered, "You've been saying all along that Neck was going to give up and that we'd be leaving him. But now that he *has* given up, you want to stay. Is it because you told him about Veracruz and now you're worried he'll tell?"

"No. Now get some sleep."

She knew that he was telling the truth. "What, then? Why the change of heart?"

"Marines don't leave their wounded on the battlefield."

Had it come from another man, Kate would have doubted the sincerity of the statement. But her husband, although prone to make cheesy, preachy statements that tended to embarrass her in public, was a man of conviction. And I love him for it, she thought before she succumbed.

Snuggling her, Darren considered his responsibilities. The kid had more than done his part. Now it was Darren's turn. He couldn't afford to sleep—someone had to stand fire watch. He thought about the climbing guide who stayed with his dying client at the peak of Everest and lost his life there, too, though he might have blamelessly left the man to die alone. Why should two people die when one is gone already? *Duty.* The culture of the Corps told Darren he had a duty to safeguard Neck. And when he delivered the kid to the National Football League, Darren would finally join those honorable ranks he so desperately admired.

Or he would die trying.

Darren jolted upright with Kate still locked in his arms, twisting his head around for signs of the intruder. But the forest was silent except for piercing beeps. "Easy, cowboy," said Kate groggily. "Just our watch alarms."

"Damn it. I fell asleep."

"That was the plan."

"Not mine," he said, stretching.

Both of their minds were still thick, and they dulled the pain that was knocking and demanding notice, permanently grafted to their beings. Kate

helped Darren to his feet, and as they walked up to get Neck she grunted every time her feet struck the forest floor.

"Ow. Ow. Ow. Ow. Ow," she joked, still infatuated with her dream. She had taken a bunch of tittering models hiking on a You Go Girl! trip. No, that's not quite right, our bemused society somehow deified a lucky few as *Super*models— and we know what pets they have, where they vacation, why they love PETA, what they think about the Elian Gonzalez raid. *Those* were the women in the dream. The weather turned and Kate's little girls pushed on, but the *Uber*models died. Which will crush Darren, she thought, who kept his precious *Victoria's Secret* catalogues on a shelf in their bathroom, ostensibly for her benefit. Maybe *I'll* finally get a magazine cover, she thought. A real woman, not some twig-girl-boy feigning athleticism in her bikini so that the men can ogle her manu-factured curves as they pass the newsstand on their way to *make money* and *talk on cell phones* and *work all night . . .*

". . . just can't believe it!"

Kate vanquished the daydream and asked her husband to repeat it.

"Neck's gone!" Darren tried to run up the slope but his legs were dragging Volkswagens. He settled for a hike. "Neck!" he shouted in a hoarse whisper. "*Neck!*"

Kate watched her husband, and he seemed distraught, an otherworldly emotion for his face. Must be the sleep deprivation, she thought.

"Oh, no. No. I knew I shouldn't have slept." Darren shook his head and cursed himself. "I should have seen that coming. This is bad, Kate. This is really bad."

"Shhh. Hey. *Hey.* He's a grown man. He wanted to stay, but his mind just re-fused him. You saw how powerless he was. Disheartened. We've both been there, babe, and we both know that if he wanted to hide, then he's gone."

Darren paced back and forth and noticed the Hell Bitch encircling Neck's sneakers. *He's left us his shoes.* He walked over and saw that Neck had crafted a smiling face with ten feet of rope. The Air Starbursts acted as bookends for a message that was churned up in the wet dirt.

Good luck

Sorry I let you down,

neck

– 53 –

WEST OF TEHUACÁN, MEXICO

Roger Corwin was the only one in the team who was warm. Problem was, the Second Chance Body Armor added another six pounds to his muscular frame and he was lagging behind the others as they moved up through the pine forest toward his prize. Corwin, Saiz, and the team of special forces *Federales* had been forced to hike for several miles up from the base of the ridgeline because the pilot had refused to land on top of Saiz's coordinate. The high winds had spooked him. Corwin had wasted several hours hiking. Still, walking in back was not a bad outcome when there were men with rifles lurking everywhere.

Corwin came up on Saiz, who was in the middle of some sort of argument with one of the *Federale* soldiers. They stopped talking when he walked up, pectorals pressing the bulletproof vest on every breath. He didn't take silence as an insult. Nor was he self-conscious. Corwin considered himself the boss of the operation and it was not unusual for subordinates to be cowed.

"How far?"

"Just about there, Roger. Maybe two hundred meters," said Saiz.

One of the soldiers stood and spat. It was no longer raining, but the wind was wild. The white glob bent before it hit the ground and zipped up into the trees. "*This is what I'm talking about, sir,*" the *Federale* said in Spanish. "*You and him talk in English so you can plan your robbery.*"

"*Nonsense,*" said Saiz. "*This has nothing to do with the assassins. If you find them, you get the reward. End of discussion. We are simply going up there to have you replace Team One. I still cannot raise them on the radio, but their signal is working.*"

"Then tell me why you two are here?"

"Another matter entirely. We are here to arrest the Indian who is traveling with Team One."

"He's your informant, isn't he, sir? To be blunt, the drug agent who stole the Land Rover warned us about your plan for the money. That's why you sent the Indian along?"

Saiz put his finger in the soldier's face. *"You're a fool. You watch your tone."*

"And you watch your back, sir. You're a long way from home." The soldier gave a hand signal to his men and they spread out, moving up through the trees again. Saiz was left wondering if *El Toro* had already turned them.

Corwin put his pistol back in its holster. He had a gift for intonations and knew how quickly a battle could escalate among fools, especially foreigners, who often lacked respect for authority. "Just what the hell was that?"

"I should ask you the same question. Your agent Contreras told the team we were after reward money before he stole my goddamn truck," Saiz said. "You're sure he is headed here?"

Corwin nodded. An hour before, he had received an encrypted Black-Berry from his source in the Bat Cave telling him that Contreras was back under Susanne Sheridan's wing, along with a set of coordinates toward which he was now hiking. Corwin could not wait to flush both Contreras and Sheridan down the political toilet when he returned to D.C. An inquiry by Senate Oversight might do them nicely. "I can't tell you how I know, Eduardo, but, yes, I think Contreras is headed here. That's why he stole the truck. Question is, why are *we* headed here? You haven't had comms with Team One for several hours."

"We both have secrets, Roger. I know their location but I cannot say how. Yet somehow you also have this same location."

"Then we understand each other," said Corwin.

One of the soldiers started yelling and soon the wind was carrying all of their shouts, amplifying the panic. Corwin sprinted toward the voices, careful to stay behind Saiz. A branch whipped into his cheek and he was still cursing silently when he came upon the *Federales*. They had formed a hasty perimeter and looked like robots in their night-vision goggles. One of them jerked his thumb and Corwin kept walking, panting all the way. Saiz was standing in front of a pile of bodies stacked on a boulder. In the dim light Corwin could see the rusty streaks of blood.

Saiz made the sign of the cross. He pulled his undershirt up over his nose and stood on his toes, fixated on a stubborn turkey vulture devouring a meal on the top of the tallest boulder. Saiz cried out and the buzzard flapped its wings and caught an updraft. A slimy mass slid down the face of the boulder and plopped into the mud at Saiz's feet. It might have been a bunch of grenades for the length of his leap.

"What is it?" whispered Corwin.

"Human hearts," said Saiz before he vomited out of disgust with himself, not the body parts. He wanted to cry. If there were not other men around he would have. His wife was so very far away from him there in the high mountain woods, and the man he had hoped to be was farther still. His aspirations now had a headstone.

Roger Corwin was not fazed. His was a career on the upswing, perhaps days or even hours away from a collar or three that would cement his aspirations. As for the carnage, Roger had seen plenty of roadkill and the only thing that surprised him any more was how red internal organs looked, even at night. His own heart was not there dying in the puddle. The fact that someone had ripped them out was strange, sure, but not as weird as the time that dazed transsexual had stumbled up to his motorcycle looking for a penis after he-she had flipped his-her car on the 405. He got mucho mileage out of that tale.

"It was my fault he got out here to begin with," whispered Saiz.

"Contreras?" asked Corwin. "You think he did this?"

Saiz laughed bitterly. "If Contreras did make it here, he's in that pile. No, *El Monstruo Carnicero* did this, and now he's gone. The whole operation's gone. Now we have no way to track *Los Asesinos* or the monster."

Corwin chewed on the statement. It was not palatable, especially given the promise he had given the director. He had skirted the specifics of Saiz's operation so that if it imploded in impropriety, he would be outside the effective casualty radius. Now he was being asked to throw his own clothes in with Saiz's dirty laundry. How the hell did the Monster Butcher get in position to kill these people? Was he part of the original team?

Corwin watched Saiz pull a metallic object from the mouth of one of the corpses. A cellular phone. The Network satphone was the pink elephant that he and Saiz had never discussed, yet now he was being told that it no longer had utility. Somehow the Monster Butcher had become the key to finding *Los Asesinos*. The connection confused him. What did they have in common? He searched the compartments in his brain until he arrived at a name. Agent Jimmy Contreras.

"It's not over yet, Eduardo," Corwin said. "But if I unfuck this, I take sole credit for the takedowns. Agreed?"

"If you get my family out of Mexico in one piece, you can have all the credit you want."

Corwin snorted and walked behind a tree for some privacy. Saiz was going autistic on him and he had little choice but to carry the ball. He wanted to do a little field interrogation on the deputy attorney general while his emotions were running loose, but his instincts told him that any more information might ruin plausible deniability. This was turning into a dirty operation as it was. He needed distance. He typed into his BlackBerry.

UNDERSTAND YOUR LAST: CONTRERAS CROSSED BACK TO HER. BUT I KNEW THAT. QUESTION IS: WHERE IS CONTRERAS RIGHT NOW? GET INTEL OR FORGET ABOUT YOUR NEW LEASE. LIVES AT STAKE DOWN HERE.

– 54 –

MCLEAN, VIRGINIA

When the day turned to night, the activity had increased in the Bat Cave. He had watched several strangers visit Susanne Sheridan in the soundproof torture chamber, including three men with cropped haircuts wearing yellow visitors' badges—military operations officers.

He had been left out of the parade and was embittered. The fact that everyone else in the Cave was on the sidelines with him barely dulled the pain. They were idiots, he was on the rise. He was disappointed that he had not yet located Gavin Kelly—Sheridan had been smart enough to get the Austin DEA agent to call her back on a secure line before he gave Kelly's jail location—but he had to be very careful about how he pursued the information while inside the Bat Cave.

The Cave was built without partitions for two reasons: to encourage communication and implement the most natural check and balance in the world— eavesdropping on your neighbor. The Cave might run covert ops on the outside, he thought, but inside the environment crushed secrets. Except the one his boss was keeping right now, of course.

"Gonna be a long night," the prick seated across from him said.

"Just wish the boss would give us the scoop. Do you have any news?"

"No. Whatever she's doing she's doing on her own. I think she's protecting us, actually. This is dicey stuff. Maybe illegal. Congress would squash . . . Hey, you okay?"

He nodded and shrugged off his reaction to the pager that was now massaging his calf. He kept Corwin's BlackBerry in his sock when he was at the desk. "Just a foot cramp," he said.

He scooted his chair back and leaned under his desk, squeezing his entire torso into the cubby before he withdrew the BlackBerry and read the message. Oh, don't do this to me, he thought. You fucking bastard, Corwin. You sound worse than her. Once I have my own staff, I won't have to put up with this shit.

He emerged and randomly tapped on his computer keyboard to allow the previous conversation to gain sufficient distance before he said, "I'd still like to know where Contreras went, though. Corwin sounded pretty hot when he called in this evening, and Ms. Sheridan said he was heading back here."

"Back here?" said his colleague. "He isn't headed back here. Think about it. You think that call from DEA this afternoon looking for Contreras was random? No way. You heard the way she reacted on the phone."

"So where's Contreras headed?"

The prick shrugged arrogantly. "Beats me. Let's ask her."

———

Susanne Sheridan was trying to figure out where to put the knife when Ted Blinky and Christian Collins approached her. It was a jeweled Berber dagger that the Moroccans had given her for "diplomatic" work in the southern Atlas Mountains, wonderfully engraved to her alias: *To Lynn Graves, Friend of the King and a Terror to Pirates. Thank you for your support of the Moroccan people. Your mind is as sharp as your tongue.*

"Ignore the rubies, gentlemen. The king promised me it was valued under the seventy-five-dollar gift limit." Susanne chuckled, running her fingernails along the dagger's curve before placing it in the cardboard box next to the picture of her children and the stapler she'd been forced to purchase on her own dime during the lean years. "Anyway, it's hard to imagine a GAO investigation on a swan song."

"It stinks you have to do this in the open, ma'am," said Christian Collins.

Susanne patted the two other boxes. "My demise is no secret, gentlemen. At least I don't have the internal security section escorting me out in cuffs. Friday is the dead woman's walk."

"This is a real shame," said Blinky.

Christian Collins looked at him skeptically before saying, "I just wanted to tell you I'm with you to the end, ma'am. Ted and I know you're working something hard and we want to help."

Susanne patted Christian on the shoulder and would have done the same for Blinky if he had one. Something about their request made her paranoid. Looking at the two men, her instincts told her that one—or both—of these men was the snitch leaking information to Roger Corwin. She covered her anger with a smile. "That's sweet, gentlemen, but I'm playing without chips. Worse, someone's been looking over my shoulder. You two need to find a new sugar momma. Or have you already found one?"

It was an awkward question.

"We want to help, ma'am," Ted Blinky burst. "I'm the senior technical analyst in the Cave and I want in. I don't care about other people. I work for you."

Susanne thought about ramming the dagger into her desk for a flourish, but twenty-two years in the service had instilled a fear of damaging government property. "All right. Truth is, I can use the help. We've located Gavin Kelly and Contreras is on his way. I'm sure you've already figured that out. As for the plan, I'm going to make two trips to my car to with my personal effects. If each of you accompanies me to the parking lot, one at a time to avoid any unpleasant corroboration, you may just hear me mumble some concerns I have with the extract."

− 55 −

TAMPICO, MEXICO

The lights in the cell flickered on and buzzed. Kelly was hidden under a pile of sheets and didn't hear it for the swelling in his ear canal. Miguel Ramos tapped on the bars with a key. "Mister Callahan. Or should I call you Mister Contreras? Wake up. Wake up, it's only eleven p.m."

Kelly rolled his feet off the cot and planted them on the concrete. His head was still buzzing and his equilibrium was gone. Before his Sumo cell mate had departed, he had doled out some punishment as a farewell gift. Kelly touched his ear and cringed. A baseball-sized bruise had developed in the last four hours and he could feel the fluid dimple at his touch.

Ramos put his face up to the bars. "That's quite a black eye you gave yourself. I hope your dream was pleasant?"

Kelly fought a wave of nausea. "Yeah, well, except for that leather outfit you were wearing everything else was cool. Dreamed you were going to let me out tonight."

"Back yourself up to these bars. You have a visitor and we need to cuff you."

Kelly shook his head. "Sorry. Visiting hours are over."

"Oh, I think you'll take this one, asshole," said someone else.

Kelly closed his right eye and squinted to reduce the double vision. Standing there in a blue United States Drug Enforcement Agency windbreaker was the Hispanic agent who chased him through the streets of Cambridge. *It worked.*

"My name is Jimmy Contreras," the man said. "Funny, you don't look like my brother."

Kelly backed up against the bars and felt handcuffs click onto his wrists.

"Be gentle, Agent Contreras."

Contreras grabbed his hair and yanked his head backward as if he was trying to pull Kelly through the bars. "This is about as gentle as it'll be until you get
back to the States, Ryan. When we got word that Mister Ramos's men had finally
done what we were unable to do—namely catch your ass—I was sent here on
emergency orders. You've been cleared for priority extradition and I'm your es-
cort, just like you asked for, asshole."

The cell door opened and Contreras grabbed Kelly by the back of the neck
and walked him to Ramos's office at the front of the station house. Kelly thought
that Ramos looked as surprised as he was with the midnight breakout. The prosecutor counted out $9,323, placed it in an envelope, and handed it to the DEA
agent, then pushed a pen across toward Kelly. "Sign the receipt, please, Mister
Tim Ryan. It's a shame we didn't have more time together. Agent Contreras tells
me you are quite a catch. Our computer lit up like a Christmas tree when you
asked for your . . . *hermano*."

Kelly rotated his hips and waved his fingers. "How am I supposed to sign
this thing with my hands behind my back? You guys didn't plan this out too well,
did you?"

Ramos snickered and then stared hard at the DEA agent. "No, Mister Ryan.
We did not plan this. In fact, it was quite rushed. You must be a very bad boy. So
bad, in fact, that we are not privy to your file."

Kelly sensed a palpable tension between the two lawmen, so he filled the silence while Contreras signed for him. "Yeah, well, some customers from my
Arkansas trafficking days have come back to haunt me. I'll miss you, Mister
Ramos. Please give my best to my roommate from last night. Tell him . . . revenge is a motherfucker."

The white Land Rover zoomed north up Highway 180 out of Tampico. Behind it, a black Jeep Cherokee labored to keep up. Northbound traffic was light
but that did not prevent the impatient Land Rover from driving long stretches
on the wrong side of the road.

"Hey, man, how about you undo these cuffs," said Kelly. "Then at least I can
die properly on this highway, with my arms extended in panic."

He was buckled into the front seat next to Jimmy Contreras, sitting on his
hands. They had been driving for fifteen minutes, and he could no longer stand
the silence. At The Hague, conversation was treasured physical activity.

"You shut up, first. Then we'll talk," said Contreras.

"We're talking now."

"I know. And I told you to keep your fucking mouth shut, didn't I?"

Some spittle flew into Kelly's face, and he wiped his nose with his shoulder.
"Are you drunk? Your breath is kicking, man."

Contreras stomped on the brake and swerved sharply onto the gravel shoulder. The Land Rover lurched to a halt, and when Kelly was able to bring his head up off his lap, Contreras wrapped his hand around his throat. Kelly's eyes welled and spilled over. He wondered if it was the alcohol or the strangulation. Time to call in the understudy, he thought. I've been playing the prison bitch for way too long now.

"You listen, punk. You want to live—if you want your *friends* to live—you do exactly what the fuck I say. *Comprende?*"

"Oui, monsieur," Kelly said on the inhalation.

The inside of the cab was suddenly filled with red and blue lights. Kelly swiveled his head and saw a cop running toward them with his gun drawn. Contreras opened the glove compartment and fumbled around with the pistol.

"You're not going to kill him, are you?" asked Kelly.

Contreras pulled out the envelope with the cash and slapped the door shut. "This *policía* has been on us for thirty kilometers. Time for you to make a donation. Don't worry, you can expense it on your TAD form if you survive."

The cop shoved a bulky silver flashlight into the cab and flicked it on. Kelly could see a small revolver propped up on the stem. "*Everything all right, sir?*" the cop asked in Spanish.

"*Fine. My friend next to me talks too much. Had to teach him some manners,*" Contreras said with a wink. "*Listen, how far did Ramos tell you to follow us?*"

The cop turned his light off and whispered, "*All the way to the border, sir.*"

Contreras grunted. "*That'll take you all night. Listen, I can handle myself, friend, and I may need to teach gringo here a much longer lecture in manners, if you see what I'm saying. I'd rather not have you witness it.*" He shot his hand behind Kelly's head and tucked a wad of money in the cop's hand. "*Go home to your wife tonight and promise her something nice, courtesy of the United States government. I'll take it from here.*"

The cop turned his back, holstered his pistol, and flicked on the flashlight to inspect his bounty. "*Have a good night, sir, and get a shot in for me.*"

Contreras waited until the cop grew tiny in the rearview mirror before he unlocked Kelly's cuffs and started the Land Rover. "This little trip we're about to take is what we call 'need-to-know,' Kelly. So please don't get in the early habit of asking questions. I say, you do. When we arrive at the boat, you will give me specific directions to the landing site. I know you're familiar with jail, which may come in handy if you fail to comply with my orders."

"What kind of boat?" asked Kelly, rubbing his wrists.

"See? There you go. You are along for the ride only because Phillips may not come in if he sees me. As a former jarhead, you know how to carry out an order, don't you, Marine?"

"Spoken like a true drill instructor. You were in?"

"Yes. And I wasn't no zero. Sixty-seven to seventy-three. Back when fragging young Irish lieutenants was all the rage." Contreras popped the clutch for effect, chuckling smugly. "I don't tolerate shit when I'm in the field. You still got a grudge when we get stateside after this op, we'll settle it then."

Kelly tried to smile but it hurt. "Well, after watching you try to catch me back in Cambridge, I can't say that I'm all that concerned. Were you drunk then, too? How much did that goat rodeo cost the taxpayers?"

"Not as much as it may cost to rebuild that face of yours."

Contreras realized he had forgotten about the pistol. He reached across Kelly and grabbed it out of the glove compartment, along with a map, a Garmin GPS, and directions he had jotted down during the conversation with Susanne Sheridan. He elbowed Kelly on his way back to the steering wheel.

"Careful, I throw a mean head butt, as you can see."

Something in the rearview mirror caught Contreras's eye. Flashing police lights came up over a rise about three kilometers behind the Land Rover. Contreras swore and cut his own headlights, increasing speed. There were no highway lamps, and several southbound cars nearly drifted into them before jerking back to the right in a flurry of honks and bright headlight flashes.

"If you want to kill us, why not just use the pistol?" asked Kelly. He pulled his lap belt tighter and squinted at the dashboard, checking for a passenger-side airbag.

"I think it's that same *policía* coming after us. Something's gone wrong. We're busted." Contreras tossed the directions on Kelly's lap. "We're on one hundred eighty north. Our turn is coming up fast on the right. What's the kilometer mark?"

Kelly held the paper up to his left eye and said, "At seventy-three kilometers from the Route one hundred eighty–one hundred intersection there will be . . . looks like you wrote . . . a dirt trail? And a Volkswagen in a garage? I can't read your writing in the dark."

Contreras checked his trip odometer—70.6 kilometers—and pressed the pedal into the floorboard. "I know the rest. Go in the back, open the rear hatch, and drape the car cover over the taillights. I gotta brake soon."

"Sing out if you speed up. I don't wanna fall out."

"If I could go faster, I would."

Kelly scrambled over his seat back and smashed the interior light with his first before crawling up to the rear hatch. He popped it open in time to see the driver of a pickup truck recoiling in fear as the blacked-out Land Rover cut him off. By the time the driver reached his horn, Contreras's Rover had already barreled out of range and the honk was faint. Kelly flopped the cover out over the bumper. The wind shooting up from the tire wells billowed the cover and it flapped out horizontally, like the tail of a hunting dog. Kelly could see the sparkle of red and blue police lights trailing them. He wedged his sneaker into a side window and leaned out over the bumper, pinning the car cover to the tail-lights with his hands.

"Good to go!" Kelly shouted to the asphalt.

"What?"

"I SAID GOOD TO . . ."

The Land Rover turned sharply and nearly came up on two wheels. The entire vehicle shuddered as the friction increased, rubber peeling off the tires in long strips. Kelly dropped the cover in the middle of the highway and lunged for the door handle. His hand went sailing by it as he was flung forward. He thumped into the back of the driver's seat, popping a swollen blood vessel in his cheek. Now dust filled the cab. His hands fought for balance, but Contreras was braking even harder and Kelly was sucked into the foot well behind the front seats.

"Let's go! Let's go!" shouted Contreras.

Kelly realized the vehicle had stopped inside a garage. He heard what sounded like a jackhammer and peeked in time to see a bald man in blue coveralls, wearing a huge backpack, shutting a large sliding door with a chain. Contreras dragged him out of the Land Rover, right over the bald man now working the rear license plate with a crowbar.

"You might have told me we were stopping," Kelly said.

"Shut your mouth and follow me. Ain't you never had a hot extract before?"

"Not without being shot at, I haven't."

"This op ain't over yet," said Contreras, already trailing the bald man out the back door of the building.

It was a thirty-minute bushwhack to the ocean from the garage, but neither man seemed to be bothered by it. Contreras's legs were as long as Kelly's—two sinewy pairs that had raised the ire of many a Marine on the long humps both used to lead. They chewed up the terrain in meter-long bites. Kelly wanted to press Contreras into a conversation to explain the plan, but he knew English voices would attract attention in a Mexican coastal jungle. Soon the muddy trail became sand and revealed a silver beach that acted as a protected cove for a large Hatteras fishing yacht anchored fifty meters offshore.

"Is that our ride out there?" Contreras asked in Spanish.

"English is better for me, actually," the bald man said.

"Is that our ride?" Contreras asked again. Susanne's brief had been short on details, hastily arranged. No matter. Contreras was thunderstruck that she had plowed ahead alone into territory where doing what was right also violated orders. He assumed the bald man was either a CIA operations officer or a contractor.

The bald man pointed at a small Boston Whaler beached with its outboard up. "That's not exactly the bona fides I was briefed on, but I guess it's close enough. You'll take that Whaler out to the yacht. You can winch it up onto the bow or just trail it. Weather is supposed to turn bad tomorrow. Got twenty-knot winds coming from the east, so I guess you best be going wherever it is you're going."

The man escorted them down the beach and pushed the whaler until it was floating. He dumped his backpack inside with a thud and unzipped it, lifting a plastic-wrapped M-4 automatic rifle for show before stuffing it back inside. Kelly could not pinpoint his age or nationality in the dark.

"Got two weapons in here plus ammo and the satcom terminal. Got decent cell phone coverage along this shore so if it fails you can always phone home. There's a backup satcom in the forward berthing in the Hatteras along with all explosives and the fuses. I'd say you only need two pounds to do the job, but I packed ten. The blasting caps and remote detonators are under the steering wheel in the main cabin. We had an extra M-60 Golf machine gun so I stuffed that in the forward fish box, alongside its tripod and two thousand rounds of seven-six-two." The bald man smiled and added, "Wish I was going to the party. Need anything else?"

"I like to go into battle with a riding crop and a bugle. Got those?" asked Kelly, annoyed with the man's analogy.

"Guess you'll have to whistle."

"That's funny. What's your name? I've never met a bald Mexican before."

Contreras moved aft and flipped the engine locking lever to set the propeller into the water. The bald man just stared at Kelly in silence, shoving him out into the Bay of Campeche and deeper water.

– 56 –

WEST OF TEHUACÁN, MEXICO

Neck limped for two miles on his bare feet, driven by a ravenous hunger for sleep that was so powerful he twice walked in a circle before orienting himself and pushing on. If Darren and Kate found him they'd make him hike. If he hiked, he would die.

He crossed a dirt road and scoured the terrain for a flat spot on which he could sleep. Nothing else mattered. He saw a cemetery atop a small hill in the distance and trudged through a cow field up among the crosses. The cows looked like giant spiders and he hoped they were not poisonous.

The wind was up again and he saw the aftershock of the squall approaching from the west this time, as if the mountains had repelled the cumulonimbus clouds and sent them back in full retreat, the sky darkening and thick again.

He stumbled to a small, flat oval full of gravestones. There were no crosses. The graveyard was the size of a boxing ring, encircled by a three-foot wall of slate stones that reminded him of his grandfather's house outside of Newton, which was outside Boston, which was outside Massachusetts or something. It was all very confusing.

Distant lightning flashed and illuminated the tiny yard. Neck managed to clamber over the wall after a serious struggle, complete with a rest stop where he sat straddling the wall, wondering how in the world he had ever come to believe he could play professional football in the first place. What a crock. Vincent Cappucco was a quitter.

He lost his balance and thumped on the other side where he curled up tight and out of the wind, melting into the ground. Before the thunderclap from the bolt reached him, Neck was in a deep sleep.

———

Neck slept so soundly that his dreams piled up in his head like a car wreck, one layered on another: Kate, ESPN Draft Day, the Backstreet Boys, the Wolverines, the shoot-out in front of the cop station, the trip to Pasadena for the Rose Bowl, a toy horse he had as a boy, his ex-girlfriend, the rapids, voracious dogs, his mother's laugh, chickens . . .

A giant chicken, as fast as a dog. Yellow and fluffy. No, not a chicken, a chick, pecking him on the cheek. Chicken, chick, cheek. Peck . . . PECK . . . *PECK!*

Neck swiped at the chick and his hand was stung by a wasp. It wasn't a chick, he could see that in the back of his eyelids easily enough, it was a wasp. A talking wasp! He shook his head and when he opened his eyes he inhaled and his nerves came alive. Every fiber, every tendon, every bone, every muscle screamed. The Sleep Monster grabbed him and shook him up, but a stronger sense dispelled it. Fear.

He sat up against the cemetery wall.

The thunderheads covered his plot like a blanket and the stars were gone again. Neck squinted around the grave markers but it was too dark to see more than a few feet. Rising above the general deluge of throbbing, his hand caught his attention and he studied it in the black, bringing it right up against his face. He'd cut it in his sleep. Just a scratch, really, an inch long. He dragged his fingers around in the dirt next to him—*probably a piece of glass from a broken brew bottle*—and the dirt was cold and smooth. Soothing. He was asleep before his head bumped the wall behind him.

His eyelids snapped up. Was he talking in his sleep? Probably. Somebody was. Thunder rumbled in the eastern sky but the graveyard was still. He held his breath and all noise ceased save a pesky cricket that freaked him out. He imagined Jiminy Cricket playing a fiddle.

Then the cricket stopped chirping.

Was there a giant cricket on the other side of the rock wall? Was it a *person* who was talking to him? He tried to stand, but his right thigh tightened and cramped wickedly. He flopped back, growled, and dug his thick fingers into his quad, trying to relax even as the ripple began to creep around to his hamstring like ice slowly freezing a pond. A knot the size of a volleyball swelled in the back of his leg. Tears would have leaked from his eyes had it not been for the fact that he was bereft of excess fluid. Neck managed to grab his toe and he pulled back, angling his foot. In a minute the cramp abated, but like a foul tide it left torn muscles behind when it receded.

Neck limped to the wall and sat down with his back leaning against the wall and his right leg extended. He checked his watch. Kate was right, just a two-hour nap and he felt much better. The NFL was a possibility again. Maybe if he slept some more, the old ass-kicking Neck would reemerge from the ashes like the fiery Kleenex or whatever. He closed his eyes. A flash turned his lids from black to red and when he opened his eyes, the lightning lingered long enough for him to notice the boy. He was standing behind a grave marker not twenty yards away inside the wall. Next to him, a dog sat on its haunches, panting.

The curtain fell quickly and Neck had lost his night vision. When the spots imploded and were gone, he looked near the gravestone. The boy was gone. No, it was not a boy. He had a beard. A tiny man. Neck pulled himself up and sat on the wall, then pushed himself to his feet with a painful shove. He could not put weight on his right leg.

"*Hola, señor!*" Neck called out to the dark.

Flight was out of the question. Neck could barely stand, let alone run. Anyway, he wasn't afraid, not of a tiny farmer. Farmers usually had warm milk and maybe even a hot daughter, who would bathe him and give him a happy ending. "*Hello,*" he called again in Spanish.

Up behind the ridge, lightning flashed erratically like a strobe light, one bolt after another. Neck saw the man-boy pop out from behind a headstone and start for him. He was walking, *strolling* really, but the flashes made his movements look jerky and mechanical, like a toy clown. Saint Elmo's fire snaked blue around his belt buckle, then disintegrated.

There was a respite and Neck lost him in the dark again. His head swiveled to follow the imaginary man on his path, but when the next bolt shot up, the graveyard was empty.

"*Hello,*" came a high voice in Spanish next to him. Neck jerked back and spun. Somehow the man had snuck around behind him.

"*Hello.*"

"*You speak Spanish?*" the man asked.

Looking down at him, Neck thought that he barely cleared five feet four inches. Just like Michael J. Fox or Tom Cruise, he thought, remembering his team's meeting with Jay Leno before the *Tonight Show Rose Bowl Special.* Big Jaw had irritated him when he told Neck that he was too big to be an actor. "You'd just be a caricature," Leno had told him, whatever that was. "Fact is, all the great actors are short."

"Not Arnold and Clint," Neck had responded, "and they rule, bro." His cunning observation must have stunned Leno. It solicited a raised eyebrow and nothing more. When Neck retired as a Hall of Famer, he planned to go into movies. Yeah, boy! His nap had allowed the dream of professional football to take its rightful place after its sleepless hiatus. He *was* an army! And now he was a step closer to home.

"*Yes, I speak Spanish. Italian, too,*" Neck told the dark little man, waiting for the Mexican to ask him if he was an *Asesino* or a hostage.

"*Storm coming,*" said the man, who smiled, stroked his beard and said nothing else. He had a head like a giant nutcracker. Neck wondered if the Guinness Book paid for world record entries.

Neck waited for the questions, but they never came. This is strange, he thought. Even if he *is* a farmer without a TV or anything—and hasn't heard about *Los Asesinos*—he should at *least* be a little *curious* as to why a soon-to-be American *pro football player* is sleeping in some *cemetery* in the middle of *Mexico* in a *heat lightning storm!*

"*I'm, uh, lost,*" Neck offered, struggling a bit with his Spanish. It was irritating because it was the one subject in which he excelled. "*Which, how do, does one find a big town? With hotels and people?*" Neck was tired, but he remembered Darren's instructions. "*A phone? Do you have a phone?*"

The little man took the beard and popped it into his mouth. I wish Darren Phillips could see this guy's nasty growth and grooming habits, if he thinks goatees are bad, Neck giggled to himself. The man's head was too large for his skinny body and he was smiling. His forehead is fucking weird, thought Neck. I wonder if he's ever seen a white man. Certainly not one as big as me! I wish I had some candy or a mirror I could trade for food.

"*I call the police for you. Yes?*"

"*No,*" Neck said quickly. "*Uh, no, thank you, sir.*"

The man raised his eyebrows but they had a long way to go up that head. "*No? Why not? They'll help you.*"

"*I don't have . . . need help, thank you.*"

The man laughed and hit a high octave, tripping over it. Forget the food, Neck thought, I just want him outta here. I'll find my own way in the morning. "*Took me a long time to wake you, friend,*" said the man. "*I was almost going to shave you. I'm still considering it. You want that? A clean face?*"

Neck was confused and thought he must have misheard the Spanish. "*I don't understand. I'm sorry.*" Lightning illuminated them with a flurry of flashbulbs and Neck noticed that the man had muddy sneakers on. Something began to bother him and he took a step back to gain some distance.

He stepped on the dog's tail, and it howled sadly.

"*You understood. Like this.*" The man mimicked a shaving motion. "*With a knife.*"

El Monstruo Carnicero slipped Bear Claw from his belt. Yes, it would be perfect for a boy this size. He held the big Malaysian parang up, twisting it so the boy could marvel the width he had so precisely refined. It was pattern-welded thick enough to support the pressure required to take the skin from an animal as big as a bull. Like this blond boy!

"*I made this myself. See the top? Gave it a finely serrated bite. I could chop a tree with Bear Claw. What do you think I could do to your legs?*"

He was eager to test Bear Claw on someone so big, but steeled himself for disappointment. This boy, just like the soldier and all of the others, would shake in fear when he finally recognized that the taste in his mouth was unavoidable death. Then he'd go weak and the begging would start.

Of course, this one was *already* beaten. He could barely move! *El Monstruo Carnicero* watched the boy limp toward the middle of the graveyard. His right leg did not bend. *El Monstruo Carnicero* did not have to rush to keep up with his massive prize.

"*I . . . have to leave, now,*" said the blond boy, looking over his shoulder.

"*Stop there, boy,*" hissed *El Monstruo Carnicero*.

"*No. I'm sorry. I have to leave. I am walking tonight . . . to the house of my friend.*"

El Monstruo Carnicero was irritated by the callow lie and even angrier that the boy was already trying to run. This wasn't going to be pleasurable at all. Well, that's not true, he thought, don't be rash. There is still Bear Claw's work to keep me sane!

El Monstruo Carnicero reached for the small of his back and produced Falcon. He stroked its titanium nitrate coating and then found its tail. He watched the boy's right leg and when it planted and held in place for a second, *El Monstruo Carnicero*'s arm bent, cocked, and snapped the steel through the air. Falcon whistled as it flew. The blade penetrated deep into the boy's big calf and put him down. When the boy fell, he took a headstone with him and dirt was catapulted into the air. *El Monstruo Carnicero* was amazed at his size—it was going to be like killing a bull.

"*When I talk to you, you look at me,*" he hissed over the boy's English babble.

"Fuck you, motherfucker!" screamed the boy in English. "I'm going to fucking kill you, you rat fuck!"

"*I'll teach you how to cry out in Spanish.*"

The blond boy rolled to his knees and wrenched the blade out of his calf. Bear Claw was waiting for the move and the parang scratched the boy hard on the hand, raking off a finger. *El Monstruo Carnicero* snatched Falcon off the ground and backed away. It was best not to get close to a boy that size, he knew from experience. He was thin and in many fights he had been bruised, but the wounds were sustained for a reason—to deal a killing strike, you had to get close, and sometimes the victim got in a final kick or punch.

"You listen, boy, or I cut your whole hand off next time. You . . ."

"I said to GO FUCK YOURSELF, YOU BITCH!"

The boy lunged at him, but *El Monstruo Carnicero*, though surprised—shocked!—leapt back like a cat and crouched. The boy fell on his face. *El Monstruo Carnicero* studied the blond boy for the first time. Really looked at him. Beyond the hair and the tan there was true rage, and that was all that mattered. He chortled with anticipation as he watched the boy crawling after him, hand swiping like a giant rattlesnake.

"A fellow warrior!"

Neck rolled onto his knees. The little man kicked him right in the face, but Neck absorbed the blow easily and tried to grab the man's leg. If he caught him, he would snap the motherfucker in half. The little bastard was fast, though, and danced backward again. Neck struggled forward, but his body was broken and he suffered the indignity of this little thing laughing at him.

"Olé!" the Indian yelled. *"Come on, bull! Huitzilopochtli is howling for you!"*

"Dead man. I'm talkin' to you, motherfucker," Neck said. The lightning erupted again and he saw the little man laugh, moving in spasms in the light. Saw the big machete, too, and it quieted him.

"You know where you are, yanqui? You're in an Aztec cemetery. We build them circular, like this one, except these headstones aren't ours. The Spaniards just put them in later. The crosses you see sprinkled outside the wall there? Those are the tainted, either my people who caught sick from the Spanish and died, or trembled at the roar of their cannons and lost their will to attack, or were corrupted and converted like stupid dogs, or the conquistadors themselves. You know who I am?"

Neck shook his head and thought about the toppled gravestone and his days as a discus thrower. How far could he toss it, given his leg? At least fifteen feet.

"No," Neck lied.

"I am called the Monster Butcher. I am pure Aztec. Mexica's finest warrior."

"That's funny. You look like a small bitch."

It caused a long pause in the interaction. *El Monstruo Carnicero* wondered if the boy's Spanish was just faulty, or if he really had the *cojones* to say such an odd thing. He was acting differently than most opponents. So pompous in his dyed blond hair. *"Think you can beat me? I give you a chance, then I'll carve you up and bathe in your blood and taste you while you watch. You have heard of Aztec human sacrifices?"*

"Let's do this," the boy said. He sounded eager.

"If you can make it out of this ring of death, outside the wall, I won't torture you. I'll hack off your head with Bear Claw and be done with it. Otherwise, yanqui, it will take a while. And I'll take your heart out while you're still breathing."

El Monstruo Carnicero expected the babbling would start now—the weak protests, calls to one god or another. Instead, the boy nodded and managed to stagger to his feet, hopping on one leg.

"I've played Bull in the Ring, before, bitch. When do I go?" the boy whispered.

El Monstruo Carnicero raised his eyebrows and waved Bear Claw as a matador might wave his cape to the crowd, bowing his head and sweeping the parang across his body, extending his arm like a wing. Yes, he thought, Bull in the Ring is exactly right. *"As you wish, boy."*

"Just you?" asked the boy. *"Or you call a hundred little Aztec friends first?"*

It surprised *El Monstruo Carnicero,* and he felt a frisson of joy because his temper was rising, each of the boy's words as grating and spirited as a hair plucked from his chin. The boy hopped behind a gravestone and then bounded toward the far wall on one leg. *El Monstruo Carnicero* cut him off and jabbed at him once, just to test the boy's reactions. The boy had more furor, it was true, but his instincts were the same as all the others—where the knife moved, his body jerked away.

"Just me, boy. Just you and me."

El Monstruo Carnicero watched the boy's arms and decided to play a little. He closed like a cat and decided to take a deep slice from the boy's forearm, anticipating the boy's reaction to the attack. *El Monstruo Carnicero* aimed for a point in the dark that was empty until he feinted. The boy did the expected. He jabbed with Falcon, slid right, and when the machete barreled though the night the boy's arm came to meet it, not vice-versa. There was a thick thump when Bear Claw tasted bone.

The boy roared. His other arm shot out and snatched *El Monstruo Carnicero* by the wrist, the luckiest grab *El Monstruo Carnicero* had ever seen. The grip was as powerful as it was unexpected. Before he could bring Bear Claw in for another bite, *El Monstruo Carnicero*'s wrist was broken and he was hurtling through the air.

El Monstruo Carnicero tumbled across the dirt and smacked into a grave marker, bruising his back and stealing his wind. His lungs burned as he watched the boy hop for the wall. He found Bear Claw and stood to give chase, but the boy was bounding away like a giant kangaroo.

El Monstruo Carnicero would keep his promise to the boy, and he regretted the fact that there would be no interrogation. The boy would get free of the wall. He had hoped to listen to stories about the girl Kate North. He raised Bear Claw above his head and screeched, trotting toward the boy's back, focusing on his thick neck. He wondered if he could take the head off given its diameter.

Neck saw the wall careen closer. He was happy that he had won. Even if the man hit him with another throwing knife he was confident that he'd make the wall. He wasn't the first to underestimate Neck Cappucco! Little fuck! But what did that get him? A quick death, the Monster Butcher had said, and what good was *that*? He was to be cut down like a cow after he vaulted this wall! By that little man-boy!

El Monstruo Carnicero was in a near sprint. He was thinking about the extension he'd need to reach up to deliver the killing blow when suddenly the boy turned shy of the wall and faced him. His big body was heaving and his teeth were clenched. What's this? *El Monstruo Carnicero* wondered. He gawked at the pose—and the size of the boy's teeth—but his momentum carried him forward even as the boy did the unexpected. *He's charging!*

The boy hit him like an oak door and broke a rib that sounded like a breaking branch. *El Monstruo Carnicero* was in his huge arms now, up in the air and rushing backward, riding his shoulder. He jabbed Bear Claw into the boy's back, but before he could jam it to the hilt he was flying again like a cornhusk doll. He impacted the wall head first and his vision blacked for a second before the boy, the *wildest* boy, filled his eyes once more.

And once more a charge.

El Monstruo Carnicero managed to get a foot up. He coiled his leg and kicked the animal in the face. It did nothing. The boy's thick neck acted as a shock absorber and he swatted *El Monstruo Carnicero*'s leg as if it were a nuisance, his tree-trunk arms slithering across and finding his face. And then hands found his neck. It was like being choked by a wolf trap. He grabbed at the boy's smallest finger, but it seemed as thick as a tire iron and was just as pliable. When the boy cut off his airway, *El Monstruo Carnicero*'s vision closed in. He saw Bear Claw halfway imbedded in the boy's back, dangling and bouncing along with the fight like a *banderilla* doing its damage on a bull. This *is* a bull fight.

But bulls do not choke. I cannot breathe.

The dog howled and howled, eager to join the wrestling match.

El Monstruo Carnicero found the parang's handle and twisted it as hard as he could. He heard the flatulent sigh of a lung bursting. The boy collapsed on his lap.

El Monstruo Carnicero rolled the big animal onto his back and straddled him. "*You fight hard, boy,*" he gasped. "*Huitzilopochtli will be pleased!*"

The boy just stared, concentrating on his own breathing.

El Monstruo Carnicero stroked the boy's cheek. "*Look at you. Worked so hard for that tan. Don't you know that the conquistadors avoided the sun and protected their pale flesh for status? Don't you know that even today rich Spanish cunts carry parasols with them on sunny days to avoid the sun you lust after?*"

The boy was gurgling, working to expel the blood from his throat. *El Monstruo Carnicero* couldn't waste any more time, though he enjoyed the boy's company. He sheathed Bear Claw and removed Barracuda for the surgery. "I ask *questions only once. Not like your movies where I beat you up, or shock you, whatever. If you lie once, I start to cut your skin off. Where is the girl Kate North going?"*

"*Mexico City,*" the boy whispered.

The boy reacted violently to Barracuda's movements and *El Monstruo Carnicero* was happy some nerve endings were still alive. It made for better interrogations. "*No. You're too far off course. Where?*"

"*Mexico City.*"

El Monstruo Carnicero was satisfied that the boy was truthful. He'd never seen a man hold fast to a lie without a personal stake. Still, a flick of the wrist confirmed it. "*Where?*" he asked for good order's sake.

"MEXICO CITY, YOU FUCKING ANIMAL!" Neck gasped in English.

"*Who is she meeting when she gets there?*"

The boy's eyes were rolling like a crazed horse's. *El Monstruo Carnicero* pushed him on his side so he could spit some blood and breathe. When he rolled the boy back, he was smiling broadly, red splotches on big white teeth like cherry Popsicle stains. "*I miss my mom anyway.*"

El Monstruo Carnicero slapped the bull hard across the face. "*Who is she meeting?*"

The big boy said, "*I almost won, even with my hurt leg and your knife.*"

"*Who is the girl Kate North meeting?*"

The boy's eyes rolled back into his head, and all he said before he died was, "*Just wait until you meet my friends, bitch.*"

THURSDAY

In humans, short-term sleep deprivation leads to sleepiness, mood disturbances, and performance deficits. When sleep deprivation is prolonged for more than a few days, as can be done in rats, a physiologic syndrome develops . . . increased food intake, loss in body weight, and increased energy expenditure culminates invariably in death.

—G. TONONI, C. CIRELLI, AND R. SALAZAR,
*FUNCTIONAL CONSEQUENCES
OF SLEEP DEPRIVATION*

- 57 -

ORIZABA, MEXICO

The moon rose up over Orizaba's 5,610-meter volcanic peak at 0122. There were no clouds—the system rolling in from the Caribbean had cleared them away in preparation for its arrival. In the ribbon of night light that rippled down the slopes of the volcano and out over the high desert, a couple limped along in silence. In the ground behind them lay one companion and two former lives. Neither the man nor the woman knew if they would get them back again.

Three days earlier, her feet were size eight. Now they had swollen to ten and were dressed in men's size-fourteen sneakers, toes stuffed with crabgrass to temper the friction. Her arms and legs had become perpetual pendulums and her hands were as fat as her feet, the size of small baseball mitts. The blood engorged her nerve endings and even the soft heads of the cattail field made her grind her teeth.

"Are we there yet?" she whispered.

It was a joke familiar to anyone who had ever used terrain to punish their body.

"Just over the next hill," the man said.

_____

The sun rose at 0527. The high mountain range of the Sierra Madre was at their backs as the couple began the long descent to the Atlantic. Lush flora started to emerge from the earth along the Jamapa River that they were tracing to the east. The sparse green patches appeared gradually, first as freckles on a dry brown landscape, then, just a daydream later, the ground was covered in a thick blanket of greenery. It was a cruel game of hide-and-seek. The clime looked benign, but the relief was still severe—steep, convex fingers ate what was left of their quadriceps and calves, deep draws burned the ligaments along their ankles and nourished their blisters.

The woman could no longer see the mountains, but she still felt them. The downhill mashed her rotting toes into the front of her oversized sneakers. She concentrated on kicking her heels hard into the weeds before she set her soles down, but instead of dispelling her pain, she redistributed it.

They came to a wide bend in the river that looked safe because of its beauty. The water lapped gently over polished rocks that had been washed for hundreds of years. The couple pushed through a cluster of bright green, prehistoric ferns and knelt on the bank, lapping at the water like happy dogs.

"It's beautiful, isn't it?" she said between gulps.

The man just nodded and stuck his face back in the glacial runoff to cool himself. His mind was capable of attaching just a single emotion to the wild: dread. The terrain in front of them was a crucible, not an idol. It was the enemy.

She watched a lovely blue parrot land on a spruce tree overhead. She listened to its song and smiled, wondering if she could kill it and eat it. But her throwing arm no longer had the strength. Besides, she had done enough killing. She tossed the stone into the brook and watched the tiny shock waves expand in concentric circles.

"We may not be in 'SundayStyles,' but I'll bet we're in the *Times*," she said. "Dad will be pleased."

The man grunted, busy digging into a beetle nest hidden in the soft dirt. He handed her two writhing insects and several worms. She crushed them to stop movement and swallowed them like vitamins.

"We've killed some innocent people, Darren."

"In war, innocents die. Now help me find some more protein."

"Is Neck home by now?"

It hurt him, and he took a moment. "Yes, baby, I think he is."

The moon set at 1117, but the couple did not see it disappear from the baby blue sky. When they entered the jungle it had swallowed them whole, a living organism of triple canopy foliage that absorbed them reluctantly and now seemed to be fighting to rid itself of the foreigners that had infected it. Hiking along an ancient overgrown river trail, the couple had to lean into the slippery bush to keep momentum.

A long, thin branch snapped into the woman's cheek like a whip.

"Ow! Watch it," she whispered.

She couldn't see him in the thick greenery, but a voice said, "Watch what?"

"The branches! Hold them until I grab them!"

"Sorry."

She sighed and tried to step forward. A tangle of wait-a-minute vines had her by the shoulders and her legs buckled. She was so exhausted that she just melted into a popcorn bush and sat there breathing.

"I need fifteen minutes to silence my barking dogs."

The man fought through the vines and knelt beside her. That she was asking for a stop before him gave him urgency. He stroked her forehead and said, "Homestretch, baby. Pretty soon we'll hit one of the big rivers running from the mountains all the way to the Veracruz. We'll just float downstream."

She leaned back and raised her leg, biting her lip. "Something's wrong with my feet. Can you take a look?"

"Blisters?"

"I wish."

He untied her right shoe and loosened all the laces so that the shoe could slip right off, but her foot was so engorged that she still yelped when he pulled the Nike free. He grabbed her leg by her ankle and his fingers sunk an inch into the cellulitis. He peeled off her sock as delicately as he could, cringing at both the odor and the understanding that he was peeling her skin.

She bit down hard on the branch between her teeth. "And I thought a bikini wax was bad."

He grunted. The bottom of her foot was a mix of black and purple, splashed with patches of green where the bacteria had not yet destroyed the epidermis. The contour was ragged and pockmarked where little pieces of her skin had been killed and replaced with pus. Trench foot forms when feet are kept damp for long periods and become breeding grounds for infections. It is a living bacterial infection that resembles frostbite and can eventually mutate into gangrene if left untreated. Unfortunately for her, treatment was fifty miles away.

She saw his reaction and said, "Trench foot, right?"

"And it's a doozy of an infection, babe."

He ran a twig down the length of her foot, and she jerked it from his hand. She felt like he was cutting her tissue with a straight razor. It was a good sign; her nerve endings were still alive, warring against the infection.

"I don't give your feet much time," he said, angry that she was hurt instead of him.

"Then we better get moving."

———

The sun set at 1742. The woman limped along behind the man with her hand on his shoulder, gripping his exposed trap when she needed a crutch or a tow. They had distanced themselves from the river an hour earlier when they heard the shouts of rafters playing on its currents, moving up past the bank where the vegetation was thick.

They were totally emaciated, all hollow eyes and gaunt limbs. Sinewy tendons could be seen vibrating and rolling just underneath the surface of their paper skins. Bark, grass, grasshoppers, worms, and dragonflies were slowly sizzling in their stomachs.

The pain was fading in the woman's feet. With it went the ability to walk. She felt as if she were hiking down a steep trampoline in roller skates. Soon both her hands were on the man's shoulders, and eventually her feet were wrapped around his waist, too. She held onto him and did not want to let go.

The man did not mind. Indeed, he felt as if he were slowly paying down some crushing debt he had incurred over the years. Tiny calcified granules of tendonitis that had built up under his plastic kneecap were sawing into his tendons. And he relished them.

"We're moving too slowly," she whispered in his ear. "You can't keep this up."

"No, but I can make it just one more minute. And another minute after that."

She kissed his neck. "I love you, baby."

"I love you, too."

The thick smell of vanilla hit the man's nostrils when he pushed through a wall of weeds and tumbled onto his face. The woman fell on top of him and started to talk, but he had a hand over her mouth. The jungle had ended. They were lying at the high edge of a huge clearing, easily a kilometer long and about 400 meters wide, filled with neat rows of some waist-high shrubbery. The giant crop was surrounded by a mountainous jungle that ringed it like a gigantic football stadium. At the opposite edge of the plantation sat a white mansion and two black cars that glinted in the sun.

"We just found our ride to the beach," he whispered, noticing the group of heads that were bobbing among the plants below him, workers picking a crop. Most of them were carrying burlap sacks from the hedgerows to a truck that was slowly circling the crop on a dirt firebreak.

"Must be a vanilla plantation. Smell it?" she said. Her tiny stomach groaned. She fought the urge to low-crawl down into the basin and pop some beans into her mouth, so great was her sugar craving. A vanilla ice cream sundae with snowcap sprinkles appeared in front of her in the dark, and she tried to vanquish the hallucination, transforming it into a box of vanilla wafers before she managed to focus her eyes on a massive spigot that must have been used for irrigation.

"We can't risk it. We'll sleep until midnight, then go grab dinner and a car. He'll be waiting for us at the beach come daylight."

"What if he's not there?"

"He'll be there."

"And then we'll find Neck?"

"Yes, that's the first thing we'll do."

FRIDAY

These were sacred dedications to sacred destinies: the boy-child to warriordom on the field of battle, the girl-child to weaving by the hearth and to constant sweeping to secure and preserve her small corner of the social world.

—INGA CLENDINNEN, *AZTECS*

– 58 –

GULF OF MEXICO

A crescent moon popped free of the horizon just after midnight and illuminated the Hatteras cockpit with a shimmering glow. For sixty miles Contreras had been driving parallel with a cruise ship, carefully tucked in its radar shadow as it headed south, but his GPS alarm had just sounded. He eased back on the throttle and let the big ship slip away, then powered up and cut right, pitching perpendicular across its huge wake on a course of 250 degrees. That ought to wake Kelly up, he thought happily. Contreras had spent a long day listening to Kelly's blather. He had been tempted to throw a barb about Kelly's Somalia fuckup to silence the kid, but he knew better than to criticize the combat actions of a fellow Marine, police action or not. Contreras had banished him to the cabin instead.

Contreras gripped the rubber ball handles of the twin throttles and slowly pulled them up until they clicked into apogee. The eight hundred horses that powered the Hatteras instantly responded to the tug on the reins and the propellers stopped spinning. Contreras clicked the key to the left and savored the sounds of the thick, steady crush of water as the yacht sloshed in the waves.

The wind was raging ahead of a low-pressure system that was approaching the Gulf. Warm air was screeching across the beam at over twenty-five knots and rocking the boat from side to side. Contreras set the autopilot, then stuck his head outside the bridge. He closed his eyes and faced the breeze, smelling the salt air, squinting when the droplets peppered his bare skin. Reveling. In just under six hours the sun would rise and the operation would reach its culmination. The harsh weather helped Contreras get into character, and he felt all those old butterflies come to life. The enemy. The unknown. The weather. *Retribution.*

"Yo! We there?" shouted Kelly, who had climbed up the ladder to the flying bridge with the green satcom radio in his hand, parachute antenna deployed.

"We're about twenty miles east-northeast of your extract site," said Contreras, annoyed that Kelly seemed as comfortable in the thrashing boat as a monkey on bars. Maybe he wasn't lying about all the fishing stories. "We'll spend the night here. If someone runs up on us, we won't bust the beach landing site. Go set the anchor."

"The anchor? Sorry, skipper, it'll never hold in this weather. What's our depth?"

"Kelly, have you ever read *Message to Garcia?*"

Kelly had read it but he was curious. "No."

"My C.O. made me read it when I was in country. He . . ."

"What country?"

"Vietnam, that's what country. What other country could I be talking about?"

"Kuwait. Somalia. Bosnia. Afghanistan."

"I'm talking about *real* combat, Marine. Anyway, the point of the story is that a young officer is given an extraordinary task and he just does it—no questions asked. So, youngster, when I tell you to set the anchor, *set the fucking anchor.*"

Kelly smirked for a protest—Contreras was running the op and internal friction wouldn't help anything. The important thing was to get Darren and Kate safe onboard. He handed Contreras the satcom. "Your CIA-DEA-NSC-PAP lady boss wants to speak to you."

Contreras was so angry he snarled. "Don't you *ever* mention those agencies again, Kelly. You understand me? I'm sick of your little questions about this op. Your fucking sole concern is to lead me to Darren and Kate Phillips so I can recover a phone. That's their price of freedom. Doesn't matter where I'm from. What's the PAP, anyway?"

Kelly swung around the outrigger pole to the gunwale, careful to keep the balls of his feet firmly planted on the nonskid tape. "It's a gynecological examination, skipper. Figured I'd enlighten you since you work for a woman. What does she look like? No, don't tell me. I love her voice. You and me, Contreras, we're like reverse Charlie's Angels."

Kelly slid down the ladder and went rummaging around the cabin looking for material suitable for a sea anchor. He remembered the giant duffel bag that held the plastic explosives he had discovered while snooping earlier that night.

He assumed the explosives were for an emergency scuttle. They didn't need their carrying case.

He opened the floorboard and reached into the bilge, slowly removing the plastic-wrapped yellow packets and stacking them above the propeller shaft. He felt something smooth and round, like a duck pin bowling ball, and removed it. It was a human skull.

"Kelly, get up here!" Contreras shouted from above decks. "We've got a boat inbound!"

Kelly dropped the skull and tipped the plastic explosives back into the bag. His mind was racing, but it was too hard to concentrate with the wave action and Contreras's warning. When Kelly returned, a big swell pitched the yacht sideways and Contreras had to hold on to one of the bolted chairs to stay on his feet. Kelly ambled over without any difficulty and peered at the black crystal radar display. When the glowing green sweep came around toward Veracruz, a green splotch appeared. Above it, the intruder's distance and speed appeared.

"Twenty-two knots is fast for this sea," said Kelly. "That's a powerful boat."

Contreras handed Kelly the satcom. "Take this and hide it away with the rifles. Four miles. I figure we got ten minutes. I'll grab the equipment up here, you grab the fish below. We got two that are still alive. Gaff one—make sure it's a nice hole—and put it in the ice chest along with one of the dead ones. Then you stay below and do just like we planned. Remember the code word?"

"Chesty."

"Do NOT—I repeat, DO NOT—do anything absent my lead. Go."

Kelly rushed belowdeck, stashed the weapons and the radio, and opened the cooler. There were twenty-four pints of O+ blood and six liters of saline fluid stacked in the crushed ice among the fish, and he was careful not to rip any of the packages when he pulled a thirty-pound red snapper free. He dragged the fish up the ladder and found his balance before stepping out onto the open deck.

The wind stung Kelly's face, but it soon went numb with windburn. He grabbed the flying gaff and sunk it deep into the snapper, then plopped it into the fish box. Next he straddled the live well and gaffed one of the two fish that was still swimming, dumping it in beside the other. When he looked up, Kelly could see the hazy white-and-red running lights of the approaching boat not two kilometers off the stern, blinking because of the harsh wave action. He turned in time to see Contreras tumble across the slimy deck.

Contreras slid for a few feet before crashing shoulder-first into the port gunwale. The rod he was carrying popped free and the treble hook caught him in the webbing between his left thumb and index finger. He growled and tried to reach the rod rack but the swell passed under the boat and the hull pitched the other way, sending him careening back across the bloody deck—snapper mixing with human—toward Kelly, who caught his free hand on the fly and helped him to his feet.

"Hooked my goddamn hand!" Contreras shouted into the wind. He had his fingers extended and separated and was studying his trembling red hand as if in a biology class.

Kelly braced his feet against the fish box. A wave came over the side and he stepped in front of Contreras to absorb it. It shattered on his back. "Barb's pretty big. I'm going to have to cut."

"My hand!"

"No. The barb!" shouted Kelly, glancing over his shoulder.

Kelly bounded over to the stern, opened the tackle box, pushed aside one of Contreras's spare pistols, and returned with a Leatherman. "Hold steady!" he shouted as he positioned the cutters and snipped the tip of the hook. He snaked the rest of the hook free and tied it to the reel, then stuck the rod into a rod holder.

Contreras pressed his bloody hand into his armpit and leaned into the gunwale as a wave took the Hatteras higher and slammed it down again. "Here they come! Go below!"

Kelly shook his head. "They'll never buy it. Why don't I . . ."

"GO, YOU ASSHOLE!"

Kelly was inside the cockpit when the spotlight lit the deck. *Whoever it is, they must have increased their speed to reach us so quickly,* he thought. He peeled back the mattress from one of the cabin racks. Stabs of artificial light brightened the cabin, then disappeared, then brightened it again as the swells tossed the yacht and its new companion. There was a steel O-ring connected to the wooden baseboard and when he lifted it he was staring at four weapons: a high-powered hunting rifle with a scope, two M-4s, and an M-60 machine gun. He chose what he knew best and grabbed six full magazines of 5.56-mm ammunition for the M-4, stuffing them into the pockets of his cargo pants. He checked to make sure a round was chambered and crept halfway up the ladder with his weapon at the ready.

———

Contreras opened the package of squid and spilled them onto the deck just before the thirty-four-foot steel police cutter wheeled next to the Hatteras and shined its spotlight down. *Too late at night and too terrible a sea for the regular shift,* thought Contreras as he shielded his eyes to see. *This will be some junior snuffie working with minimum crew.*

A young man wearing a tremendous orange life preserver stumbled out onto the cutter's deck. He was carrying a red-and-white megaphone and trailing a strap that Contreras assumed was a safety harness, though he could not see where it was connected. The man raised his megaphone and twice was unable to speak because of the pitching and rolling. Eventually he locked his legs around the rail and raised the megaphone. *"What is your business here?"*

"Just some fishing!" shouted Contreras.

The kid looked perplexed. *"In this weather?"*

Contreras shrugged and jerked a thumb at himself. *"Oh, I've seen much worse. I'm not doing bad, either. I got enough red snapper to feed all four of your men."*

"Only got two with me tonight. We thought we'd pulled some bad duty, but look at you! You do this for fun?"

"Man has to feed his family, friend."

The police cutter was blowing down on the Hatteras yacht, so the young man was closer now. With the timing of the swells, he and Contreras looked like they were having a conversation on a seesaw. *"Listen, I have a job, too. We have orders to keep this coast clear and search vessels. I have to ask you to follow us back to Veracruz."*

"You're joking. I'm on a hired charter right now. It will make my month."

"I'm sorry about this. The entire coastline is on alert, if you can believe it."

Somehow word has leaked out of Tampico, thought Contreras. *"For what?"*

The kid's eyes walked across Contreras's deck, and then he took in the entire yacht. His eyebrows slanted toward his nose. *"Where's everyone else?"*

Contreras laughed and shouted, *"My customer went to sleep. Seasick, you know? Up to me to catch some breakfast. The fact is, the damn engine was giving me trouble and it was too dark to fix it, so to save some embarrassment I told him we'd night-fish."*

"What's the problem? Maybe we can help."

Clever, thought Contreras, but with a crew of three it's just a bluff. *"The out-valve on the fuel pump probably got snagged again. Just give me a few more hours! When the sun comes up, I'll fix her and we're off. I'll be gone by seven, okay?"*

A large swell lifted the cutter, and for a moment Contreras thought the two boats would collide. The cutter's engines gargled and the boat backed away from the Hatteras just before impact. Spray flew over the cutter's pilothouse and doused the young man on deck. He shivered and when he spoke again his pitch was up. *"Listen to me, friend. I need you to follow us into Veracruz harbor. It will only take a few minutes when we get there . . ."*

"Don't say this. Give an old man a break."

"I don't have a choice."

"And I told you the damn fuel pump's clogged, sir. You'll have to tow us. Could

take hours in this sea and it will greatly embarrass me. I say it again—this is how I feed my family, sir. You will harm my reputation as a captain. Certainly you understand!"

Contreras stared hard at the young officer and watched as a big roller popped over the cutter's rail and doused the young man again. He gripped the rail just before his legs shot out from beneath him, then scrambled quickly to his feet.

"You said you were doing well with snapper, didn't you? In this sea! But your bait's all over the deck and you have only one rod. So show me a snapper."

Contreras smiled at the officer and stumbled over to the fish box. *"How about two snappers!"* he shouted, hefting two of the fish free of the cooler. One was still alive and it thrashed wildly, its tail curving against its red scales and gills before snapping to the other side like a fire hose gone wild. It wriggled free and bounced on the deck, flipping itself several times as it gyrated toward the fish gate in the stern.

"Okay, consider this your last warning, crazy. I'll be making this run at dawn, and if I find you here I'm towing you in and impounding that boat of yours. Understood?" shouted the officer.

Contreras nodded several times. *"Thank you, sir! I will be gone at first light!"*

"You better be!"

The officer faced his pilothouse and gave a hand signal that Contreras missed because of a breaking wave. White foam washed up over his sneakers and the fish continued its flopping slide. When the sting from the saltwater in his eyes abated, Contreras wiped his face and watched the cutter disappear into the black. Then he went to find the satcom and tell Sheridan that someone had been tipped.

– 59 –

ARRILLAGA PLANTATION, MEXICO

Sergeant Mauricio Gutierrez pressed his eye socket into the rubber cushion on the end of his AN-PVS9c nightscope. The sight gathered the ambient light from the stars and moon, amplified it, and bathed the field in sparkling crystalline green. In the oval, Gutierrez watched the wind blow the vanilla plants erratically. The artificial shadows the scope created flickered and blinked. No movement. Gutierrez removed his eye, washed it with his eyelid, and yawned.

"Gettin' sleepy on me, Mo?" Staff Sergeant Dave Crawford asked him.

"I don't sleep, Staff," whispered Gutierrez. "You know that. I'm a creature of the fucking night."

Crawford grunted his agreement. All the soldiers in his team were hardcore—you weren't selected by SouthCom for one of its Joint Task Force counter-narcotics missions if you carried even a whiff of laziness—but Gutierrez was a different breed. He held the most assiduous sense of duty that Crawford had ever seen: The kid volunteered for security watch when it wasn't his turn, cleaned his big sniper rifle twice a day, checked the sensors and the claymores that surrounded the hide before he allowed himself some sleep, never was caught with both boots off while he changed socks, and had even volunteered to police the dreaded *shit trench*. Crawford had never seen anything like it. The kid watched that goddamn vanilla field every second, as if he were waiting for Santa to come down the chimney.

Crawford tapped the kid on the thigh. Gutierrez was a sergeant by rank, but he was *still* just a kid—he'd been meritoriously promoted so fast through the ranks that his years hadn't caught up yet. Crawford remembered how he'd complained about taking a kid on the team, but he was a Puerto Rican and fit the mission profile better than anyone else: Spanish speaker, indigenous looks, great shot, and, most important, a disciplined soldier who wouldn't do anything stupid to jeopardize the United States' presence in another country. At twenty-two, Gutierrez was already a career man who understood rules.

"My turn to watch," whispered Crawford. "You get some sleep."

Gutierrez checked his watch. "Still have four minutes to go, Staff Sergeant."

The kid shouldered his massive Barrett .50-caliber sniper rifle and put his eye up to the scope for a last glass. Incredible. Crawford remembered his first mission, when his imagination was still able to beat back the boredom of observation, the same struggle performed by night watchmen, security guards, and probably even Secret Service officers. Now the JTF counter-narc missions had become routine. He no longer fantasized *this* would be the night when he would go to guns. No, with the rules of engagement as strict as they were, the chances of coming into Mortal Danger were nil. He sighed and rolled his shoulders to stretch.

"Time's up, young stud."

Crawford saw the kid's fist held high in the air and he froze. What the hell?

Guttierez strained to follow the two people in his 50X scope. At just over 500 meters, their figures filled his sight picture, bouncing erratically until he found his breath again. He heard the thick arms of the bipod sliding across the dirt as he swiveled, as quiet as it was. The first man wore a pack. A bald black guy.

Infiltrator? Buyer? Hiker?

The man was limping badly, but the rest of his movement was clean and efficient. He navigated down a row of waist-high plants, studying the ground, then turned around and gave a hand signal.

Pointman of a rival cartel force?

A second man emerged from the jungle and trudged down the hill in what looked like a terribly painful gait, dragging his left leg as if it was dead. He was barely ambulatory. He looked like some undead zombie in a monster movie.

Car accident? Hiking accident? Was his leg broken? Had they been tortured?

Gutierrez put the cross hairs on the second man and saw that it was not a man at all. He tilted the big rifle ever so slightly so he could see her face, but Gutierrez was fighting a losing war against his racing heart. The edges of the sight picture were jumping all over the place. When he settled down, he saw her terrible grimace as she staggered along. It's her, he thought. The girl from the picture! *Man, she's one hurting unit.*

Then she smiled. Gutierrez watched the man's hand come into the picture to stroke her cheek. She nodded—*she's telling him that she can make it*—but a few seconds after the hand retreated, when the man had turned around so she could grab his neck for support, she started to cry.

"You're not gonna fucking believe this, Staff," whispered Gutierrez. "But you remember the brief on that American couple we're supposed to be on the look-out for? The Assassins?"

"Affirm."

"I'm pretty sure they're walking across the field toward Arrillaga's mansion."

– 60 –

ZAMPEDRO ARMY BASE, MEXICO

Roger Corwin locked the door of the bathroom in Eduardo Saiz's office. He was about to make a casualty call and he was nervous. Too many bad memories. He hoped the Mexican coroners would at least put a few stitches in the kid to hold him together before the identification viewing.

He checked his BlackBerry for the third time in an hour, holding it outside the window to ensure he had a signal. Nothing. He had sent two recent messages to the source but had received nothing. The source didn't have the gall to go to sleep without the pager alarm turned on, did he? Not if he wanted a job he didn't.

Corwin organized his thoughts while he brushed his hair and applied a spot of makeup from his compact travel kit. It wouldn't do to have circles when the tape ran for the nation the next morning. He knew from the source that Contreras had sprung Gavin Kelly from prison on the east coast, presumably to use as a guide to meet *Los Asesinos*. But why was Kelly driving a boat to begin with? Because he was going to smuggle them out by water. Problem was, he had no idea where or when.

Goddamn, but Sheridan had some balls, didn't she? The Church hearings would be nothing compared to the new testimony he would bring to bear. It might cripple the CIA for good. Corwin was tempted to inform the director about the rogue operation, but he wasn't going to stake his career on unconfirmed information from a lemming who believed he was a tiger. The coastal alert Saiz had rammed through would have to suffice short term.

What Corwin needed was to catch Contreras in the act. Then at least he'd have a vigilante arrest, assuming the director would allow the information to go public. Of course, if he caught Contreras and *Los Asesinos,* his combat tour would be up and his rise would be secured. Whether or not Saiz could deliver the Monster Butcher was questionable now, especially given the body count. Best to steer clear of that mess.

Saiz was waiting for Corwin when he stepped out of the bathroom. "You ready?"

"This can't look like a setup," said Corwin.

"No worries. I lectured the reporters on discretion."

Corwin nodded and peered through the glass windows into the conference room where the family had gathered to wait for news. Two of the football players were chatting with Cappucco's father, undoubtedly crafting another crazy theory about the location of *Los Asesinos,* or where the boy Cappucco would go if he escaped. Their optimism made it harder. This was his doing and he knew it.

Eduardo opened the door, and five heads snapped up. Neck's father saw the camera crew and breathlessly said, "Is he gone?"

Eduardo took a long pause for the camera with his head bowed, then walked over and placed his hand on the fat man's arm. They'd grown close over the last day and a half, or so this man kept telling him. Eduardo wasn't a tactile man by nature, but he knew that the Americans watching would respond to it. He was fully cognizant of the power the lens behind him carried, sickened to be beholden but compelled to use the man's grief to prevent his own. "John, I'm so sorry to tell you this, but we've found Neck. He was murdered by *Los Asesinos* sometime Wednesday night. He's gone."

The man did not go pale but reddened. He burst into tears and shouted, "How! How could they do that? Oh my God, no!"

One of the football players started to destroy a chair in a rage. The other just stood and mumbled. Eduardo embraced John Cappucco and held him tight. In the big man's arms Eduardo suddenly felt safe. He started to cry with him. It was not an act.

Corwin was about to step into the frame for some face time but when he heard Saiz blame the murder on the couple he recoiled and stepped back out of the room. That was not what they had agreed. Hell, the poor kid might have been killed by the monster. It made no sense for the couple to cut him up like that.

There was quicksand in the hangar, and it had muddied his shoes. If he was not careful, it would swallow him whole. He had known all along that Saiz was covering his ass, but the extent of his filth had eluded him. Was this a righteous hunt? Yes, it was. Darren and Kate North were mass murderers and his government wanted them to face justice. He typed a message into his BlackBerry, pressing down hard on the keys.

SEND ME CONTRERAS LOCATION RIGHT FUCKING NOW.

- 61 -

MCLEAN, VIRGINIA

He was too busy to respond to any of Corwin's paranoid demands. If the guy wasn't reasonable over the pager, imagine how he'd be as a face-to-face boss. Still, the position he was dangling was succulent and he wasn't even doing anything illegal in return. Quite the opposite. The whole purpose of Homeland Security was to force the big bureaucracies to share information, and here was his own boss acting on her own. That went directly against the wishes of the president himself. The CIA and FBI needed to share, and if he was needed to force-feed perspective so be it. History would write about him as a visionary, someone who leaked secret information to further the national interest, just as Ellsberg had done in 1971 with the Pentagon Papers.

He was sitting in the torture chamber with his soon-to-be-ex-boss. Deputy Director Sheridan's desk had been cleared and she had spent the day wandering like a ghost, saying her good-byes. It was pretty sad. He liked her and everything, but if the tech revolution had taught the world one thing it was that loyalty—to both organizations and individuals—was inefficient. She herself had said that she didn't want anyone going down with her when her clock ran out at eight that morning, in five hours.

Sheridan set down the phone and asked, "You get the frequency dialed in?"

He had been summoned to set up the satcom for her again. From what he overheard, it sounded like she had been on the phone with the same DEA who had called two days earlier looking for Contreras. Now she wanted to relay the information to Contreras via the satcom.

He'd have something hot for Corwin if he could pry it out of her.

He stayed so she would hear him over the white noise. "I can stay and help you out, ma'am."

"No, sorry to be a pill, but it's for your own good."

She hung up the phone, waited for him to leave, then checked to make sure the privacy light was illuminated on the satcom line. The million-dollar encryption fill in the satellite communicator could be rendered useless by some random Cave dweller clicking on the wrong phone line. She keyed the tone alert a few times.

"Jimmy, are you there?"

"Hey, Charlie," said a voice she had come to recognize as Gavin Kelly's. "I'll go wake him. It's two in the morning and you know how grumpy he gets, so beware, over."

"Actually, I do," she chuckled. "Who's Charlie?"

"I like your voice. You from the south? Over."

"Just go get him please."

He clicked off and a minute later, Contreras said, "Whatcha got, boss? It turned really nasty out here. Waves must be ten feet."

"Jimmy, I'm going to be giving you a patch through directly to one of the army counter-narcotics surveillance teams working for your buddy at DEA. They may have your targets in sight."

"You're kidding. Where?"

"I'll let you figure it out. SouthCom has agreed to give you strategic control of the team, call sign Texas Two. Your handle will be Rattler. Stand by for the patch."

"Strategic control? That's incredible. By the way, have you silenced your snitch? Bad enough he alerted the coastal patrols. Last thing we need is to get this op quashed."

"I'm on it," she said. "Good luck."

———

Susanne walked over to the glass wall and got Ted Blinky's attention by waving. "Shut the door behind you," she appeared to lip-synch when he entered.

He glanced around conspiratorially and sat under the white-noise speaker bank, hoping she would have to lean in extra closely. She set her hands on both arms of his chair and put her nose an inch from his. He had wanted proximity, but this made him uncomfortable.

"Any way we can get local Mexican television station coverage beamed here?"

"Depends. What city?" he asked.

"Cancún, Mexico. We've got an agent down there on a beach with a camera, but his uplink is out. He has access to local television equipment. Can we see what he sees?"

"Cancún? Is this about Agent Contreras?"

"You know that's out of bounds, Ted. But you can draw your own conclusions. Go figure out what you need and I'll swing by in a moment. This stays between us."

Susanne watched him retreat to his desk. He chatted with Christian Collins and began hacking away at his terminal, grinning from ear to ear. Was that how he was communicating with Corwin? No way, she thought. He's too smart for it. She could have his email history on her desk in five minutes.

Christian Collins poked his head inside the torture chamber. When she nodded, he walked over and said, "Ted says he's working on something time-critical. Can I help?"

"You're not missing anything. Have you noticed him making any strange phone calls? Say, using a cell in the cafeteria?"

"I don't exactly pal around with him, ma'am, but yeah, he does all of the above."

"Go home and get some rest, Christian. I'm turning in my badge at eight o'clock if you want to see me off."

"With all due respect, ma'am, I'd prefer to spend tonight here working."

"You're twenty-nine," said Susanne. "Your nights are best spent sleeping with the opposite sex. Once you men hit thirty it's all downhill."

Collins grimaced. "What's wrong with wanting to help?"

"All right then, be a doll and get me a map of Tampico, Mexico. Specifically, I need to know about its harbors. I'm thinking of taking an urgent vacation on a big yacht."

Susanne watched him walk out onto the floor of the Cave and felt a tickle of anxiety. She could not place the source of the emotion, but there was something about the interaction that seemed forced. She had spent the bulk of her conversational currency on men over the years and took pride in her ability to tune in to even their oddest frequencies. It was certainly nothing to worry about, but she could not fight years of trade craft and a faulty marriage partner. She picked up the phone and dialed the station in Mexico City.

"Hello?" said a junior duty officer.

"I'm going to need immediate information on unusual police or army activity at one of two cities on the east coast of Mexico. Prepare to copy."

– 62 –

ARRILLAGA PLANTATION, MEXICO

They sat Indian-style in the field and plucked beans for thirty minutes, chewing ravenously. When they were full, Kate grabbed Darren's hand and tried to stand. Her right foot sunk deep into the mud of the vanilla plant basin. When she compensated, her left foot—her dead one—found a sprinkler head. She nearly fainted. It felt like a nail being pounded deep into her tissue. Her head tingled. She collapsed to her knees on the dirt access road and vomited a quart of crushed vanilla beans. The wind whipped some of it back into her face.

"Oh my God. Are you okay, baby?" whispered her husband.

"Sorry," she managed, breathing in jags. "Now I'll have to eat another bushel to gain some strength."

He removed his soiled shirt and wiped her mouth and face clean. He carried her back into the field and set her down between two bushes, noticing the dark streaks running up from her trench foot to her knee. "You rest here and eat. I'm going to go hot-wire that truck and come back to grab you. We'll be outta here before anyone wakes up. We're driving to the beach."

She touched his bare chest. "If I'd known I was going to get a little show, I would have puked earlier in the trip."

"I'll be right back."

She grabbed his arm. "No, I'm coming with you."

"Not without antibiotics and two days' bed rest, you're not. That infection's not going to allow you to walk."

"Hurry up, sweetie," she said. "I miss you already."

"This nightmare ends in an hour."

Darren crouched and moved over to the long irrigation ditch that bordered the access road. The truck was parked fifty meters away from the mansion, behind a corrugated tin storage shed. With the wind shaking the trees and bushes so violently, he doubted the residents would even hear the engine turn over. He searched for a rock big enough to break the ignition tube and shuffled down the ditch in a hunch like a primitive hunter approaching a sleeping tiger.

- 63 -

ARRILLAGA PLANTATION, MEXICO

Since Staff Sergeant Crawford was busy dealing with the higher-ups, Sergeant Gutierrez used the spotting scope to watch the couple. In the green night vision they looked like wild animals in one of them *National Geographic* specials, all bent over and dirty, picking beans off the bushes and then greedily sucking water from the sprinkler heads like dehydrated hamsters at a water bottle. He felt bad. Staff had told him not to form an opinion about guilt or innocence, but what he saw disturbed him. He did not know what he would do if ordered to shoot them. Hell, they were so sickly he figured they might die right in the field.

Gutierrez watched the man disappear behind some defilade, out of sight. When he panned back to the woman, she had her face in her hands. "I'm thinking we should go grab them," he whispered. "She's in a world of hurt, Staff."

Crawford shushed him with a simple hand signal and concentrated on the voices in his earpiece. What a clusterfuck. His initial request was simple: *Los Asesinos* had been identified and he wanted his team to make the grab. The captain in El Paso did not have decision-making authority and had passed the request up to JTF headquarters in Key West. It was too big for them, so it traveled to Southern Command headquarters in Miami, where the DEA in Washington was called for approval. Now somebody called Rattler from a different agency entirely was on the hook, probably calling from the White House. If the voice did not have a Hispanic accent, Crawford would have believed it was the president himself, as long as it had taken to get an answer.

"Texas Two, how many men do you have?" the voice asked. What a crock.

Here was some government desk jockey who had no idea what his makeup or mission was.

"Rattler, we have four, over."

"Where is your relative position?"

"I say again, on a hill about one hundred meters above and four hundred twelve meters away, over."

"Okay. Get down there and snatch Phillips. He may be armed, so proceed very carefully. This guy killed a bunch—"

Crawford cringed as an argument broke out on the other end of the satellite transmission. Talk about junior varsity, he thought. They don't have their act together.

"What's up?" Gutierrez asked him.

"They're trying to get unfucked," whispered Crawford. "Sounds like they're fighting, I shit you not. They say the couple may be armed. I guess they're not sure if they're bad guys or not."

"Yeah, well, they're Americans sitting in a cocaine crop. I say they get the benefit of the doubt. Tell 'em."

Crawford was surprised to see the kid so passionate. Must be the pressure, he thought. He keyed his handset. "Rattler, I'll take two men with me but will leave my sniper behind as overwatch. Over."

Gutierrez swung his lens to the right, scanning the jungle behind the woman. One of the bushes had shifted. Another man would have missed it—the wind coming in ahead of the storm was thrashing everything that wasn't nailed down—but in scout sniper school he had been taught to use the rods and cones in the corners of his eyes, where night vision was clearest. He blinked and held the scope steady. No, it wasn't that one of the bushes had shifted, it was that one of the bushes *wasn't moving at all.*

Gutierrez had been using one of the weaker lenses to widen his field of view. He clicked the aperture bezel ring, increasing the magnification by a factor of three, and zoomed in on the hedgerow. It was so shaky that he put the scope on the ground for stability and slithered in behind it. A boy wearing a suit of leaves was standing in the middle of the field, staring at the woman. His face was painted. He was holding a rope and Gutierrez followed it down to a hound dog.

"Staff, we got company!" he hissed. "Or, they got company, I mean. There's a kid with a dog about seventy-five meters from the woman. I don't think it's that Michigan football player, neither."

Crawford repeated the report and listened to the response his satcom handset gave. He turned to Gutierrez. "You're sure it's a boy? Sorry, but they want to know."

Gutierrez tapped the scope and studied the boy's face. "Negative, sorry. He's got a long beard. And a tall head. He's a man. Big fucking hook nose like an In-dian. He's creepy, Staff. I'm lasing and measuring . . . he's twenty-point-two inches tall in the scope . . . and the multiplier is three at this distance."

"Roger. Sixty-one inches tall. Five foot one. Is he armed?" asked Crawford, doing his best to relay the information to Rattler.

"There are holsters on his belt, but the handles are straight. Like knives, maybe, instead of curved like pistols. No long gun. He's not wearing a shirt that I can see, but he's got some sort of camouflage leaf thing going."

Crawford waved the handset around to indicate his frustration with his new superior. "Sorry, Gutierrez, but you're *sure* he's an Indian? Does he have any tattoos?"

Gutierrez snorted. "Yeah, he's a fucking Indian all right. But can you tell them at five hundred meters I can't exactly see—well, okay yeah, there's some dark splotch on his chest. Could be mud. Could be a birthmark. Could be a tat."

Crawford relayed the message, then grew quiet for a long period. When he finally spoke, Gutierrez detected such a drastic change in pitch that he took his eyes off the scope and turned around. Crawford was shaking his head.

"You're not going to believe this," Crawford said.

"We gotta stand down?"

"Nope. We've been ordered to shoot the Indian."

- 64 -

GULF OF MEXICO

Jimmy Contreras was holding the satcom terminal in one hand and the handset in the other, fighting the urge to squawk for an update. The silence was killing him. It was not an admission he expected to make anywhere within Kelly's fifty-meter conversational kill radius, let alone standing right next to him, but it wasn't every day that a serial murderer welcomed an explosive-tipped, .50-caliber round with his bare chest. The anticipation in Contreras's mouth felt as thick as cotton. He wanted to scream, What's your status? Is *El Monstruo Carnicero* dead and gone? Yet he was not sure if he could find the words. Three hundred dead women and a dead partner seemed to be looking over his shoulder. If telepathy was a reality, he would have burned a hole in the terminal with his eyes.

"You holding that thing on the azimuth?"

Kelly was pointing the parachute antenna at the sky, his instinct to look at the frothy ocean fighting a war against his concentration on the Southern Cross. A swell lifted the boat beneath him, and he counterbalanced like a blind surfer. "Goddamn right I am."

"Well, where the hell is Texas Two?" asked Contreras.

"How long has it been since you were in the field?"

Contreras was considering using the handset as a club on Kelly's head when it crackled with preemptive static. "Rattler, this is Texas Two, over."

"Texas Two, tell me you plugged him," Contreras practically screamed.

"Negative. Lost him in the bushes. We have a team moving down to grab the girl, but it could take a while. I think the Indian may reach her by then. Should I fire a warning shot?"

"Goddamn him to hell!" Contreras screamed into the wind. He kicked at the wooden cup holders next to the desalination tank until they were pulp.

"Hey, cool out," said Kelly. He had had a vicious argument earlier when Contreras told the soldiers that Darren was an armed threat to them, and now the DEA agent seemed to be coming totally unglued. "Get that kid to fire a warning shot like he asked. This thing's gonna go down quickly. We need to get Darren back to her before the monster does."

"You shut your fucking hole, Kelly!" Contreras screamed. He caught his breath before he depressed the rubber talk switch, still glaring at Kelly. "Texas Two, is the Indian moving up on the girl?"

"Rattler, this is Texas," the radio crackled. "I am on my rifle now and I can't see as good. Field is narrowed to about five meters. But, yeah, I assume he's stalking her. Over."

"Okay, listen up, Texas. I want you to put your sight right on the girl. When the Indian comes up on her, shoot him dead. How copy, over?"

Kelly kicked Contreras to get his attention and set the antenna face down in the captain's chair. "Have you lost your fucking mind? You're going to use Kate Phillips as bait to kill a bounty hunter? Are you crazy? Tell him to fire now."

Contreras lunged at him, but a wave twisted the hull and so slowed his approach that when the two men collided it was more hug than collision. They grabbed each other's backs, struggling for balance like bad dancers. "You don't know the first thing about that Indian," Contreras shouted. "So stay the fuck out of this or I'll hurt you bad."

"Have him fire the warning shot!"

Contreras shook his hand in front of Kelly's face. "Let me give you the priorities here. First, that Indian. Second, a cellular phone. Last, your friends. If this sniper is good, that girl out there has nothing to worry about. Stand the fuck down or you're going back to jail."

The strong hiss of the radio got their attention. "That's a solid copy, Rattler, but if he comes in from behind it's gonna be a tough shot. There's a row of bushes . . ."

The boat rocked again. Kelly grabbed Contreras by the shirt collar, squatted, and rolled backward as the boat tipped through horizontal. Contreras tumbled over him and slammed into the bulkhead. Kelly bounded up the steep slope of the heel like a bear on all fours. He grabbed the handset and said, "Texas, fire your warning shot. Fire! Fire!"

Contreras grabbed his legs and took them out from under him. Kelly ripped the parachute dish from the terminal and tossed it out off the flying bridge. The wind caught it immediately, and it went flying off in a right angle above the ocean.

"You stupid motherfucker!" Contreras screamed. "I'll kill you!"

Contreras grabbed Kelly by the neck and tried to find just an instant of balance to slam his head into the fiberglass, but the boat tossed him into the console. His head impacted one of the knobs on the cabinets. His vision sparkled and dampened. He grabbed the steering wheel and when he struggled to his feet, Kelly was standing there with his legs spread and his fists up. Contreras tried to defend himself, but the boat tilted and his left hand went down to the wheel just as Kelly's right smashed into his temple.

Contreras shivered to his senses five minutes later. He was lying facedown on the deck. Kelly had finished binding his wrists to his feet behind his back with forty-pound test. Now Kelly took the fishing reel and spun more line around a chair pedestal, working like a spider obsessed with its web. He took some more turns around Contreras's wrists and disappeared. He returned with a bucket of crushed ice and stuck his arm in up to his elbow.

"I think I busted my hand," Kelly said.

Contreras tried to flip over onto his back, but he was tied too tightly to the chair.

"Sorry about that, but I had to secure you for sea, so to speak," said Kelly.

"You don't know what you've done."

"I've given my friends a chance."

Contreras seethed, jerking at the line like a tethered animal. "You arrogant fuck. You've just traded another hundred women away, and for what? *Two murderers.*"

"Darren and Kate are not guilty, asshole. I have no idea about a hundred women."

"Not guilty? I'll show you a tape when you're in jail that proves the opposite. They killed those people, and don't give me any bullshit about self-defense. Were the people on the bus a threat to them? Bullshit! That Indian out there is a serial murderer. He's killed over three hundred people and you just saved his life. You're the asshole here, Kelly, and my only mission after I kill *El Monstruo Carnicero* will be to see you burn."

Contreras clenched his teeth and put his feet on the pedestal. He tried to push the line apart, but Kelly had wound it too thick. Contreras went into a rage, kicking and flopping more violently than the snapper had two hours before.

When he tired, Kelly said, "You have epilepsy?"

"Did you set up the spare radio? What happened out there? What happened!"

"I have no idea. I was too busy hog-tying your ass. We'll both just have to trust that soldier to do the right thing."

– 65 –

ARRILLAGA PLANTATION, MEXICO

Sergeant Mauricio Gutierrez brought his right knee up and found his shooter's position. He hefted the big sniper rifle and placed the crook of his shoulder into the butt of the weapon, leaning his body weight onto the bipod and rocking forward into place. He plopped his cheekbone on top of the stock and slid his face forward toward the barrel. He blinked his eye and found the proper sight relief. The woman was still there eating vanilla beans. Gutierrez concentrated on his pulse, slowing it, feeling it thump in his fingers. He slowed his breathing and allowed the tranquil haze to take hold. Now the world was yin and yang, black and white, targets and friendlies.

Gutierrez triggered the AN-L2 laser range finder slung below the barrel and 364 popped up in the scope. At that range, most rifles would need a sight adjustment to compensate for the steep trajectory and the slight crosswind. But the Barrett .50 was not a normal rifle. The heavy, armor-piercing rounds—fitted with explosive tips—would fly straight and flat at over 2,000 miles per hour across the field. *If* he decided to fire.

Rattler had fallen silent. Staff Sergeant and the team were en route to the field. It was up to him. He tried to put all the conflicting thoughts in order, but it was too much. He wanted to be a soldier. Maybe he should follow orders like a good soldier and wait until the Indian appeared in the sight picture behind the woman. The Indian was the mission. Rattler had added something at the end, but it was unintelligible.

Gutierrez's eyes snapped shut and he thought about his wife, Cindy, jogging at Benning. When he opened his eyes he was back on a drug plantation outside of Veracruz, Mexico, and the order made no sense.

He put the crosshairs on the woman's chest, then shifted until he was aiming at a thick row of plants just thirty feet behind her. His extended trigger finger twitched and began to curl toward his face, as if beckoning an enemy to a fight.

"Stay low, lady," he whispered, "because here comes the thunder."

- 66 -

ARRILLAGA PLANTATION, MEXICO

Darren was approaching the truck when he heard the flat echo of the shot rip across the basin. Hunting rifle, he thought. Very large caliber. He wheeled and saw that a bush was on fire near Kate. He sprinted back to her, cursing himself for having left her side again. He heard the sharp snap of another round passing through the sound barrier and then a thunderclap when the bullet slammed into the ground and flashed.

Exploding rounds. Sniper. Please, God, let her be alive.

A third bullet flashed deep in the heart of the field and backlit his wife. Her silhouette was covering its head with its arms as if hopelessly protecting against the falling sky, but the next shot was even farther away.

Is the sniper friendly? Darren wondered.

He picked Kate right up off the ground and threw her over his shoulders. She was so light and bony. "Hold on!"

"They're shooting at us!"

"No, he's not."

Darren bulldozed through the bushes. He was closest to the shooter's side of the field and he gambled, hurtling the hedgerows on his way toward the jungle where he had seen the muzzle flashing. Two sets of headlights illuminated the field. He dove behind a hedge, careful to absorb the impact on his chest. He heard engines gunning down the access road from the mansion, then a skid, then voices. Two black Cadillacs parked twenty meters apart were turned toward them, cutting off their escape route.

A spotlight snapped on, and their section of the crop was awash in light, like a prison yard, the plants alternating from black to bright blue to black again. A circle of light slowly moved across Kate's patch of earth, and she froze, staring at the strange plants that carpeted the basin floor. A thick swath of softer, leafy plants lay under the vanilla plants and stretched as far as she could see. She plucked one of them and smelled it, pungent but sweet, like sugarcane. This was not a waste of her time—she wanted to know what had finally killed her.

"We're in the hornet's nest," she said quietly. "The vanilla is just a cover."

Darren reached out and touched her hair. "I figured. We're charmed, I guess."

A stitch of bullets cut through the air three feet above them. She felt the waves of pressure beat down into her lungs. Still, she knew that it was just general fire to flush the intruders, not point-targeted. The bullets were not as big as the hunter's. Just three days and I can differentiate in a gunfight, she marveled.

A third car came roaring up the other firebreak, behind them, and joined the Cadillac headlights illuminating the crop.

"They're encircling us," Kate whispered.

"What are they saying?" Darren asked, trying to figure out why the sniper had fired in the first place.

She listened to a man shouting just fifty feet away, between them and the hunter on the hill. She parted one of the plants and squinted into the headlights—he was standing behind an open car door with a black gun in his hands. "He wants us to stand."

Darren looked for an escape path. A line of men was moving across the field, carrying an assortment of rifles, flashlights paving a steady path toward them. On the road that encircled the field, the pickup truck rumbled by and cut off the far end of the field. Only a matter of time, he thought. The line of men would soon squeeze them out into the teeth of the road.

"They're going to flush us out and kill us, right?" she asked.

"Listen, I'm going to make a run across the field. When I go, you crawl back into the jungle. Kelly's only ten miles east of here," said Darren.

Kate grabbed his wrist and dug her fingernails in to hold him. "What is it with you? You're not leaving me. Not ever again."

He shook his head. "I can't save you. I can't save anyone."

"You saved me, baby. I love you."

"I love you too, Kate. More than you'll ever know."

She grabbed his hand and whispered, but he couldn't hear her. He just smiled sadly. He thought that it wasn't right, how it had turned out. She deserved so much better. For Darren, well, there were worse places to die than on a drug ranch in Mexico.

They heard a low growl a few hedgerows away. Darren slithered forward a few feet on his belly and saw the flash of a dog's paws when a spotlight passed over it. If it's a guard dog, why isn't it attacking? he wondered. He turned to shrug at his wife and saw the man with the Uzi submachine gun standing over her, looking the other way. Darren scrambled to shield Kate with his body. The flashlight beam seemed to come around in slow motion, and when it caught the couple the guard looked as surprised as they were.

Then his chest popped like a water balloon and blood sprayed in a gush that painted the plants and Darren's cheeks. Another Uzi fired wildly, but it sounded like a corn kernel popping compared to the deep crack of the sniper bullet. Darren reached out for the dead guard's Uzi and tugged at it, but its strap was wrapped around the guard's shoulder and one of the bushes shook loudly.

Another guard charged toward the sound with his flashlight extended. His shoulder exploded and his arm was gone. The flashlight tumbled through the air and settled at an angle, illuminating the dying man. He sank to his knees and gasped when he glimpsed the damage. His blood seemed to be fleeing him by way of a hose.

The report from the big rifle echoed again and drowned the Uzi chatter, but the pitch from the throats of the men in the field increased in volume, tone, and tempo. A bullet exploded in the engine block of one of the cars and set it on fire. The flashlights snapped off and the headlights followed. The field was dark and then completely silent, save the flickering light from the fire and a few terrified whispers that floated among the rustling plants.

They're as surprised as we are, Darren thought. *Who is that?* He was still tangled in the crisp branches of a plant and he didn't dare move. He strained his eye back toward the closest car. On the hill behind it he saw a wink of orange fire. Got you, he thought. You've got some kind of nightscope, don't you? You can see us.

The round ripped through the air and exploded somewhere next to the car. A man started screaming, *"Mi pierna! Jesucristo él disparó mi pierna!"* It sounded more like a wild animal being mauled than a human being.

Darren used the noise cover to roll out of the bush. "Let's go!" he whispered.

"*Toward* the car?"

"That's where our guardian angel wants us. He's clearing the path."

They crawled as quickly as they could and paused when they were ten yards from the Cadillac. Next to the tires, keeping the car between themselves and the sniper, men were lying prone with their rifles.

"Get your head down," whispered Darren, pumping his arm up and down in the dark, then pointing at the guards with an exaggerated tomahawk chop.

"Why?"

"Because he'll go after the car next."

A bullet shattered the car window and glass pellets plunked down around them. The guards rolled away and sprinted twenty meters up the road toward the second Cadillac, dragging the one-legged man along with them. Darren smelled the acrid smoke of melting rubber.

For some reason a man standing behind the second car returned cover fire, spraying the distant hill carelessly with an Uzi. A different weapon Darren recognized as an M-16—probably the sniper's security team—unleashed a steady barrage of 5.56-mm bullets into the surviving Cadillac. The ricochets whined off the metal and sparked when they deflected back into the air, singing as they bounced back into the thick air. Two other M-16s cracked to life and the basin was filled with the steady *pop! pop! pop! pop!* of gunfire muted only by the occasional thundercrack of the sniper's cannon. Red tracers zipped into the field and careened off at wild angles. Some guards ran full bore in hunches, zigzagging back toward the mansion. Others just stayed in place and screamed.

"That's our cue!" shouted Darren, grabbing her around the waist.

They scrambled to the edge of the road and ran right up on a guard who was cowering in the irrigation ditch, unarmed, hands covering his ears with his eyes closed. He didn't hear them approach and he didn't hear them pass. Darren leaned forward into the vines and when they broke, the jungle welcomed the couple back into the fold.

———

They managed only 400 meters in an hour. In the darkness the flora reached out to them from all angles. Rosewoods grew out of the jungle floor like volcanoes, cedar chijols seemed to be growing sideways, and chaca trees had their roots in the canopy above. Kate gripped Darren's shorts by the waistband and leaned on him for support, favoring her eroded foot.

"Let's take a listening halt," whispered Darren. "I thought I heard something."

"That's just my foot crying, babe."

He faced her and she smiled. What does she look like when I'm not watching? he wondered.

"You saw the irrigation ditch. River's got to be around here somewhere. When we find it, it'll lead us right to the ocean."

There was a crash in the jungle above them. Darren and Kate crawled carefully to a tiny clearing behind a large cedar tree trunk. Something thumped, like a stack of newspapers dropped on the cement. A twig snapped—closer this time—and Darren heard the steady plod of footsteps. He's got the stealth of a drunk water buffalo, thought Darren. He's an American soldier all right.

- 67 -

ARRILLAGA PLANTATION, MEXICO

Gutierrez felt the soil under his left heel give. He couldn't reach out to arrest his fall because he had been taught to protect the Barrett. He hugged his thirty-pound rifle like a baby and tumbled down a game trail into a wall of thorns.

Godammit! he thought. Leave it to me to patrol with a fucking .50-cal!

Not that he had a choice. He had watched Staff Sergeant Crawford's team get sucked into a draw on their way back to the observation post. They were still beating brush on the other side of the hill when one of the sensors had tripped. *Los Asesinos* were right below him. Gutierrez knew he was in for a dime now anyway, might as well toss in the dollar and guide the couple in himself.

Gutierrez stuffed the rifle through the curtain of branches and turned his body sideways so he could slide through. A thorny vine caught a nostril and cut the inside of his nose. He twisted his head back to cushion the cut, and when his eyes darted back down the slope he saw a little man and a dog standing still under a tall jungle tree. The man made a throwing motion and Gutierrez's right shoulder blazed hot before it died. He tried to find the trigger housing, but his shooting arm swung down, straight and limp. Lifeless.

I've been shot! He's charging!

Gutierrez dropped to a knee, tilted the rifle toward the man and pulled the trigger with his left index finger, using his body to angle the rifle. The shot was high, and a tree branch above the man's head exploded with a flash and started a slow burn. The man somehow dodged the second bullet and a machete blade came down and hacked deep into Gutierrez's left shoulder.

"Fuck! Help!"

Gutierrez reared his leg back to kick, but the man was too fast. He heard the whoosh of the machete followed by a thump as it cut through his Danner combat boot and imbedded itself in the middle of his ankle. Gutierrez tried to punch, but both arms were streamlined against his sides, useless. He was too shocked to feel anything yet. It was as if a shark were chomping on him. The man stomped on Gutierrez's shin and pried the machete free with a grunt, working it loose with two sawing motions.

"*Stop! Stop!*" Gutierrez screamed in Spanish. "*You're making a mistake! I'm an American!*"

The man straddled his chest and sat down hard, clamping hold with his legs like some awful insect. He was shirtless and light. Gutierrez thought of his boy, Eddie, when he crawled on him. Was his will in order? Yes, the captain had made sure of it. SGLI death benefits were $200,000. They'd be okay.

Then Gutierrez recognized him.

It was the Indian with the big head he was supposed to shoot. The Indian reached past Gutierrez's head and strained at something. Gutierrez turned his head and saw that the Indian was trying to free some sort of throwing knife from his shoulder. A goddamn throwing knife! What's happening!

"*Listen to me! Hold it! Listen. Arrillaga is fucked. You want to go to jail? You leave now and I never saw you!*"

El Monstruo Carnicero spit in the American soldier's face and dragged his stringy beard across his lips. "*I don't even know who Arrillaga is, bitch. Where are Los Asesinos? Are you here to pick them up?*"

The American started to lie, so *El Monstruo Carnicero* pulled Falcon from the soldier's shoulder and sunk it deep into his eye. The soldier writhed and screamed, but it didn't bother him—his ears were still ringing because of the cannon that the boy had shot. Damn his ears hurt!

Somewhere beyond the tone in his ears, *El Monstruo Carnicero* heard the dog barking. Had the damn dog been barking the whole time? He followed the dog's gaze and saw the blur just before it crashed into him. *El Monstruo Carnicero* jerked to his feet and sliced across his body with Bear Claw, but the man was fast. A foot smashed into his ribs and three of them cracked. It was as if he had been kicked by a mule. He flew for five feet and his head bounced hard against a tree. He staggered to his feet and the ground tilted and pitched him backward, where he grabbed a branch and fought to gain his balance. His vision sparkled for an instant.

When it cleared, the man was on him again. *El Monstruo Carnicero* saw the roundhouse sailing toward his head. He brought Bear Claw up with a deft rush of motion to block the blow, ducking at the same time. He felt the big blade glance off the man's arm. That will stop him, he thought, just before his head ran into a savage uppercut that had been waiting for him on the other side. The big fist slammed into his ear, sealed his ear canal, and exploded his eardrum. His head roared and he stumbled behind a tree and vomited.

Still the man advanced. Shirtless. Black skin. Oh, how he was going to enjoy cutting that black skin. He would slow him down with Falcon, spike it deep into his guts. He shifted Bear Claw into his left hand, ignoring the pain, and slipped his right into his belt, unsheathed Falcon, and cocked his good arm. It was a lightning movement that belonged in a magic act.

The tree exploded next to his head, and the concussion blew him onto his back. Chips of bark were stuck like pins in his face. He saw a girl advancing with the great rifle, the flash of flame, a second round cracking over his shoulder like a thunderclap. The rifle blast put the girl on her ass, but still she leveled the barrel, relentless in her attack.

It was the girl Kate North.

El Monstruo Carnicero rolled behind a thick cedar tree trunk as she fired again. The blast concussion stabbed deep into his broken ear. He gasped for air, but his broken ribs bent him double when he inhaled. He took a last look at the two-headed beast and scurried into the brush. He sprinted until his damaged equilibrium robbed him of his feet. After that, he crawled alongside the dog, forced down on all fours like an animal.

———

Gutierrez was in terrible pain, but felt ashamed watching her limp over to him. She could barely walk. Thin red thorn scars criss-crossed her bare legs. She set the Barrett next to his head and said, "Darren. Will he have a first-aid kit?"

"There should be a square, plastic container on his cartridge belt."

Darren grabbed the rifle, ejected the thick magazine, and replaced it with the spare that Gutierrez kept on his belt.

Gutierrez looked around wildly and asked, "How am I?"

Darren kneeled next to him and helped Kate press bandages into his wounds. "No spurts from your shoulders. Arteries are fine. You'll live."

Kate patted Gutierrez on the forehead and said, "Can you sit up? So we can wrap you tight?"

Gutierrez did a sit-up and the action seemed to jolt his senses. An electric wave of pain splashed into his ankle and shoulders. He held Kate tightly as Darren wrapped him like a mummy. She whispered some comfort in his ear and he burst into tears.

"He stabbed my fucking eye! Who would do this? He was looking for you." Gutierrez felt embarrassed for crying in front of a fellow soldier, but the woman hugged away his shame.

"I'm so sorry," she whispered.

"Where're the rest of your team?" asked Darren.

Gutierrez clenched his teeth and writhed as she packed gauze into his eye socket. "Unh. They're coming."

"How far's the coast, Sergeant?" asked Darren, glancing at his insignia.

Gutierrez didn't even pause. "Opposite side of this hill there's a draw that leads down to the Pasa Limon River. Ocean's seven miles away downstream. I got a map in my butt pack. And a Magellan GPS."

"You got ibuprofen in your first-aid kit?" Darren whispered.

"Oh hell, yeah . . . Hey, here they come."

There was more crunching near them. Darren grabbed the Barrett in one hand and dragged Gutierrez behind a tree with the other. Kate rifled through his gear, stuffing some items into Darren's pack. She popped open a bottle of pills, shook several into her mouth, and gave the bottle to Darren.

"What's your challenge?" Darren whispered, pointing the Barrett upslope.

"*La Isla Bonita*," said Gutierrez.

Darren cupped his hands and placed them around his mouth to direct his shout. "LAH EELSAH!"

Gutierrez heard Staff Sergeant Crawford yell, "*Bonita!*"

"Halt where you are," Darren shouted. "There is enemy close by and you have a man down. Have one man advance slowly to be recognized."

Darren bent over Gutierrez and handed him the Barrett. "Thanks for that shooting, soldier. See you back home."

Gutierrez watched Darren and Kate limp back into the darkness of the jungle. When he could no longer hear them, he turned to his teammates and yelled, "You gonna come down and get me, Staff, or you want an invite?"

– 68 –

MCLEAN, VIRGINIA

He had long ago reached the conclusion that Susanne Sheridan disrespected him. But her puerile trap was evidence that she underestimated his intellect, as well. It was maddening. Did she really think he was going to go raising warning flags about some random Mexican city until he was certain Contreras was heading there? Unlike Sheridan, he did not make irrational, hair-trigger decisions. He used deductive reasoning and logic. If Sheridan was a true professional she would have just asked him if he was sharing information with the FBI. But of course she was not, just a gunslinger who played fast and loose with both rules and emotions.

The clumsily baited task had snapped something in his head. Here she was breaking the rule of law and she was trying to trap *him?* It was so totally insulting that his first instinct when he walked out of the torture chamber was a phone call to the Senate Select Committee on Intelligence. Let's just make this all public and see who is on the side of right. But when he settled into his chair he realized that the best way to slap her down was to give Roger Corwin exactly what he was asking for. He had minimized Corwin's recent pages, but now he grabbed the task with both hands and yanked it in close where it hurt. *Jimmy Contreras, where are you?*

His weapons of choice were the secure duty phone with the CIA caller identification stamp and his Palm Pilot. Sheridan had sent him on a grueling, monthlong dog and pony liaison trip to a slew of infernal military and civilian law enforcement bases in preparation for her chop to Homeland Security. His detailed report was probably dead two months now—glanced over, shredded and forgotten, he suspected—but his list of contacts was secure inside his electronic assistant.

It took him two hours and twenty-seven phone calls to six different commands before he got whiff of an emergency extraction of a U.S. soldier working for a joint counter-narcotics task force in Mexico. Once he had a conversational entry point, it took only two more phone calls before he learned about the sighting of Darren and Kate Phillips.

The mixture of pride and bitterness in his blood was so intoxicating that he did not bother to duck under the desk to send the message:

CONTRERAS IN VERACRUZ

- 69 -

GULF OF MEXICO

Kelly had spent three intense hours at the controls of the Hatteras, getting a feel for its capabilities as he maneuvered behind a bluff just outside a surf zone in the dark, ten miles north of the beach extract site. He had struggled to stay off any radar scopes that might be bouncing energy into the storm in search of a reflection, twice backing up over waves that were trying to take the sixty-foot yacht along with them into the beach. The yacht was nimble for all its power.

The sun had already risen, but the thick marine layer and the storm clouds above it absorbed most of the rays, turning the ocean gray instead of blue. The wave interval was narrower now that the system was approaching landfall but there was no rain yet. The yacht bobbed violently in the suds. Kelly planned to roar up to the beach at exactly six to minimize his exposure to patrols, and he had just finished fueling the whaler that sat atop the bow deck under the mini-crane.

At five-thirty his Oakley watch alarm beeped. Let's do this thing, Kelly thought, cognizant of the odd mix of elation and terror. He hoped for a clean extract with no death, but his penchant for calamity had put a 9-mm pistol on his belt and an M-4 on his back. He pressed the throttles forward and cut south, accelerating to twenty-five knots when the hull found its plane.

"How you doing?" he asked Contreras. They had not spoken since Kelly debriefed Texas Two over the backup satcom and learned about Darren and Kate's escape.

"Untie me now and maybe they'll cut a year off your sentence."

"Darren and Kate would be dead if it was up to you."

"Yes, and a year from now a hundred parents would still have their daughters."

The black ocean pounded both men. Kelly steered a vigilant course, alternating his eyes between the hazy shoreline and the depth sounder. So he didn't see the police cutter until the collision alarm on the radar screeched. He swerved out to sea and threw the engines into neutral.

"Come to your senses?" asked Contreras when Kelly approached with the knife.

"Got a police boat half mile and closing."

"Well, hurry up, asshole."

"I am. My hand is broken. Proof of a hard head."

When he was free, Contreras massaged his wrists and scowled at Kelly, who had already accepted some form of retribution so their relationship could move back to barely functional. But he did not expect his testicles would be grabbed.

"You want your friends to live, you do what I say," Contreras hissed. He released his grip and shoved Kelly in the back. "Now go hide."

———

The pilot of the police cutter didn't cut his engines until he was ten meters away, choosing instead to swerve to a halt just upwind of the Hatteras. His boat ripped a curtain of skin from the ocean. The wave splashed Contreras and forced him to a knee, molding his hair flat to his skull.

The same young officer appeared at the rail in his orange lifejacket. *"This is bad, my friend. I gave you a break and you spat it in my face! Follow me into Veracruz harbor immediately and maybe you'll get away with only a day in jail!"*

A seasick policeman with a green face walked up unsteadily behind his captain, an M-16 slung around his shoulder. He was clearly seasick. He knelt down on the nonskid, braced his knees against the railing, and tried to point the M-16 at Contreras. But the waves were fierce and the rifle was soon waving all over the place. The man vomited over the side, holding the clanking rifle by its hand grip.

"Okay! Okay!" screamed Contreras, hands extended to show he was frightened. *"Do not shoot! I will follow you directly!"*

Contreras watched the young officer closely. When he saw the kid's eyes shift above his head to look at the shore he felt the old electricity invade him: His senses were sharpened, every sound magnified, every sight clarified, a wild animal seconds away from the sprint, the image of the pistol in his head now—stay on the front sight post, don't anticipate the recoil, kill the officer first if he draws.

"Are you here to pick someone up?" the officer shouted.

"We are dangerously close to the surf here to talk."

The sick policeman pulled himself up with great effort and stumbled back around the pilothouse, returning a moment later with a damp piece of paper. The officer snatched it, straddled the rail for stability, and squinted at Contreras. Spray crashed up under his chin as if it were jetting from a broken hydrant. His mouth opened slowly into an O shape until his chin seemed flush with his Adam's apple.

"*Is your name James Contreras?*" he screamed.

"*No,*" said Contreras. He could hear the crash of the surf on the beach.

"*Put your hands up! I'm arresting you!*"

Contreras snatched the pistol from his waist band and shouted, "CHESTY! CHESTY! CHESTY!" He thumbed the safety and clicked back the hammer. He was forced to grab the gunwale to keep from falling and his pistol was totally unsteady, its aiming point swinging across both police officers, over the pilothouse, up to a cloud, back through the height of the boat, into the ocean, and back up again. "*Put your hands up and get your other man out here!*" he screamed.

"*Shoot him!*" the officer screamed at his mate, who had already showed his palms.

"*Sir?!*" the mate shouted.

The officer flopped flat on his back and fumbled with his jumpsuit zipper, trying to grab his own pistol. "*I said, shoot him!*"

"*Don't!*" screamed Contreras. "*I'll kill you!*"

The officer paid no heed, so Contreras leveled his pistol and squeezed the trigger. The round sailed well high and Contreras tried to time his next round with the roll, snapping it into the steel hull where it sparked orange and yellow. The police cutter's engines roared and the steel boat spun away from the Hatteras. The officer freed his own pistol, rolled onto his knees and fired, joining Contreras in a battle more of luck than skill, both of them waving violently at each other atop an ocean that was more violent still, trying to impact targets that the barrel flames alone could nearly reach. They squeezed their triggers wildly, but the crazed pendulums veered the shots.

The mate with the M-16 remained frozen flat on the deck. He appeared to be trying to become one with the steel.

Now Kelly came sprinting out of the cockpit with his weapon shouldered, bounding across to the gunwale in fluid strides. He put a single round in the officer's shoulder, hoping he was wearing body armor. White stuffing that looked like wisps of cotton spewed out of the officer's life jacket. He tumbled over the side, but the cargo strap caught him before he splashed. His body clanged against the pitching hull like the hammer striking a church bell. Kelly looked for blood but saw none.

The cutter reversed hard and Kelly emptied his magazine into the hull, careful to keep the barrel away from the pilothouse. The cutter snaked erratically away from the yacht, careening toward the shore where a plunging wave caught it. The boat rose in the moment before it went over the crest.

"This is bad shit!" screamed Kelly. "Those are good guys!"

"I'll worry about that. You get us out of here," Contreras said. "They'll be radioing others."

Kelly was totally distressed. He had just shot a Mexican national and had no idea why. The wrong people always died in war—innocents, children, heroes. He was sure of it. "I didn't have a choice but to shoot. Shouldn't we call headquarters?"

"Not if we want to finish this operation. You want to save your friends?"

"Yessir," Kelly replied out of habit.

"And I want to kill an Indian."

– 70 –

VERACRUZ, MEXICO

The water that carried them had melted from Orizaba's slopes only twenty-four hours earlier. The crisp chill would have been refreshing four days earlier, when they still had fat stores, and tolerable two days earlier, before their bodies started to consume their muscles for fuel, but now the glacial runoff tightened their skins right over their skinny limbs and caused them to hyperventilate. The pack bobbed between them as a float, each of them holding a shoulder strap. The river sucked them toward the Gulf of Mexico at over eight miles an hour, well high of the mix of boulders below.

"Meltoff must be high this year. We're in luck."

"Oh yeah, Kate," said Darren. "We must be the luckiest couple on the planet."

A rock jolted her feet before she could respond. Her focus turned inward for the duration of the swim and she thought back on her thirty years. How had it come to this? A wild ride on some Mexican river in the middle of the night! Pursued by the police and a hunting party and an Indian! Married to a black Marine! Adventure racer! Killer! Shot a helicopter down! *The fat girl from Spence!*

So full was her memory that when the couple emerged from the river thirty minutes later, Kate had only gotten up to that time in eleventh grade when Ms. Kastagenhogen had told her that she was "lucky to have been born smart because only pretty girls can get away with being dumb."

Darren checked the GPS. "We have to get up this bank. Then I figure it's one-point-three miles to go. We made it, babe."

She accepted his hug but didn't have the strength to return it. She was experiencing what other athletes called "bonking" or "smashing into the wall." Kate called it a "catastrophic body event," and whatever burst of adrenaline she manufactured when she heard that the finish line was so near was swallowed by the implosion occurring right then in her body. She bent over and retched violently. She tried to pinpoint the sickness and a few seconds later, when the blood brought the feeling back into her feet, she found it. She hopped up and down on one leg.

Darren felt helpless watching her struggle. With her soles filleted, her nerve endings were exposed and frayed. Each step was like fire walking. Darren had seen some of his toughest Marines drop out of humps when the first pinpricks of immersion foot radiated north, and here was his own wife who had been walking on barbed wire for over forty-eight hours. Her racing career is probably over, he thought gloomily, and she knows it. Of course, I'm not exactly electable anymore.

"Climb up," he said.

She piggybacked him, but even her one-hundred-odd pounds were enough to tip him over into the steep bank. His face slapped into some damp sand and he came up spraying it from his mouth. He smelled rotting wood and her bile.

"You just start up and I'll grab your pack," she whispered.

He started up the bank, tugging her behind him, using the thin saplings that dotted the side as pull-poles. He heard her muted squeals and it totally distressed him. But what other choice did he have? Her feet were being slowly eaten by a fungus, and he was too weak to carry her for a long distance.

Kate had had a catastrophic body event only one other time, at the finish line of the Hawaii Ironman World Championship. She knew her body was reacting the same way—with the finish line so close, her brain was finally sending the signals of proximity and her defenses were disappearing. In the same way a person's bladder or nausea-control mechanisms are weakest approaching the bathroom, so, too, is an athlete's ability to sustain a taxing pace toward the end of a race. She knew she had been redlining for at least a day. Now, with fifteen minutes to hike, her mind was waging war with her body.

She lapsed into a dream state and just staggered along until she heard an engine racing toward her. "Motorcycle," she gasped.

Her husband put his big hands on her shoulders and squeezed them lovingly. "Shhh. We made it. Listen."

Kate heard what sounded like a car crash. Then another and another. She put her face up close to a pine tree where some sap had trickled out of a knot, and inhaled as sharply as she could. Her eyes watered and she reveled in the tangy spirit. She heard the crash of the surf.

When she saw the Gulf of Mexico, her pain subsided so quickly that she felt guilty for having nearly succumbed to it. And when she saw the white yacht floating just offshore the pain disappeared altogether.

"My God. Is it him?" Kate asked.

"That's him all right," said Darren.

They walked to the edge of the bluff together. A fifty-foot cliff separated them from a narrow beach, steep enough to require the rope. The froth from the surf was rising up as mist in the harsh wind. Kelly was standing on the bow deck of the yacht, swinging a small boat on a crane. When he saw them he just waved and continued his task.

"Happy to see you, too, Gavin," she said.

"He knows us too well to be surprised," Darren said. "Say good-bye to the Hell Bitch." He removed the rope and started to uncoil it.

"At least she has a lovely resting place. It's beautiful here."

Darren fastened a roundturn and a bowline to a pine tree, backed it up with an overhand, then walked the Hell Bitch over to the edge and tossed it off. It unraveled cleanly and thumped to a halt on the beach.

Kate was first to snap into her harness. She wove the rope through the figure-eight descender and clipped it to a caribiner on her waist.

"I'm going to miss this rope," she said as she backed up to the edge.

"You haven't humped it for three hundred miles," said Darren.

"But she saved us more than once, didn't she?"

"Yes. She did."

Kate kissed her husband on the cheek and leaned over the cliff. The portion of rope between her and the trees rose up off the ground, levitating and then stiffening with her weight. She saw beads of water pop free as the fibers stretched themselves dry.

"See you on the beach."

Kate bent into her rappelling form and started down the cliff, taking her time to avoid any additional pounding on her feet, moving steadily but very slowly, keeping close to the wall, feeling the burn in her hand as the Hell Bitch slithered through.

Darren sat on the edge of the cliff watching her proudly. In four days, all his dreams for the future had been crushed except one, and Kate stood tall among the ruins.

A dog growled. Darren dropped his harness and spun. The bearded Indian was standing in the treeline holding a machete in one hand and a leashed bloodhound in the other. He's the one who's been tracking us, thought Darren. And he's come alone for some reason, probably the reward. He's the Monster Butcher. *He's* the Monster Butcher.

The Indian yelled at the dog and it strained against the leash and barked savagely. He worked it into a frenzy and swiped the machete across the taut leash. The bloodhound surged forward, low to ground, gathering speed, baring its teeth. Darren braced himself and put his damaged left forearm forward to absorb the attack. *This arm's useless anyway.*

The dog leapt when it was close and snapped its teeth around Darren's forearm, jerking wildly, digging its fangs into the solid meat. He punched the dog in the head with his free hand, but it rolled back its eye and shook more violently. Darren felt no pain but the stab of fear. He backed close to the cliff's edge and spun like a discus thrower. When the centrifugal drag of the spin was greatest, Darren yanked his arm back. Patches of his left arm disappeared over the cliff with the dog.

He turned to kill the butcher next.

The man stepped out into the sunlight and slowly angled his big blade. Darren watched the square patch of light glide along the grass and crawl up his body to his face. The reflection was blinding. When Darren shaded his eyes, he saw that the little man was laughing. Darren bent over the pack and pulled out the broken Corona bottle, holding it by the neck in his right hand. He couldn't make a fist with his left hand, but he could use the bloody arm as a club and a shield. It was gone now.

"You want to play?" he asked. If I can buy enough time, he thought, Kate can get down safely. He crouched into a fighting stance and took a step toward the man.

"*Si usted me luchará, usted'll necesita un mejor cuchillo que eso. Trate esto.*"

The man made a sudden lunge, as if he were snapping an imaginary whip, and Darren just managed to twist sideways before the silver missile slammed into his left side. Pain exploded in his shoulder and raced to all the nerve endings in his body. He couldn't stifle the scream. A wave of heat rushed to his head and forced him to his knees. His vision was dotted with shiny black spots that blossomed like flowers and dissipated. When it cleared, he saw some kind of throwing blade sunk deep into his shoulder. Blood was spitting out of the spiked wound, oozing down his triceps and trickling off his elbow.

Darren reached across his chest with his right hand, grabbed the blade's steel handle, and pulled. It did not budge. He bit down on his own teeth and twisted the knife hard, wrenching it free. His vision went dark again and he fought the nausea, trying not to faint. The wave passed and Darren found himself lying facedown in the grass. His memory came rushing back and it startled him—the chase, Kelly in the boat, Kate on the rope . . . *the Monster Butcher.* His left arm was immobile, so he rolled on his side and snatched up the throwing knife, on his feet now, lunging forward to meet his attacker.

El Monstruo Carnicero watched Darren Phillips stagger toward him. He was impressed at how quickly the man had fought his way back to his feet. His face was grizzled and saliva dripped freely from his mouth. This savage brute broke my ribs, he thought. *El Monstruo Carnicero* thought that he was fighting an animal, just like the American football player. Only more cunning! A bull who might not rely only on strength. A great black bear, a true hunter and a fitting appetizer.

El Monstruo Carnicero snatched Barracuda from his belt and held the filet blade next to its fat brother, Bear Claw. He breathed deeply to taste the excruciating pain where his splintered ribs scraped against his lung. The charging bear wasn't going to get close enough to wound him again. He darted to get an angle on Darren's bloody, wounded side and poked Barracuda into the open shoulder wound. His first lesson. More to come!

But the black bear didn't even flinch, a testament to the purity of Falcon's flight, *El Monstruo Carnicero* thought. Falcon had killed the bear's arm. *"Aprecia usted eso, la ramera?"* he asked. He hoped Darren understood some Spanish. He wanted to watch the reaction to the word the boy had taught him. That a man could be a bitch tickled him.

"Come get some," said Darren.

El Monstruo Carnicero saw the black bear sneak a glance at the rope, saw the eyes narrow down toward its snout, saw the puzzlement on its slobbering face. *El Monstruo Carnicero* took a step back and realized why the bear had been so clumsy on his run. He was protecting the rope. The rigid rope. *The girl Kate North is on the rope.*

Darren advanced, leading with his pulpy left red arm. *El Monstruo Carnicero* lashed out with Bear Claw in a counterstab, just to test Darren's reactions, and he was able to steer the Marine like a personal puppet. Just like all the others.

El Monstruo Carnicero twisted the black bear by following through with a swipe on the back swing, forcing it to duck. Barracuda was waiting underneath and it bit through the black bear's hide and tasted its rib cage.

"Usted're no tan rapidamente cuando usted se pone 'T me sorprende en la noche, soy usted ramera?" *El Monstruo Carnicero* said to the bear.

The thing spat red and mumbled something in English. Its tongue snaked out and slithered across its bloody lips, then retreated back to its hole. Wretched beast, thought *El Monstruo Carnicero.*

"Matarlo es fácil," said *El Monstruo Carnicero.* *"Tomaré más largo con la chica Kate Norte."*

Darren's eyebrows rose when he heard his wife's name. He mounted a desperate, stumbling charge. *El Monstruo Carnicero* flung Eagle to ward him off. The knife whistled cruelly and disappeared in Darren's stomach. He tipped lower and lower to the ground. *El Monstruo Carnicero* realized he was not falling but building momentum and leverage into the attack. *El Monstruo Carnicero* went flat on his stomach to meet him, extending his two blades.

It was like a car wreck. *El Monstruo Carnicero*'s head was stuffed into his torso. Teeth shattered in the collision. Some of his lowers crunched all the way up into the roof of his mouth. When his collarbone snapped it sounded like damp wood popping in a blaze.

Darren tumbled over the Indian and rolled for several meters. There was a filet blade stuck between two of his knuckles. He pulled it out gingerly, wincing and cursing, and dropped it in the grass. A paralyzing cramp spread across his stomach. He bent over to relieve the pressure, inspecting the thin slice where the throwing knife had entered his abdomen. There was no sign of it, and he didn't have time to go fishing.

The Indian was on his feet spitting blood and white chips. He stumbled to the edge of the forest, listing sideways as if he were drunk, holding his jaw. Darren started to chase him but stopped when he realized where he was going. The rope was still rigid. *Kate's still on the goddamn rope.*

- 71 -

GULF OF MEXICO

"*Hold it* steady, Kelly!" Contreras screamed. "Hold it so I can kill him!"

Kelly was pinning the barrel of the Winchester rifle to the guardrail so Contreras could shoot, but with the boat rocking so wildly it was impossible. The wind was up with the sun and the Gulf of Mexico was littered with whitecaps and airborne droplets. Long strings of bubbly froth ran perpendicular to the swell all the way to the horizon, as if the ocean had racing stripes.

They were anchored just offshore where the rollers began their final run into the beach. The anchor acted like a bit in a bronco's mouth, holding the bow fairly steady, but leaving the stern free to kick high in the air as each swell rolled underneath. Each time Contreras put some weight on the trigger and centered the crosshairs on *El Monstruo Carnicero,* he was pitched forward or back, and the crosshairs danced onto Phillips or into the trees.

"No way, we're rocking too much! Let's launch the Whaler!" Kelly shouted.

Kelly saw the little man on the bluff run to the woods. He felt as if he were watching some terrible videotape, removed and helpless as tragedy unfolded. Except this one starred his best friend.

"Shit! Inbound, a mile away," shouted Contreras.

Kelly followed Contreras's extended arm. Two black jeeps were racing up the beach, blue lights blinking in the sun, huge plumes of sand spraying as they fought for traction.

"Get on the machine gun," said Contreras. "I'll grab the explosives."

Kelly knew that he was no longer part of a sanctioned operation. Contreras had become increasingly reckless the closer he got to his Indian, and now he was gundecking. Kelly could tell because he himself had done it so often. The choice was clear: the Phillipses on one side, and any poor bastard who happened to threaten their extract on the other, complicit or not. Contreras had lost it.

Maybe he never had it.

"Now hold on just a second," said Kelly. "What are our rules of engagement?"

"Rules? Stop those jeeps and get to the beach. Those are the rules."

– 72 –

VERACRUZ, MEXICO

Roger Corwin was glad he brought his yellow-tinted Oakley shooting glasses with him to the beach. He and Eduardo Saiz were standing in the back of a black *Federale* jeep racing north toward the small cliff where they had spotted *Los Asesinos*. The wind was raging and with the fifty additional miles per hour of speed the jeep added, the sand was slashing his cheeks and building up as wet sludge along his lips.

Corwin kept spitting sand. He was able to stand the pain only because of the eye shields. His hands were otherwise occupied, madly gripping the roll bar so as not to be bounced out of the jeep as it swerved in the deep sand. He had no idea how Saiz and the poor soldier who was supposed to be manning the up-gun .50-caliber machine gun were hacking it. He tucked his head into his body-armor shell like a turtle so the Kevlar collar covered his ears.

Corwin leaned close to Saiz. "You're sure that was Monster Butcher up there?"

Saiz tried to speak but gulped a tablespoon of sand instead. He nodded vigorously.

"Could be any vigilante! You're sure, now?"

"It was him!" screamed Saiz. "We got all three, Roger! What about the boat?"

"You let me worry about the boat!"

Corwin loved his grim yellow world, stark and crisp in his polarized sunglasses. With his binoculars bouncing on his armor vest he felt like Rommel riding across the North African desert. Outfoxed them in the end, didn't you, Dodger! The yacht anchored offshore had scared him at first, but what a rush he had felt when he raised the binoculars and saw that *Los Asesinos* and the Indian were still on the bluff.

In the CHP he and his fellow motorcycle patrolmen had instituted the annual kebab competition—how many motorists could you nab at one time with a single speed trap? If Jimmy Contreras was in the yacht anchored offshore, and somehow managed to get to the beach, Roger Corwin would skewer the mother of all kebabs and quite possibly go international in terms of recognition.

Something blinked in the back of the yacht. Is Contreras giving them a warning signal? Corwin's stomach rolled at the thought of Contreras racing out to sea and the couple disappearing back into the jungle. He squinted, trying to decipher the winking orange signal. Is it Morse?

Corwin heard a sharp crack and thought they had blown a tire. Then the dirt bluff in front of him opened in a thin line, as if someone were ripping an invisible rope out of the dirt. The concussions reverberated gently in his chest. He kicked frantically at the driver's rear window and eventually had to put his steel-toed assault boot through the glass to get his attention. "Stop!" he screamed. "Stop the jeep!"

The jeep rolled up over a small dune and skidded down the front slope. Corwin leapt out of the back and rolled across the sand, slipping his hand into his holster and yanking his pistol when he was flat on his belly. Seeing him, the other jeep stopped and every passenger fled, seeking cover behind wheels or dunes.

"What is it, Roger!" shouted Saiz.

"He's shooting at us!"

Saiz's eyes widened, and he peered around the jeep at the boat. He watched for a few seconds before he shrugged. "Well, they've stopped now. You are sure?"

"Hell yes, I'm sure!"

"What should we do? I have more jeeps coming! Should I wait?"

Corwin wanted to scream, You blow the hell out of that boat, that's what you do, imbecile! But he couldn't. Not in the presence of the junior FBI agent Modinger, whom he had brought along as a reward. That Contreras had opened fire on Mexican federal police officers was shocking. He had changed the rules and radically altered Corwin's plan. What the hell is he doing? Corwin wondered. Regardless, Corwin did not dare order Mexicans to kill Americans.

Corwin reverted to the decision-making skills he honed three times a year at the Hogan's Alley shooting range, where officers parsed good and evil in microseconds as cardboard threats popped up all around them. Three possibilities. First, Contreras was acting alone and had lost all perspective along with his goddamn mind. Second, Contreras and Sheridan were running an illegal, unsanctioned operation on their own. This had been his theory. Problem was, even

Sheridan was not reckless enough to have given the green light to fire without authorization. That left the third option and it literally sickened Corwin. He thought he might puke in the sand. Is someone big pulling their strings, he wondered. *Am I being backdoored?*

Corwin wanted no part of this fight. Whatever happened, happened. He'd come in as the cleaner when the time was right and put a palatable dress on whatever transpired, take what credit he could, deny what needed to be denied. It was out of his hands now that he sensed a more powerful political force looking over his shoulder.

"Agent Modinger, stay low and stay put!" Corwin shouted at his man.

"What shall we do, Roger?" shouted Saiz.

"I got you this far, Mister Deputy Attorney General. Rest is up to you."

Saiz licked his lips and shook his head. Get going, damn you, Corwin thought, or you'll lose them all. Corwin pulled his pistol against his chest so Modinger could not see, and tapped it urgently with his free hand. Fire, he mouthed to Saiz.

Saiz stood and shouted curt orders at his troopers. One *Federale* hopped up behind the mounted machine gun and squeezed off an exploratory burst. There was no return fire from the ocean. The *Federale* gave a triumphant yell and fired again. Suddenly all the *Federales* were up and piling into the jeeps. Their engines gunned and their wheels spun, sending rooster-tail jets of sand into the sky before finding traction and speed.

Corwin low-crawled behind the dune where Agent Modinger was hiding. "We gonna help them, sir?"

"Help them with what exactly?" Corwin asked.

"Isn't that boat out there shooting at them?"

Corwin removed his sunglasses so the kid could see his blue eyes. "What boat?"

Modinger tried to push up onto his knees so he could see the ocean, but Corwin placed a firm hand on his lower back and flattened him. "I told you to stay low. Keep your head down until I tell you."

"I saw a boat out there, sir," said Modinger.

"In that rough sea? At that distance? On that wild ride? Was it a pleasure boat, a fishing boat, a ferry, a government boat, or a military boat?"

"I have no idea, sir. Too far."

"That's my point. There *is* no boat until I *tell you* there's a boat. You understand that and you got a future. Now get your head down."

- 73 -

VERACRUZ, MEXICO

Darren watched the Butcher limp toward the trembling rope, holding the big machete like a bouquet. When he reached the anchor point, the Butcher raised his machete and smiled at Darren, who had no idea how high his wife was on the cliff. Darren tried to stand, but the cramp in his stomach forced him to hunch. The Butcher seemed to wait for him to lunge at the rope before severing it.

He wants Kate alive.

"I'll kill you!" Darren screamed.

Kate's weight came alive in his hand, pitching him forward and dragging him toward the edge of the cliff. Darren was pulled fifteen feet toward the ocean before he dug his heels in and stopped the slide. He leaned back and squeezed the rope as hard as he could, wrapping it around his forearm until the blood supply was totally pinched.

Darren heard his wife scream in surprise somewhere down the cliff.

"Get down, Kate! I got you! Get down!"

El Monstruo Carnicero limped up to him and patted him gently on the head. With his right arm tied up and his left arm dangling useless, Darren was defenseless. The Indian spat in his face. Darren felt the little hard chips impact like chicklets. He could not move, not with Kate on the rope, so he steeled himself for torture by focusing on his wife, surely approaching the beach now. *Save Kate and you've done it right.*

The little man squatted in front of him and whispered, *"Permita's ve cuán largo usted puede aguantar, el oso."* He held the filet blade in front of Darren's eyes, and then poked him in the cheek. The blade glanced off a molar and cut into his upper gum.

Darren roared with pain and cursed the thing that God had placed on the earth for his redemption. He would die so another, better person would live. His own wife.

He's cutting my teeth out, Darren thought. *Focus on the rope.*

Then the rope went slack. Darren freed his arm and rolled away from his torturer. "She's down and free. Now it's just you and me," he said from his knees. The cramp in his belly was worse now and he could not stand. He spat a mouthful of blood and smiled, genuinely content with his ending.

Until he saw movement at the top edge of the cliff. A hand came up and raked at the grass, then another, and then Kate flipped her torso up onto the bluff and wriggled forward like a seal out of water.

"Kate, no! Go down!" Darren screamed. But he knew his wife too well to believe she would listen. He tried to stand, but it was as if someone were prying open his insides with a crowbar. He collapsed on his face, weakly waving Kate away with his good arm.

− 74 −

VERACRUZ, MEXICO

Kate had descended thirty feet when she heard the dog bark. She arrested the rappel, tied off her rappelling device, and looked up the cliff face. A writhing dog flew just ten feet from her on its way down to the beach. She saw its bloody jowls flapping as it fell past. It tumbled along the cliff and miraculously survived the fall, taking a moment to bark once more before limping down the narrow beach.

"Darren! What's happening!"

He did not answer. Kate pushed off the rock face and twisted to look at Kelly's yacht. There was a man there with a hunting rifle aiming at the bluff.

Get up there. Kate reinforced the knot on her Figure 8 and grabbed the rope. Using it as direct aid, she swung her right foot up into a crack and twisted her ankle to gain a friction hold. In one fluid motion she yanked on the rope and put enough pressure on her foot to gain a few feet of height so she could start the exhausting process over again. She was near the top when the anchor gave way and she slid fifteen feet, clawing painfully at the face of the cliff. One of Neck's sneakers came loose and tumbled into the ocean. Kate heard Darren yelling, unintelligible save for the obvious panic.

When Kate crested the cliff, the sight so startled her that her hand went to her mouth. Darren sitting by the rope crying, holding his stomach, his entire body red with blood, cheek, chest, legs, arm . . . *everywhere.* Behind him, the Indian from the night before stood up and bowed.

"Kate, no! Go down!" Darren screamed.

Oh my God, help us.

The little man laughed and said in Spanish, *"You married a little bitch, didn't you, Kate North? But guess who's my bitch now? Maybe you, girl?"* The man had no teeth. His gums were still bleeding, but the crimson smile that outlined his lips had caked like dried cherry frosting. His head was shaped like a milk carton, made more rectangular by his long beard and nose. She could see that he was hurt.

"Get away from him," she said softly in Spanish.

The Indian raised his eyebrows. *"Oh, that's what I thought! You want to fight me, don't you?"*

Kate nodded and limped away from her husband to attract the Butcher, dragging the Hell Bitch behind her like an umbilical cord. The Indian followed, replacing the machete in his hand with a thinner knife.

Darren gasped, "Kate, no. Please run away from me. For me." The ground was listing and blurring as he fought for consciousness. His emotions were burning far more than his physical wounds, so terrified for his wife and so deeply disappointed in himself for putting her in this position that, when he passed out, he knew he had failed in life.

Kate wanted to rush over to her husband, gather him up, hold him close, and cry. Was he dead? "Darren!" she screamed. "DARREN!" She had to know.

His hand twitched first and he rotated his head up to look at her. A thick strand of blood and dirt stretched thin between the ground and his lower lip.

El Monstruo Carnicero considered ending the black bear right then—maybe sticking Barracuda through his thick neck—but he thought the girl Kate North would scrap better if she had something to live for. He flicked Barracuda back and forth and sliced the air, marveling at the sound of the wind rush and trying to gather himself. Huitzilopochtli was pounding an invisible spike into his head as punishment for his great hunger. He had broken his ribs and his shoulder for having allowed the soldier and now the black bear to continue breathing the air of Mexica. *It won't be long now.*

The girl Kate North was furious. Her great black eyebrows tipped down and came together. She limped toward him—no jukes, no feints, no catlike approach. It surprised him. No man had ever approached him so directly, let alone a *woman*. He held the knife high in case she had somehow missed it.

"Kate North! Are you blind?"

But still she came. She said something in English to the dying black bear. He wiggled around on his broken belly, reaching for the rope. *El Monstruo Carnicero* saw the slimy trail his guts painted as he slithered in pain. He laughed.

"I already cut him good, Kate North. If you gonna play my bitch you better pay attention to Barracuda. I don't want you all cut up, too. Not yet."

Stupid, stubborn girl. Here he thought Kate North would give him a struggle. Instead, she'd charge like a dumb cow and cut herself. He watched her bare shoulders, watched the sweat as it trickled down the length of her nose and dripped next to her erect nipples, saw that sweaty brow of hers with her black hair slick wet in a ponytail, saw her legs tighten and her thighs shake frozen and hard when she planted them. He decided to paralyze her arms first, then drag her to the woods, but not so far that the man could not watch.

"*You got nothing to say? Well, I fix that fast, bitch.*"

El Monstruo Carnicero was irritated with her silence. He decided to sting her and get her talking. He jabbed at her right shoulder with Barracuda to force her left, leading the dance as he had led all the others, waiting for her twitch so he could get in a poke.

But she didn't react.

In the instant it took him to shake off his surprise, the girl Kate North moved toward the blade and grabbed it. *El Monstruo Carnicero* was stunned. He jerked Barracuda hard, but she came with it, clasping his blade like an eagle would clasp a fish.

His mouth opened in shock. He grabbed Barracuda with two hands, pulling and twisting. The blade was deep inside her fleshy palm. He felt the grind as the blade squeaked and squealed across her bones. Still the girl held on, tears streaming from her black eyes and those great white teeth clenched and the air filling her cheeks as she seethed and gasped and raged.

El Monstruo Carnicero saw her other hand shoot up and then his airway was sealed shut. The girl leaned in next to his reddening face. He could hear her snorting, felt her hot spittle spraying his fluttering eyelids. Her fingers pressed his windpipe flat and now she was digging her nails into his neck. The strength of her was in him.

He realized he was moving.

El Monstruo Carnicero released Barracuda and grabbed at her rippled back. He punched her head, but her strength closed in on him, as relentless and horrible as the walls closing in his vision. She was shaking him by the throat like a rabid fighting dog. His Adam's apple popped and folded into his throat. He felt himself go weak and he scratched at the devil girl's face, then grabbed her hair in a full wrap and tried to bend her head back.

He had no leverage. One of his feet lost the ground and pedaled the air. He heard the roar of the waves below him. Now the other foot was aloft. I'm at the cliff, he thought. *This cannot be happening.*

El Monstruo Carnicero twisted the devil's hair tighter and tighter. Where he went, so would she. But he was falling, so sure of it, panic shooting up his spine and his bladder emptying and the terror of permanent regret and then finally the girl's words, not screams but harsh whispers.

"*Quién's la ramera ahora?*" she hissed. "Who's the bitch now?"

75

GULF OF MEXICO

Contreras and Kelly were awestruck watching Kate climb the cliff, but her next challenge diminished the act and they never spoke of it. When she confronted the Indian, both of them cried out, as helpless as Darren to do anything.

"We gotta get up there!" Kelly screamed. "She'll be killed, too."

"She's dead already," said Contreras, watching Kate approach *El Monstruo Carnicero* in his scope. "Best hope now is, when Monster Butcher kills her, we open up with everything and try to kill him. Hope for some luck. Then we get the fuck out of Dodge."

"Those are my friends!"

"Those were your friends."

Contreras was floating in the whaler just aft of the Hatteras stern gate where Kelly had mounted the machine gun for better stability, improving accuracy from impossible to ridiculously poor. His initial burst of rounds was meant to be a warning, but with the pitch and roll he was not certain if the jeeps even knew he existed.

A shot from a heavy machine gun cracked overhead, and the two men ducked instinctively. The government jeeps had stopped five hundred meters down the beach after Kelly had fired. Now they were moving again.

"Shit," said Contreras. "Pin them down for good so I can run into the beach."

"Warning shots only, okay?" said Kelly, clearing some black 7.62-mm links from the M-60 feed tray.

"Whatever you say, Kelly." Contreras reeled the small boat in by its bowline and then cursed himself. "Hey, I forgot something. Go to the ice chest and dig way down. You'll find a bag of hands that I may need. I'll explain later."

"Hands? Get it yourself," said Kelly, already swiveling the machine gun.

Kelly aimed in front of the two jeeps and loosed a string of tracer rounds that stitched the sand in small geysers. His eardrum popped and there was only *dddeeeeeeee* where the engine noise had once been. The two jeeps halted short of the impact area. Kelly saw their mounted guns flashing at him, but never heard the bullet cracks.

"My God, she's got him! Dragging him to the cliff!" shouted Contreras.

Kelly looked in time to see Kate wrestle the Indian to the edge of the cliff. They teetered, and then she leapt off with him. "Holy shit!"

The rope attached to her harness jerked taut and swung her hard against the face, ten feet below the lip. The man tumbled down the cliff like a broken doll and landed feet first in the sand. One of his legs shattered and he lay face down in the sand, flopping like a fish. Phillips was seated atop the bluff with the rope wrapped around his torso like the anchorman in a tug-of-war. He was clutching his stomach with one hand, breathing hard. Incredibly, his wife climbed back up and came to him.

"You see that! They're alive!" shouted Kelly.

"So's my little friend," said Contreras, staring at the writhing figure on the beach. "Keep them pinned down. I'm gonna go get mine."

Kelly yanked the machine gun off the tripod and threw several bandoliers of ammunition over his shoulders. "Fuck that. I'm going in with you."

Kelly followed Contreras into the whaler, just barely leaping into the bobbing boat before Contreras depressed the throttle. Kelly was thrown onto his back. He angled the M-60 into the center console to give him a handle. The light boat accelerated right up to, and then through, the boundaries of control in a matter of seconds. It raced into the surf zone at thirty knots.

"Jesus slow down! Aren't we swimming in?" shouted Kelly.

"Shut up!" said Contreras. He tried to time the entry, but waves were breaking all around him.

The whaler vaulted a plunging swell and left the water, propellers whining in protest as they grabbed at the air, rpms accelerating out of control. The boat crashed into the middle of the heavy surf zone, rocketing sideways across a second face that tried to keep it parallel to the shoreline. The wave crested and the stern was pulled up toward the foamy lip of whitewater. Contreras spun the wheel and pounded the throttle forward, pinning it flush to the dash. The blades dug into the water and found their grip. The bow rode back to perpendicular and when the wave broke, the whaler moved through forty knots and planed up through the shallows on a cushion of foam, decelerating hard across the beach but not before it cleaved *El Monstruo Carnicero*'s right leg in half at the knee.

The bow crunched into the base of the cliff. Kelly snapped his nose on the pistol grip of the machine gun and then fought to orient himself. The boat was marooned in the sand ten feet above the high-water mark.

Contreras vaulted the gunwale and walked up to *El Monstruo Carnicero* with his pistol drawn. He had rehearsed the speech for fifteen years, but could no longer remember it. "*Remember Luis Gonzalez?*" he said in Spanish.

"*Help me. The assassins are up top the hill,*" the Monster Butcher whispered.

"*Remember Luis Gonzalez?*"

"*My leg is broke. Wrap it.*"

"*Do you ask God's forgiveness?*" Contreras asked.

"*I do not know your god.*"

Contreras forced the pistol barrel into *El Monstruo Carnicero*'s mouth. He noticed that the Indian had no teeth. "*No? Well then, let me introduce you.*"

The bullet took the monster with it into the earth.

————

Darren was being lowered down the cliff face. It was a wild scene below, but after the fight with the Indian he wondered if he would ever again be capable of surprise. In just thirty-three years Boston University hockey players, Iraqis, Somalis, and now Mexican Indians had all tried to kill him. His college roommate was kneeling behind a beached boat, firing a machine gun at two black jeeps. Another man put a pistol in the dying Indian's mouth and pulled the trigger. Life was murderous chaos. So be it.

"Up here," Darren called.

Kelly turned around and winked, then put his cheek back on the gun. A pile of brass shell casings had already built up in the sand next to him. The other man helped him untie the chest bowline.

"Your stomach is bleeding," Contreras said to Darren when he was down, tucking him into a small depression that provided cover from the bullets. He opened the tackle box, grabbed the largest pressure bandage in the kit, and pressed it hard into Phillips's gut. "Hold this tight. Where's the satellite phone?"

A round slapped into the cliff just above their heads. Darren brushed away the bandage. "Cell phone's in the pack, but my wife's up there!" he gasped. "I need a weapon to cover her."

"You new Marines Corps are pains in the ass. Now do what the fuck I tell you."

"You don't understand. MY WIFE'S UP THERE! Who are you anyway?"

Contreras scowled, checking to make sure the phone was functional. He was stuffing it back into the waterproof pack when a handful of pebbles dropped onto his head. Kate was on rappel. He shouted at Kelly with his hands cupped. "We need total suppression!"

Kelly reloaded and waited until the jeeps were 300 meters away before he broke the trigger, aiming low to compensate for their speed. He walked the rounds in with bursts, careful to keep his eye focused on the front sight post and the red tracers stretching forward in excess of 2,000 miles per hour. He felt the metallic scratch of the recoil spring as it crushed and expanded right under his cheek. He smelled the smokeless powder, sharp against the salty air.

A trio of rounds impacted the radiator grill of the jeep closest to the water-line. Kelly held the trigger back and the hood erupted in a bevy of sparks. The windshield crumpled and the jeep swerved into the ocean. The soldier on the mounted up-gun hesitated, then swung his machine gun around.

Kelly did not want to kill him, but he was already in deep. He needed the freedom to concentrate on the second jeep. This was war. He triggered a burst to find the range and triggered a second to end the threat. Why didn't you just dive into the surf? he wondered. By the time he swiveled, the second jeep had pulled into a nook and unloaded its soldiers. They were scrambling along the bluff in an erosion gully, protected from Kelly's gun by dead space.

Contreras tapped him on the shoulder. "They gone?"

"Negative. Got at least ten moving toward us up the beach, hugging the cliff. Very bad news."

"I'll take over. Your mates are prepped for the swim. Get them to the boat and I'll catch up. Phone's secure in your buddy's waterproof pack, so don't touch the duffel bag. I inserted the blasting caps already."

Kelly handed over the M-60 and low-crawled to Darren, who was sitting down on a rock in the bottom of the depression holding his stomach. His eyes were closed.

"How's he doing?" Kelly asked Kate.

Darren opened an eye. "Me? How about you, Kelly?"

Kelly smiled and slipped his fingers under the myriad of pressure pads, checking the ACE wraps on Darren's body. "Not so good, actually. I think my nose is busted. Sucks because I was just starting to really score at B school, you know?"

Darren took his bait. "Nose? Nose! That dead Indian put a *knife* in my stomach, and it's still there. Not to mention a torn-up arm."

Kelly looked down at *El Monstruo Carnicero*'s corpse. "Who, conehead, there? He doesn't look so tough."

"Yeah, well, he could throw a knife, that's all I know."

Kelly glanced at Kate and noticed she only had use of a single hand. The bandage wrapped around her other one was soaked red. "When'd he get so thin-skinned, Kate?"

"It's his time of the month."

Darren started to laugh, but his stomach ached so he stopped. "Oh. Very funny. Very funny." The crap that was slung by just one of them was bad enough, but when they tag-teamed it was just merciless. And wonderful. Darren took Kelly's hand and stood with a gasp.

"I knew you'd be here. Good to see you," Darren said.

"You, too, Darren. You, too. It's time to go," said Kelly.

He put on the pack and led them down to the waterline in a crawl along the gunwale of the Whaler. Ten-foot plunging waves were building quickly and folding on top of themselves. Occasionally a bullet popped into a cresting face with a crack that sounded like a towel snapping.

"Surf alone could kill us," said Kate. "This is dangerous."

"Yeah, I know how much you two hate that."

Darren was hunched over in pain on the sprint into the water. When they were waist-deep in the Gulf of Mexico, Darren keeled over and floated on his side, allowing Kate to grab him in a lifeguard tow hold. Harassing fire started to snap more regularly into the whitewater around them. Kelly shouldered the M-4 he was carrying and emptied a magazine at the muzzle flashes blinking from the base of the cliff a hundred meters away. Waves were coming over his back in bunches.

Kelly screamed, "Contreras! Let's go!"

Contreras fired his last belt of ammunition and tossed the machine gun in the sand. The barrel was glowing hot pink and it steamed when a wave hissed over it. He grabbed the electric detonator and hunched behind the whaler, occasionally firing his M-4.

"Hey! Don't!" screamed Kelly.

Contreras waved him off. "You need cover fire or they'll cut you to pieces! I'll swim out when you get them clear!"

The wave action was vicious. It was also great cover. Even within the foamy surf zone where current was most directional, the swells seemed to be rolling in from all sides, forming a sea of peaks and pockets like the inside of an egg carton. Kate scissor-kicked as hard as she could between the incoming waves, taking Darren with her underwater as they slammed past.

"What about him?" Kate yelled when they were through the surf zone.

"He's swimming out," said Kelly lamely. He turned around and treaded water. It was like a giant wave pool that reminded him of Hong Kong harbor with all the cross chop. He could only see the beach in short intervals, when one wave or another lifted him high enough. He glimpsed Contreras in the boat digging into the duffel bag. When the next swell elevated Kelly, Contreras was firing his pistol at a group of ten soldiers not fifty feet down the beach. There were more jeeps roaring down the beach.

The last time Kelly saw Jimmy Contreras, the DEA agent was waving at him, but at the distance Kelly was not sure if he was giving an order or a farewell.

Contreras was vaporized in a ring of fire that consumed everything on the beach. Kelly saw a shock wave ripple up and over the grassy bluff, expanding like a relentless ring of smoke. Bark and fiberglass fluttered down onto the black sand like a ticker-tape parade. On the beach, nothing moved save the granules that were swirling in the wind.

Kelly was distraught. Why didn't he pull the fuses and run the gauntlet? *Because once he killed that Indian his life was over, too.*

Sound enveloped him. Kelly dunked his head underwater, but the shock wave was so powerful it popped his ears. Kelly feared it might rip Darren's wounds open. It shook all of the swimmers, rolling deep into their bones and organs, ten times as loud as a close lightning strike.

"What was that!" screamed Darren, with closed eyes and resurgent pain.

"That was a Marine," said Kelly.

76

MCLEAN, VIRGINIA

Deputy Director Susanne Sheridan was thirty minutes away from losing her title, yet her sadness was born not out of personal regret but from the loss of another. When Kelly had radioed with the news of Jimmy Contreras's death, she felt deeply responsible. She had used his obsession to grab the phone, knowing full well what she would reap once watering the seed. But Contreras had chosen his path, and with vengeance realized he had chosen sacrifice.

It was the loneliness of a silent death that bothered her. Jimmy Contreras would be chipped into the memorial wall as an anonymous star, but the cause for which he fought would reverberate deeply in so many lives, an ethereal presence that they would feel but not see. And Jimmy would never know that his actions had been sanctioned, not rogue.

The monster was gone. The Network would follow.

She walked out of the torture chamber and set her new attaché case on Ted Blinky's desk. He and Christian Collins were sitting side by side, watching television. "Thanks for the case, guys. I may have found a use for it."

They sat immobile, mesmerized by the plasma screen. *Men.*

"So the moment I leave, you two abuse the taxpayers and watch television on their dime?" she asked.

"Depends what it is, doesn't it, ma'am?" Christian Collins said curtly.

Blinky said, "This is Television Mexico, ma'am. I've got the translation scroll on. Eduardo Saiz has announced that they've killed *Los Asesinos.*"

Susanne forced down a smile. Saiz had no other choice but to toe the line, she thought. *He must be following your advice, Roger. Now let's find out who else is in a prom dress waiting for your return.*

"Oh, that's terrible news," she said, smiling now. *Some master of deception I am.*

On the screen, there was a helicopter shot of a smoldering bluff. A deep crater in the sand was encircled by charred burn marks. Wind was carrying the gray smoke horizontally into the woods.

Rest in peace, Jimmy, Susanne thought. Good on you.

The caption read:

> *. . . the site of the final gun battle between the assassins and Mexican federal police officers who had cornered them on this beach in Veracruz. Initial reports indicate that a federal police officer's bullet struck the gas tank of an escape boat killing the assassins.*

The shot switched to a beach view of the combat zone. Police were moving quickly in and out of the cordoned area. The caption continued:

> *How the assassins managed to find a boat has not yet been revealed, but Deputy Attorney General Saiz and his men were not the only ones who followed the assassins' trail to this remote beach. Police investigators have now confirmed that the body of the serial killer known as "The Monster Butcher" has been found at the scene of the fight. This revelation has touched off wary celebrations in Juarez City, where the killer has stalked young women for a decade. But how did a wanted serial killer end up here, on a deserted beach with a wanted American couple?*

Deputy Attorney General Saiz appeared onscreen, flanked by a troop of uniformed officers that included a sweaty-faced Roger Corwin. Saiz was wearing a suit and tie but Corwin was wearing jeans, an armor-plated vest, and an FBI windbreaker. They were standing in ankle-deep sand staring solemnly into a bank of cameras. The caption scrolled up:

> *Very easily, according to the Deputy Attorney General Saiz, who ran the operation. "As you know, when we announced the award we had all manner of people out looking for the assassins. That a wanted murderer joined the hunt is surprising, but not overly so. We received a tip that this murderer was close behind the assassins, so with the help of American FBI officials, we set a trap for both parties. That we were successful brings great credit upon our*

friends in the FBI and especially the young federal judicial police officers who sacrificed their lives to bring these killers to a final justice."

Ted Blinky threw his arms toward the screen in disgust. He tried to roll his chair into the corner but Susanne caught him by the head-rest and spun him around. "Hold on there, cowboy. I want to talk to you. Both of you."

"That's not true, is it, ma'am?" asked Blinky.

"You don't seem unhappy," Christian Collins said to Susanne.

"If they say the case is closed then the case is closed. Oh, you two aren't truly surprised, are you? Roger Corwin is the kind of guy who will always end up on top. Or should I say that *one* of you is not surprised?"

Her subordinates stared at her.

"If you think that's surprising, listen to this," she said, clapping her hands once. "I have a new opportunity for you two. There's no job security. I could screw up and be out on my ass in a week. Oh, and I'll be my usual bitchy self. But it's cutting edge."

The men looked at each other.

"Is it CIA?" asked Ted Blinky.

"Nope," she said. "Listen, you two are dead meat here. You're forever associated with the queen bee. Most of this unit will shift to Homeland, Corwin will be in charge, and you'll be permanent GS-13s counting paperclips. So how about it? No risk, no reward."

The men looked at their feet. She placed her hand on Christian Collins's shoulder.

Collins shoved it away roughly. "Take your hand off me!" he said, chest heaving. "Difficult though it may be for you of all people to believe, Ms. Sheridan, Christian Collins does run risks for his country and is treated as an equal by people more powerful than you. And with more feeling. When I manage a division in Homeland—and I will—I'm going to treat my people with *respect*."

"Is that what Corwin promised you?" she asked.

"That's no longer your business. You're out of here."

"Does this mean you're not coming with me?"

Collins shook his head in disgust. "Your sense of humor sucks, by the way."

"That hurts coming from a man with such good taste. Give my regards to Roger. Ted, I'll be at the memorial wall for a few minutes if you change your mind."

———

Ted Blinky rode in silence with his once-and-future boss until he caught his breath. He had labored over the decision as if he was writing a complex encryption code, the career choice having a finite set of realistic outcomes to which he assigned various probabilities, each of them branching out from the nodes into a decision tree that resembled a pyramid of lightning bolts. He had been forced to rush, feverishly working his mechanical pencil under a pessimistic cloud of Christian Collins's dismissive comments.

Ted Blinky had decided that there was a 55 percent chance his lifestyle and happiness would be increased if he went with her and quite literally followed his gut out the door of the Bat Cave, down the corridor, and through the glass entryway doors to where his boss was waiting in a black Lincoln sedan with government plates.

"Christian surprised me," Blinky said as they crossed the Potomac.

"He's weak." Susanne saw that Blinky was troubled by this, so she added, "And foolish. What did Corwin offer you?"

Blinky's face reddened. "A chance to run operations. Said I was good at simplifying complex problems. I never even considered it, ma'am."

She smirked and patted his knee. "You made the right choice. Oh, and tell me if you think I'm too tactile, will you?"

"I'll let you know, ma'am."

Susanne handed him a dark blue Macy's gift box with a sticker that read: "Ted—Thanks for your loyalty." He opened it and removed a blue blazer and a white dress shirt. "Hurry up and put them on, Ted. There's a tie in the jacket pocket. I won't look."

Blinky felt his carotid artery hammering inside his neck. She had known ahead of time that he would join her. Wait, he thought, don't flatter yourself. She probably has a gift hidden away for Collins, too. He fumbled with the pins in the dress shirt and quickly yanked it over his torso, so filled with anticipation that his chubby fingers were glistening.

"So where are we going, ma'am?" he asked while adding the final touch to his tie.

"The chief of staff is expecting us. Susanne Sheridan and Edward Blinky."

Blinky was concentrating on his knot. He thought Susanne was addressing him until he saw the uniformed White House secret service officer lean in through her window. "Got you right here in the computer, ma'am," the guard said. "You two are already on the staff roster. Have a nice day."

Blinky had not been to the White House since 1971, when he was a sophomore in high school. He expected it would look smaller and perhaps even banal to a man with twenty-two years of pension points under his prodigious belt, but when the car pulled up and the Marine guards in dress blues standing under the columns came to attention and snapped razor salutes in his direction, he felt intensely proud and more than a bit overwhelmed.

"We're working *here?*" said Ted.

"I've been named a special advisor to the president," Susanne said. "But I'm afraid CIA disclosure policies remain. Our roles will not be publicized and I'll need you to be totally discreet in everything we do. Understood?"

Blinky nodded. He began to piece together her mysterious behavior during the last three days. A conclusion emerged like a car rolling out of an assembly line. "You weren't conducting an unauthorized operation. You were acting on orders from the director of Homeland Security and probably the White House. They could not sanction the operation because too many players were against it, including Corwin at FBI. So they fired you as a cover—you could *act* the rogue and they'd have plausible deniability. You took a risk, you won, and now the president is cashing your chip."

Susanne prodded Blinky out of the car. It was a crisp day but she felt warm. "Sounds like a conspiracy to me, Ted," she said, straightening his tie.

"Tell me one thing, ma'am," Blinky said. "Did the couple live? Did we get the phone?"

"That's two things, Ted. But your answer is yes. Now drop it. *Permanently.*"

Roberta Kennedy walked between the Marine guards and grabbed Ted Blinky's clammy hand. "Welcome. You must be Ted Blinky."

It was not every day that the White House chief of staff called you by name. "Yes, ma'am."

"Hi, Susanne."

Susanne stepped forward and said, "Hello again, Ms. Kennedy."

The women shook hands, smirking at one another for a moment before Kennedy said, "I don't know how you pulled this off but congratulations. He needs to be surrounded by people who speak their minds. I would have arranged a press conference, but he thought it best to keep this under wraps. I guess, instead of Special Advisor to the President, we'll have to change your placard to Secret Advisor to the President."

"Thank you, Ms. Kennedy, but there'll be nothing secret squirrel from me."

"That's encouraging," Kennedy said, already walking back into the White House. "I think. Squirrel? Anyway, let me show you to your office. Ted can stay and get settled, but, Susanne, I'm afraid you're wanted at Camp David. I need your running-shoe size so I can call ahead. You know how he is. Just remember to pace yourself by keeping chatter to a minimum."

Walking into the White House behind the two women, Ted Blinky realized that Susanne had not phoned Kennedy from the car. Susanne *had* known ahead of his decision that he would join her. He made a mental note to spend more time thinking outside the box now that he was going to be indirectly advising the president of the United States.

– 77 –

GULF OF MEXICO

Darren awoke slowly. His mouth was thick with cobwebbed strands of saliva that stretched from pallet to roof. He blinked several times and tried to clear the crust from his eyelids. His head was so heavy he could not lift it. His left arm was throbbing relentlessly, but that meant it was alive. The terrible pain had a numbing effect, dimming the disappointment that was returning with his memory. He had been unable to protect her.

Again.

Darren felt his wife grip his hand, and he squeezed back lovingly. "Hi, baby. I missed you. How long have I been out?" he croaked.

Kelly patted him on the head and whispered, "Six hours, snuggle cakes."

"Get away from me, Kelly."

Kelly winked at Kate and said, "Told you he couldn't tell the difference."

Darren tried to yank his hand free, but he was too weak and Kelly held even tighter, still stroking his goddamn head. Kate was ten feet away, sitting behind a stainless-steel steering wheel with her hand covered in bandages and an I.V. antibiotic drip stuck in the crook of her arm. Darren took in the array of electronics before realizing he was on a boat. Now he felt the steady rumble of engines below him.

"Maybe these are the latent tendencies he suppresses when he's lucid," Kate giggled. She had laughed a lot during the boat ride, cracking up at the stupidest jokes. Either Kelly was hilarious or Percocet was potent.

Darren groaned. He put his chin on his chest to see if Kelly had just set him on fire as a joke. "My stomach is killing me. Oh man, it burns."

Kelly glanced at Kate and then held up a beautiful throwing knife. "Took this splinter out of you and replaced it with a liter of blood and three liters of fluid." Kelly tapped an I.V. bag that was dangling from the overhead. "Got a surgeon en route to the ocean rally point."

"We going home?" Darren asked.

Kelly deferred, so Kate said, "No, babe, we're not. But Gavin tells me that the phone bought us someplace we'll like."

"Who was that guy on the beach?" Darren mumbled.

"He caught me on my way down to get you," said Kelly. "I'll explain it later, but you're dead to the world now. If you're caught as yourselves, you'll be extradited to Mexico for trial. Too many dead."

It was a crushing statement to so goal-oriented a man. Darren felt sorry for himself for a brief moment—he would never run for office, he would never, in fact, *be* anybody—before remembering that Kate had dreams that had died in the Sierra Madre as well. They still had each other. He would learn to be thankful for an anonymous family.

"How many dead?" Darren asked.

"That's not important."

"How many?"

"Thirty-four. Not including the three Michigan kids."

"Oh my God. Neck?"

His wife kneeled next to him and nodded sadly. Darren felt the physical impact of despair. He started to cry, ashamed that he was caught up in self-pity moments before learning that he had failed a teammate so miserably. Neck was his man, and he was gone. He managed to put a hand over his eyes so he could weep in darkness.

Eventually Darren said, "You said we can't be 'ourselves.' What's going to happen to us? Certainly somebody saw the boat."

Kelly pulled the satphone from his vest pocket. "This baby has bought you some cooperation. I think they're going to set you up in another country. As for the extract, it really doesn't matter who saw what. The two governments will cut some back-office deal. I figure they'll find skulls, we'll fax them your forged dental records and send a team south to identify the remains, and both sides will put this to rest. You were killed by some valiant Mexican soldiers. That's best for both sides."

"What country?" Darren croaked.

Kelly pulled out the couple's waterproof pack. He unsnapped the top pouch and opened it. It was filled with packets of Australian bills.

"This is just a signing bonus. I got Kate's dad to transfer over a million to a numbered account. You guys are set."

Darren realized what was going to happen. "Families and friends?"

"They were vague on the radio, but it doesn't look good in the short run."

"Yeah, Kelly. We're *set*." Darren tried to sit up, but had no strength in his stomach. He traced his fingers across the sheets and felt a long series of stitches. "How many stitches?"

"Over two hundred in your body right now, but that's nothing. I'm told you'll get a nose job, some light facial reconstruction, hair dye, maybe even a breast job for Kate."

"Fat chance," she laughed. "They'll slow me down."

"Think of your country, Kate. I'd be willing to size some up for you," said Kelly.

Darren growled. "At ease. I'm not sure how inconspicuous a black man's gonna be in Australia. Especially with a white wife and all the nasty scars you've cemented. I'm just not sure a nose job's gonna do it."

Kelly laughed. "No, a nose job won't hide you, as ugly as that mug is. The scars will be lasered away but you're right about your skin color and your generally salty demeanor. So two things: First, you'll be going through sensitivity training to learn how to reach in and touch your soft side, and second . . ."

"Oh, screw you, Kelly."

". . . And second, the spooks on the radio told me that the plastic surgeon who'll be meeting you at the rendezvous is incredible. You'll be a new man. Just ask his last client."

"Who's that?"

"Michael 'Tee-Hee' Jackson, baby. They think they can get you to coffee-colored. Hello, pigment change!"

"Oh, screw *you*. Is he serious Kate? I never know with you two. Coffee-colored? Let me tell you both something, I like my coffee black."

Kate laughed, lovingly patting her husband on the head. "So do I, baby, so do I."

- 78 -

CAMP DAVID, MARYLAND

He had left basketball behind twenty-five years and two arthroscopic knee surgeries ago, but his loping stride remained, punishment for many a Secret Service officer or cabinet member selected to accompany him on his daily run. Today, both his companions, however, were steeled in the belief that fitness was a manifestation of discipline. So while it was not easy for the Director of Homeland Security and the newest Special Advisor to keep up with the president, they managed.

The running path was freshly groomed. The odd rock or stick had been cleared by the Marine platoon an hour earlier before most of them had suited up for security patrol. The other six were standing alongside the path in their woodland camouflage uniforms in mile-long intervals, waiting for the runners to pass. The president was a fanatic about splits.

"Phone?" the president asked.

George Henry was reveling in the run—the Homeland Security stand-up had kept him pinned to his desk for months—so it took a moment to realize the inquiry was his. "In friendly hands soon, sir. When our team links up with the couple in the Caribbean."

"You're sure we can't just welcome them back? It seems tragic that they be shipped somewhere undercover. They're good people."

"I'm sorry, sir, but that's the only option," said Susanne. "Saiz and Corwin swallowed the scripted ending. Darren and Kate Phillips are dead."

"Corwin?" asked the president.

"Lacks integrity, sir," said George Henry. "He's hit terminal rank. I'm sure he'll have a bestseller out in a year about tracking serial killers."

The trio rounded a bend in the trail, and George Henry saw a Marine who seemed to be gaffing his duty, fidgeting around with his wrist instead of saluting the president of the United States. Henry was about to sprint ahead and warn the Marine when the kid looked up and shouted, "Six—thirty—nine on that one, sir. Twenty-seven minutes elapsed time! Ooo-rahh!"

The president picked up the pace. His companions had been warned about the last two miles, but the increase was more than expected. They took off downhill under a row of dogwoods that were fully bloomed.

"What about their friend?" asked the president. "Gavin Kelly, right?"

His long legs were churning over so much space that Susanne couldn't answer. When she finally reached a flat section, she had just enough spare oxygen to say, "That young man has potential, sir."

About the Author

Owen West attended Harvard College on an ROTC scholarship and served as a Marine infantry officer for six years. He was co-president of his Stanford Business School class. He is currently a commodities trader for Goldman, Sachs and recently took a leave of absence to return to the active Marine infantry forces. A top endurance athlete, Owen has raced in six Eco-Challenges and reached 28,000 feet on the north face of Everest. His first novel, *Sharkman Six,* won the 2002 Boyd literary award for best military novel.